Bethany Blake is the author of

Death by Chocolate Lab

Dial Meow for Murder

Pawprints & Predicaments

A Midwinter's Tail

Something Borrowed, Something Mewed

Published by Kensington Publishing Corporation

Something Borrowed, Something Mewed

Bethany Blake

KENSINGTON BOOKS
KENSINGTON PUBLISHING CORP.
www.kensingtonbooks.com

KENSINGTON BOOKS are published by

Kensington Publishing Corp.
119 West 40th Street
New York, NY 10018

All Kensington titles, imprints, and distributed lines are available at special quantity discounts for bulk purchases for sales promotion, premiums, fund-raising, educational, or institutional use.

Special book excerpts or customized printings can also be created to fit specific needs. For details, write or phone the office of the Kensington Sales Manager: Attn.: Sales Department. Kensington Publishing Corp., 119 West 40th Street, New York, NY 10018. Phone: 1-800-221-2647.

Kensington and the K logo Reg. U.S. Pat. & TM Off.

First Printing: June 2019
ISBN-13: 978-1-4967-1735-1
ISBN-10: 1-4967-1735-X

ISBN-13: 978-1-4967-1736-8 (eBook)
ISBN-10: 1-4967-1736-8 (eBook)

10 9 8 7 6 5 4 3 2 1

Printed in the United States of America

Chapter 1

As June rolled toward July in the quaint, pet-centric town of Sylvan Creek, Pennsylvania, the whole community rallied to prepare for the annual weeklong Wags 'n Flags celebration of our nation's independence, a tradition that dated back farther than even the oldest old-timers could remember.

As always, the balcony of the historic Sylvan Creek Hotel was draped with old-fashioned bunting, the gazebo in Pettigrew Park was strung with red, white and blue lights, and nearly every storefront featured patriotic, often pet-related displays, like the one at Fetch! pet emporium, where owner Tessie Flinchbaugh had dressed her shop mascot, a life-sized plush Irish wolfhound, exactly like Uncle Sam, right down to his cottony beard.

Unfortunately, the patriotic decor was being carried a bit too far at one local Pocono Mountains establishment: the mansion that housed Artful Engagements & Events, where, for better or for worse, my sister, Piper Templeton, was holding her wedding rehearsal dinner on the night before her marriage.

The ceremony, which would unite my sensible veterinarian sibling and her compatibly pragmatic, sweater-vest-loving fiancé, Roger Berendt, had originally been planned for October. However, the date had changed when Roger, a professor at nearby Wynton University, was offered a last-minute opportunity to guest lecture for the fall term at Manchester University—in England, not New Hampshire.

Deciding they'd rather start their temporary long-distance relationship as husband and wife, instead of postponing the wedding until Roger returned in late December, the two had announced that they would tie the knot in early July, right before Roger left for Europe, where he would have just a few weeks to settle in and prepare to teach.

As Piper's maid of honor, I was scrambling to help plan the nuptials, which was a challenge, given that my pet-sitting business, Daphne Templeton's Lucky Paws, was booked solid, and my bakery for pets, Flour Power, had just been commissioned to bake three hundred cookies shaped like hot dogs and flags for the annual dog-friendly Fourth of July All Paws on Deck Rowboat Regatta on Lake Wallapawakee.

I probably should've been happy that Piper's and my mother, Realtor Maeve Templeton, had teamed up with Roger's mom, Beverly Berendt, to bring in reinforcements, in the form of wedding planner Abigail Sinclair, of Artful Engagements. But as I stood with Piper and my best friend and fellow bridesmaid Moxie Bloom in the heart of Abigail's garden, where she often hosted catered affairs, I couldn't help thinking that Abigail had gone a *tiny* bit over-board, like half the costumed dogs in the regatta would eventually do.

"I feel like I'm an extra in *Yankee Doodle Dandy!*" Moxie exclaimed, gazing around the candlelit garden, where guests mingled, chatting and eating hors d'oeuvres under a canopy of American flags, which were suspended among the trees. Several wrought iron tables, clustered on a brick patio, were bursting with shiny centerpieces inspired by exploding rockets. And each chair was festooned with a big, star-spangled bow.

Even the large fountain that gurgled at the center of the lush landscaping had been decorated in patriotic fashion. A trio of once-naked cherubs, who poured water from cement casks into a wide, low basin, now wore blue-and-white sashes and top hats, while the water had been dyed a bright shade of red that was actually a little off-putting to me.

"I half expect Jimmy Cagney to come bursting in, dancing a jig to 'You're a Grand Old Flag'!" Moxie added, clasping her hands in front of her chest. As a fan of all things vintage, from the film she was referencing to the 1950s sleeveless cocktail dress she was wearing, Moxie was obviously delighted by the prospect of a flag-waving chorus line stomping through the shrubbery. "It's like the musical has come to life—only with *more* pageantry!"

All at once, I heard a rumbling sound, very reminiscent of a groan, coming from near my feet. Looking down, I saw that my taciturn basset hound sidekick, Socrates, was hanging and shaking his big, dappled head, like he disagreed with Moxie and thought the spectacle was too much. Socrates was not a fan of ostentatious events. Nor was he happy about the fact that, as honorary "grooms-dog," he would have to wear a bow tie during the ceremony at the stuffy Sodgrass Country Club. And, last but certainly not least, he really didn't like mingling—especially since his "puppy love," a poodle named Snowdrop, was home with doggy sniffles.

"This whole thing is a train wreck," Piper said grimly, scanning the party, which was also bigger than the average rehearsal dinner. Being Sylvan Creek, where everybody knew everybody, the shindig had taken on a life of its own, and the garden was full of people and dogs, all of whom shared some sort of history with the bride, groom, and usually me.

Looking around at the guests, too, I quickly spotted Moxie's boyfriend, groomsman Mike Cavanaugh, and his mischievous little pug, Tiny Tim, as well as Tessie and Tom Flinchbaugh, who were gathered around Roger. Although he still had a bachelor party to attend that evening, Piper's reserved hubby-to-be already looked exhausted to be the center of attention. His smile didn't quite reach his brown eyes, and he kept rubbing his neck, messing up the collar of his dress shirt.

"The whole thing is completely over-the-top—an over-priced scam, in Roger's opinion," Piper noted, as thunder echoed ominously in the distance.

"Scam" was a harsh term for a normally mild-mannered man like Roger, and I winced at the word, and at the noise from above.

"I will never understand how we got roped into having a theme wedding," my understated sister added, picking at a plate of too-colorful canapés. Even the food, supplied by Snowdrop's person, chef Daisy Carpenter, was on theme, and in some cases, appearance had taken priority over taste. "It makes no sense!"

"Really? You don't know how this happened?" I asked, glancing over at the buffet, where our mother was laughing it up with Beverly—not that either of them was actually smiling. The two women eschewed wrinkle-causing expressions. Instead, they conveyed whatever mirth they felt by tossing back their heads so their matching angular bobs swung and lightly touching each other's arms. They were also remarkably similar in terms of wardrobe. In spite of the heat, both had chosen to wear black pencil skirts and white shirts, accented with blue-and-red silk scarves—the Fourth of July, as interpreted by Ann Taylor.

"I thought they would hate each other," Piper noted, watching them, too. "I mean, Beverly is practically a rival.

And Mom *crushes* rivals. Yet they've been inseparable since the engagement party."

"Maybe they bond over having one 'perfect' and one 'wayward' child," I suggested, balancing my own plate and popping a cheesy wonton "firecracker" into my mouth. The appetizer—one of the less patriotic, and more tasty, choices—was aptly named. Herbed and spiced cream cheese burst out of the crisp wrapper, and I covered my mouth as I spoke. "Speaking of which, is Roger's supposedly 'rebellious' sister coming tonight? Because I am dying to meet the missing bridesmaid."

"Ooh, me too," Moxie agreed, her green eyes glimmering with interest. As the owner of Sylvan Creek's unique salon for people and pets, Spa and Paw, she was also the chief conduit for local gossip. "Dorinda Berendt sounds like a very intriguing person!"

"She's a very *troubled* person," Piper clarified. "And I don't expect her to show up tonight. From what I understand, Dorinda had a run-in with Abigail when she came here to pick up her bridesmaid dress yesterday." Piper rolled her eyes behind her wire-rimmed eyeglasses. "And don't even get me started on those hideous things—"

"Smile, bride and company!"

For a second, I thought someone honestly wanted Piper, especially, to cheer up. Then, as Moxie took me by the shoulders and spun me around, dragging me next to her and my sister, I realized that we were about to be photographed.

Before I could even steady my plate full of tiny nibbles, a flash blinded me. And I was still blinking when Abigail's official photographer, Laci Chalmers, turned her camera around so we could all *try* to see the image she'd captured.

"Talk about a 'magical memory,'" Laci said, sounding a touch sarcastic when she alluded to the Magical Memories scrapbook that came with every Artful Engagements wedding package.

At least, Mom had touted the binder as a selling point when she'd unleashed Abigail on Piper.

"You all look marvelous," Laci added, with a wink that said otherwise.

Moxie, who did look great, took the compliment seriously. "Why, thank you," she said, lightly touching her hair, which she'd dyed a quirky, cool color she called "something blue."

While not pushing any fashion boundaries, Piper also looked nice in a crisp, sleeveless sheath, so I was pretty sure Laci's wink had been aimed at me.

In the split second before she turned the camera back around, I saw that my grayish-green eyes had been closed and my dirty-blond curls were going crazier than usual, thanks to the rising humidity. I also noted that my floral sundress, which I'd purchased at the Tuscan equivalent of a flea market, was wilting in the heat, so it looked only a notch above Laci's fitted black T-shirt and cargo pants.

I assumed that Abigail allowed the young photographer to wear the casual outfit because Laci moved around a lot and carried a lot of gear.

Or maybe Laci was breaking the rules because she was a short-timer.

"You are shooting the wedding tomorrow, right?" Piper asked, so I knew she was thinking the same thing as me. Which was rare, given that my sensible sibling and I were complete opposites. "You'll be there, right, Laci?"

"Only as a favor," she said, absently rumpling her dark hair, which was cut in an extremely short pixie that accented her high cheekbones and blue eyes. "I collect my last paycheck from the wicked witch of the Poconos tonight—assuming I can pry the cash out of her grasping hands."

Laci was grinning, but the comment was still pretty harsh, though justified.

"Lucky for you, you're friends with my new boss, so I am happy to help out," she added, jerking her thumb in the direction of Gabriel Graham, who was owner of and formerly sole reporter at Sylvan Creek's *Weekly Gazette*.

Gabriel, whom I used to date, off and on, had his arm around his more serious girlfriend, gorgeous television executive Elyse Hunter-Black.

"Of course, we'll pay you," Piper promised Laci. "We don't expect you to work for nothing!"

Laci, who had an acerbic personality that would dovetail well with Gabriel's edgy wit, was already backing away, and she waved off the offer with a wry grin. "I'm just happy to be free of these gigs, and Abigail's clutches, forever. This one's on the house. In fact, my presence at the wedding, which will *kill* Abigail, will be payment enough!"

"Wow, no love lost between Laci and her boss," Piper said quietly as Laci disappeared into the crowd.

"I guess not," I answered my sister, but my attention had already shifted back to Mom and Beverly Berendt, who had their heads bent together, like different witches. Ones who might be brewing up some scheme to take over the world. Or at least dominate the local real estate market.

"What are the odds you'd marry the son of a bossy, scarf-wearing Realtor from the next town over, huh, Piper?" I mused, shaking my head. "It's like you're getting a double dose of Mom!"

Down by my feet, Socrates huffed softly. Given that he avoided my mother whenever possible, I suspected he was already dreading future family gatherings.

"I didn't know Mrs. Berendt sold real estate, too,"

Moxie said, sounding delighted by the terrible coincidence. She plucked a cocktail in the party's signature colors from a tray carried by a passing server. "Where?"

Piper slipped a blueberry from a skewer that also held chunks of watermelon and feta. The appetizer was festive, and contrasted with my sister's glum tone when she told Moxie, "Beverly has an office in Zephyr Hollow."

"Oh, I love that town!" Moxie cried, missing the point—which was that Piper's mother-in-law would be way too close for comfort. "It's so artsy and weird!"

All at once, lightning flickered in the distance, drawing my attention to the darkening sky.

"Friar Tuck over there would fit right in at Zephyr Hollow," Moxie added, seemingly apropos of nothing. But when I looked at my best friend again, I saw that she was pointing to a balding, bearded man who wore a brown robe that did appear monkish, if only because it was tied with what appeared to be a rope, albeit a colorful, decorative one. A pair of Birkenstock-style sandals added to his monastic mien.

The strange man, whom I didn't know, stood near a rose-covered arbor, chatting with my part-time, nearly certified accountant, Fidelia Tutweiler.

Abigail's young assistant, a dark-haired young man named Dexter Shipley, who probably shouldn't have been mingling, rounded out the strange trio.

Shaking her head, Moxie made a tsk-tsking sound. "Too bad the monk is messing up the *Yankee Doodle* party with an outfit that's totally off theme."

"Let's just hope he doesn't mess up the *vows*," Piper said, handing her empty plate to another passing server. "Because, believe it or not, that guy—'Brother' Alf Sievers, from Graystone Arches Gateway to Eternity 'monastery'— is *performing the ceremony*."

I hesitated for a long moment, not sure if I should give

Ms. Peebles for the next week. You're the only sitter who *understands* her."

I suspected that I was the only person who would repeatedly stick my arm into a chimney flue to pull Ms. Peebles down. But before I could mention that, the smile disappeared from Abigail's face, and, as thunder shook the mansion, she suddenly shifted the conversation to a topic I'd been dreading, and trying to avoid all night, for a number of reasons.

"So, Daphne," Abigail said, crossing her arms and tapping her red nails against her crimson suit, "is Roger's best man going to *show up* for the wedding? Or is your Detective Jonathan Black *still missing in action*?"

Chapter 3

When the storm that had been brewing all evening finally hit, it struck with a vengeance, drenching the buffet table, which Abigail had stubbornly insisted on restocking until the bitter end, and sending the few remaining guests, who had lingered too long, running for their vehicles.

As maid of honor, I'd felt obligated to stay until nearly the last minute, although I'd bolted before a few stubborn guests. Even so, Socrates and I had endured a harrowing ride back to our home, Plum Cottage, which was located on Piper's property, Winding Hill Farm.

By the time my pink 1970s VW Bus had slipped and slid its way up to the isolated, tiny house, tucked away in a forested part of the property, the power was out and hail was clattering on the tin roof.

Thankfully, I was well stocked with candles, and, after changing into a comfortable pair of cotton pajamas, I knelt before the arched stone fireplace, lighting enough votives and pillars to cast the room in a soft, flickering glow.

Soon, the sturdy cottage felt snug and secure, the sound of the rain and thunder joined by Socrates' soft snores as he dozed on his favorite rug by the hearth. Yet I couldn't shake a feeling of unease, and not only because Piper's wedding seemed plagued by problems, from an unhappy groom to a disgruntled, "troubled" bridesmaid and a minister whom I thought was sketchy, to say the least.

I was mainly worried because I hadn't been able to answer Abigail Sinclair's very reasonable question regarding the whereabouts of Detective Jonathan Black, who had seemingly dropped off the face of the Earth in the days before he was supposed to serve as best man.

Shuffling to the kitchen in my favorite pair of fluffy slippers, I put the teakettle on the gas stove, then picked up my phone, which I'd left on my spindle-legged antique table. Poising my index finger over the screen, I prepared to tap in a familiar number. Then I paused, and my gaze cut to the potted herbs on my deep kitchen windowsill, where a surly, black Persian cat was half hidden, the better to watch me with big, orange, *critical* eyes.

"You don't think I should call Jonathan again, do you?" I asked Tinkleston, whose tail was twitching. "You think I'm starting to seem desperate, right?"

Tinks meowed loudly in reply. I was pretty sure he agreed that I had called Jonathan one too many times, without getting any response from the handsome, sometimes enigmatic homicide detective I'd started dating over the winter.

Things between us had been going great—until March, when Jonathan had left for San Diego, where he was working as a consultant on a naval base that had suffered a series of suspicious deaths.

The temporary job, and Jonathan's ability to swing a leave of absence from the local force, were testament to his growing reputation as a detective and the respect he'd earned in his past life as a SEAL. I was really happy for him, and for his two dogs, Axis and Artie, who had gone along on the adventure. However, in spite of having a PhD in philosophy, which had taught me the value of patience,

I had to admit that I also missed Jonathan. Especially since he had gone *completely silent* in recent days.

"What if something happened to him?" I mused aloud, while lightning crackled outside. I was sure that the storm was contributing to my unsettled feeling, but I couldn't help worrying. "It's not like Jonathan to leave Roger, especially, in the dark on the eve of his wedding!"

I hadn't expected a response from Tinkleston, but he made another almost plaintive sound, which probably just meant he was hungry.

Setting down the phone, I retrieved some homemade Something's Fishy Snacks, made with sardines, carrots and sweet potatoes, from the old-fashioned icebox and offered three treats to Tinks.

While he ate, I pulled the whistling kettle off the burner and poured myself a big mug of chamomile tea. Blowing out all but one candle, I picked up the one that still glowed and collected my tea and my phone, then juggled everything the whole way up the iron spiral staircase that led to my loft bedroom.

Setting my supplies on my nightstand, I climbed into bed, pulling the covers over myself, because the night was getting a little chilly as the storm roared past overhead.

A few moments later, Socrates came padding upstairs, headed to the purple velvet cushion where he usually slept. He was still settling in for his nightly meditation when Tinks joined me, too, hopping onto the bed and curling up near my feet.

"Please don't stare at me like you disapprove," I whispered to Tinks, so as not to disturb Socrates. The hail had stopped, and rain pattered softly overhead. Reaching past the flickering candle, I picked up my phone. "I can't help it. I have to make sure Jonathan's okay. And I need to know why he's disappeared."

When I said that word, "disappeared," against a low

rumble of thunder, I suddenly got a sick feeling in the pit of my stomach, recalling a conversation I'd once had with Gabriel Graham. The savvy reporter, who sometimes clashed with Jonathan, had reminded me that everyone had secrets. Especially Navy SEALs who'd seen combat, and who didn't like to talk about the past.

But if Jonathan wasn't who I believed him to be, I'd made a huge mistake, falling for him . . .

"No," I whispered, causing Tinks's ears to twitch. "I can trust Jonathan."

I promised myself that, and yet, once again, my phone call went directly to voice mail—as I simultaneously received a text.

Fumbling, I quickly switched to my messages, only to realize that Jonathan and I didn't have our wires crossed.

"Oh, rats," I mumbled, unable to contain a twinge of disappointment to see Daisy Carpenter's name on my screen, followed by a message that expressed her continued agitation with Abigail Sinclair.

Don't take the cat sitting job for Abigail. Return the keys ASAP and tell her firmly: NO DEAL! Seriously, do it now!

I sympathized with Daisy, but I didn't want to get dragged into a feud. I also wanted to get some sleep, because I had a big day looming. Still, I felt like I should at least offer to listen if she needed to vent, so I quickly texted back, *Need to talk? I am here.*

I expected my phone to ring right away, but in a few seconds, the screen went black and stayed that way.

Setting it on the nightstand, I took a sip of tea, blew out the candle and snuggled under a cotton sheet, hoping that the increasingly gentle noise of the rain and the softening rumbles of distant thunder would lull me to sleep. But my thoughts, and later my dreams, were troubled. It hardly felt like I'd dozed at all when I woke to the sound of my phone ringing, right near my ear, as if I'd reached for it again during the night.

This time, I didn't jump. I knew from the wedding march ringtone that I shouldn't expect to hear Jonathan's voice when I tapped the receiver icon.

"Piper?" I asked, sitting up straighter and using my free hand to rub my eyes. Then I pulled the phone away from my ear for just a moment, checking the time, in case I'd somehow overslept. But it was still early, and I returned to the call. "What's up?"

My sister didn't exchange pleasantries, or even greet me.

"Get up, get dressed and get over here to the Sodgrass Club," she ordered, sounding like a bridezilla. Except I knew she was distressed, not being a diva, when she added, "This wedding's no longer a train wreck. It's completely sunk, like the *Titanic*!"

didn't answer my questions right away. Halting directly before me, she looked me up and down, her brows knit together. "Why are you wearing your bridesmaid gown— which makes you look like the Statue of Liberty?"

Looking down at myself, I picked at the bluish-green, toga-like garment that Abigail had insisted we bridesmaids wear, along with spiky crowns of gladioli, one of which was perched on my curls. "Um . . . When you said get dressed . . ."

"Never mind." Piper waved away my explanation. "Your outfit is the least of my problems!"

The room was pretty loud, but I heard Socrates make a huffing sound. He'd probably known all along that I should've worn regular clothes. Either that, or he was again expressing his disdain for the hideous garment, which made it look like I'd just stepped off a pedestal and waded through a harbor to reach the country club.

Ignoring him and adjusting my tiara, I said, "Please, tell me what's happening. Because I am completely in the dark."

Before my sister could answer, Roger joined us, threading his way through the clusters of shocked and disgruntled people. "Piper and I stopped by this morning to make sure everything was in order, and it appears that Abigail Sinclair promised this room to six different bridal parties," he explained, mopping his brow with a handkerchief, like the Sodgrass manager. Roger's face was an unpleasant shade of gray that clashed with his pale yellow polo shirt, and two dark half-moons, smudged under his eyes, made him appear even more sickly. If I hadn't known better, I would've guessed that my sister's fiancé, who never had more than a cocktail or two at any gathering, hadn't exercised his usual self-discipline at his bachelor party the night before.

"Are you okay?" I asked, resting my hand on his arm. I was confused by the news about the wedding mix-up, but more worried about the groom, whose flesh was clammy. "Do you need to sit down somewhere?"

"I'm fine," he insisted, folding up the handkerchief with hands that shook a little. Roger was usually very calm, like Piper, but he seemed to have been pushed to his limits. His brown eyes appeared tired, but there was anger simmering there, too, and he amended his earlier assurance. "Well, I am sick over the fact that, as I predicted, Abigail Sinclair turned out to be a scam artist."

"Let's not jump to that conclusion," I urged, trying to be the calm voice of reason, which was not usually my role when I was around Piper and Roger. "Abigail has a good reputation in this area. This has to be a mistake."

Piper shook her head. "No, I've got to agree with Roger. Abigail told me and a bunch of other brides that she'd reserved the outdoor amphitheater here for the wedding, and this room for the reception. But, according to the manager"—Piper gestured to the panicked man in the suit—"she never contacted the resort."

"I guarantee you that she cashed the deposit checks," Roger noted. "I'm sure that money's gone."

Down by my feet, Socrates snorted loudly. I was pretty sure he was trying to say, *"I told you so."*

"Not the right time," I told him, meeting his droopy, knowing eyes. Then I addressed the humans again. "Abigail has been in business for years. Why would she suddenly pull a stunt like that?"

"Because she's been in business for years," Roger said, turning my statement on its head. "She probably got sick of dealing with persnickety mothers, fussy flower girls, unreliable vendors and, worst of all, bridezillas." He raised his hands to Piper. "Not you. You have been a patient saint throughout this whole debacle our mothers foisted upon us."

I could hear other couples around us snapping at each other as they tried to figure out what to do next, and I was glad my sister and Roger still had a unified front. I also had to admit that Roger had a point. Last but certainly not least, I finally realized that someone would have to break the news to a *pair* of persnickety mothers, if best buddies Maeve and Bev were still in the dark.

"Do the women who wrote the checks to Abigail know what's happening here?" I asked, looking between Piper and Roger.

My sister might've been rattled, but she still had her wits about her. She shook her head again. "No. They have not been contacted yet."

"Good thinking," I said. "We should probably—"

I was going to suggest that we talk through how to let two demanding and take-charge women know they might've been swindled, because I knew they would not take that news well. But as I was speaking, Dex made his way over to us, breaking into the conversation.

"I'm trying to contact Abigail and straighten this out," he promised, giving us only half of his attention. His eyes were trained on his phone. Socrates wisely took a few steps back, so he wouldn't accidentally get stepped on. "I'm sure this is all a big, if very regrettable mistake," Dex added, rubbing his jaw. "Abigail has been under a lot of pressure lately. Errors happen."

Roger opened his mouth, like he was about to make another accusation.

I didn't think that would be productive, so I spoke first. "If it was a mistake, what's your theory?" I asked. "What could've gone so wrong? Because booking six weddings for one place . . . It *does* seem a little odd."

"Perhaps her planner glitched," Dex noted coolly. He couldn't have been more than twenty-six or twenty-seven, but he was handling the chaotic, confusing situation with admirable composure—which didn't surprise me. I'd dealt with the tall, handsome planner-in-training several times, as maid of honor, and I was always impressed by his ability to cope with Abigail's mercurial moods and endless demands without getting flustered. "Strange things happen," he added, twisting his wrist to check the time. However, he wasn't wearing a watch, and he muttered, "Force of habit." Then he finally gave us his full attention, so I could see his blue eyes, which were impressively impassive, given the tension in the room. Lowering his voice, he spoke confidentially. "As I noted, Abigail has been very stressed lately. I wouldn't be surprised if she's not answering my messages because she's knocked out cold with sleeping pills. Which also cloud her judgment."

Roger, Piper and I exchanged puzzled glances, like none of us was sure what to make of that information. Socrates also looked disapproving, as if he thought Dex had shared too much.

And before any of us figured out how to respond, Abigail's right-hand man added, "I'll let you know as soon as I have more information." Smiling in a reassuring way, he gave Piper's arm a quick squeeze. "Just hold tight, okay? I'll do my best to salvage your big day."

"I don't think that's poss . . ."

Roger tried to protest, but Dex was already striding off. We all watched him for a few moments, until Piper drew our attention back to her, noting, "Roger, you're right. There's no way this 'big day' can be saved at this point. Which means we need to start calling guests to let them know that the wedding is postponed."

My sister sounded disappointed, but it wasn't her nature to fret or sulk. She was the type of person to face crises head-on. Roger seemed to pull himself together, too.

"You're right," he agreed. "We have to contact Daisy Carpenter, too. She's no doubt cooking already, but maybe we can stop her before she's done too much. I'm sure our mothers won't get their money back, but at least we won't waste Daisy's time or more food than necessary."

"We need to call our mothers, too," Piper reminded us. "There's no avoiding it." Then she looked at me. "Daphne, can you help us, if I promise you don't have to break the news to Mom?"

I hesitated for a moment, because I really did want to fulfill my maid of honor duties and be of assistance. But while Piper and Roger had been making plans, I'd had an idea of my own. One that might actually provide us with some answers.

"I will make some calls, and enlist Moxie and Fidelia, too," I promised. "Just give me a half hour to run an errand of my own."

My sister might've been my polar opposite, but she also knew me pretty well, and she watched me with suspicion. Socrates seemed skeptical, too.

"Where are you going?" Piper asked.

I stalled again, because neither my sister nor my canine companion was going to like the answer. And Roger clearly objected, too, when I finally admitted, "I'm running out to Artful Engagements—I have a key, and Abigail's permission to go inside."

Chapter 5

"I think this is actually a very good idea," I defended myself to Socrates, who was harnessed in the VW's front seat. We were driving down the long, tree-lined lane that led to Artful Engagements, and I could tell that he thought we were on a fool's errand. Which didn't stop me from trying to explain my rationale for visiting the mansion. "Dexter Shipley said Abigail might be passed out. I think somebody should at least check on her. If she's been acting erratically, and taking sedatives, maybe she's in trouble."

Socrates swung his head around to give me a baleful look, and I knew he agreed with Piper and Roger, who thought Abigail had skipped town with a bunch of brides' and grooms' money. The fact that Abigail had actually told me she was leaving town that very day only added more weight to that theory.

"Well, if she has bolted—which I will admit is possible—I should at least check on Ms. Peebles," I told Socrates, pulling off my ridiculous crown of gladioli. I wasn't sure why I'd worn it as long as I had, and I wished I could've changed out of the dress, too. But I felt like I should go directly to Artful Engagements, on the off chance that Abigail really did need medical attention. "Abigail asked me to stop by today," I added, tossing the tiara into the back seat. "Albeit, a bit later than this."

Socrates woofed loudly, and I thought he was continuing to disagree, until another noise met my ears: the roar of a motorcycle engine, coming out of nowhere—and quickly drawing closer.

My heart racing, I jerked the steering wheel, guiding my van to the very edge of the narrow road just in time for the snarling, black bike to tear past, at a speed much too high for the twisting lane.

Hitting the brakes, I rested one hand on my chest, catching my breath and checking the rearview mirror. But the helmeted rider was long gone, and I turned to Socrates again. "Are you okay?"

Needless to say, he didn't respond, except to look at me placidly. "Well, thanks for trying to warn me," I added, before taking one more deep breath and putting the VW in gear.

A moment later, we rounded a slight curve and pulled up to the mansion that housed Artful Engagements, where I immediately spotted something that seemed a little . . . off.

"I know this is technically a place of business, and usually unlocked, but Abigail doesn't seem like someone who would leave a door ajar," I told Socrates, who stood with me on the semicircular driveway in front of Artful Engagements. I could see part of the garden at the side of the building and glimpsed the flags, now drenched and dragging, hanging from the trees. "And it's hard for me to believe nobody cleaned up after the party, in spite of the storm. This property is always perfectly maintained."

Socrates whined softly, and I could tell that he thought the wise course of action would be to turn around and leave. And seeing his lowered head and stiff tail did cause me to hesitate for a moment, because the last time he'd warned me about wandering around an old house, I'd stumbled across a body.

Then I remembered all of the baffled brides who were also wandering—around the Par Four Room of the Sodgrass Club. And I couldn't leave before I made sure Abigail was okay, especially since I increasingly felt something was amiss.

"I've got my phone," I reminded Socrates, showing him the device, which I held in my hand, because my dress didn't have pockets. "If there's any trouble, I'll just call 911."

Socrates didn't appear reassured, but I was determined to make some effort to track down Abigail. Hiking up my long, voluminous skirt with my free hand, I mounted three short steps to a small porch. Without checking to see if Socrates had followed, I pushed one of the doors open and leaned into a quiet, dim and blissfully cool foyer. "Abigail? Hello?"

No one answered. In fact, the house was deathly quiet, the only sound the faint ticking of a clock from a distant room.

"I don't think anyone's here, but I'm still going to have a quick look around," I told Socrates, with a glance up a staircase that led to Abigail's private quarters. The day was bright and sunny, but what little I could see of the second floor appeared dark, as if the blinds were closed or the doors were shut. I was starting to think Roger and Piper were right, and Abigail had swindled everyone and bolted. "I'm getting a little worried about Ms. Peebles," I added. "I'm assuming that she was left behind, if Abigail really did ditch town. And you know how she tends to get stuck in high places, or wedged under furniture."

Socrates made a sound reminiscent of a sigh. But he followed me upstairs, which was where I usually found Ms. Peebles, although she had the run of the whole building.

"Ms. Peebles?" I called softly, moving from room to room.

As I'd expected, the curtains were drawn, and everything seemed very neat, even for an orderly person like Abigail. The upstairs kitchen, which was smaller than the commercial-grade one downstairs, didn't have so much as a crumb on the marble countertop.

"She really took off," I muttered, poking my head into her bedroom, where I often found the tiny, tawny cat with the big green eyes cowering on top of a tall antique wardrobe.

However, the feckless feline wasn't waiting on top of the wardrobe, and she didn't yowl from inside the closet, where she was also often trapped. But I did find something interesting. Two suitcases, both on the bed. One, which was closed, was black and shiny. The other was open, the lid thrown back, but I could see the distinctive signature Louis Vuitton pattern on the sides. Piles of neatly folded clothes waited to be tucked inside on top of the shoes that were already stashed away in plastic bags.

"What the . . . ?" I looked down at Socrates, who was sticking close to me. "So she's not gone yet!"

I thought that was a good sign, but I could tell by the way Socrates shuffled his paws, and from the deep furrows in his already wrinkled brow, that he disagreed.

"Ms. Peebles?" I tried one last time.

My soft call was met with more silence. Except for another ticking sound, from a timepiece on Abigail's nightstand, which also held a book and a tube of hand cream with water lilies on the label.

I looked down at Socrates. "There's nothing more to see here. Let's go downstairs."

That suggestion seemed to appeal to my low-slung sidekick, who trotted off, his big paws thudding loudly on the stairs as we both descended to the rooms that Abigail used for her business.

"I'll make this quick," I promised, poking my nose into a parlor—which was now a different kind of seating area, for client meetings.

Not seeing the cat or Abigail, I next checked a former library that now housed her office. The space was tidy, like the rest of the mansion, with two exceptions.

The first was a tilting pile of papers on Abigail's desk.

Moving closer, I saw that the document on top was a photocopy of what appeared to be an old edition of the *Weekly Gazette*. A grainy image, made worse by duplication, showed a bunch of people standing on the shores of what appeared to be Lake Wallapawakee.

I had no idea why Abigail would read about what I assumed was a drowning, given the way the people were milling around.

I could better understand her interest in two travel brochures, advertising a romantic island in the Caribbean. I was sure Abigail planned plenty of destination weddings, and I turned my attention to the other slightly messy part of the room: a corner where Abigail had stashed a bunch of baskets. The containers overflowed with wedding-related items, like cake toppers and little pillows with ribbons to keep rings in place.

I supposed the props were used in emergencies, like if a bride forgot to bring her own special pillow for the ringbearer. Abigail to the rescue.

"So what happened today?" I muttered, suddenly sick on Piper's behalf.

Even if I did find the missing wedding planner, Piper and Roger were already calling guests to let them know the ceremony was canceled. Not that my sister had wanted the patriotic-themed extravaganza anyway.

Sighing, I again hoisted my shiny, bluish-green skirt

and headed down a corridor to the kitchen where I'd last seen Abigail arguing with Daisy Carpenter. Socrates trotted along behind me. Failing to spot Ms. Peebles there, I moved on to the back door, which was also open.

"That's weird," I said, fighting off a sudden sense of foreboding as I pictured the motorcycle driving swiftly away. The mismatched pair of suitcases, which I'd initially thought were a good sign, suddenly seemed ominous, and my fingers curled more securely around my phone. Then I reminded myself that I was probably jittery because the time I'd searched a similar large, lonely property, on the shore of Lake Wallapawakee, I'd found a body. In fact, I'd probably met my quota for murder victims, and I shook off my nerves and pushed the door open wide enough for me and Socrates to pass through.

I thought he seemed relieved as we stepped into the sunny garden, where my ears picked up two more sounds.

The faint trickle of the fountain—and the soft yowl of a cat.

"Let's go save Ms. Peebles," I said, following the distressed cry, until we reached the center of the garden, which was a *disaster*.

Socrates and I both stopped at the edge of the brick patio, where the tables were strewn with plates and cups that had been hastily abandoned when the storm had cut loose. The flashy centerpieces had been blown over, and some of the soggy flags had also fallen from the trees. One lay crumpled on the ground, one had landed on the buffet, and a third was clogging up the three-tiered, perhaps six-foot-tall fountain, where Ms. Peebles had somehow managed to climb atop one of the cherub's heads.

"Good grief," I said, setting my phone on a table and dragging my skirt across the bricks, while Socrates hung back. "How did you get up there?"

The little cat blinked down at me with her green eyes, as if she had no idea how she'd crossed the pool of water, which was still red, and climbed atop a baby angel's smooth head. The top hats and sashes had apparently blown away in the storm.

"Come on." I raised my arms and waved my hands, urging her to jump to me—only to suddenly freeze in place when, out of the corner of my eye, I spotted something peeking out from under the flag that, upon closer inspection, was draped lumpily, but perhaps too neatly, across the lowest basin.

The half-concealed object looked a lot like a *hand*, with a big diamond ring winking on one finger.

"Oh, no," I cried, instinctively wading into the pool and dragging the sodden flag off Abigail Sinclair, who lay sprawled in the water, like some twisted part of the decor, from her white limbs to her red suit—to her face, which was an unnatural and alarming shade of blue.

Chapter 6

After I called for help, there was nothing to do but wait, so I sat stiffly on a wrought iron chair near the fountain, along with Socrates. Ms. Peebles had jumped down by herself, at some point, and run off.

I was tempted to keep myself busy by cleaning up the mess of plates, cups and soggy food, but I'd already disturbed the scene enough. I knew from experience that I would get in trouble if I kept moving things around.

I also wanted to go inside, where it would be cooler, and where I wouldn't be able to keep glancing at Abigail's body, which was still half-submerged. However, I felt a duty to stay with her, keeping vigil, although I knew there wasn't anything I could really do.

"I can't believe how this day turned out," I said softly, just as I heard the muted sound of an approaching vehicle.

For a moment, I got nervous, thinking the mysterious motorcyclist, who might very well have been a killer on the run, had returned. But as the noise grew more distinct, I could tell it was very different from the deep, loud rumble of the bike's engine.

Then the motor cut out, followed shortly by two sequential

slams of a car door, or doors, while sirens finally sounded softly in the distance.

Standing, I smoothed my sweaty palms over my already limp, damp dress, as Socrates rose, too, his manner suitably somber—unlike the demeanor of an excited, gleeful, one-eared, drooling Chihuahua, who suddenly burst into the garden, running straight for his best basset hound buddy.

I was still trying to process Artie's inexplicable presence at Artful Engagements when his chocolate Lab "brother," Axis, came loping behind.

Then, as realization set in, I felt my heart pounding as someone else joined us.

Jonathan Black, who first grinned at me, only to have that smile slip away while he took in the scene before him.

"Daphne?" he asked, greeting me with confusion, instead of the warm embrace I might've daydreamed about, once or twice, since he'd left town. He took a step closer, his dark blue eyes scanning everything, no doubt recording details, before he met my gaze again. "What in the world *happened* here?"

Chapter 7

"Honestly, Daphne, it's one thing to find bodies on normal days, but to ruin your sister's wedding day!" My mother made a tsk-tsking sound as she clumsily attempted to pick up a slippery water chestnut with a pair of chopsticks.

Maeve Templeton had conquered the local real estate market, but foreign foods and the implements used to cook and eat them were her Achilles' heel. She battled daily with the Italian espresso maker that she used without permission at Flour Power, and she was struggling mightily with two thin balsa wood chopsticks at Typhoon, a funky little Chinese restaurant in the neighboring town of Zephyr Hollow.

In a rare moment of agreement, Mom and I had decided that Piper should get out of her house and enjoy a change of scenery after a day spent at Winding Hill calling friends and family to explain that her wedding had been canceled. To our surprise, Piper had agreed. In fact, she seemed more calm and upbeat than our mother.

"For goodness sake," Mom complained, slapping down the chopsticks. I wasn't sure if she was still frustrated with me, or if she was now more vexed by her inability to eat her

Shanghai shrimp. And things didn't get any clearer when she added, "This whole day has been a disaster!"

With a slight lift of her hand, Piper caught our server's eye from across the room, then pantomimed eating with Western-style utensils. The waitress nodded and hurried off, while Piper returned her attention to the conversation. "I think the day was destined for disaster, even before Abigail's disappearance and, apparently, murder," she noted. "Things started going downhill the moment Abigail handed me the 'dossier' full of red, white and blue 'inspiration images.'"

Although a candle that flickered on our table was reflected in her eyeglasses, I could tell that Piper glanced at our mother.

"Sorry. I don't mean to sound ungrateful. Especially since you are probably out a lot of money, thanks to whatever scam Abigail was pulling."

Piper was the favorite child—we all acknowledged it—and our mother came very close to smiling at my sister's sympathetic comment. She reached across the glossy mahogany table and patted Piper's hand while the server silently slipped a fork next to Mom's plate. "Don't worry about me, dear," Mom said, while I gave the waitress a nod of gratitude. "I took out wedding liability *and* cancellation insurance. And if I sue Abigail's estate, as I intend to do at this point, I'll more than recoup my investment in the event."

I overlooked the callous comment about the lawsuit, which Mom was planning less than twenty-four hours after Abigail's death, because I was too focused on the other source of my mother's potential windfall.

"Wedding insurance is actually a *thing*?" I asked, struggling a bit with my own chopsticks and a spicy dish called "dragon noodles." In spite of spending quite a bit of time in Thailand, I hadn't mastered the art of dining with chopsticks, either. However, I was determined not to give up, unlike Mom, who was digging in with her fork. "What made you think to even find out if it existed?"

As soon as the question came out of my mouth, I regretted asking it.

"I protect *all* of my investments!" Mom shook her head at my ignorance. Her signature asymmetrical bob swung, and the cut was so razor sharp that for a second I feared she might slash her cheek. "Who would plan a wedding without insurance?"

"Piper, are you sure you're okay?" I asked again, turning the subject back to my sister's state of mind, which was at least outwardly stable. "You're fine?"

Expertly plucking a peanut from her plate of kung pao chicken, Piper shrugged. "It's not like Roger left me at the altar. We're still in love, and we'll still get married . . . at some point. I'm incredibly disappointed that the wedding didn't take place today, and I'm angry at Abigail, although that seems wrong. But I'm coping. And Roger is less frazzled, too, now that he's gotten a little sleep."

"That must've been some bachelor party!" I reached for my water glass, because the dragon noodles were causing me to breathe fire. Whoever had placed the little flame icon next to the dish on the menu hadn't been kidding. Before I doused my tongue, I quickly added, "He seemed pretty wiped out this morning."

"I don't know why he looked so ragged." Piper snagged another peanut, while I lost a whole pile of noodles I'd been about to cram into my mouth. I credited Piper's dexterity to her surgical experience and tried not to feel badly about my relative incompetence. "Maybe he did cut loose, a little, at the Lakeside."

I wasn't surprised to learn that Roger and his groomsmen had gone to that particular bar, which wobbled atop a sagging pier in Lake Wallapawakee. The Lakeside, which only served boxed wine and beer—along with the freshest seafood around—was a popular haunt, especially during the summer.

"Roger also mentioned that he didn't sleep well, because he felt like something was going to go wrong with the wedding," Piper added. "Apparently, he tossed and turned all night."

I raised my eyebrows with surprise. "Roger Berendt, half of the world's most rational couple, had a *premonition*?"

Mom waggled her fork, a dismissive gesture. "Roger doesn't believe in voodoo, Daphne."

I had not mentioned a belief system that, as far as I knew, didn't involve prognostication. But there was no sense in mentioning that to Mom.

Piper also overlooked the disconnect between Mom's comment and mine. "He never trusted Abigail. And he was really out of sorts near the end of the dinner at Artful Engagements. I think something, or everything, about Abigail rubbed him the wrong way . . ."

Piper's voice faded out as she realized she'd just admitted that her fiancé had been on the outs with the victim of a homicide. And having all been murder suspects before, our small party got quiet for a moment.

Surrounding us, servers bustled around the crowded, dimly lit room, which was painted a deep, vibrant red that popped against lacquered black trim. Red paper lanterns hung from the ceiling, where a hand-painted dragon seemed to dance above us.

Because the town was something of a quirky artists' enclave, the main street, visible through a big window, bustled with tourists. I watched people stroll past in the steamy evening, some of them stopping to check a flyer that was taped to Typhoon's glass door. I'd noticed the advertisement, too, for business called the Owl & Crescent Art Barn, which hosted painting parties for small groups. Although I had no artistic talent, I thought gathering some friends to paint and drink some wine sounded like fun. Of course, I had more serious matters to attend to right then, and I broke the silence, asking, perhaps too casually, "Roger probably called you when he got home last night, right?"

I didn't suspect Roger Berendt of homicide, but there was a good chance Jonathan and his partner, Detective Fred Doebler, would question all of the disgruntled brides and grooms—and likely focus on a groom who had been at Artful Engagements right before the murder. Piper must've been thinking the same thing, because some of the color drained from her face. "No, I told him not to call. I wanted to turn in early."

"Piper, dear!" Mom interjected. My less-than-subtle attempt to ensure that Roger had an alibi hadn't escaped her, either. She shot me a dark look, silently chastising me, even as she reassured my sister. "Roger didn't harm anyone. The killer was almost certainly that person on the motorcycle Daphne nearly crashed into." Of course, I'd told Mom and Piper all about my discovery of Abigail's body, including my strange encounter on the narrow lane. Then Mom pointed her fork at me. "And Daphne, I am going to kindly request that you don't drag yet another perfectly innocent member of this family into one of your capers!"

I wanted to protest that Jonathan, and just plain circumstance, had roped us into the last several local homicide investigations. But there always did seem to be some shreds of evidence, or potential motives, linking us to killings in Sylvan Creek.

Thankfully, Piper spoke up first to defend me. "It's really not Daphne's fault, Mom. We seem to be at the wrong places at the wrong times lately. And Jonathan Black's presence on the local force has upped the investigative game."

"Speaking of Detective Black . . ." Mom's voice iced

over, just a touch. She respected, and possibly even liked, Jonathan, but she'd probably never forgive him for buying the gorgeous A-frame house *I'd* found for him after he'd rejected the "golf course living" condos Mom had tried to foist upon him when he'd first moved to the area. Not that she would ever admit that I'd basically sealed the deal. "Where in the world was *Roger's best man* for the last few days?"

"Driving as fast as he legally could, all the way across the country," I informed my mother.

Piper already knew that part of the story. Jonathan had stopped at Winding Hill, looking for me, the moment he'd reached town. He hadn't been responding to my 911 call when he'd found me at Artful Engagements. He'd just been tracking me down, only to find me in the midst of a mess.

"Well, why did he fall off the face of the Earth for the last few days?" Mom pressed. "Who in the world can't take time for a quick call or text?"

I was still wondering that myself. Piper had been too busy contacting every person on her wedding guest list to do more than tell Jonathan my whereabouts. And Jonathan and I hadn't had a moment to catch up before some EMTs, coroner Vonda Shakes and Detective Doebler had arrived on the scene, interrupting our reunion, which hadn't turned out the way either one of us had anticipated. At least, I hoped Jonathan had also been looking forward to something a little more romantic than a hurried exchange at the scene of a likely homicide.

That a murder had been committed seemed pretty clear to me. But as far as I knew, Jonathan, who'd asked me to take Axis and Artie for the evening, was still sorting out what had happened back at Artful Engagements.

"Well, Daphne?" Mom asked again. She'd set down her fork, folded her arms and was tapping her red nails, which almost matched the wall color, against her upper arms.

Clearly, Jonathan had lost a few points in her ledger. "Why didn't he call?"

Piper looked understandably curious, too.

I wouldn't have minded an answer myself. And, thankfully, before I had to admit that I had no idea, my phone pinged.

Normally, I would've waited until after dinner was finished to answer, but I knew the police might be in touch again. So at the risk of being rude, I rested my chopsticks on my nearly empty plate and dug into my pocket to see who had contacted me.

The number wasn't familiar, but the texter had identified himself in the message, which said, *Can we talk tonight? Jonathan*

Chapter 8

By the time I'd finished dinner and hitched a ride with Mom and Piper back to Winding Hill, where I picked up Socrates, Axis and Artie, it was nearly nine o'clock. However, as I drove down Sylvan Creek's main street, some of the shops and all of the restaurants were still open to serve the summer tourists who were meandering down the sidewalks on a balmy night. But, as I turned onto the lane that ran past Pettigrew Park, headed for a parking lot near the gorgeous, Italianate public library, the town grew quieter and darker. The library was, of course, closed, the many windows in the wedding-cake-like facade dark, too.

Jonathan's black truck was the only vehicle parked in the small lot, and I pulled up next to it. He wasn't inside, so I hopped out of my van and released all of the dogs, who ran off toward the creek that ran inky black and silent on the other side of the park.

When I couldn't see them anymore, I spun slowly around, wondering where Jonathan was. Then I spotted him, rising from the library's steps, where he'd been waiting.

The moon was full, but it was still difficult to read his expression as he walked toward me.

Neither one of us spoke, and, even as my heart raced

with anticipation, I felt a knot form in the pit of my stomach.

Jonathan obviously hadn't been pleased to find me at the site of another suspicious death, and, although I kept trying to explain away his lack of contact, I couldn't help suffering nagging doubts about the state of our long-distance relationship.

That evening's terse text, from an unfamiliar phone, wasn't helping matters.

Then, just as I was about to ask if everything was all right, or all wrong, he drew close enough for me to read his eyes. And, although Jonathan Black was very good at concealing his emotions when he wanted to, I could tell exactly what he was thinking when he looked down at me—right before he pulled me close and kissed me in a way that dispelled all my fears.

"I can't believe your phone is at the bottom of the ocean," I said, enjoying the feel of Jonathan's fingers interlaced with mine as we strolled down Market Street under trees strung with hundreds of tiny white lights. After letting the dogs run in the park for a while, we were heading to Daisy Carpenter's new restaurant, In a Pickle, to celebrate her grand opening with a drink on the patio, where canines were allowed. "It was really nice of you to take Artie to see some sea lions," I added. "That sounds like something he'd like."

"Yes, he enjoyed it a little too much," Jonathan noted, glancing at the Chihuahua, who trotted jauntily at the end of a leash, his little tail whipping back and forth and his big eyes bulging with happiness.

Axis and Socrates were walking without leads, but Jonathan was making Artie regain his trust after having darted out onto some slippery, perilous rocks to greet a bunch of lounging marine mammals back in California. Lunging after the little dog, Jonathan had dropped his cell phone into the Pacific—which honestly sounded more like something I'd do.

"That was our last stop on the way out of town," he added. "I didn't want to waste hours buying and setting up a new phone, since I was already cutting it close to get here in time for the wedding. So I borrowed a phone, called the only Sylvan Creek number I knew by heart—my own, at the station—and told Adele Ashbee, who picked up, to let you know I was on my way."

I looked up at him with surprise. "You really didn't know my phone number?"

Jonathan arched an eyebrow. "Do you know mine?"

Heat crept into my cheeks. "Well . . ."

Trotting along at my side, Socrates snuffled, like he'd understood the exchange.

"It's the curse of relying on contacts," Jonathan noted. "And, apparently, I can't rely on our administrative assistant, either."

I frowned. "It's too bad the trip turned out to be a total waste of your time."

"Hey, Daphne . . ." Jonathan tugged my hand, so we all stopped under one of Sylvan Creek's iconic, old-fashioned streetlamps, right near Piper's practice, where the window boxes on the pretty blue clapboard overflowed with red and white petunias and impatiens.

Patriotic lights twinkled in the windows of other shops, including Flour Power, down the street, and the marquee at the Bijoux theater advertised an upcoming showing of the movie Moxie had just mentioned, *Yankee Doodle Dandy*.

The summer scene was charming, but I couldn't stop studying Jonathan, hunting for changes that I might not have spotted when we'd Skyped over the last few months. But he looked reassuringly the same. In spite of having been working on a military base, he continued to wear his dark, nearly black hair a little longer than when he'd first moved to Sylvan Creek. And I could just make out the scar on his strong jaw, which was stubbled, as if he hadn't shaved in the wake of his long drive, the last day of which had been made longer by his unexpected arrival at the scene of a murder.

I did notice that Jonathan was a little leaner than usual, which had worried me at first. A tiny part of me had feared that his temporary disappearance had been related to the return of a rare form of cancer he'd already battled twice. A relapse wasn't the type of news Jonathan would share from across the country, and in a few dark moments, I had imagined him taking time to come to grips with the diagnosis before returning here to share the news.

But as I searched his eyes, I finally put those fears to rest.

And yet, I could tell that *something* was on his mind.

"What were you about to say, a moment ago?" I asked, sensing the mood shifting between us.

He spoke quietly. "Just that driving here wasn't a waste of time." He hesitated. "I wanted . . . needed . . . to see you."

Feeling my cheeks redden again, I squeezed, then released, his hand, signaling that we should resume walking. Socrates, who didn't like public displays of affection, even with Snowdrop, was giving me warning looks. Artie was also getting antsy, while Axis, always well-behaved, waited patiently until he got the signal to go.

"I've missed you, too," I told Jonathan, tucking some of my curls behind my ear. A nervous gesture. "And I'm sorry you found me tangled up in another murder. I suppose this is a mess for you." All at once, I realized what might be worrying him, and I looked up at him again. "Am I a suspect?"

Jonathan shook his head. "No, I don't think so. I think Doebler's given up on trying to pin homicides on you. For the time being—at least until Vonda calls time of death—the focus is on identifying the mystery motorcyclist you saw driving away. Plus, you called 911, then waited by the body, while inexplicably wearing a *Statue of Liberty costume*—"

"That was my bridesmaid gown."

Jonathan again quirked an eyebrow. "You're joking, right? I thought you were doing something related to Wags 'n Flags . . . maybe taking part in a parade I didn't know about . . . and just hadn't changed for the wedding yet."

"Nope. That *wasn't* a costume. Nobody wears those except dogs, during All Paws on Deck."

A glimmer of amusement returned to Jonathan's eyes. "Yes, you and Moxie can dress up Artie."

"Really?" We'd reached the lovely brick, Victorian building that housed In a Pickle, and I glanced down at the Chihuahua, who was spinning happily at the end of his leash, like he'd understood the conversation. Artie was a big fan of costumes. Socrates, on the other hand, made a soft, groan-like sound, while Axis, who was also a bit reserved, wisely stayed quiet. "I'm sure Moxie will dream up something special for you," I told Artie, who yipped and bounced on his tiny paws. "We'll just have to find someone with a boat."

"And someplace else to get a drink," Jonathan noted, nodding to a sign on In a Pickle's arched doorway.

CLOSED—SORRY FOR ANY INCONVENIENCE

Stepping back from the doorway, where a banner that hung above us paradoxically announced the restaurant's grand opening, I finally noticed that the building's tall, narrow windows were all dark, just like the window at Flour Power, across the street.

"Sorry, Socrates," I said, looking down at the stoic basset hound, who'd hoped to see Snowdrop. He was trying to hide his disappointment, but his tail drooped lower than usual. Turning to Jonathan, I frowned. "I wonder if this has something to do with Abigail and the wedding disaster."

"How so?"

"Daisy Carpenter was supposed to cater Piper's wedding," I explained, suddenly recalling the strange exchange I'd witnessed back at Artful Engagements, when I'd thought Daisy might've been crying. I didn't believe in keeping secrets from Jonathan, but I didn't like gossip—or casting suspicion on friends—so I decided to keep that information to myself, unless Jonathan gave me good reason to share it. "She might be dealing with a bunch of wasted food."

The street had grown quieter, and Jonathan bent to unclip the leash from Artie's collar. The Chihuahua did another happy dance. Then, on some unspoken agreement, we all began to move toward Flour Power, where the Italian coffee maker and some freshly baked treats for pets, and usually people, waited. "What better place to get rid of food than a restaurant?" Jonathan observed. "Shouldn't she be open, if she has a lot to spare?"

As we crossed the street, I glanced over my shoulder at the dark restaurant, feeling a touch of concern. "Yes. I suppose so."

"So, what will happen, with the wedding?" Jonathan asked when we stopped at the door to Flour Power, where the dogs were already waiting. "Will it take place before Roger leaves the country?"

"I doubt it," I reluctantly conceded, digging into the pocket of my jeans to find my keys. "We don't even have a venue. And everything is booked in the middle of summer."

"But if you had a place—"

"That would be fantastic, but probably impossible," I said, selecting the right key. I shook my head as I tried to unlock the door. "Not that Piper wanted to get married at the Sodgrass Club. That was Mom and her new best friend Beverly Berendt's idea, in collaboration with Abigail."

Standing behind me, Jonathan dragged his hand through his hair. "There *are* a lot of suspects in this case, but I can't deny that your family and friends are mixed up in yet another homicide."

All at once, my hand froze as I pictured Roger's ashen face the morning of the murder. After a night when his whereabouts probably couldn't be verified, following his party.

Roger, who'd been upset with Abigail about the wedding, and her treatment of his sister, Dorinda . . .

"What are you thinking about, Daphne?" Jonathan asked. "I can tell you're formulating some kind of theory, or considering a clue."

"It's nothing," I told him, shaking off my concerns and opening the door so the dogs could all trot into the dark, mod-themed bakery. When Jonathan and I were inside, too, I turned to him before I even switched on the lights. Moonlight streamed in through the windows, casting half of Jonathan's face in shadow. "At least, there's nothing I want to tell you right now, if that's okay."

Jonathan didn't say anything for a long time. I wondered if, like me, he was thinking about how our relationship always seemed to walk a tricky tightrope, one that stretched between our personal lives and his job, making things difficult for both of us. But especially for him.

"Daphne," he finally said quietly. I could tell that he was choosing his words carefully. "You *do* know that I'm technically still on leave, and not really assigned to this case—which *would* create a conflict of interest. I just helped out earlier because I was at the scene."

My mouth opened and closed a few times as I realized I might've deluded myself a little. "I . . . I guess I did know that, on some level," I said. "But for some reason, I assumed you would stay until the case was solved . . ."

He was shaking his head. "No, Daphne. Regardless of whether or not *Doebler* solves Sinclair's murder, I'll need to return to California in less than two weeks."

A bigger, heavier silence fell between us, punctuated by the steady click of my cat-shaped clock's swinging tail and rolling eyes. Even the dogs had the sense to disappear behind the counter into the kitchen, leaving me and Jonathan alone, surrounded by displays full of treats and the sixties-inspired flowers Moxie had painted on the walls. In spite of the cheerful, comforting surroundings, I felt a weight growing inside of myself that was as ponderous as the silence. Maybe I was having a premonition. Or maybe I was just getting better at reading the complex emotions reflected in Jonathan's eyes.

"Jonathan?" I took a step closer to him. "What did you want to talk about earlier?"

He looked away from me, out at the festive street, where twinkle lights glowed in most of the windows and a few tourists still strolled. Fireworks, set off by revelers getting a head start on the holiday, crackled softly in the distance. Meeting my gaze again, Jonathan said, "We should probably sit down. There are things we need to discuss."

In spite of how he'd kissed me, and the way we'd just held hands, I felt my heart sinking like a rock to my favorite Mexican sandals. "Just tell me what's up," I requested. "Please."

Jonathan again took a moment to think. And when he spoke, his voice was low and measured. "I haven't made a decision yet. I wanted to consult with you. And take time to weigh my options."

My stomach was really twisting. "Options? For what?"

Jonathan took a step closer and gently clasped my arms, so I could feel that he didn't want to lose our newly reestablished connection, even as he told me, "I have an offer for a permanent position—with NCIS in San Diego."

Chapter 9

"Daphne, you know that I'm a little bit psychic, and I have a very strong feeling that Jonathan isn't going anywhere," Moxie said, her serious proclamation at odds with the way she was crossing her eyes, the better to thread a needle by the dim light filtering through my sister's living room windows on a hot, overcast day.

Although I used to live in the farmhouse, it felt odd to be there while Piper was out for the afternoon, attending to a guinea pig who'd eaten a bunch of Styrofoam packing peanuts. In her absence, my sister had asked me, as maid of honor, to help her deal with a few remaining things that needed to be done in the wake of the wedding debacle.

My first task was to sort through a bunch of gifts that were piled in the farmhouse. Some of the presents had been mailed earlier by well-wishers who lived out of town. Others were from sympathetic guests who kept stopping by Winding Hill, insisting that the couple accept the items they'd already purchased, because they knew Piper and Roger would get married eventually. And a few boxes and bags had ended up at the Sodgrass Club, too, in the previous day's confusion.

Piper, at least, felt weird about using anything until she was actually married, and she'd asked me to catalog everything so she could write thank-you notes. Then I was supposed to store the gifts, which were no doubt constant reminders of a day gone wrong, in the barn.

Moxie, meanwhile, was sitting cross-legged on the floor, crafting a costume for Artie to wear to All Paws on Deck. She'd leaped at the chance to dress up her favorite "model" again and had devised a plan within hours after I'd texted her.

Socrates, on the other hand, was expressing his disapproval of pet costumes, and probably decorated rowboats, by pretending to sleep near the fireplace.

I really thought that, like Jonathan, he should just give up and accept that dogs in Sylvan Creek dressed up and paraded around.

"My sixth sense tells me that your relationship with Detective Black is just fine," Moxie added, stabbing the needle into khaki fabric. I had no idea how she planned to dress the Chihuahua and Mike's pug, Tiny Tim, who would both ride on a boat owned by one of Mike's relatives. The costumes were supposed to be a surprise, even for me. She held up her handiwork, inspecting her stitches, but I couldn't even guess what her ultimate goal was. "Trust me. I would feel it, if Jonathan was going to take that navy job. Which sounds like a step down to me. I mean, I've seen *NCIS* on TV, and it's not *that* interesting. I don't even bother with the spin-offs!"

My best friend said a lot of kooky things without even realizing it. But she and I—and probably Socrates, too—knew that investigating crimes for an agency with international reach would be an exciting challenge for a guy who thrived on challenges, and who'd only reluctantly abandoned the risk and endless adventure of life as a Navy SEAL.

Along with making more money and having more room for advancement, Jonathan would also be returning to a brotherhood he'd loved, in one of the most beautiful places in the country, if not the world . . .

"What about going with him?" Moxie asked, reading my thoughts, which had just drifted to sunny San Diego. "I would miss you, but I couldn't blame you for following your heart."

"We didn't even talk about that possibility—which isn't really possible at all," I told her. "I signed a three-year lease on the bakery, and I have Lucky Paws clients who count on me. I have serious commitments, not to mention friends and family here."

"Well, then, he'll just have to stay in Sylvan Creek," Moxie said firmly, as if she'd settled the issue.

"It's not that simple." Moving to Piper's coffee table, I reached for a pitcher of freshly brewed iced tea, infused with sprigs of mint from Piper's expansive garden, and I poured two tumblers full, the ice clinking into the glasses. "As Jonathan pointed out last night, he would've had to *again* recuse himself from a case, if he was officially back on the local payroll. He's starting to worry that he knows too many people—or at least people who get mixed up in murders—to do his job here."

Looking up at me, Moxie gnawed her lower lip. "That *is* kind of problematic. You, especially, do find a lot of bodies."

"Yes, it's like I'm accidentally pushing him away," I agreed glumly. "Ironically, the thing that brought us together—involvement in murders—is now threatening to help send him across the country, permanently."

Moxie shook her head. "It's like no good *ever* comes of homicide."

I wasn't sure how to respond, so I took a sip of the cool,

refreshing tea, then set my glass down next to a plate of freshly baked cookies—one of which had been nibbled.

Glancing around the room, I spied a naked tail slithering under the couch. In the past, I would've shuddered to know that Moxie's white rat, Sebastian, was creeping around the room. Having grown fond of him, I was instead slightly irritated that he'd ruined a perfectly good lemon meltaway.

"So are you going to solve *this* case?" Moxie asked, oblivious to her pet's petty crime. "Because it seems like, once again, people you're close to are prime suspects."

I'd returned to the gift pile and was about to check the contents of a huge white bag, but I stopped to look at Moxie, who was rooting around in the antique hatbox that served as her sewing basket. "Who comes to mind first, for you?"

Moxie had brought up the subject of suspects, but she didn't seem eager to answer. A silence fell over the room as she continued digging in the box.

"Who, Moxie?" I asked. "Spill."

Finally looking up at me again, she worried her lower lip. "It's not like I believe he did it . . ."

I was afraid I knew who she was about to name, because I couldn't stop thinking about a certain person's quite obvious motive and recent state of mind myself—even though doing so also made me uncomfortable.

"You're thinking about Roger, aren't you?" I asked quietly, digging into the white sack and pulling a heavy gift from a nest of white tissue paper. The marble wine cooler, which wasn't even in a box, screamed "regift." Checking the accompanying card, I muttered, "Really, Aunt Noreen?" Then I bent to pluck a notepad off the sofa, quickly jotting down my relative's name and a description of the object, which I doubted Piper and Roger would ever use, either. "I've thought about him as a suspect, too," I added. "But for once I agree with my mother. It's almost impossible to believe Roger Berendt could commit murder."

Moxie had pulled some gold thread from her sewing kit, and she used her teeth to tear off about a foot from the spool before reminding me, "But we *both* thought about that possibility."

"It's hard not to, given that Roger was angry the night before Abigail's death, and he looked so ashen and exhausted back at the Sodgrass Club."

As we talked, I reached for another gift bag, which was one of several silver sacks, and, like the wine cooler, probably not new. There was a stain on the bottom. Then I dug into the tissue paper and found the source of the mark. Something *damp*.

That didn't seem promising, but I nevertheless pulled out the object, which turned out to be a purple, lacy garter that looked about seven sizes too big for Piper's leg, because the elastic was destroyed. Setting down the bag, I dangled the ruined accessory from my index finger, showing the weird present to Moxie. "What do you make of *this*?"

Moxie made a show of shuddering before returning her attention to her project. "I don't think I want to know."

I dropped the odd, somewhat icky gift back into the bag, which had a small stamp on the interior, near one of the handles: *The Gilded Lily*. Fishing around some more, I failed to find a card, which was okay. I didn't think Piper owed the giver a note of gratitude. I pushed the bag aside. "I don't want to know the story, either."

Socrates must've agreed. He made a soft, almost growling sound, so I knew he'd been faking his nap.

I wiped my fingers on my jeans. "Getting back to Roger . . . It's a little bit too easy to imagine a scenario in which he went to Artful Engagements to complain about the wedding and Abigail's treatment of his sister—"

"Are we ever going to meet Dorinda?" Moxie interrupted. "What's her story?"

"I have no idea." I pulled together some of the presents to take to the barn. "But Piper said Abigail was very rude to her, which also upset Roger."

"Gee, I didn't even know about that part, and I already expected him to be investigated!"

"Yes, if I were Detective Doebler, I'd have to conclude that Roger had motive. Especially if he'd somehow known about Abigail's plan to disappear with his mother's money." I looked around the room, even though I knew we were alone. Still, I dropped my voice to a whisper. "Which seems possible."

"What do you mean?"

"Piper has twice mentioned that Roger didn't trust Abigail and believed she was ripping them off."

Moxie had resumed rooting around in the sewing kit, but her hand suddenly froze. And when she slowly raised her eyes to meet my gaze, I saw that she seemed uncertain.

"What's wrong?"

"It's just that . . . Well, Mike said Roger called Abigail a 'scam artist' when they went out for drinks." She spoke quietly, too. "And I wasn't going to share the rest of what he told me, because it's probably nothing . . ."

I heard a jingle of tags and looked over to see that Socrates had raised his head, like he couldn't contain his own curiosity, even though he normally disapproved of gossip.

"Maybe you should tell me," I suggested. "We both know, from experience, that it can be problematic when information trickles out during a murder investigation."

Moxie hesitated. Then she confided, "Mike was the designated driver that night. Which was kind of a joke, because Roger and Gabriel don't really drink. Except maybe Roger, that night."

"*Roger* got drunk?" I frowned. "That's hard to believe, too."

"Well, it wasn't like Roger got *ossified*," Moxie clarified, using a vintage *word*, which I was pretty sure meant "drunk," based upon context. Abandoning her sewing project, she held out her hand so Sebastian could climb on board. I hadn't even seen him sneak out from under the couch. As she delivered the rat into her sewing kit, where he sometimes traveled, Moxie continued her story. "But I guess Roger hadn't eaten much at the party, and after a few beers, he seemed a little tipsy. And more agitated. So, about an hour after Mike dropped him off, he called Roger's cell phone *and* landline, just to be a good groomsman, you know? He wanted to make sure Roger was okay and remind him to set his alarm for the following day."

"But . . . ?"

"Roger didn't answer either phone."

I took a moment to think, then said, "He could've been asleep."

Moxie shrugged. "Yes, probably."

We were acting like we agreed on that scenario. But I could tell that, like me, Moxie was also imagining an alternative. One in which Roger, his inhibitions lowered and his judgment clouded, had gone back out . . .

"Nope," I said firmly, cutting off my own speculation. I bent to pick up the gifts I'd just cataloged. "No way!"

"Yes, we got a little crazy there!" Moxie agreed, sounding relieved to dismiss our ridiculous suspicions. She tucked the materials for her project into the box and rested the lid lightly on top, leaving a gap so Sebastian could breathe. Then she uncurled her legs and stood up, dusting off her 1950s pedal pushers, although Piper's floors were spotless. "As former murder suspects ourselves, we, of all people, shouldn't be speculating about our friends, no matter how terribly guilty they look. We should be trying to figure out if there's any way we can help Piper and Roger get married before he has to sail to England."

Moxie was so stuck in the past that I wondered if she subconsciously thought Roger might actually be taking a boat to Europe. She probably pictured us all waving him off as he stood at the rail of a 1930s Cunard luxury ocean liner, confetti raining down around him and champagne corks popping.

Socrates, who had also risen and shaken himself, gave Moxie a funny look, like he thought the comment was odd, too.

"As I told Jonathan, I really doubt that it's possible to throw a wedding before Roger *flies* off in less than two weeks," I said, leading the way to the kitchen, where the back door was located. "We don't have anything in place. Not even venues for the wedding *or* reception—"

All at once, I lost my train of thought, and I abruptly stopped in front of Piper's kitchen window, causing Socrates to bump into my leg.

The day was overcast, but the scene outside was still lovely. Piper's restored red barn, where she kept an antique truck parked, was hung with festive bunting, in anticipation of the holiday, and a field of daisies danced in the light breeze.

"What's out there?" Moxie asked, joining me at the window. She craned her neck, frowning. "I don't see any-thing."

"Nothing," I said, because I wasn't sure if I wanted to share my idea yet.

It might be too crazy, especially since I already had so much to do. The Wags 'n Flags celebration would kick off in a few days, bringing more tourists to town. And I was still overbooked with pet-sitting clients . . .

Chapter 10

"This *hopefully* isn't going to take long," I told Detective Fred Doebler, who was accompanying me and Socrates into Abigail's mansion.

The building's interior technically wasn't a crime scene. Only the garden was officially sealed off with yellow tape and still under scrutiny by a few members of the investigative team. But Jonathan's partner, who was overseeing activity at the site, had intercepted me before I could open the front door. He'd made it clear that he didn't want me nosing around Artful Engagements or Abigail's private living quarters and had insisted upon tagging along as I checked on Ms. Peebles. In fact, if I hadn't reminded him that someone would need to clean her litter box and possibly extricate her from some potentially perilous situation, he would've just opened a can of cat food himself.

"I'll honestly just be a few minutes," I added, leading the way into the dim, cool foyer. Detective Doebler was close on my heels, but Socrates lagged slightly behind, like he was still reluctant to enter the building. "Unless poor Ms. Peebles is *really* stuck somewhere. Which happens. A lot."

"You're taking the cat with you, right?" Detective Doebler

asked. "So you"—he glanced down at Socrates—"and your *dog* don't need to keep coming back here."

I was pretty sure Socrates knew he'd been insulted, but he clearly didn't care about Detective Doebler's opinion and was completely ignoring him.

"So, the cat's going with you, correct?" Detective Doebler repeated, as if saying it twice would make me agree.

Unfortunately, that wasn't my plan. "I don't think I can do that," I told him. "I'd like to get her out of this big, lonely house, but I don't have a foster home for her. And I don't think my cat, Tinkleston, would give her a very warm welcome at Plum Cottage."

Socrates, who had been listening, made a disapproving snorting sound, while Detective Doebler scratched his head, which was crowned by a receding thatch of sandy hair. "Aren't you on the board of directors of a *cat shelter*?"

I was, indeed, one of the administrators of a shelter called Whiskered Away Home, but I didn't think many people knew about my involvement. "Yes," I told him. "But how did you know that?"

I hoped he was going to say that Jonathan talked about me all the time, but, of course, since Jonathan rarely shared anything personal, that wasn't the case.

"I dug into your life the last few times you were involved in killings." Detective Doebler's voice was flat, and I could tell he still considered me a suspect. "So. Are you going to take the cat to the shelter? Or will you have to return here every day to feed it?"

"For now, I plan to keep Ms. Peebles here, because at this point, I don't think she's up for adoption," I told him. "Maybe Abigail had provisions for her in her will."

Detective Doebler opened his mouth, so for a second I thought he was going to order me to take Ms. Peebles home. But he didn't really have that authority.

"Just make it as quick as possible, okay?" he requested, tapping his wrist to get me moving.

It struck me that the middle-aged, paunchy sleuth had gained a bit of an attitude since Jonathan had been away. In past investigations, Jonathan had definitely been the dominant partner. However, while Detective Doebler had also stepped up his wardrobe game, with a better-fitting suit in a shade other than brown, I suspected that he would again take a subordinate role when . . . *if* . . . Jonathan returned to his old job. A decision that would again team Jonathan with a partner who wasn't always pleasant to be around.

"I'm going," I agreed with a sigh, because it seemed even more likely that Jonathan would take the position in California.

Detective Doebler wasn't listening. He'd been distracted by something on his phone, and he didn't follow me upstairs, like I'd expected. He remained in the foyer, his head bent over his screen and his thumbs fumbling, while Socrates wisely tagged along with me.

"Where do you think Ms. Peebles is wedged today?" I asked him, starting a game that my prescient canine friend and I had played more than once at Artful Engagements. But before I could guess "flue of the upstairs fireplace," I heard a muted, panicked mewling sound, coming from Abigail's bedroom.

Heading right for that door, which was ajar, I pushed it open and listened more closely, because I didn't see Ms. Peebles anywhere.

Mrrow . . .

The familiar, still-muffled cry of distress drew my eyes to the bed, and my spine stiffened with surprise.

My hand still resting on the door, I glanced down at Socrates, who shook his head with clear disbelief.

Then, much as I hated to do it, I called over my shoulder, "Detective Doebler? You might want to come here . . . and I guess I *will* be taking the cat."

Chapter 11

"Are you sure you can't keep Ms. Peebles at the farm-house?" I asked Piper, my gaze darting between Tinkleston, who was hunkered down in his favorite spot on the kitchen windowsill, and Ms. Peebles, who sat on top of the old-fashioned icebox.

Tinks was hissing like an angry general defending his miniature turf, while Ms. Peebles was blinking her wide eyes and licking a paw, seemingly oblivious to her tempo-rary housemate's extreme displeasure at having a second cat in the house.

I sort of envied Socrates, who had headed straight up-stairs the moment we'd come home, to avoid the conflict.

"Seriously, Piper," I said, shooting my sister, who sat at the kitchen table, an imploring look while I dug my hand into a canister of freshly made Salmon Snackers. I proba-bly shouldn't have been rewarding Tinkleston's behavior, but as the one-sided feline fight and the afternoon wore on, I felt like I needed to resort to bribes. Setting two treats in front of Ms. Peebles and one in front of Tinkleston—who batted his to the floor with his black puffball paw, a look of indignation on his smooshed-in face—I continued pleading with Piper. "Wouldn't you like to have a cute, wide-eyed cat around for a few days?"

"Although I know that I owe you for all you've done as maid of honor, including sorting through the gifts—"

"Some of which were very strange," I interrupted, thinking of the soggy garter.

"Including the strange ones," Piper continued, digging into a slice of her favorite pie: peach cream, made from our grandmother Lillian's recipe. "In spite of all that, I'm afraid that, between everything happening in my personal life and guinea pig emergencies, I can't handle a pet right now," she said, repeating excuses she'd already listed. Then she glanced at Ms. Peebles. "Especially one who gets herself zippered into suitcases."

"That was no accident," I said, joining her at the table with my own slice of the simple but delicious pastry, made with cinnamon, sugar, cream and fresh peaches from a local orchard. "Between the time I found Abigail's body and the time I returned to Artful Engagements, someone took one of the suitcases that was on the bed and sealed Ms. Peebles in the remaining bag."

Piper covered her mouth with her hand, because she'd just taken a big bite. "Are you sure there were two bags on the bed the first time you went through the house?" She raised her voice, speaking over a new round of complaints by Tinks, who was yowling. "It *was* a pretty stressful day."

"No, I'm not wrong about the suitcases. I remember them both, because one was Louis Vuitton, in the classic pattern I always associate with Mom, and the other, now missing, was basic black."

Piper set her fork on her empty plate and sat back in her chair. "Daphne, I can tell you are starting to investigate, and, although you have had some success in the past, I wish you wouldn't do it."

"I simply went to care for a cat," I reminded her. "The

suitcases just happened to be there. Now it's impossible not to speculate."

Piper wanted to object, because every time I got mixed up in a murder, I seemed to nearly get killed. But her logical side also loved solving puzzles, and she quickly abandoned the lecture and started surmising herself. "Let me guess. You're thinking that Abigail planned to travel with someone—maybe a romantic partner—and that person came back after Abigail was killed to reclaim his or her luggage and sneak away."

Keeping one eye on Tinks, who had finally grown quiet and hopped down from the windowsill, I nodded. "Yes. And it's interesting that you think the person might've been a woman. To be honest, I was only picturing a guy—maybe because I also thought the motorcyclist who nearly crashed into my van was male. Which might not be right. I didn't really get a good look at him. Or her."

Piper had been scraping her fork across her plate, rounding up the last few crumbs, but she stilled her hand. And when she looked up to meet my gaze, I thought she seemed troubled, for some reason. "Do you really think the motorcyclist was male? Not female?"

"In retrospect, I'm not sure," I admitted, pushing my plate, which held the last slice from the pie tin, across the table. I loved the dessert, which I only made a few times each summer, when the fruit was at its peak, but Piper was fanatical for peaches. She accepted the offering with a nod of gratitude while I continued kicking myself for being shortsighted. "I've been making gender-based assumptions that might very well be wrong. I'm glad you reminded me that Abigail might have had a girlfriend, not a boyfriend."

"Or neither," Piper reminded me. "We're just speculating here. And the motorcyclist and suitcase owner aren't necessarily the same person—or even the killer."

"True," I agreed, working hard to both focus on the

conversation and continue to monitor Tinks, who had eaten his treat. The stealthy, surly Persian was stalking around the floor while Ms. Peebles continued to groom herself on the icebox. I didn't intend to interfere unless a real fight broke out. "But most homicides are committed by someone close to the victim."

Piper stood up, like she was getting ready to leave. "Which might be a good reason for a secret lover to quietly gather his or her things and make an exit before the police even knew about the relationship."

"So, as far as you knew, Abigail wasn't involved with anyone?"

"No." Piper picked up the plates and carried them to the sink. "But I didn't know her that well. You would probably know more than me, since you spent time in her personal space."

I pushed back my chair and stood up, too, which sent Tinks scampering from the room. I considered that a good thing. "I don't recall anything that would indicate *anyone* ever visited Abigail, let alone spent the night."

As I said that, I pictured the room as it had looked the day I'd found Abigail in the fountain, and I had this nagging feeling that I was overlooking, or forgetting, something. Maybe a clue to the suitcase owner's gender. But I couldn't put my finger on what I was missing.

I also suddenly felt sorry for Abigail.

"It's kind of sad, to think that she planned so many weddings but never got married herself. Looking back, it seems like the upper part of the mansion always had a lonely, sterile vibe."

Piper was washing the plates, but she looked over her shoulder at me so I could see when she rolled her eyes. "You and Moxie and your 'vibes'! You're probably just feeling mushy because Jonathan's back in town. It's funny how being in love makes you wish everyone was feeling the same way."

I hadn't yet told Piper about Jonathan's job offer, because she had enough on her mind without listening to my problems. Grabbing a dish towel, I turned the conversation to *her* love life.

"So, have you and Roger decided whether you'll try to cobble together a wedding in the next week or so?"

The amusement I'd just seen in Piper's eyes flickered out. "It's impossible, Daphne. And, although I've tried not to make a big deal out of it, especially to Mom, I really am disappointed." She shrugged. "It's hard to explain, but it would have meant a lot to me if we'd been married when he was overseas, even if that had meant jumping through hoops in Abigail's star-spangled circus, with a cult leader for a ringmaster."

"So you know about Brother Alf's organization?" I asked, glad that Piper had brought up the man in the monk's outfit who would've presided over her ceremony.

I'd been shocked when Piper had told me he was a member of Graystone Arches Gateway to Eternity, a community that occupied a compound located about fifteen miles from Sylvan Creek, deep in the Pocono Mountains. I'd never been there, but I'd heard rumors that the "brothers" and "sisters" did more than bake amazing bread—and craft handmade zithers—at their monastic estate. From what I understood, from both local gossip and an exposé Gabriel Graham had printed about the group shortly after he'd taken over the *Gazette*, the leaders *brainwashed* acolytes into staying on the property.

"I take it you've heard the rumors?" I added, accepting a wet plate from Piper.

"Yes, of course," my sister informed me. "I read Gabriel's story. But most people around here knew the place, which is half-monastery, half-dojo and *all* cult—"

"What do you mean 'dojo'?" I interrupted. Having taken a weekend krav maga class at a community center in Israel, I was intrigued by the martial arts.

"I don't think they break any boards," Piper said. "I've just heard that they get different-colored belts for their robes, based upon their loyalty and service—and, I'm sure, financial contribution—to the 'community.'"

I recalled that Brother Alf had been wearing a decorative rope around his waist at the dinner, but I couldn't remember the color. "How high up is Alf? You said he's a leader, right?"

"Not only a leader but the founder. Don't you remember when he performed that *mass wedding* on the shores of Lake Wallapawakee?"

I nearly dropped the plate. "No! How did I miss *that*?"

Piper looked to the ceiling, thinking back. "I think you might've been on one of your overseas jaunts. To Istanbul, I believe."

"Oh, yeah!" I smiled at the memory of impressive minarets and medieval architecture, which I'd greatly enjoyed until I got food poisoning from cheese-filled *börek* pastry sold by a somewhat shady street vendor. Shaking off the memory, I set the dry plate on the counter and returned my focus to the present. "So why did you ask Brother Alf to marry *you*?"

"Believe it or not, he's Roger's uncle." Piper rinsed the other plate. "There was really no other choice, unless we wanted to cause a family rift. Just like I had to ask Dorinda to be a bridesmaid."

"About Dorinda . . ."

Piper shut off the tap—and that line of discussion. "Let's not get into that mess right now, okay?"

"Fine," I agreed, accepting the second clean plate. "But who knew mild-mannered Roger Berendt had such a complex family!"

Piper pulled the old rubber stopper out of the drain and watched the water swirl away with a wistful expression on her face. "You know, I would've endured it all, to be married before Roger goes away." Her shoulders lifted and fell. "It'll sound stupid, but it would have been easier, somehow, to live apart if I knew he was my husband and we had that solid connection."

It was not like my rational sister, who had just accused me of being fanciful about love, to get sentimental about the special union shared by spouses, and I had to resist the urge to tease her. I also understood what she meant. Jonathan and I weren't on the verge of getting married—maybe the opposite was happening—but for once in my life, my previously commitment-phobic self could understand how one might want to forge an even deeper bond with a partner before being separated by many miles.

"So why not elope?" I asked, opening a cupboard and putting away both plates. "You have the license."

I thought I'd come up with a great idea, but Piper offered me another wry grin. "Have you met Bev and Maeve? Do you think they'd take kindly to me and Roger running off? Their 'status' in the community demands that their children have a suitable wedding that serves as a public showcase of their financial means and good taste."

She was right. Eloping would definitely be frowned upon.

Then again, Piper and Roger could have a *real* Fourth-of-July-themed wedding. One that made a statement about the couple's future independence from two domineering real estate agents. But I knew rule-following Piper would never do that.

"Sorry." I handed her the towel so she could dry her hands. I also needed to free my own hands so I could answer my phone, which was pinging in my pocket. As I pulled out my cell, I reluctantly agreed, "I guess you're right. Eloping is out of the question."

I was talking, but distracted by a message from Jonathan. One that read: *Take a ride with me to Crooked Creek Lane?*

I was just about to ask Piper if she'd ever heard of that road when a black whirlwind flew past our feet and Tinkleston finally launched himself at the world's meekest, most clueless and most accident-prone cat, who went flying off the icebox with a familiar, plaintive yowl.

Chapter 12

"Where are we going?" I asked Jonathan, who hadn't answered that question the five other times I'd posed it since hopping into his truck about fifteen minutes, and ten miles, back at Winding Hill, where Piper had finally agreed to keep Ms. Peebles for at least a day or so.

"You are persistent," he noted, grinning as he negotiated a narrow, curving road that passed through an isolated, deep valley I couldn't ever recall exploring.

I almost felt as though he'd conjured up the bright green acres of farmland and shaded forest that passed by on either side of us, the setting sun adding depth and vibrancy to the palette of summer hues.

The truck's windows were open, and I stuck my hand out to catch the breeze, not unlike the three dogs who were sitting in the back seat, sticking their noses out to sniff the scents of cows and flowers and freshly mown fields. Checking the rearview mirror on my side, I saw that even Artie, who was awfully short, had managed to get in on the action, squishing next to Socrates, whose ears were flapping in the wind.

"Can you at least give me a hint?" I requested, facing

forward again and trapping my wildly whipping curls with one hand. "Or a small clue?"

Jonathan downshifted to second so we wouldn't skid around a particularly tight turn. "We both know you take small clues and *attempt* to solve big crimes. So, no. I'm afraid you'll have to remain in the dark for now."

I sat up straighter. "Speaking of big crimes . . . have you heard anything about Abigail's murder investigation? Because I find it hard to believe that Detective Doebler keeps *you* in the dark, even if you're technically not on the case."

I immediately wished I hadn't mentioned the part about Jonathan being on leave, because so far, we'd avoided talking about whether he would *ever* solve another case in Sylvan Creek. I knew we needed to discuss that topic at some point, but right then, I was just enjoying the ride and wanted to live in the moment a bit longer.

Maybe Jonathan felt the same way. He overlooked my comment about his continued leave of absence. "There's been some progress," he informed me. "The coroner's office has determined cause of death."

I shifted in my seat, facing him as much as I could within the constraints of my seat belt. "Can you tell me anything?"

"I suppose so, since it's all going to be in the *Gazette* tomorrow anyway. Graham's new protégé, whose name escapes me . . ."

"Chalmers." I filled in the blanks. "Laci Chalmers."

I'd forgotten all about Laci, whom I'd last seen at Artful Engagements the night before Abigail had been murdered. If I remembered correctly, Laci had called Abigail a witch—and said something about prying her last paycheck from Abigail's grasping fingers after the event was over. A time when everyone else, with the exception, perhaps, of Dexter Shipley and *maybe* Daisy Carpenter, would've gone home . . .

"Do you know something about Ms. Chalmers?" Jonathan asked, his gaze cutting to me again for just a moment. "You're awfully quiet."

"I barely know Laci," I said, sidestepping the question. I wasn't going to implicate a young reporter who was relatively new to town based upon some wisecracks she'd made on the last day of a horrible job. However, I did tell him, "I noticed she has an edgy sense of humor, like Gabriel. I thought they'd get along."

Jonathan could tell that I was holding back, but he didn't press me to share more. We might've been dating, but we had certain unspoken rules when it came to investigating murders. There were limits on what he could tell me. And he probably knew by then that I would follow up on any hunches I had and let him—or, this time, Detective Doebler—know if I found a real lead.

"So, what will I read in the *Gazette*?" I asked, suffering a sudden twinge of concern. "Anything about my friends? Or family members?" I hesitated, then added, "Or maybe something about *potential* family members?"

Jonathan shook his head. "Doebler wouldn't speculate about suspects, Daphne. Not with a reporter."

"What about with you?"

Jonathan's fingers flexed on the steering wheel, and he didn't answer right away. Then he glanced at me again. "It would be nice if Berendt had a better alibi."

That was all he needed to say. All that he *would* say. "I'll keep that in mind," I muttered.

Jonathan acted like he didn't hear me, and I understood that, if I was ever asked—which I wouldn't be—that brief exchange never happened.

"You *will* likely read that Abigail was murdered around one a.m.," he said, slowing the truck and turning onto a dirt path that was bordered by a field of daisies on one side and a bubbling brook on the other. I wanted to insist that he tell me where we were headed, but I also wanted to learn more about the investigation. "There was evidence of a significant struggle, during which her assailant attempted to strangle her, after knocking her over and ultimately drowning her in the fountain."

Jonathan spoke evenly, with enviable clinical dispassion, while I rubbed my throat, which had gotten tight.

"In spite of the fact that the wounds had been submerged for quite a long time, Vonda was able to find white and blue fibers in a series of tiny lacerations on her neck," he added.

"You mean from the flag that was draped over her?"

"Doubtful," Jonathan said, as we passed under a copse of trees that arched above the road. The dogs had pulled their heads in, and they also seemed anxious. Or eager, like maybe Axis and Artie, at least, had visited this spot before. "The fibers are likely from whatever object the killer used to strangle Sinclair," Jonathan noted. "Doebler's waiting on lab results that will hopefully reveal what, exactly, that weapon was."

I had a lot more questions, but we had emerged from the trees, and I forgot about the murder for a moment when I saw that we had reached a dead end. The lane stopped at the edge of a pond, just past a ramshackle white building with peeling paint and sagging shutters.

"Um, Jonathan?" I ventured, when he parked in front of the dilapidated structure. I glanced back at Socrates, who was also eyeing our destination warily. Then I turned back to Jonathan, who was getting out of the truck and releasing the dogs, who ran directly for the pond. Socrates seemed to forget his misgivings and chased after his friends. I exited the vehicle, too, with less enthusiasm. "Did you bring me to *another* crime scene?" I asked, slamming my door shut. "Because this looks like the perfect setting for a homicide."

"There are rumors of a great tragedy that took place

here," Jonathan said, coming around to the front of the truck, the better to view the building. Then he grinned at me. "But it's also, in my opinion, the perfect place for you, Moxie and your crew of other bridesmaids to hold Piper and Roger's *wedding ceremony*."

"Granted, this place is kind of amazing," I admitted, wandering around inside the abandoned chapel, where legend said a woman had flung herself—or been pushed— from the steeple that rose crookedly above us. To this day, those who wandered by the boarded-up chapel late at night were said to hear mournful cries and the clanging of long-silenced bells. At least, that was the story as related by Jonathan, who seemed to know quite a bit about the old church, which was in much better shape inside than out.

Dappled sunlight, filtering through arched windows that probably only required a good cleaning, illuminated rows of honey-colored oak pews and a simple wooden altar, set upon a wide-plank floor that was scuffed in a charming, rustic way.

I looked up at the arched ceiling, which was strung with cobwebs, thinking that, with a little elbow grease and a coat of white paint applied over the course of a day or two, the interior could, indeed, be perfect for the simple type of ceremony I knew Piper would love.

But the *exterior* . . .

I turned to Jonathan, who was leaning against the wall near the door, his arms crossed over his chest, as he awaited my verdict. Which was mixed, to say the least.

"You can't be serious about bringing wedding guests here," I said, still not convinced he wasn't pulling my leg. "I mean, once people were inside, they'd think it was lovely. But the outside is scarier than the old story about the haunted steeple."

"I suspect any mournful cries come from owls, roosting above us," Jonathan said, looking up at the rafters. Then he met my gaze again, and I saw amusement in his eyes. "I wouldn't worry about ghosts crashing the ceremony."

"Haunted or not, how in the world did you even find this place?" I asked, running one hand along the back of a pew. Against my better judgment, I was totally falling for the chapel's interior the longer I remained in the space. I withdrew my hand, forcing myself to focus on reality, as opposed to imagining an evening ceremony, lit by candles I could tuck in each of the narrow, peaked windows that lined the walls. "And who the heck owns it?" I added, suddenly worried that we were trespassing. "Tell me the whole story, please, before I get my heart set on this spot—for Piper."

I added that last part because, for a second, I'd been imagining my own dream wedding—and, like Piper, I wasn't the type of girl who daydreamed about white dresses and veils. My fantasies usually involved passports and plane tickets.

Plus, the only guy I'd ever truly wanted any kind of commitment with was likely moving *three thousand miles away*.

"So, what's the story?" I repeated. "What first brought you here?"

Jonathan leaned against the back of the pew and crossed his arms again. "I was looking through some cold case files when I first came to Sylvan Creek, and I found the story about the steeple intriguing. So one day, I came out here to walk through the scene." He shrugged, like what he was about to say was inconsequential, although I found it more fascinating than a long-forgotten tragedy. "Ever since then, I come here sometimes, to think. In spite of the chapel's supposedly sad history, I find it strangely peaceful. Enough so that I bought the land, about a year ago."

My jaw nearly dropped to the dusty floor. "You *own* this place?"

"And a few other parcels in the area," he noted, like that was no big deal, either. And maybe it wasn't to Jonathan, who came from a family wealthy enough to send him to boarding schools and then Yale, before he'd dropped out to join the navy. He grinned at my continued surprise. "Please don't think I purchased this property just to meditate. This was a good investment. At least, according to your mother, who struck what I believe was a great deal with the farmer who wanted to divest himself of this unused acreage."

My eyes must've been *huge*. "Mom never breathed a word."

"Realtor-client privilege," Jonathan said, referencing a doctrine my mother often invoked, and which I was still certain she'd made up. "She's very serious about it. And I'll admit, I don't talk about my investments very often, either."

"No, you don't. Which is okay," I assured him. "My finances are only an open book because the story is so short. And edited by Fidelia Tutweiler, whose passion for accounting is not necessarily matched by her skill level."

Jonathan laughed, his white teeth flashing in the chapel, which had grown dark. We both seemed to realize that at the same time, and we made our way down the aisle to the door, which Jonathan opened for me.

I stepped past him out into a cool breeze, which carried the sound of the dogs playing near the pond, crickets singing and the soft, spooky hoot of an owl. The waxing moon glowed in a clear, star-filled sky, bathing the old chapel in a forgiving glow.

Taking a few steps back from the building, I let my gaze travel from the crooked, plywood-sealed steeple to the peeling paint and sagging steps.

Jonathan joined me, studying the building, too.

"It really is oddly peaceful here," I said. "I can see why you come here to clear your mind. But can you really fix this place up in the brief window of time we have to hold the wedding?" I suddenly thought of a factor that might influence that timeline, or derail the ceremony. "That is, assuming Roger is cleared of all suspicion, related to Abigail's homicide."

I supposed I was trying to get some assurance from Jonathan, but he didn't exactly offer me that. "Let's hope for the best and assume he'll be able to travel as planned." Before I could ask more questions, he added, "And I won't be repairing the chapel alone. I'll have help."

I glanced at the pond, hoping he wasn't referring to Axis and Artie, who, along with Socrates, continued to sniff around at the water's edge. "From who?"

Jonathan answered my question with a question. "Remember how I hired some ex-convicts to work on my barn?"

Of course I recalled that Jonathan had given some former prisoners the opportunity to gain work experience by hiring them to construct the beautiful barn that sat behind his home. "Yes, but can you count on them again?"

"Two of the men started a construction company together." Jonathan smiled. "They're very grateful for the fresh start, and they said they'd be more than happy to undertake what they consider to be a relatively simple project—which mainly involves scraping paint and adjusting a few boards. I told them the steeple doesn't have to be perfect, as long as the plywood is down so people can see the bell. They also know a landscaper who can clear some brush from around the pond and plant some flowers, last-minute."

I had to admit that Jonathan's plan sounded realistic, and I finally let myself fully envision Piper and Roger standing at the altar, while the candles I'd imagined glowed softly on the deep windowsills and the scent of wildflowers and sounds of soft music filled the cozy space.

And I knew the perfect spot for the reception . . .

"Just have a little faith in me, okay?" Jonathan added quietly, interrupting my daydream.

He sounded different—his voice lower and more serious—and when I turned to him, looking up into his eyes, I knew we weren't just talking about a renovation project anymore.

"Daphne . . ." He reached for one of my hands and laced his fingers with mine. "About the job in California. I don't want you to worry about *us*."

I searched his eyes, looking for reassurance again. "How can I not?"

Jonathan used his free hand to rub the back of his neck, a gesture that meant he was struggling to find an answer, too.

I looked away for a second, and he took my other hand, drawing my attention back to him. "We'll figure something out."

"Yes, of course," I agreed, hoping that didn't count as a fib. Because the more I thought about it, the more convinced I was that he'd take the California job and that what we would "figure out" would be a long-distance relationship doomed to failure. Still, I heard myself bending my rules about lying by saying, "Everything will be fine, I'm sure."

Jonathan didn't reply. He drew me closer to himself, so I could feel the warmth of his body and smell his familiar spicy, masculine cologne. I wanted him to kiss me. But as he wrapped one arm around me and bent to make that wish come true, I stopped him with a firm hand to his chest and a firmer, single-word command that I couldn't believe escaped my mouth.

"Wait."

Chapter 13

"While I'm very grateful for Jonathan's offer, and your willingness to help out, I honestly don't think we could pull this off," Piper said the next day, while looking over a list of things we'd need to accomplish if we were really going to hold her wedding and reception in less than two weeks. She set the paper on the butcher block work surface at Flour Power, where I'd also summoned Moxie and Fidelia Tutweiler for an emergency bridal party meeting.

The small space wasn't optimal, but I really needed to decorate some of the three hundred cookies that would be handed out to dogs at the All Paws on Deck regatta. Plus, I knew that Maeve Templeton would only venture to Flour Power's kitchen twice a day, at regular times, to use the coffee maker. Otherwise, the room was like a secret bunker, safe from meddling mothers and mothers-in-law.

"There's just too much to do," Piper added, sitting back on one of the high stools that ringed the island, where cooling racks held about three dozen cookies shaped like flags and little hot dogs. Picking up her phone, she once again checked a photo of the chapel I'd snapped and sent to everyone in the room. "It's a lot to ask of Jonathan, and you three have already done so much, too. We can't throw a wedding on such short notice!"

I hated to bring up a bad topic, but I had to ask, "Are you sure Roger is really leaving in a few weeks? We all know that he wasn't involved in Abigail's murder, but I think everyone who was upset with her is probably under investigation. Do you think he might be detained in the United States longer than expected—which would mean we had a little more time?"

I tried to put a positive spin on Roger's status as a suspect, and Piper didn't seem overly concerned anyhow.

"I think he'll be traveling as scheduled," she said. "He hasn't mentioned anything about Detective Doebler lately. It seems that the investigative focus has turned elsewhere, thank goodness."

Given my recent conversation with Jonathan, who had indicated otherwise, that news surprised me. Moxie seemed doubtful, too. She was making herself useful by squeezing squiggles of mustard on the mini-wieners, but she looked up from her work to meet my gaze and shake her head slightly, as if to say, *"Piper's being too optimistic."*

I was working on the flags, piping red "icing" made with beet-tinted yogurt onto the cookies, and I shrugged, messing up a line. Setting aside my mistake, I said, "Well, for now, let's work with the existing timeline."

"I think this is all very exciting!" Fidelia said, reaching for the list. Then she shook her head and sighed. "And it's so romantic, too, with the mysterious chapel."

"Yes, it's like *The Birds* meets *The Father of the Bride*," Moxie agreed, referencing two classic movies that, if I recalled correctly, featured little white churches—one of which had been infested with a nightmare's worth of murderous crows, while the other had served as the backdrop for a dream wedding.

I wished Socrates could've been there to roll his eyes, but he had chosen to stay home with Ms. Peebles and Tinkleston rather than listen to one more wedding-related discussion. I suspected that the reserved basset was also avoiding Mike Cavanaugh's prank-loving pug, Tiny Tim, whom Moxie was watching that morning.

Glancing over my shoulder, I was relieved to see the tawny, impish dog in the *PUG NATION* shirt snoring near the back door, his little paws in the air and his tongue darting in and out of his pushed-in muzzle.

"I love Daphne's idea about the barn, too," Moxie noted. "It's going to be perfect for the reception."

I'd first thought of holding Piper's post-wedding party in her picturesque, classic red barn the day I'd warehoused her early wedding gifts. But, lacking a venue for the ceremony, I'd pretty much dismissed the idea—until Jonathan had promised to deliver a church. Then I'd quickly contacted his ex-wife, Elyse Hunter-Black, who produced a TV show called *Wondrous Weddings* for her network, Stylish Life. Fortunately, Elyse, who had impeccable taste, had been thrilled by the prospect of transforming the barn with lights, flowers and music.

"It's going to be magical," Fidelia agreed. "I've been checking out dream wedding websites myself, and you should see how beautiful a barn can be in the hands of a skilled decorator!"

Moxie, Piper and I exchanged surreptitious glances, and I knew they were also feeling a bit badly for Fidelia, who had a romantic streak, but who had never had a date, let alone a proposal, since moving to Sylvan Creek. We all knew that, because Fidelia complained endlessly about her lack of a romantic life.

Then I took a closer look at my part-time accountant, noting that she was wearing a surprisingly bright yellow blouse and blue shorts instead of her usual palette of brown.

I'd never known Fidelia Tutweiler to wear so much color, let alone bare any skin, and I gave myself a mental pat on the back for setting her up with two handsome dance partners at the holiday Bark the Halls Ball. I swear, twirling around the floor with Jonathan and Gabriel Graham had boosted her confidence.

In fact, a moment later, I suspected that she might have her sights set on a man. And a handsome one, at that.

"Do you think maybe we should ask *Dex* for some assistance?" Fidelia mused, sounding a bit too casual when she spoke the young wedding planner's name. She was also overly focused on the list of tasks, which we intended to divvy up. I got the sense she was trying to avoid meeting our eyes when she said, "Dexter didn't try to cheat anyone. And he'd probably feel badly enough to help us out. Because this list is pretty long."

Moxie had a gleam in her eye that told me she agreed that Fidelia might have a crush on Dex, who'd chatted with Fidelia at Artful Engagements.

As I pictured that exchange, I suddenly realized that Dexter Shipley might take over the business in the wake of his boss's death. If that was the case, he would be out from under Abigail's oppressive, demanding thumb *and* owner of an established, lucrative enterprise.

Interesting.

"Well?" Fidelia prompted, sounding hopeful. "Should we contact Dexter?"

I wasn't sure about that idea, and I deferred to the bride. "What do you think, Piper?"

"Even with help, you're all attempting the impossible," Piper insisted again. She reached across the island and plucked the list from Fidelia's fingers. "Flowers. Photographer. Minister! Nothing's in place!"

Fidelia seemed disappointed by Piper's dismissal of her idea about Dexter, while I couldn't believe my can-do sister was acting so defeated. "I can easily contact Alf Sievers and Laci Chalmers," I volunteered, setting a completed flag cookie onto a drying rack. I looked to Piper. "That is, if you still want both, or either, of them involved in the ceremony."

"I doubt Laci will be interested." Piper reached for one of the strawberry-lemonade slushies I'd whipped up in Flour Power's blender. I'd expected the kitchen to get hot. "And it's almost impossible to call Alf."

"Who the heck is 'Alf'?" Moxie asked, without looking up from her work, which was impeccable. I would never understand what had gone wrong with my van. "I don't recognize that name."

"He's Roger's uncle," I explained, since Piper wasn't rushing to brag about her odd officiant. "He was dressed as a monk the other night. And he's kind of famous for performing a mass wedding on the shores of Lake Wallapawakee a few years ago."

"It was a blatant publicity stunt." Piper shook her head. "Two hundred couples getting married at once. Why would *anyone* take part—or be involved with Graystone Arches Gateway to Eternity?"

Moxie seemed oblivious to Piper's disapproval. Her eyes lit up. "Oh, I love that cult! They make the best sourdough—and zithers!" She'd finished decorating all the cooled hot dog cookies, and she set down her piping bag so she could make a tossing motion. "I just throw away the flyers that invite you to live with them forever as a hostage when I buy the bread at the farmers' market."

Fidelia, who had also spoken with Roger's uncle at the party, made a face. "I thought Brother Alf was very sweet. I can't imagine he'd take anyone hostage."

"I doubt the residents are actually held against their will,"

Piper said. Then she changed her tune slightly. "Although, Daphne, you might want to avoid the compound. You do have a habit of getting yourself into sticky situations."

I hadn't planned to drive to the isolated property, and I frowned. "Why did you say I can't just call?"

"There's only one phone at Graystone Arches. If you call someone, the monk on duty may or may not bother to track down the person you're trying to reach. And you'd have to hand *your* phone over if you went there. They took Roger's away when he visited a few weeks ago to ask Alf to marry us."

I set down my piping bag, too, and licked some yogurt off my fingers. The beet mixture was surprisingly tasty. "Are you sure you can't use another minister?"

Piper shook her head. "No. I told you, it would cause a huge family rift. So, please, just forget this crazy wedding idea!"

"Let me at least ask Laci and Brother Alf if they're available," I said. "It can't hurt."

Piper sighed. "Fine. If you insist. But please don't go to too much trouble. You're all very busy!"

"If you aren't detained at the cult, could you please pick up some bread?" Moxie requested. "I'll pay you back."

"Umm, sure," I agreed, while Piper shot Moxie one of her signature funny looks.

Fidelia didn't seem to think the comment was odd. She was too enthralled by the growing intrigue surrounding the wedding. "Has anyone else realized that, between all of us, the monk, Laci . . . and *possibly* Dexter"—she wasn't giving up on her plan to loop in Abigail's assistant—"we're reassembling the people who were at Artful Engagements the night before Abigail's murder? And, if things go as planned, we'll all meet at an abandoned chapel where someone went missing years ago." She shuddered with what I thought was a mixture of dread and glee. "I feel like I'm in an Agatha Christie novel, and the killer will be revealed at the wedding!"

Fidelia had made the observation, but Piper looked directly at me. "Please tell me that's not your plan, Daphne."

I raised my hands, protesting my innocence. "I just want to return safely from Graystone Arches. I am *not* investigating anything."

Piper continued to appear doubtful. Shooting me one more warning look, she read the next item on the list. "We'd need a cake, too!"

Moxie's hand shot up. "I can do that. I've finished Artie's and Timmy's costumes for the regatta, so I have some free time."

"Will you please tell me how you're dressing the dogs?" I asked, reaching for my own slushie. As I'd expected, it had grown warm in the kitchen, where an antique fan, set on top of a cupboard, created the only breeze. "Are they, like, part of a pair?"

"Yes, they have matching costumes," Moxie confirmed. "But I'm not telling you anything else. I want it to be a surprise when you set sail!"

Swallowing a sip of the icy drink, I blinked at her, confused. "When *I* set sail?"

Moxie nodded. "Yes, of course. You'll be captaining the *S.S. Tiny-tanic*, which is not so much a luxury liner as Mike's cousin's rowboat."

Piper groaned, while Fidelia clapped her hands together. "Oh, what fun, Daphne! You always have the best adventures!"

"I don't even know how to row . . . And that name, *Tiny-tanic* . . ."

Moxie spoke right over me. "You don't need to worry about a thing. The boat's real name is *Something's Fishy*.

Mike's cousin Fred just jokes that it's the *Tiny-tanic*—because it sank once. But he's plugging all the leaks as we speak. You will be good to go by All Paws on Deck!"

I didn't see how *Something's Fishy* was much better than the nickname, but my shoulders slumped with resignation. "Will you be 'sailing' with me?"

Moxie made a mock shudder. "No, thank you. There are turtles in that lake." She had a severe case of chelonaphobia. "Plus, I'll be busy baking the wedding cake. I'll probably just pop by in time to see you and the dogs floating by."

I couldn't deny that Moxie would be preoccupied. And she was doing me and Piper a lot of favors by making Artie's and Tiny Tim's costumes *and* baking what I knew would be a beautiful cake. Moxie had once re-created all of Sylvan Creek in gingerbread, her details so accurate that a missing light in a window had helped to solve a homicide.

"There is so much going on," Piper noted, sounding concerned again—while I got a little worried, too, because Tiny Tim had woken up and was heading for the glass counter, which was stocked with treats. "And I hate the thought of Jonathan fixing up a chapel just for me and Roger. That's a big favor."

Reluctantly setting down my cold, sweating glass, I followed the pug. "Jonathan said he needs to repair the building anyway. And he promises it won't take long."

"I think we can all trust Jonathan Black," Moxie advised, as I stepped into the public part of the bakery. "He *always* comes through. Remember the time he saved you from your own refrigerator, Daphne?"

I was well aware that Moxie was urging me to have faith in more than Jonathan's ability to slap some paint on an old church. I had already told her about how I'd pushed Jonathan away with the weak, but somewhat true, excuse that Piper and Roger should share the first kiss at the chapel. The *whole* truth was that I fell harder for Jonathan every time he so much as took my hand in his, and I wasn't sure that was a good idea, for the time being.

Needless to say, Jonathan's and my ride home had been quiet, and the kiss I did receive, at Plum Cottage, had been planted respectfully on my cheek.

"I'm sure the chapel will be finished," I promised, pretending I didn't catch Moxie's deeper meaning. Continuing to keep one eye on Timmy, who'd passed the counter and moved to the door, I spoke over my shoulder. "In the meantime, we also need a caterer. It seems as if Daisy Carpenter has disappeared."

Back in the kitchen, Piper responded to me, but I didn't catch what she said, because all at once, Timmy popped up onto his hind legs, pressed his paws against the glass, and started barking in an urgent, excited staccato.

I *really* didn't want to pay attention to those yips, because the last time Timmy had summoned me in a similar way, he'd dragged me into the middle of a murder investigation. Yet I found myself joining him at the door, where I looked across the street.

Then I turned back again and said, more loudly, "Correction. I don't think Daisy has vanished. I think she's just been *hiding*!"

Chapter 14

"Hey, Snowdrop," I called softly, poking my head into In a Pickle. The poodle, who was probably violating a bunch of health codes by exploring the dining room, dropped down to all fours and turned away from the window, where Tiny Tim had obviously spotted her before I did.

Her tail wagging, Snowdrop hurried to me on her delicate paws, her nails clicking on the whitewashed pine floor.

"Socrates and I have both missed you," I whispered, offering her a treat I'd grabbed from Flour Power before darting across the street. Snowdrop's puffball-topped tail was wagging hard, so I knew she'd missed us, too. I had to resist the urge to pat her head, because the fur between her ears was also perfectly teased, and I didn't want to mess it up. Instead, I asked, "Where's Daisy?"

Snowdrop seemed to understand the question. Her eyes alight, she turned toward a discreetly placed swinging door on the opposite side of the pretty restaurant, which was decorated in an upscale country style that accurately reflected Daisy's innovative farm-to-table cuisine. Exposed brick walls surrounded a scattering of scarred walnut tables, above which metal pendant lights dangled from an original punched-tin ceiling. Old pickle barrels flanked a bar where customers could have a glass of wine or sample from glass jars of tempting homemade pickles in flavors ranging from sweet-and-sour to garlic dill and spicy habanero.

Offering Snowdrop another treat, I picked my way through the tables, which were preset with gingham place mats. As I drew closer to the door, I heard clinking, clanging sounds coming from the kitchen, like Daisy was finally going to have her grand opening.

Thinking I'd congratulate her and offer to help before bringing up the catering job, I pushed open the door—only to discover that the young chef wasn't chopping, stirring and sautéing. In fact, there was no food in sight. Only plenty of utensils, which Daisy was tossing into bus pans that were lined up on her shiny silver prep area.

"Daisy, what are you doing?" I asked, one hand still on the door.

She wheeled around, her eyes wide with alarm. Or guilt. Maybe both.

"What's going on?" I inquired again, stepping into the kitchen and letting the door swing shut behind me. I didn't mean to exclude Snowdrop, but, having read a few pages from the health and safety manual that governed local establishments, I was sure dogs weren't welcome in commercial *kitchens*.

"Please, go, Daphne," Daisy requested, without greeting me. She resumed piling gleaming utensils into the gray pan. "Just leave me alone!"

I overlooked that plea, because she seemed awfully distressed. Then my gaze darted to two cardboard boxes that also sat on the counter. One of the cartons, which, according to its label, should have held tomatoes, was filled with linens. A stack of striped terry cloth towels was about to topple over. "Are you *packing up your kitchen*?"

Daisy wasn't cooking, but she'd covered her hair with a

wide headband and donned her chef's coat, probably out of habit. Swiping the sleeve under her nose, she spoke in a choked voice that told me she'd been crying. "I have no choice!"

I was seriously starting to wonder if Daisy might have had a hand in Abigail's death. I couldn't imagine the petite brunette with the wide brown eyes and heart-shaped face killing anyone, but she'd gone into hiding right after the crime, and it looked like she was fleeing town.

"Why don't you tell me what's going on?" I suggested, keeping my voice even and standing very still, so I wouldn't provoke her or make her dart off. "Maybe I can help."

"There's nothing you can do," she said, her bow-like lower lip quivering. "The police already suspect me of killing Abigail—and they haven't even figured out the secret she held over my head, using it to *blackmail me*!"

The case against Daisy seemed to be getting stronger, and I probably should've run away. But the fear I felt prickling in my veins was balanced by an equal tingle of curiosity, and I heard myself asking, "What secret, Daisy?"

She suddenly seemed to grasp that she'd unburdened herself too much. Her jaw hung open for a moment. Then she must've figured there was no going back. Or maybe she needed to confide in someone, because all at once she blurted the truth.

"Abigail knew about the *poisonings*, Daphne! The ones I hid for two years!"

Chapter 15

"You have got to give me the recipe for the spicy habanero, and the other varieties, too, if you don't mind," I said, taking a sip of beer from a frosted mug. I set the drink on the gleaming bar and swiveled on my high stool. "Like everything you cook, your pickles are delicious."

Daisy smiled, but wryly, and her eyes were still rimmed with red. "I'm surprised you're not scared to eat here—like everyone else will be, when word gets out that dozens of people got deathly ill from my food."

Poor Daisy hadn't purposely poisoned anyone. Something had gone wrong with potato salad she'd prepared for a summer wedding back in her hometown of Narrowsburg, New York, in the Catskills. She'd come to another tourist-friendly community—Sylvan Creek—in hopes of making a fresh start. Unfortunately, she hadn't moved quite far enough to escape the gossip among small-town wedding planners on the East Coast. The planner who'd booked Daisy for the fateful reception had contacted Abigail, warning her about the disaster.

Abigail had been savvy enough to realize that the incident, which had stemmed from a server's failure to fill an ice tray under the salad, wouldn't happen again. She was also smart enough to grasp that she basically held Daisy's reputation in her hands, and she'd used that power to force Daisy to work for next to nothing.

"I thought if I could just handle Abigail's abuse until I had a loyal customer base and firmly established this place . . ." Daisy waved her hand, gesturing to the welcoming restaurant she'd created. Snowdrop, who sat at the foot of Daisy's stool, clearly understood her person's mood. She lay down and whined softly. "I was convinced that I could stop catering," Daisy continued, "and Abigail would lose her power over me."

Pushing away my empty plate of pickles, I rested my arms on the bar. "Daisy, maybe nobody has to know what happened in the past. I can't imagine that Detective Doebler would go blabbing about an incident he uncovered during a murder investigation. I've been involved in a few cases myself, and it seems to me that detectives are pretty discreet."

Daisy hung her head and picked at the hem of her white coat. "The story will get out somehow." She smiled again, but she still wasn't amused. "It's ironic, how Abigail actually kept the tale in check by maintaining power over it. She would've lost her slave labor if anyone else ever found out the truth."

But if Abigail was dead, Daisy would be free, and the secret would be buried, too . . .

"I know what you're thinking," Daisy said quietly, watching me. "You're wondering if I killed Abigail after I staged that pathetic rebellion the night of Piper's party. And then I sent you that text when I was so angry."

I didn't try to deny that I had doubts. "What happened in the kitchen at Artful Engagements? And what was up with the message?"

Daisy looked away, across the bar, at a mirror that reflected us both. My curls were more wild than usual, thanks to the humidity in Flour Power's kitchen, and I had a smudge of flour on my gray T-shirt, which featured the bakery's paw-and-peace-sign logo. Daisy's cheeks were pale, and she had dark circles under her eyes. Her headband, which she kept pushing with the back of her hand, was askew. In short, both of us looked like we could use a shower, and possibly a nap.

"I didn't want to see Abigail push you around, like she did me," Daisy finally said. "I heard her bullying you into watching the cat, and, even if she wasn't blackmailing you, I didn't want you to get stuck under her thumb."

"I probably should've been more firm about refusing her," I agreed. "But it's very hard to argue with a person who basically ignores your protests. Which is how Piper, who is pretty direct herself, ended up with a theme wedding."

"Not only was Abigail forceful, but I'm pretty sure she was starting to wield her power over me just for the fun of it," Daisy noted. "She knew that storm was coming, but she kept pushing me to stock the buffet."

"And you tried to fight back."

Daisy nodded. "Yes. When you came into the kitchen, I nearly blurted that she didn't pay me enough to boss me around like that. But I saw the disbelief, then challenge, in her eyes, and I knew she'd destroy my business if I defied her. So at the last second, I held my tongue and did as I was told." Daisy raised a hand. "And you need to believe that I didn't know she'd overbooked the Sodgrass Club and was about to skip town. I had no clue! I was one of several caterers she booked that day. We all lost money, buying food and wasting our time, preparing for events that never happened."

"Sorry," I said. "Piper was afraid that was the case." It was my turn to study Daisy. "So what happened after the storm cut loose? How long did you stay at the mansion?"

Daisy drew back on her stool, suddenly putting up her guard. "Are you trying to convict, or help, me? Because I know you have a reputation for solving murders—sometimes to protect your friends. I followed the story about Moxie last winter. I read in the *Gazette* that you helped solve the case because the evidence pointed toward her. But I'm not one of your good friends, like Moxie. And *someone* goes to jail when a murder is solved. Maybe you think it should be me."

She was putting me on the spot, but she had a right to ask about my motives, since I was snooping around, asking a lot of questions I really had no right to ask. I needed to make a decision, and I glanced at Snowdrop, who wagged her tail again when I caught her eye.

No one in Sylvan Creek had wanted the once-high-maintenance poodle, who had previously belonged to a woman who'd basically tried to ruin the town before ending up dead under a Christmas tree. Only Daisy had stepped forward, and now Snowdrop was well adjusted, her days of diamond-studded collars long behind her.

Her tail still carving short arcs, Snowdrop next gazed up at Daisy with the sort of worshipful look that dogs reserve for their most important person.

I met Daisy's eyes again. "I believe you're innocent. And if I can help you, I will. But you need to be honest with me."

Daisy nodded, accepting those terms. Then she said, "I've already told Detective Doebler everything that happened that night. Not that I think he believes me."

I'd taken another sip of beer, and I swallowed quickly so I could sympathize. "He never believes me, either. Don't feel badly."

"To be honest, I don't know why he *wouldn't* suspect me," Daisy admitted. Her brow creased, like she wasn't sure of her own innocence. "Things got so strange after that storm broke."

"How so?"

Daisy had sort of drifted off, and she shook her head, snapping back to reality. "I'm sure you remember how the guests who were still there just took off." A faint, more genuine smile played at the corners of her mouth. "I remember seeing the monk waddling away."

I could also picture Brother Alf's hasty departure, his retreat hampered by his sandals and the long ends of his belt swinging.

"I kept running back and forth between the buffet, the kitchen and my van," Daisy added. "I was trying to salvage at least some of the food, but it was really too late, once the rain and wind started. It was just chaos then."

I had questions, but I let her keep talking.

"I know that Dexter tried to be helpful," she said, looking off into the distance. "I saw him with an umbrella, escorting somebody to the parking lot. But I had no idea who it was, because he was hunched over the person, his free arm outstretched to shield him or her from the wind and the hail. Then Dex seemed to disappear."

I couldn't help chiming in. "Where was Abigail during all this?"

Daisy's pale cheeks flushed, and she turned her face away. Snowdrop whined again, clearly sensing that her person was agitated.

"What did you see?" I asked Daisy. "I can tell you're keeping something back."

Daisy faced me again, and I saw misery in her brown eyes. "I haven't even told this to Detective Doebler, because he didn't ask the right questions. And I don't want you to run to him—or Detective Black—if I share this with you. Because I don't know what Laci has admitted to the police. And her story is *her* business, and hers to tell."

Maybe that was the case, but Daisy must've been sick of carrying Laci's secret, on top of her own, because without waiting for me to make any promises—and I wouldn't have been able to—she confided, "The last time I saw Abigail, the power had gone out at the mansion. I was fumbling my way down the hallway that runs past Abigail's office, trying to get to the front door and go home. As I passed the office door, lightning flashed, and in the split second the room was illuminated, I saw Abigail—and Laci. And even in that tiny moment, it was quite clear that they were arguing, when I thought Laci should've already been long gone. It was her last night working for Abigail, and the party was over."

"Laci mentioned something about staying to get her check."

Daisy shook her head. "I don't think she meant that literally. When Abigail *did* pay us, she sent checks in the mail."

I didn't know what to make of that, and it was time for me to go. Hopping off the stool, I dug into the back of my jeans, pulling out some cash to pay Daisy for the beer and pickles.

Daisy stood up, too, being careful not to step on Snowdrop, who'd waited patiently on the floor. Then she waved off my offered money. "No, this was my treat." She suddenly seemed to realize her predicament again, and the light that had sparked briefly in her eyes flickered out. "I'll be looking to get rid of my inventory soon anyhow. If I'm not on trial for murder."

I stuffed my money back into my pocket. "Don't give up the restaurant or worry too much yet, okay? My mother, Moxie and Piper have all been in deeper trouble than you. Or, at least, as deep. And they were dealing with Jonathan, not his partner. Just stay the course for now, okay? Hold your grand opening!"

Daisy didn't seem convinced. She moved behind the bar, clearing off my empty plate and mug. "I don't know . . . I can't imagine that word about my past won't get out somehow." She reached under the counter, grabbed a rag and cleaned up the ring of condensation left behind by my drink. "I feel like I'm destined to be ruined here and should prepare to move on."

Snowdrop whimpered, as if she understood the conversation, and I suddenly realized that, if Daisy really did move, Socrates and the poodle would be separated again. I *needed* Daisy to stick around.

"I can help you restore your reputation," I promised. "I'm not as powerful as Abigail, but I do know just about everybody around here. And I can offer you a job that would introduce a lot of influential local people to your food and prove that you can safely cater a big summer event."

Daisy's head jerked up, even as her hand kept swiping circles. "What do you mean?"

"We're trying to regroup and hold Piper's wedding this summer. If you're available, we'd like you to cater the reception."

Daisy was feeling defeated, but she was a chef at heart, and she couldn't help being interested. The little spark in her eyes came back. "What were you thinking?"

"Unlike Abigail, who forced you to create a bunch of red, white and blue stuff that didn't really represent *your* food, I'll leave most of the menu up to you," I told her. Then I was struck by an idea, and I told her, "But there's one thing you *have* to serve, if you accept the job. And I won't take no for an answer!"

Chapter 16

"I honestly think Daisy and Snowdrop are going to be fine and stick around Sylvan Creek," I told Socrates as I hauled open the door to Piper's barn, trying not to drop a bunch of rags I'd brought from Plum Cottage or lose Ms. Peebles, whom I'd picked up from the farmhouse.

I'd spent my ride back to Winding Hill debating whether to tell Socrates that Snowdrop might be leaving town again, because the poodle had disappeared once before, when she'd been part of a complicated estate settlement. Ultimately, I'd decided that Socrates would rather have time to prepare, emotionally, if he and his puppy love were going to be parted—which I didn't *really* think would happen.

"Daisy is very invested in In a Pickle," I reminded the stoic basset hound, who followed me into the barn, where the table full of gifts waited. The pile would need to be moved again before the reception. I turned to close the door, then changed my mind, deciding to let the evening breeze clear the air. "Once Daisy successfully serves potato salad at Piper's reception and all of the guests are wowed by her food and flock to the restaurant, she'll regain her confidence and realize that she's going to be successful in Sylvan Creek."

"Woof!"

Socrates' rare vocalization, which I assumed was a re-minder that Daisy was also under investigation for murder, startled me, causing me to drop the old towels—and Ms. Peebles, who leaped from my arms and ran across the wooden floor.

The barn, with its exposed rafters, sharp tools and open hayloft, was probably a terrible place to bring the world's most accident-prone cat, but Piper had made me promise I'd take responsibility for Ms. Peebles again. And I didn't feel good about leaving her alone at Plum Cottage with Tinkleston while I began cleaning up for the reception.

"I'm sure Ms. Peebles will be okay for an hour or so, right?" I asked Socrates as I knelt down to pick up the rags, which I planned to use to wipe dust from the antique truck that was parked in the barn. I'd mentioned the vehicle, which was red, with wooden slats around the bed, to Elyse, and she'd suggested that we might bring it outside and decorate it with flowers, creating a photo op for guests. Grabbing the threadbare dish towels, I continued trying to reassure Socrates. "And Daisy *didn't* kill anyone . . ."

I let that thought trail off for two reasons.

First, Socrates was wandering away, headed back out-side, presumably to meditate while the sun set.

I also grew quiet because, all at once, as I grabbed the rags from the floor—and recalled how Daisy had wiped down the bar at In a Pickle—I felt a cold knot form in the pit of my stomach.

Still kneeling, I flashed back to the box of towels I'd seen in the kitchen, too . . . and a cloth Daisy had used at Artful Engagements, when she'd wiped down the counter there.

All of the rags were the same, presumably purchased in bulk at a restaurant supply store.

Crouching on the rough boards, I also heard Jonathan's voice echoing in my mind.

"Vonda was able to find white and blue fibers in a series of tiny lacerations on her neck . . ."

"Daisy's towels were all blue and white striped," I whispered, talking to myself.

Or, at least, I thought I was alone, until I heard a soft *mrrrow*, coming from right next to me.

"Hey, Ms. Peebles." I glanced at the curious cat, who blinked at me with her huge eyes. Then I dropped all but one of the dish towels back to the floor. "You're going to think this is crazy. But I have to check something."

Feeling a bit silly, I nevertheless wrapped the towel around my throat and tried to pull it tight.

There wasn't much leftover fabric to hold on to, so I wriggled a bit, trying to determine if an assailant could've really kept a grip if someone struggled.

"Mrrow!"

Ms. Peebles's eyes were *huge*, and she backed away, like she thought I'd lost my mind.

And she wasn't the only one to question my investigative tactic.

As I fought even harder against myself, I heard someone call to me from the doorway, his normally steady voice uncertain, "Daphne . . . Are you *strangling* yourself? Because I don't think that's going to work!"

Rising, I pulled the towel away from my throat and turned to greet my rational future brother-in-law with a sheepish smile. I held out the rag. "I was just . . ."

I planned to explain what I was doing, until I saw the look on Roger's face as he stepped closer to me.

"What's wrong?" I asked. "Are you okay?"

Roger Berendt was one of the most solid citizens I knew. A guy I respected and trusted, from the top of his conservative haircut to the pennies in his loafers. So I was very surprised when he swallowed thickly, then admitted, "I've been lying to Piper, Daphne. And I can't do it anymore."

"I understand that you wanted to spare Piper any more stress," I told Roger, who sat next to me on the bed of the antique truck, our legs dangling down. "But you need to be honest with her. She thinks you're pretty much free and clear, and no longer on Detective Doebler's radar."

"That is not the case at all." Roger bent his head and rubbed his temples. "I think I'm a *prime* suspect." He let his hands drop to his sides and turned to me, misery clouding his brown eyes. "I can't believe I'm coming to you about this."

That was a bit insulting, but I understood what he meant. Roger and Piper considered themselves the problem solvers—except when it came time to handle murders, at which point I was clearly the expert.

"I'm hoping you can offer me some advice," Roger said. "I'm not sure what to do at this point. I've never had any scrapes with the law. Nothing more than a traffic ticket. And suddenly, on the eve of my marriage and a fantastic opportunity to teach overseas, I may be arrested for *homicide*."

I'd never heard Roger Berendt sound shaken before, but, having seen Piper crack when under suspicion of murder, I knew what the pressure could do to even the strongest person.

"Why don't you tell me everything that happened after the party at Artful Engagements?" I suggested, hopping down off the truck and grabbing one of the rags, which had been piled next to me. I planned to listen carefully, but there was a lot to accomplish, and the sun was setting on one of our precious few days to get things done. Shaking out the towel, I added, "And why did you think Abigail was running some sort of scam before the day everyone found out?"

Roger pinched the bridge of his nose and grimaced. "I regret ever using that word. I'm usually so careful with language."

I began polishing a fat cherry red fender. "What *did* you mean?"

"I just thought Abigail's entire business was more style than substance," he explained, hopping down, too, and brushing off the back of his trademark khakis. He also wore a short-sleeved, plaid summer shirt and loafers. I wasn't surprised that he considered Abigail's enterprise frivolous and ostentatious. Roger grabbed a rag, too. "She overcharged our all-too-willing mothers for things that we could've done ourselves, like booking a room at the Sodgrass Club. And her ideas weren't particularly original. Just showy—like red water in a fountain ringed by cherubs dressed as Uncle Sam. Not to mention brides-maids' gowns that turned out to be cheap costumes!"

My hand jerked to a halt. "What?"

"The dresses Abigail ordered weren't 'designer exclusives,' like she claimed. I did an Internet search on the label, and, like I expected, 'Shakespeare's Closet' caters to community theater leagues and schools putting on inexpensive productions. Your dress was cheap nylon."

"Yet Moxie made it look good, at our fitting," I mused, looking around for Ms. Peebles, who had disappeared. That didn't bode well.

"I can only imagine how much money Abigail has pocketed over the years, passing off low-quality items to brides and grooms with stars in their eyes—not to mention status-obsessed parents with deep pockets. And we fell prey to her 'grand finale.'"

"My mother is usually so shrewd," I noted, shaking my head, then shaking the dust out of my rag. "Then again, she stands to make money on the swindle."

Roger must've known about Mom's plans, because he didn't ask for an explanation. Instead, he patted the truck. "Why don't we just run this thing through a car wash?"

That was a reasonable question. "Piper's afraid a modern car wash will destroy the old wood. And it's not really dirty. Just dusty."

Roger seemed to accept that explanation. He resumed working, running his rag along the wooden slats that surrounded the truck's bed.

"So, you really didn't know that Abigail actually planned to leave town?" I asked, awkwardly climbing onto the back of the truck again so I could wipe down the roof of the cab. "You were as surprised as anyone else that day?"

"Of course," Roger said. "If I'd known anything in advance, I would've had *harsher* words for Abigail Sinclair, the night . . ."

I turned to look down at Roger, who seemed to have realized that he'd slipped and nearly said something important. The sun was very low, casting shadows in the barn, but I could see regret and self-reproach in his brown eyes.

"You and Abigail had a confrontation? The night she was killed?" I asked, ignoring the soft meow I heard above me.

Roger's mouth was a thin line. He nodded. "Yes. I did call her after Mike, Gabriel and I had drinks at the Lakeside."

I abandoned cleaning the top of the truck and knelt

down in the bed so I could see Roger, who'd moved to the back. He was twisting the rag in his hands.

"You didn't *go see* Abigail, did you?"

He shook his head. "No."

I remembered what Moxie had said about Mike's unanswered calls. "You went somewhere, though, didn't you?"

Roger nodded. "Yes. I did go back out for a while."

"Where?"

Piper's fiancé averted his gaze. "I told Detective Doebler most of this."

"Roger, you came to me for advice. And, speaking from experience, I suggest that you tell Detective Doebler—and Piper—everything. Even if you don't want to tell me."

He faced me again, and his voice was tight. "I can't. I need to protect her."

He was wrong. "Piper can handle whatever you have to say."

But Roger was shaking his head. "Not Piper."

"Who?"

"My sister," he confided. "She's the reason I called Abigail—not the overall wedding. That whole affair was ridiculous, but it was our mothers' folly, not Piper's and mine. I contacted Abigail about *Dorinda*. And that's who I went to see after my bachelor party—where I had *two beers*. No more. The detective keeps making it sound like I was drunk!"

Above us, the mewing grew louder. I still didn't look up.

"Why aren't you telling Detective Doebler *all* of this?" I asked, wishing I could see Roger better. The barn was nearly dark. "At least, I assume this is what you've been holding back."

"I can't tell him anything about Dorinda." Roger's voice was even more strained. "She has a record."

Piper had called Roger's sister "troubled," but I was still

surprised to learn that she'd had at least one serious run-in with the law.

"And Dorinda has a problem with being . . . *misunderstood*," he added. "She gets agitated, then defensive, and blurts things out. I need to protect her for as long as I can. Keep her out of the investigation until the real killer is caught."

I swung my legs off the back of the truck again, still trying to see Roger better. "I'm not sure I understand why that's so important."

Roger took his time before explaining. Then he told me, in a whisper, "When I went to see Dorinda, late that night, she threw her bridesmaid dress at me. She wasn't angry with me. Just frustrated. That's how I saw the label, when I folded up the gown."

My fingers, wrapped around the edge of the truck bed, tensed. "Why was she so upset?"

"It's not important," Roger said. "All I can tell you is, after she hurled the dress, Dorinda told me that she wanted to *kill* Abigail Sinclair. That's the type of thing my sister says when she's angry. And it's why I have to keep her away from the police."

Roger's explanation—and Dorinda's threat—hung out there for a long time, the quiet that descended over the barn punctuated only by the continued soft yowling from the rafters.

"People say things like that all the time without acting on them," I finally said. "Maybe I should talk to Dorinda. I do have a good track record when it comes to sorting out situations like this."

Roger didn't embrace that suggestion right away. In fact, he didn't say a thing.

"Just tell me where to find her," I suggested. "If nothing else, I need to ask if she still wants to be a bridesmaid."

Roger stammered, clearly taken aback. "You'd . . . you'd still consider that, after everything I just told you?"

His voice was thick with emotion, and, while I always liked Roger well enough, I suddenly saw him in a new light. He was a loyal brother, and I prized allegiance to family and friends. I also admired people who looked out for lost souls, whether they were siblings or Chihuahuas and pugs with oversized personalities. Or very insistent cats.

I finally looked up to see that, as I'd expected, Ms. Peebles was trapped on one of the barn's exposed beams. But she wasn't in any imminent danger and could get herself down if she'd just keep moving, so I returned my attention to Roger.

"Of course, Dorinda should still be part of the wedding party," I told him. I felt fairly confident that I could speak on Piper's behalf. "She's family." I cringed, feeling sheepish. "To be honest, we probably haven't tried hard enough to include her in the planning, up to this point."

Roger stood in the gathering darkness, and I thought that, in spite of being grateful for my willingness to reach out to Dorinda, he might still keep her contact information a secret. I was glad when he said, "She probably wouldn't respond if you called or texted. I'll send you her address." Then he took a step back, turning toward the door. "And thanks, Daphne."

"No problem. I look forward to meeting your sister."

I was being truthful. I was very intrigued by Dorinda Berendt. But Roger paused at the door, like he was trying to decide if I was being sarcastic. He also had something else on his mind. Something that must've been bothering him. "I may be way out of line," he noted. "But do you think I could ask *one more favor*, on Piper's behalf?"

I had a lot on my plate, but I *was* a maid of honor, entrusted with making the bride happy. "Sure," I agreed, speaking over increasingly strident mews. "What do you need?"

Roger made his request, which turned out to be quite big, but also sweet. When he was gone, I took a deep breath, reminding myself that my sister's wedding was a once-in-a-lifetime affair, and that Piper was lucky to have such a thoughtful future husband.

Then I finally, reluctantly raised my eyes to the rafters again—and groaned.

"Oh, Ms. Peebles! *Seriously?*"

Chapter 17

"I don't understand how you ended up *hanging upside down*, like a bat!" I told Ms. Peebles, whom I'd just rescued with the aid of a wobbly wooden ladder I'd found stashed in a corner of the barn. The catastrophe-prone cat, whom I'd carried back to Plum Cottage after locking up the barn, seemed to have forgotten her recent peril. She followed me around the house as I opened some windows to let in the cool night air. "Cats are *born* to walk on things like beams!"

Tinkleston, who was perched on the mantel, made a hissing sound that was more like a snicker than a threat. I got the feeling Tinks, who didn't seem capable anymore of sustaining rage the way he used to, was already starting to find Ms. Peebles more entertaining than infuriating. It was probably a relief *not* to be the cottage's primary trouble-maker.

Socrates, on the other hand, didn't seem amused by Ms. Peebles's mishaps. He rolled his brown eyes and trundled up the spiral staircase, turning in for the night after eating his favorite summer snack, a Fruity Pupsicle.

I was pretty sure the contemplative basset was also

quietly worried about Snowdrop's possible move. I certainly understood where he was coming from.

Moving to the steamer trunk that served as my coffee table, I picked up my phone to call Jonathan. Then, at the last minute, I dialed a different number, for the Owl & Crescent Art Barn in Zephyr Hollow. A few minutes later, much to my relief, I was able to check off the latest item on my long to-do list.

"A wine-and-painting party sounds like a nice bridal shower, doesn't it?" I asked Ms. Peebles, who continued to trail after me. Tinks had run upstairs, too, while I'd been talking to the studio's proprietor, Willow Bellamy, who had been happy to accommodate a last-minute gathering. I turned out a light that burned in one of the living room windows, telling Ms. Peebles, "Roger's right. Piper deserves a *nice* party, even if it's small. And I like the fact that we'll tie in another barn. It's like a preview of the bigger party."

Ms. Peebles flicked her tail, which might or might not have indicated agreement, although her big eyes always gave the impression that she was interested in whatever was going on.

Snuffing out the rest of the lights, I followed Socrates and Tinkleston upstairs. Ms. Peebles joined us, but wisely curled up in a cozy wicker basket full of clean clothes, rather than joining Tinks and me on the bed. I was sure Tinkleston's lukewarm welcome would turn icy, if not violent, if Ms. Peebles set one paw on the crisp cotton sheets.

Climbing into bed, I set my phone on the nightstand and soon fell into a deep slumber. I didn't even hear my phone sound off with messages until well after sunrise, although some of my contacts had been busy overnight.

The first message was from Roger, as promised.

You'll find Dorinda at the end of Loudpipes Lane, off

Route 23. If she's not on the first floor, as is likely, try the second.

"Where the heck is that lane?" I muttered, scrolling on to the next text, because I seriously doubted that Tinkleston, Ms. Peebles or even Socrates, who was fairly well-traveled, if only locally, would answer me.

Opening the second text, sent by Moxie, I discovered only emojis and one punctuation mark, which was repeated at least five times.

 ?????

Then I finally opened a message I might've been putting off reading, because it was from Jonathan, whom I hadn't heard from in over a day. And when I read the text, I wished I could've delayed even longer, although there was nothing inherently troubling in the short missive, which said, simply, *Daphne, we need to talk.*

Chapter 18

"Maybe . . . we went . . . the wrong way," I told Moxie, who was pedaling next to me on Route 23, a shady, quiet, but hilly road that was popular with local and visiting cyclists. Men and women in spandex kept darting uphill past me and Moxie, who were both wearing regular clothes.

Well, my jeans and peasant blouse weren't exactly re-markable. Moxie did stand out a bit in a vintage, crisp, white-collared blouse and pedal pushers that matched her lemon-drop yellow antique Schwinn.

The bike had fat tires and no gears, yet my best friend wasn't breathing hard or sweating, unlike me, who had borrowed Piper's twenty-one-speed touring bike for a ride Moxie forced me to undertake each July. Just like she dragged me to Pinchwater Pond every Christmas to go ice skating. She was nothing if not a fan of tradition—and obviously way more coordinated and in better shape than I was.

". . . I think . . . we should . . . turn back," I suggested, gulping air in between every pair of words that wheezed out of my mouth. Front wheel wobbling, I managed to steer to the side of the road. "I can . . . get my . . . van . . . to find . . . Dorinda!"

Moxie breezed up beside me and braked to a halt, checking her Mickey Mouse watch. "I *do* need to run home soon to feed Sebastian." She leaned over her handlebars and opened the lid of a wicker basket. A little white head popped out and a twitching pink nose tested the air, then Moxie's rat dropped back into his carrier. She shut the lid. "He's eaten all of his snacks, which means he'll soon start eating the basket, and eventually drop to the road!"

"We don't want . . . that to happen," I noted, catching my breath and trying to sound more concerned than relieved, although I was mainly the latter. Usually Moxie insisted that we cover at least five miles before turning back. I'd hoped to cut the actual riding part short and kill two birds with one stone by adding a stop at Dorinda's, where I'd intended to invite her to the shower in person. "I'll text Roger later to ask for more clear directions."

Moxie began to scooch her bike around, readying herself to coast down the winding road, which was flanked by thick woods. "I'm sorry we didn't find Piper's mysterious sister-in-law-to-be. But the hunt definitely added a bit of extra fun to the ride."

"Better fun than distance," I noted, awkwardly turning my bicycle, too, and facing downhill.

I could already imagine the breeze in my face and feel my legs regaining some strength when all at once I heard the rumble of an engine coming from the bottom of the long rise.

A moment later, as the noise grew louder, a motorcycle came tearing around a curve.

Moxie and I both pulled our pedal-powered bikes farther off the road just in time for the *motorized* two-wheeler to roar past.

"Yikes!" Moxie cried, turning, like me, to watch the black bike crest the hill—where, hardly slowing down, the leather-clad rider cut sharply into a lane I hadn't noticed before.

I continued to observe a cloud of settling dust, but my thoughts were elsewhere. Back at Artful Engagements, where I'd had a similar encounter, right before I'd found Abigail's body.

Only, this time, I was fairly certain of the rider's gender.

Then I peered more closely at the top of the hill, noticing a small sign on a metal post. I could only make out a few letters on the marker, but I turned to Moxie, telling her with a sigh, "You go on home, for Sebastian's sake." I climbed off my bicycle and, with one last longing glance at the downgrade, began trudging uphill. "I think I've found the missing bridesmaid, and she might have some explaining to do."

Chapter 19

The Wild Hog Bar & Grill had a somewhat mythical status for most local folks, and as I pushed Piper's bike toward the tilting, ramshackle, pale green building, I could understand why few people actually ventured to the remote establishment, where a half dozen motorcycles were clustered like a line of defense in a gravel parking lot. The bar itself seemed to be uniting with the surrounding forest, which pressed in from nearly all sides. What looked like years' worth of rotted leaves smothered the rusting tin roof, and dark green beards of mold crept down the walls, growing from under air conditioners mounted on the rotting sills of tilted windows.

I'd spent a lot of time in low-budget hostels during my travels, and I knew that looks could be deceiving. But I had to admit that I was nervous as I parked my bike, which suddenly seemed spindly and ridiculous standing next to a gleaming machine with an engine that was still radiating extra heat into the summer air.

Swiping my sweaty palms on my jeans, I stepped up onto a porch where a small wooden sign, which looked like it had been carved with a jackknife, gave the only indication that the structure housed a business.

WILD HOG. CASH ONLY OR ELSE!

Checking my pockets, because I wanted a cold drink, I was relieved to discover a twenty-dollar bill. Then I took a deep breath, and, reminding myself that Roger wouldn't have sent me there if he'd thought I'd be in any real danger, I pushed open a screen door, then a sticky wooden door.

Stepping inside, I was momentarily blinded by darkness, while my other senses were assaulted by the odors of smoke and grease and the sound of someone *singing* to the accompaniment of a guitar. I paused to listen, thinking the person had a lovely voice. Then I took another step into the bar, and the performance stopped abruptly when the screen door snapped shut behind me. In the wake of that noise, which echoed like a shot, I heard the creak and scrape of chairs being moved on the floor, and I was well aware that everyone was turning to stare at me.

Shading my eyes, which wasn't helpful at all, I tried to peer into the gloomy room. "Hello?"

No one answered. The silence, and the darkness, continued to surround me.

"I'm looking for Dorinda Berendt," I said, blinking hard, to no avail. "Is she—?"

I didn't get a chance to finish my question. All at once, I heard a new sound. A clattering noise, like tiny footsteps coming toward me, and a throaty, but feminine voice—that of the singer—yelling, "Lady! You better run!"

"You're lucky Harley didn't really attack," Dorinda grunted, leaning back in her chair and stroking an adorable little pig who sat on her lap, his mouth permanently turned up into a self-satisfied-looking grin and something like amusement in his bright eyes.

Clearly, the cute but pugnacious porker was proud of his attempt to shove me out the door by butting his little black-and-white head repeatedly into my shins.

And apparently no one at the Wild Hog gave two hoots about the presence of a pig at one of the bar's mismatched, wobbly wooden tables. The bartender who had delivered our drinks hadn't batted an eye at the "customer" who was breaking at least six health code violations, just by sharing a chair with Dorinda. Instead, the bearded server with the greasy T-shirt and scraggly beard had seemed disapproving of *me* when I'd attempted to order iced tea before settling on a random soda he'd dug up from heaven knew where.

Fortunately, I wasn't fussy about animals in eateries, or expiration dates, because I was pretty sure if I searched the can I was popping open, I would find a "best consumed by" date of nineteen-seventy-something.

Setting her pet on the floor next to her open guitar case, which held a few coins, Dorinda leaned forward and cupped her hands around an icy mug filled with beer, the better to study me with brown eyes that were remarkably similar to Roger's. I could tell she was trying to intimidate me, but it was hard to be cowed, given the many similarities she shared with her quiet, measured brother, from the shape of her nose to the color of her longer, wavy hair.

Of course, Roger would never live in an apartment over a dive bar, or be covered with ink, like Dorinda, who was tattooed nearly head to toe. Black spiders danced across her hands, and a majestic pink-and-purple unicorn reared up between her wrist and elbow.

All at once, I noticed the bottom half of a human face on her upper arm.

"Is that *Roger*?" I asked, leaning closer to view the portrait, which was peeking out from beneath the sleeve of her black T-shirt. "Seriously," I said, barely resisting the urge to grab her wrist, because she was pulling back from me. "Do you have your *brother* on your arm?"

Dorinda didn't answer me. Jutting her chin, she tugged down her sleeve, obscuring the image with her shirt, which featured the Harley-Davidson logo. Her acoustic guitar, which was propped against a chair on a makeshift stage, was plastered with similar stickers.

Clearly, Dorinda was loyal to her brother and her brand.

"What do you want here?" she demanded. Crossing her arms, she turned away from me. "Please tell me it's not more of this stupid 'bridesmaid' stuff."

I'd only known Dorinda Berendt for about five minutes, so there was a chance I was reading her wrong. But I was pretty sure she was dismissing the "bridesmaid stuff" because she wanted to be part of it and feared that she was going to be shut out. She was rejecting me, Fidelia and Moxie before we could reject her, just like Abigail, and probably a lot of other people, had done.

Or maybe not. Maybe she just hated weddings.

Dorinda faced me again, her eyes glittering with anger. "If you've come here to grovel, I'm not interested in putting on a fancy dress and dancing like a chicken at some stuck-up country club."

Under the table, where he was restlessly rooting around for fallen French fries and crumbs—of which there were quite a few—Harley snorted, like he agreed with his person.

"I really don't think we're doing the chicken dance," I informed them both, thinking I wasn't a fan of bending my arms into "wings" and shaking my tail feathers, either. "And the reception will be held at Piper's farm, Winding Hill. It's going to be really nice, but not 'stuck up'. And it would mean a lot if you would help me and my friends plan everything. We're kind of overwhelmed."

Dorinda snorted, a defensive laugh. "So, you need free labor?"

"No, we need *help*," I clarified, "to give your brother— and future sister-in-law—a really nice day they'll remember for the rest of their lives."

I could tell that I'd cracked Dorinda's heavy armor by appealing to her love for Roger. But she still peered at me suspiciously from over the rim of her beer as she took a sip, stalling.

I also took a drink of my flat cola and shuddered, setting down the can and pushing it away. If I hadn't been facing a long bike ride home, I might've ordered something in a frosted mug, too.

"What would I have to do?" Dorinda finally asked, staring at a wall full of neon beer signs again. Refusing to make eye contact seemed to be one of her defense mechanisms, and she was quick to let me know that she wasn't agreeing to be of assistance. "Not that I'll do anything. I'm pretty busy, taking care of Harley and all."

The pig in question was snoozing on the dirty floor, and given that Dorinda was hanging out in a bar before noon, I didn't think she was overbooked with activities. I was pretty sure she could fit in the tasks that I suspected she *would* eventually complete.

However, before I asked Dorinda to contact a florist and finalize the menu with Daisy Carpenter, I had two questions for her.

Leaning forward, I waited until she grew uncomfortable enough with the silence to meet my eyes again, so I could see her reaction when I asked, "Can you attend a bridal shower on Thursday evening? And what in the world were you doing at Artful Engagements the morning I found Abigail Sinclair's body bobbing in a fountain?"

Chapter 20

"I didn't know that was you driving the old bus," Dorinda said, pushing aside her beer, which was like the last vestige of the tough exterior she'd started shedding the moment I'd brought up her visit to the scene of a homicide. She leaned forward, her eyes darting back and forth. She wasn't avoiding me anymore. She was making sure no one else in the dim, hazy space could hear her over a classic rock song playing on a jukebox that glowed in a dark corner, near an unused pool table. Satisfied that the few other patrons were preoccupied, she added, "I've been wondering when I'd get found out. I didn't think it would happen *today*, when you stumbled in here."

"Did you really not see my name on my van when you drove past?" I asked, with a quick glance at Harley, who was snuffling in his sleep. "It's painted in huge letters!"

"I was going pretty fast," Dorinda reminded me. "All I saw was a horse."

"That's actually a dog," I said. "But it's a common mistake."

"Why do you have a big dog on your van?"

"I'm a pet sitter. And I own a bakery for cats and dogs. Didn't Roger ever mention that?"

Dorinda shook her head. She couldn't have been more than twenty-two, and she was starting to look her age as she let her defenses down and the hard edges she'd put up softened. "No. Roger doesn't talk much about you. Mainly Piper."

"Well, I didn't know you sang, either," I told her. "You sounded great."

She shrugged. "It wasn't even really a gig. Sometimes I just play. My own stuff, or covers." She nudged the guitar case with a booted foot. "People toss me some coins or buy me a beer if they like what they hear."

Dorinda was acting humble, but I could tell she was proud of herself.

"You have a real talent," I said.

"Yeah, well, watching pets is cool, too." She looked down at Harley. "I like animals. They don't judge."

"I like that about them, too," I agreed, forgetting for a moment that I was worried Dorinda had strangled a wedding planner.

I wanted to steer the conversation back to murder. However, at Dorinda's insistence, we had ordered lunch, which was probably a terrible mistake, and we stopped talking for a minute so the bartender, who was also the cook, could set down two plates. I'd ordered the only vegetarian thing on the limited menu—a grilled cheese sandwich with potato chips—while Dorinda had opted for a cheeseburger and fries.

When Dogtags—that was the bartender's nickname—was out of earshot, I asked again, "Why were you at Abigail's place?"

Dorinda reached for a bottle of ketchup without taking her eyes off me. And she didn't answer my question until she'd poured a red puddle onto her plate. Even then, her response wasn't direct. "Roger says you solve murders sometimes."

I was glad my future brother-in-law had said *something*

about me. And, unlike my mother and sister, apparently he didn't disapprove of my sleuthing.

"He says you helped Piper and your friend Dixie—"

"Moxie."

"Moxie. You helped *Moxie* beat a murder rap."

"It didn't get quite that far," I said, taking a tentative bite of my sandwich, which was *amazing*. And, while I didn't eat meat, I thought Dorinda's burger looked good, too. I shifted in my seat, giving Dogtags a thumbs up.

He was leaning against the bar, wiping glasses with a stained towel. "Muenster."

I didn't understand. "What?"

"The secret is Muenster," he said, more loudly. "It melts very nicely."

"I'll remember that," I promised, turning back to Dorinda, who was slipping fries to Harley. The little pig had woken up and was rooting around under the table again.

"Dogtags was a cook in the army," Dorinda explained. "The kitchen is cleaner than the front of the house."

"Good to know," I said, viewing my plate with more enthusiasm. I had suffered a few bouts of food poisoning, including the incident in Istanbul, and I wasn't eager to go through the experience again. Then I lowered my voice. "I do sometimes solve homicides. And if you're asking if I can help you—"

"Like I'm helping you, as a bridesmaid."

Dorinda wasn't as tough as she pretended, but she had chosen, for some reason, to live in a pretty rough environment, and she was savvy. I nodded. "Yes. Although I don't really think of it as some kind of bargain. I'd try to help you even if you bailed on being a bridesmaid—as long as you're honest with me, and give me all the facts as you remember them."

Dorinda pondered her options over a big bite of her

burger, which was about an inch thick and topped with a slab of tomato. She set down the sandwich and licked her fingers. "There's not much to tell," she finally said. "I was up all night, thinking about what that witch said about me, right to my face—"

"What happened *before* the morning we nearly ran into each other?" I interrupted. I remembered how Roger had said Dorinda had thrown her dress at him, and I cautioned, "And try to stay calm, okay? Getting upset doesn't help anything. As Saint Francis de Sales said, 'Do everything quietly and in a calm spirit.'"

Dorinda wiped her mouth with a napkin she'd plucked from a dispenser in the center of the table. "Roger said you're a philosopher, too."

"Yet he never said 'pet sitter' or 'bakery owner'?"

"Nope. Just PI and philosopher."

"Interesting," I said, through a bite of gooey cheese and buttery, toasted bread. "Now, about what happened between you and Abigail . . ."

Dorinda tossed down the napkin. "When I went to pick up my gown, which was *stupid*, by the way—"

"Because it was a costume."

Dorinda rolled her eyes, like she'd known that all along. "Duh. That was obvious!"

I really regretted wearing the outfit for an entire day.

"So, I stopped by the dead lady's giant mansion—before she was dead," Dorinda clarified, bending to set her plate onto the floor. I could have sworn Harley's curly tail wagged as he chowed down on what was left of his person's meal. "And she told me I should use makeup to cover my 'nasty' tattoos at the wedding." Dorinda scowled. "I told her the idea was idiotic." She held out her arm with the unicorn. "Like there's makeup that would cover *that*. If I even wanted to do it, and pretend to be somebody I'm not. Which I *don't* want to do."

I had to agree that Abigail's plan had been flawed, but I let Dorinda keep talking as I mentally added details to the altercation Roger had mentioned.

"We started arguing, and she called me 'trashy' and a 'lowlife'!"

Dorinda's voice spiked, and I made a patting motion with my hands, urging her to tone it down, because some pretty big guys in leather jackets had turned to look at us.

Dorinda realized her mistake, and to her credit, she controlled her temper and leaned forward, speaking more softly again. But there was a glimmer of anger in her eyes. I couldn't really blame her for being upset, especially when she confided, "High-and-mighty Abigail Sinclair told me I should skip the wedding. That if I showed up, I'd 'disgrace the whole affair.' Those were her exact words."

Dorinda's eyes suddenly gleamed in a different way. Tears brimmed at the edge of her lashes.

"Like I don't get enough comments like that from my *mother*," she muttered, leaning back again.

I gave her a second to compose herself, then pushed aside my completely empty plate. I was pretty sure Dogtags had made the wafer-thin chips by hand. "Why did you go back in the morning?"

"I was gonna take back her cheap costume and tell her where she could stick it."

I winced at the image, and the reaction I imagined Detective Doebler having if Dorinda was questioned.

"Then I was going to make her give back Roger's money," Dorinda added. "Because he paid for my gown." She swiped a finger under her eye, wiping away leftover tears. She was no longer close to crying. Just angry again. "And I bet she overcharged him, too. She acted like those dresses were worth a million dollars!"

"Yeah, she definitely ripped us off," I agreed, as Dogtags, who'd emerged from behind the bar, cleared the table

and bent to pick up Harley's empty plate, too. Thanking him,
I watched him carry the dirty dishes back to the kitchen,
thinking there had to be rules against patrons eating off
the same plates as pigs. Even cute ones. Not that I cared.
Socrates would *only* eat off dishes designed for humans. I
looked across the table at Dorinda. "What happened when
you got to Artful Engagements?"

"The place was unlocked. I walked around for a while,
looking for her."

I thought of the suitcases on the bed. "Did you go upstairs?"

Dorinda gave me a funny look. "No. I figured that was,
like, her house. I've got *some* manners. I stayed on the first
floor, then I looked out in the garden." All at once, Dorinda
blanched. "That's when I saw her lying under the flag. I
could tell she was dead, so I ran to my bike and took off."

"Did you touch anything?"

She shook her head. "No. The doors were both open.
Front and back. I figured she was airing the place out for
some reason. Until I found her body. Then I knew somebody had probably rushed in, killed her and rushed out."
Dorinda spread her hands on the table, showing off the
spiders on her fingers. "And *if* I'd touched anything, I
would've wiped off my prints. I have a record, you know."

The little pig snuffled loudly. It almost seemed like he
was proud of his person.

"What exactly did you do?"

"I was busking in Key West. Trying to get money to
return to Pennsylvania after dropping out of college during
spring break." She shrugged. "Turns out singing and playing guitar for cash is illegal there without a permit."

I was confused. "Wouldn't you just get fined for busking?"

Dorinda sank down in her chair. "I punched the cop who
told me to get lost."

She definitely had a temper. But I had a feeling it stemmed

from holding in a lot of anger not toward Abigail Sinclair, but toward her mother. It was just a hunch.

Digging into my pocket, I put the twenty on the table, certain it would cover our dirt cheap meals, including tip. "Dorinda, you have to tell the police everything you told me."

She reared back, clutching the table like I was about to drag her away, and Harley squared off against me, too, oinking loudly. Dorinda spoke over his squeals. "I don't think so!"

Everyone was staring at us, and I stood up, thinking I needed to get going. I had another appointment that evening, and I needed a shower. I wasn't sure if Dorinda would follow me, but she rose, too, and we left together, trailed by Harley.

"You know Roger's under suspicion, right?" I asked when Dorinda had closed the door behind all three of us, giving us some privacy on the shaded, sagging porch. "And he's probably making things worse for himself by trying to protect you. Which is also undermining his marriage before it even begins. He doesn't even want to tell Piper the whole story."

Dorinda shrank and rubbed her arm, where she'd inked the tribute to her brother. "I didn't know all that." She squinted out at the sunny day. "I'll think about it, okay?"

"I date . . . kind of date . . . a detective . . . a guy who was a detective . . ." Seeing Dorinda's confusion, I gave up trying to explain Jonathan's employment status, or my relationship to him. "I know some investigators in this town," I said. "I could go with you, if you want to come clean."

"Maybe." Dorinda was noncommittal, but I felt confident that she'd make the right decision.

"Hey, Dorinda?"

"Yeah?"

"I have a mother who is like a clone of yours, and who expresses endless disappointment with me. I understand why you might want to drop out of school, run away and punch a cop. But there are better options."

She didn't sound too optimistic. "Yeah. Probably."

I stepped down off the porch, thinking about Jonathan, who quietly helped troubled people, including a prickly youth who reminded me of Dorinda. But just as *two* great ideas struck me, Dorinda looked past me, frowning. "Which bike is yours?"

I turned to point out Piper's twenty-one speed—only to discover that it was gone.

"Oh, no!" I groaned, wheeling back around. "I had this bicycle . . ."

"Sorry," Dorinda apologized for her adopted tribe. The permanent piggy grin on Harley's face made it seem like my plight amused him. Maybe it did. "Stuff like that happens here sometimes," Dorinda added. "I'll do my best to get it back. Or get parts of it back."

"Thanks," I said glumly. "Can I borrow your phone? I need to call Piper for a ride."

Dorinda started to reach into the back pocket of her jeans, then she grinned. It was the first time I'd seen her smile.

"You don't have to call your sister. Bridesmaids help each other, right?"

I felt a bit wary. "Yes . . . ?"

Dorinda turned around, and I wasn't sure if she was sincerely coming to my aid or testing me somehow when she said, "I'll get an extra helmet."

Chapter 21

"That was harrowing," I told Socrates, who kept making snuffling, snickery sounds from his seat in the van. It was dark and getting drizzly outside, and there were no street-lamps on the rural road we were traveling, so I couldn't see him very well. But I could tell that the thought of me riding on the back of Dorinda's motorcycle, clinging to her for dear life, with a pig squashed between us, amused him. I clutched the steering wheel, still white-knuckling it, two hours after Roger's reckless sister had delivered me, safe but shaken, to Plum Cottage. "I was sure we were going to crash!"

Socrates tried to act suitably sympathetic, but it was clearly difficult. I was sure his spirits were uncharacteristically high because, when I'd returned home, I'd discovered a message from Daisy Carpenter, letting me know that she planned to stay put for the time being and would be happy to cater Piper's reception. For now, Snowdrop wasn't going anywhere.

"I don't blame you for being cheerful," I told him, with a sigh. I steered the van onto the short lane that led to Jonathan's A-frame house, which was tucked into the woods. Spying dim lights in the windows, my stomach twisted with concern about our looming conversation.

Socrates finally seemed to catch my tense mood. He stopped snuffling as I parked behind Jonathan's truck, and we were quiet while we hurried through the rain, which was falling harder, to the front door, where I raised my hand to knock.

Needless to say, Axis and Artie had heard us approaching and must've alerted Jonathan, because he opened the door before I could even rap.

Like always happened when I saw him, butterflies started wheeling around in my stomach—then I looked past Jonathan into his house, and my breath caught, so it took me a moment to form the question, "What have you *done* here?"

"I wanted to start a fire and have a picnic outside, but the weather ruined that plan," Jonathan explained, setting a tray with a bottle of wine and two tumblers onto the floor in front of me. The dogs had been sent off to play, to give us some privacy, and I was sitting on the antique Turkish rug that anchored his living room. Jonathan joined me, resting back against one of two leather sofas that defined the otherwise open space, which was a snug refuge from the wet night.

A fire burned in the huge stone fireplace, the sound of the crackling logs mingling with the soft patter of rain against a wall of windows that overlooked the paddock and barn he'd built for his two horses. The only other light came from dozens of candles that were tucked among Jonathan's many books, shelved on floor-to-ceiling bookcases that rose up around us—a sight that had caused me to gasp with surprise when he'd opened the door.

"I thought I'd try to give you fire and something like a starry sky indoors," he added, reaching to pour the wine and handing me a glass of deep red merlot. A wooden cutting board with a selection of crackers, cheeses and some cherries that were as dark as the wine waited by the tray, if I ever found my appetite. Jonathan rested back again. "It's a poor approximation, but I did my best."

"It's perfect," I assured him, even as a part of me wished it *wasn't*. Not that I wanted Jonathan to be a jerk, but I was trying to guard my heart, and the romantic gesture had pretty much ruined that effort, as surely as the rain had changed his plans. Taking a sip of the merlot, I set my tumbler on a coffee table he'd pushed off to the side—only to bump into a stack of papers.

Leaning over, I spied a grainy picture of people milling around a lake and jolted. "I've seen those before." I turned to Jonathan. "Where did you get those clippings?"

"They were on Abigail Sinclair's desk. Doebler initially confiscated them, then decided they weren't related to her murder."

"But you're not so sure."

"No, I'm not. So I asked if I could borrow them, just to read through." He tilted his head. "How did you see them?"

"I stopped in Abigail's office when I was looking for her. Right before I found her body. I noticed the pile because it *wasn't* neat." I glanced at the papers again. "What if you find something interesting in there?"

"*If* that happened, I'd turn everything over to Doebler."

We both realized that we'd quickly segued into the discussion I'd been worried about all day. It was probably my imagination, or the fire dying down, but the room seemed to grow darker.

"Daphne . . ." Jonathan's voice was low and grave, and I suddenly couldn't take the suspense anymore. I shifted on the floor, facing him more directly and blurting, "You're taking the job, aren't you? Which is why I couldn't kiss you the other day. And why I shouldn't be sitting here in a pretend starry meadow, because you're about to break my heart, and all this"—I gestured around the room—"is only making it harder to let you go."

"Daphne, calm down," Jonathan urged, a glimmer of amusement in his eyes. "You're getting way ahead of yourself. I'm not going to drop some kind of bombshell on you."

That was a *partial* relief. I took a deep breath. "Sorry. I've just been very worried, the last few days, about you—and Snowdrop, on Socrates' behalf."

Jonathan, who had brought the poodle back to Sylvan Creek when she'd been taken away by lawyers, frowned. "What's wrong with Snowdrop?"

Forgetting my nervous stomach, I dipped a cracker into smooth, tangy chèvre, which was a perfect complement to the sweet cherries. "Daisy Carpenter was considering fleeing town . . ."

I could tell by the flicker of concern in Jonathan's eyes that he knew Daisy was a suspect, so I quickly added, ". . . but I helped her calm down, and for now, she's sticking around."

"I assume she was leaving because she had a pretty strong motive to kill Sinclair. The blackmail about her former business."

I pulled back slightly. "I didn't realize Daisy had admitted that. And how much does Detective Doebler tell you?"

Jonathan grinned again. "He's not used to working alone. He likes to bounce ideas off me now and then."

"So what do you think about Daisy as a suspect?"

"Unlikely. And I'm basing that on gut instinct and her claim that she left the mansion before Laci Chalmers, while Dexter Shipley seemed to have disappeared—which doesn't mean he wasn't somewhere on the property."

"Daisy could be lying." I held up my hands. "Not that I think that. I really like her."

"Yet, she *was* considering running away. That's not a good sign. Maybe we're both wrong about her."

I recalled the towels I'd seen Daisy using. "Did the lab ever identify the fibers found in Abigail's wounds?"

Jonathan could tell I was asking for a reason. He put *me* under a microscope. "Not that I know of. Why? Do *you* know something?"

I thought back to my experiment, and how it seemed like it would've been very difficult for someone to use a dish towel as a weapon. And Abigail had been a tall, commanding woman, while Daisy was petite—although her arms and hands were probably strong, from chopping, kneading and stirring . . .

"Daphne?" Jonathan's voice broke into my thoughts.

"Just tell me if you ever hear about the fibers," I said. "Depending upon what they're from, I *may* have something to say."

Jonathan didn't like that deal, but he nodded agreement, while still watching me closely by the flickering light of the fireplace and the soft glow of the candles. The storm had grown worse, and rain was streaming down the windows, wind whistling across the chimney. Jonathan's eyes were nearly as dark as the sky outside, and all of my resolve to maintain a tiny bit of distance from him melted away into a big, messy puddle that I soon wouldn't be able to resist jumping into.

He must've seen me caving in, but he hesitated, sort of asking permission without saying a word. I gave the slightest nod, and he leaned closer to kiss me. My hand moved up to wrap around his neck, my thumb brushing the scar on his jaw. I felt like I could've stayed in that moment forever, which was perhaps why he pulled back. I knew he was thinking about how I'd pushed him away, the other night, and worrying that he was pressuring me into doing something I wasn't sure was good for me right then.

He was probably right, but I didn't take my hand away. I kept tracing that jagged mark while my eyes searched his.

I wanted to finally learn the story behind the old wound I'd noticed the first time I'd met him and that had intrigued me ever since. He'd never volunteered the tale, and, until recently, I hadn't felt like I could ask questions. Some instinct told me that he hadn't just cut himself shaving or something silly like that.

That night, I couldn't resist any longer. If I was going to trust him not to break my heart, he needed to trust me with his past.

"Jonathan, what happened?" I asked quietly, still studying his eyes. I thought I saw a flash of wariness, and I feared he was going to put his guard up, like he sometimes did. Then the moment passed, and I asked again, "How did you get this mark?"

He caught my hand with his, trapping it and holding it. He wasn't pushing aside the question. Just giving us room to talk. "I don't even know," he told me, facing the fire and dragging his free hand through his hair. "There were so many injuries that day. Me, and a lot of other men. And Herod, who, of course, didn't make it." Herod was the dog who'd been his canine partner when he'd been a SEAL. His voice was dispassionate, but I knew he was deliberately keeping his emotions in check, even as he made a grim joke. "It's a wonder I don't look sewn together like Frankenstein's monster. I didn't even notice the cut on my jaw, and wouldn't have gotten it stitched anyway. The medics were saving arms and legs, not looks."

There was so much unsaid in that story. So many details left out, not to mention a strong suggestion that he'd suffered injuries more serious than the one that had left a visible hint at his past. But it was the first time Jonathan had come close to telling me anything about the battle that had claimed his friends and his beloved dog, and I didn't ask for more information. I just rested against his strong shoulder and clasped his hand, both of us watching the fire and listening to the storm, until he gently moved away from me again, if only to see my face.

"Daphne, if I've learned anything from combat, and cancer—not to mention solving homicides—it's to appreciate life on a moment-by-moment basis, however trite that might sound." He grinned, teasing me. "You, of all people, should know that. In fact, I'm pretty sure you've delivered that lecture to me, backing up your argument with quotes from everyone from the Buddha to Socrates. The philosopher *and* the dog."

I'd slouched down a bit, and I looked up at him. "Somehow, my philosophical training and the counsel of a very wise canine flew out the window when you said you might move to California. Suddenly, all I can think of is the future and what will happen with us."

"Believe me," Jonathan said, "I'm giving that topic a lot of thought, too, especially when I'm working at the chapel, where my mind is free to wander. And I think the fact that we're both uncharacteristically worried about the future actually bodes well for us."

I understood what he meant, and I pulled myself back up, feeling a bit more optimistic. "So what do we do now?"

"Keep talking about our options. It's all we can do right now." He arched an eyebrow. "I don't suppose you'd even consider moving . . . ?"

My heart quickly sank again, if only because I was going to disappoint him. "I have too many ties here, including family, friends and a three-year lease on a business I just started."

He wasn't happy, but he was realistic. "I expected that answer, and I think you're right."

"Plus, I just hired a new employee. One who seems to need some guidance, and maybe a female sounding board, as much as a job." I pictured the ramshackle biker bar that

Dorinda occupied. "Well, maybe she needs the job just as badly."

Jonathan leaned forward, frowning. "Who's the mystery hire? Another formerly felonious accountant?"

"Well, she does have a record," I said. "But Dorinda Berendt won't be handling my books. She's going to be my part-time dog walker—which will actually help me out quite a bit. And hopefully help Dorinda, too."

"How so?"

Lightning flickered outside, and I knew I would be wise to get on the road before it got much later. I started to rise, telling Jonathan, "She really is a sort of lost soul, who I think is acting out against her overbearing Realtor mother by dropping out of college and living above the Wild Hog."

Jonathan managed to stand up before me, probably because I'd twisted myself into a half-lotus position, and he offered me his hand. "Sounds like you're doing a good thing. That place is pretty rough. Although the food is great."

"You've eaten there?" I accepted his offer of assistance, and he pulled me to my feet. "Why?"

"More than one homicide investigation has led to the Wild Hog," he told me. I moved to pick up the cheese board, but he clasped my arm and shook his head, letting me know he'd clean up later. "Dogtags found out I served in combat, too, and he always insists that Doebler and I eat on the house."

"Yeah, he seems like a nice guy. Unlike the person who stole Piper's bike, which I left in the parking lot while I convinced Dorinda to not only be a bridesmaid again, but to sing at Piper's wedding."

Ignoring what I thought was big news about Dorinda's agreement to share her talents, Jonathan gave me a funny look. "Since when does Piper ride a motorcycle?"

"It was a *bicycle*," I informed him. "Blue, with twenty-one speeds."

"I won't even ask why you rode something you pedal to a biker bar. And I'll see what I can do," Jonathan promised, following me toward the door. "I know some of the guys who hang out at the bar. They might be persuaded to return the bike."

"Thanks. Dorinda promised to help, too." I didn't sound or feel hopeful, and I wondered if I could put off telling Piper about the theft until after the wedding. She hardly rode her bicycle, at least not that I knew of.

We'd reached the door, and Jonathan crossed his arms and cocked his head. "How about Dorinda Berendt? Does she ride something with a little more power than an old Schwinn?"

"The Schwinn was Moxie's," I noted. "If I remember correctly, Piper has . . . had . . . a Cannondale."

"Daphne, about Dorinda . . ."

I had been stalling with the speculation about my sister's brand of bike, because I knew Jonathan was making the connection between my near-accident at Artful Engagements and Dorinda's hangout.

"Just give her a little more time, okay?" I requested. "I think she's going to contact your partner and tell him everything she told me."

"Which was . . . ?"

I hesitated, not sure how much of Dorinda's story I should share. Instead, I asked, "Vonda Shakes put Abigail's time of death at around one a.m., right?"

Jonathan nodded, but I could tell he wasn't sure why I was bringing that up, so I added, "I think Dorinda's innocent. She *was* at Artful Engagements the morning I found Abigail's body."

Jonathan clearly didn't think I was making a very good case for Roger's sister, but he let me continue.

"She drove past me midmorning. If she'd killed Abigail

in the dead of night, why go back in broad daylight, riding the world's loudest motorcycle?"

"You've heard the old adage about returning to the scene of the crime, right?" Jonathan reminded me, as the dogs all trotted into the room, led by Artie, who had an adorable string of drool trailing from his recessive lower jaw. It looked to me like they'd all been napping during the storm. Socrates' droopy eyes were sleepy. "Maybe she left something incriminating and went back to claim it," Jonathan added. "The risk of a daylight visit might've been worth it if she felt she needed to protect herself."

"That's possible," I agreed, then was struck by another thought. One that shook my faith in the Berendt family for just a moment. I quickly rejected the idea and told Jonathan, "But I still think she would've gone earlier if she'd left something."

Jonathan smiled. "I suppose you're right. Maybe you should partner with Doebler in my absence."

He was joking, but the comment dragged me back to a dilemma I'd forgotten about while we'd discussed the crime. Jonathan realized that he'd returned the conversation to a difficult subject, too. But it was one we couldn't avoid.

Or maybe we could. Jonathan took both my hands in his and drew me closer. Neither one of us seemed overly eager to speak at all.

I glanced quickly at Socrates, who seemed to realize that he and his canine buddies had returned too early. Nudging Artie, who looked like he wanted to run to us, he steered the Chihuahua and Axis toward the fire, while I looked up at Jonathan again.

"You don't have to leave, you know," he said quietly, his voice deep and his blue eyes dark again, while thunder rumbled overhead. He drew me even closer, so I rested against his chest, and he slipped his arms around me.

Bending his head, he rested his forehead against mine, his breath warm against my ear when he whispered, "Stay."

That was the best invitation I'd ever received, but it came at the worst time. And then Jonathan muddled the moment for me further by murmuring something I barely heard, because my heart was pounding so hard. Words that nearly made me accept his offer, but which ultimately sent me out the door, into the rain.

Socrates was quiet on the whole ride home, and I didn't speak, either. As the windshield wipers swiped back and forth across the dark glass, I kept replaying how Jonathan and I had parted.

And when I wasn't agonizing over our last moments at the door, I kept wondering if there was a chance that Roger, who had looked so pale and shaken on the day he should've gotten married, had confided some midnight misdeed to Dorinda. In which case, she might have rushed to Artful Engagements not to confront Abigail but to see if she could do anything to protect the brother who looked out for *her*, and whose image was inked permanently on her flesh.

Chapter 22

The sun was bright and my schedule busy enough to get me out of bed early the next morning, in spite of spending a restless night in the loft.

Feeding Tinks and Ms. Peebles, who ate their home-made Meow Mash-Up kitty chow from bowls I was slowly pushing closer together on the kitchen floor, I next gave Socrates some of his favorite PowerPup breakfast. Then I brewed some tea using an herbal blend I'd bought at the local farmers' market from a stand operated by a former hermit named Max Pottinger, who'd been brought out of his shell, and the woods, by an affable Saint Bernard named Bubba.

I wasn't very hungry, but I ate a fresh plum, also from the market, before strapping Socrates into the van, hopping behind the wheel and heading for a pet-sitting job in town. However, as I passed by Piper's farmhouse, I saw that her Acura was parked near the barn, which struck me as odd.

It was only seven thirty, but my dedicated and early-rising sister was usually at her practice by seven at the latest.

Since I had time to kill, I pulled over and let Socrates out. He went directly to the back door, like he also thought something might be amiss, and I started to get worried as

I opened the unlocked door and stuck my head inside, calling softly, "Piper?"

She didn't answer me, so Socrates and I entered the kitchen, where I first noticed a stack of mail—and a copy of the *Weekly Gazette*—on Piper's breakfast bar.

Picking up the paper, I saw that the top story was about the murder, and I didn't think Detective Doebler would be happy with the headline: *Local Cops Stymied by Red, White and Blue Slaying.*

Then I spied a smaller story that made me groan.

Area Realtors Lead Bamboozled Brides in Legal Battle for Compensation

The article was accompanied by a photo of Mom and Beverly Berendt, standing back-to-back, their arms crossed, looking something like an aging pair of Charlie's angels out for justice.

I was pretty sure they were also handing out business cards to the brides and grooms they were dragging into their class action suit, because sooner or later, the couples would get married and probably want to buy property.

I decided not to read the whole account, but I did check the bylines. Both stories were by Laci Chalmers.

"Laci is definitely hustling," I noted to Socrates, who was sniffing around the kitchen. "Gabriel must be happy."

Socrates had mixed feelings about the *Gazette*'s editor and didn't respond with so much as a look in my direction, so I set down the paper next to the stack of mail, which included a bill from the water company and a brochure that featured palm trees and a sandy beach, not unlike the travel pamphlets I'd recently seen at Artful Engagements.

Since all my mail came to the farmhouse, mingled with Piper's correspondence, I didn't hesitate to reach for the brochure—only to be stopped by my sister, whom I hadn't even heard step into the kitchen.

"Daphne! What are you doing? And what are you doing *here*?"

I looked up to see her blinking at me with mingled rebuke and surprise.

I stared right back, not believing my eyes. Socrates was observing my sister, too, his head tilted so that one of his long ears dragged on the ground.

I didn't mean to sound rude, but I had to hold back a chuckle when I asked, "What the heck are you *wearing*, Piper?"

"It's not the gown I'm going with," Piper repeated as I tugged at the zipper of a white, filmy spaghetti-strap dress, in which she was stuck. Her cheeks were flushed. "I just thought it looked pretty, so I brought it home with a few others I found at Something Borrowed, Something New. But none of them are working, and they all need to go back!"

Socrates had politely remained in the kitchen, but Piper and I were in her bedroom, and I glanced at her closet, which was open. A bunch of long white plastic bags from Sylvan Creek's only bridal shop hung inside, next to Piper's wardrobe of cardigans, blouses, slacks and capris.

"Can you please hurry?" she requested, batting helplessly at her back. "I need to get to work soon."

That was true, but I thought she was mainly embarrassed and wanted to be free of the *last* wedding gown I ever would've thought Piper would consider. The sheath was close to skimpy—*slinky*, even—and too insubstantial, let alone formal, for any wedding held in conservative Pennsylvania, by a conservative couple.

"I didn't mean to laugh," I said, finally getting the zipper to budge. I stepped back, letting Piper, who'd squirmed away impatiently, tug it the rest of the way. "You actually look lovely. It's just so different for you!"

"Well, different can be good. If not in this case."

She sounded defensive, and her cheeks were still flaming, so I backed toward the door, telling her, "I'll go brew some coffee and fill your thermos."

Piper wasn't as addicted to caffeine as our mother, but she always took a big mug of black coffee to her practice, and she nodded grudgingly. "Thanks."

I left her to change and returned to the kitchen, where I whispered to Socrates, "Something's not adding up here."

He gave a rare, low *woof* of agreement while I poured ground beans into a filter and water into Piper's workhorse traditional Mr. Coffee machine. By the time Piper emerged from her room, wearing a peach-colored, summer-weight sweater and white pants, the house was filled with the earthy, bitter aroma of Piper's favorite Colombian blend.

"Piper, again, I'm sorry," I told her. "You really did look nice."

Socrates woofed again, begging forgiveness, too.

"I'm sorry I snapped at you," she told me, opening an old-fashioned bread box and taking out a bag of English muffins. She held it up, wordlessly offering me one. I shook my head in the negative. "I just felt foolish, locked into one of several gowns that don't suit me," she told me. "And there's so much going on, with Roger and the investigation."

I didn't want to let on that Roger had spoken with me, in case he hadn't talked with Piper yet, so I said, "But you said he probably wasn't under suspicion."

Piper had placed a muffin in her toaster, and she spun the bag, sealing it again. "I was never as confident as I acted in front of Moxie and Fidelia. I just didn't want Fidelia, especially, to know how worried I am, since I'm not as close to her. Meanwhile, Roger has confided that he's quite concerned, too. Detective Doebler is hounding him about a phone call he made to Artful Engagements just before midnight. And he's determined to protect Dorinda, who was also upset with Abigail, and whose only alibi is a bunch of bikers who aren't exactly known for being forth-coming with the police."

I was glad Roger had been honest with Piper, telling her everything he'd shared with me.

"Is there anything I can do?" I offered. The coffee had stopped dripping, so I grabbed Piper's thermos from the drying rack in her farmhouse sink and filled it to the rim. "Aside from help with zippers and breakfast?"

Piper shook her head. "I don't want you to get involved in this case. I just have to trust that Roger's innocence will be enough to save the day. Just like Mom's and my inno-cence won out in similar situations."

I thought I deserved a *tiny* bit of credit for proving them innocent by catching the real killers when they were murder suspects. But, hearing the faith in Piper's voice, I mainly felt very guilty for doubting Roger, even for a moment. Socrates, who was incredibly loyal, not to mention a good judge of character, seemed to know what I was thinking. He gave me what looked like a shaming glance.

Fortunately, Piper was oblivious to all but her toast, which had popped up. Plucking the muffin from the slot, she sighed. "I can't believe I'm saying this, but I wish Jonathan was on the case."

I was setting her coffee on the counter, and my hand jerked when she added, "When were you going to tell me about his job offer?"

"What?"

"I know that he's been offered a position in California."

I turned to see Piper spreading peanut butter on the warm bread, but watching me. "How did you find out?" I asked.

"I went out to see the chapel, and he was working there.

We got to talking, and he mentioned it. He was surprised I didn't know."

I leaned back against the counter, wrapping my fingers around the marble edge. "I didn't want to add my problems to yours."

"You're my sister, Daphne. You can *always* talk to me."

Piper and I were complete opposites, and we'd taken very different paths growing up. She had always walked a clear, straight line, from high school to college to career, while I had meandered. Only lately, since I'd moved to Winding Hill and we'd gotten tangled up in some difficult situations, did we seem to be forging a truly solid bond. That was another reason I didn't want to leave Sylvan Creek, in spite of what Jonathan had said to me the night before. Three little words that I shared with my sister, since she'd offered to listen.

"Last night, Jonathan told me he's in love with me."

"I've known that since . . . well, about the time he tried to put me away for murder." She licked some peanut butter off her fingers, still watching me. Probably wondering why I wasn't jumping for joy. "What did *you* say?"

The farmhouse wasn't air-conditioned, and a trickle of sweat ran down my back as I recalled my poor response. Shrugging, I picked at my fingernails, hiding my embarrassment. "There was a lot of stammering. Before I ran away."

Socrates, who, let's face it, had heard everything from his spot in Jonathan's living room, dropped down to his belly and whined on my behalf.

"Oh, Daphne." Piper also sounded borderline exasperated with me, but, to my surprise, somewhat sympathetic. She set her half-eaten breakfast onto a waiting plate and joined me, leaning against the counter, too. Then she bent to see my eyes. "Jonathan Black is *not* like our father.

He's not waiting for some excuse to bail and fly off to the West Coast. He's looking for a reason to *stay*. Or at least a compromise that keeps you together."

Piper treated pets, not people, but after a moment of reflection, I realized that her analysis was dead-on. I shook my head with disbelief. "How did I not see that I've been waiting for him to leave? Because that's true. From the moment he went to San Diego, I've been bracing for the worst, expecting him never to come back. How did I not realize that the past is messing up my future?"

"Because you're in love with Jonathan, and that's terrifying. Especially when you don't exactly have a great male role model. I suppose that's why I wanted to be married before Roger left for Europe. I'm sure I have some subconscious trust issues going on, too."

I rarely thought of Piper as vulnerable, because she didn't like to be seen that way. I appreciated her candor. "Thanks, Piper. You've helped me see things more clearly."

She smiled. "No problem. You did keep me out of jail once. And you've been a great maid of honor."

I grinned, too, feeling lighter. "You mentioned seeing the chapel," I noted, pushing off from the counter. We both needed to get to work. "How's it coming along? And will it be done in time?"

Piper gave me a funny look. "You know, the chapel—which is *adorable* . . . You know that Jonathan's not really . . ."

I wanted her to finish whatever thought she was trying to form, but she suddenly seemed to realize she didn't have time to keep chatting. As she checked the clock on the stove, her eyes widened behind her glasses. "Oh, goodness. I am late! I'm seeing a ferret with an injured tail in ten minutes!"

"Don't forget the shower tonight," I called as she hurried to leave.

Opening the door, she turned back. "Oh, Daphne, I really wish you hadn't—"

"Your friends want to celebrate. Roger insisted, and I think it's a great idea."

Piper didn't seem convinced. Shaking her head, she departed without another word, leaving me and Socrates alone in the kitchen. I knew she didn't expect me to clean up, but I still had a few minutes to spare, so I finished her English muffin, turned off the coffeepot and wiped down the counter.

Looking around, I tried to find more ways to be useful, only to recall the dresses that were hanging in Piper's closet.

"A good maid of honor would return them, right?" I asked Socrates. "I'm driving right by Something Borrowed, Something New later today."

Socrates didn't seem convinced that my errand was a good one, but I ignored him and returned to Piper's bedroom.

I was about to pull down all the bagged dresses, but at the last second, I couldn't resist seeing the other styles Piper was rejecting.

Socrates padded to the door, watching with a skeptical eye.

"I'm not opening mail," I reminded him. "I'm just checking out a bunch of unwanted dresses. I don't think Piper would really care."

He shook his head while I unzipped one bag.

And another.

And another.

Planting my fists on my hips, I surveyed the gowns. Then I turned to Socrates, invoking the original name of the boat I'd captain during All Paws on Deck.

"There is definitely *something fishy* going on here!"

Chapter 23

"Why would Piper choose a whole bunch of skimpy dresses?" I again asked Socrates as he hopped out of the VW at Something Borrowed, Something New, where the parking lot was nearly empty. The little white shop, housed in an old one-room schoolhouse, stood alone just outside of Sylvan Creek in a pretty field that was strewn with sunflowers big and small in all sorts of cheerful shades of yellow and orange. As its name suggested, the boutique sold both new and vintage formal wear, making it one of Moxie's favorite haunts. Since I often accompanied her on shopping trips, I was no stranger to hauling the type of slippery bags I was wrangling out of the back of my van.

Still, I struggled as I kicked the door shut, my arms overflowing with Piper's *very* unusual collection of rejected gowns.

Then, just as I feared I was going to lose control of the whole pile, someone came to my rescue, hurrying out of the shop, grabbing the hangers and swooping the dresses out of my arms with a gallant offer of, "Please, let me help you!"

"Thanks, Dexter," I said, wiping my brow with my arm. The day was as hot as it was bright.

Even though he was wearing a suit, Dex Shipley didn't

seem affected by the temperature, and his smile was nearly as dazzling as the sun. "No problem." He led the way to the door, speaking over his shoulder. "Welcome to the shop!"

Socrates and I followed him inside the cheerful interior, where a seafoam-green carpet stretched between soft white walls. An ancient chalkboard, announcing a sale on fall apparel, linked the boutique to its history. "Um, are you working . . . ?"

I was about to ask Dexter if he'd already changed careers in the wake of Abigail's fraud and death, which might've spelled the end of Artful Engagements.

Before I finished my question, though, I spotted someone I knew whom I hadn't expected to be there. Nor did I ever anticipate seeing this person in a crystal-encrusted, mermaid-style bridal gown with what I was pretty sure was a princess seam bodice.

"Fidelia?"

"I could've sworn I was assigned to hunt for bridesmaids' dresses," Fidelia said after she'd changed back into her regular clothes. Two faint spots of color appeared on her cheeks, under what looked to be a trace of cosmetic blush. She was wearing colorful clothes again, too—a bright pink blouse— and I could have sworn her normally mousy brown hair was a bit darker. The color looked good on her. "I just got a bit carried away, with the wedding dress," she said, biting her lower lip. "It was so lovely!"

"You really did look nice," I assured her, flipping through a rack of gowns. Socrates, who probably feared he would be forced to try on a bow tie, had turned tail the moment he'd seen Fidelia spinning on a dais surrounded by three mirrors and was waiting outside. "And as for 'assignments,' everyone is welcome to pitch in however they can," I added. "I can certainly use the help."

Fidelia was also perusing the stock, right next to me, but I saw her gaze flick to Dexter Shipley, who was across the shop, arranging a veil on a mannequin, and I thought I knew the *real* reason she'd stopped by Something Borrowed, Something New.

"Fidelia?" I whispered. "Did you know Dexter would be working here? Do you have a *crush* on him?"

I could tell by her startled reaction that I was right. But I'd said the wrong thing.

"No . . . no, of course not," she stammered softly, backing away from the rack. She again glanced at Dexter, who seemed oblivious to us both. "I'm here to help you and Piper!"

Fidelia's self-confidence was legendarily low, and I tried to give it a boost. "Well, if you like him—and he *is* handsome, and seems nice—you should ask him to do something. Like go to the fireworks tomorrow night. Or to All Paws on Deck." I had a sudden image of myself at that event. "You can watch me sink in the *Tiny-tanic*. It'll definitely give you something to talk about."

"Oh, I don't think so, Daphne." Fidelia's cheeks had gone pale. She took another step back. "I'm not like you, dating handsome journalists and detectives." Her gaze darted to Dexter one more time. He still didn't seem to notice us, and I worried that I'd been wrong to give Fidelia advice that, perhaps fortunately, she wasn't going to heed anyway. She checked her wrist, although she wasn't wearing a watch. "I've . . . I've got to go, Daphne. I've got a class in a half hour." She must've seen the confusion on my face, because she added, "Summer session!"

With that, my part-time accountant scurried out the door, the shop bell tinkling in the wake of her departure.

"Well, I botched that," I muttered, resuming my attempt to find a dress that would flatter me, Moxie, Fidelia and

Dorinda—and which wouldn't look anything like Lady Liberty's toga.

I was so focused on sifting through silk and chiffon that I didn't even hear Dexter Shipley come up behind me until he said, gravely, "Daphne Templeton, did you chase away a potential *three-thousand-dollar sale*?"

"I'm sorry, but there was no sale to begin with," I told Dexter, who had wheeled a rack of specially curated potential gowns over to the dais where Fidelia had recently been twirling. "Fidelia Tutweiler is quite single. And very interesting. A sweet person."

I wasn't being very subtle, and Dex's blue eyes registered regret as he unzipped a plastic bag like the ones he'd just taken off my hands. "I'm sorry, Daphne. I'm not interested in dating right now. I'm just coming off of a breakup, and I'm incredibly busy with my new enterprise." His jaw clenched. "The whole mess at Artful Engagements is bogging me down, too. It seems like I'll never get out from under fixing the mess Abigail left."

"Dexter, did you really not know *anything* about Abigail's plan?" The question popped out of my mouth before I could stop it, but Dexter didn't seem upset.

"Not a thing," he assured me, holding up a pink satin sheath with spaghetti straps. The color would've worked on Moxie, but Dorinda would've looked horrible. I shook my head, rejecting the gown. "Abigail and I were in the process of separating, professionally," he added, zipping the gown back into the bag. "I had already bought this place, with the long-term goal of establishing a one-stop bridal experience."

"You mean wedding planning, too."

He nodded, unzipping another garment bag. "Yes. Abigail and I were going to be competitors. But that was far down the road. I've only owned this place for three months, and all of my focus is here. I bought the shop because old Tillie Martingale wanted to retire. The opportunity was there and likely wouldn't come again. But I have a huge learning curve when it comes to women's fashion."

Pulling a dramatic black-and-white cocktail-length dress from the bag, he glanced at the mannequin he'd just been dressing, and I looked, too. The veil was a bit askew.

"Plus, Abigail and I had creative differences," Dex continued, rehanging the second dress on the rack, too, when I again shook my head. Moxie would've hated the ultra-modern pattern. "It was time for us to part ways. I was only staying on to help with some of the weddings that were in the works when I bought the shop—mainly in hopes of persuading Abigail not to carry out some of her increasingly over-the-top ideas."

I recalled several times Dex had all but grimaced as he'd carried out Abigail's plans for Piper's wedding. "You hated the Fourth of July theme, didn't you?"

He snorted, and, in his sharp, dark suit, with his neat haircut and dreamy eyes, he was good-looking enough to pull it off. "It was gaudy and ridiculous," he said. "I hate what happened to all the brides and grooms back at the Sodgrass Club, but in a way, your sister is lucky. Especially if your mother's class action suit is successful and everyone recoups their losses."

"I guess Artful Engagements will likely be liquidated, if Mom and her fellow litigants win."

"I suspect so," Dexter agreed. "I'm incredibly lucky I got out when I did, rather than buy in as a partner."

That was a surprise. "Abigail offered you that chance?"

"Yes, I had a chance to be her full partner—which probably indicates that the business was struggling, hence her take-the-money-and-run strategy." Dexter held up a yellow dress, and, seeing crystals on the bodice, I shook my head more firmly. I couldn't imagine anything really flashy looking right in the chapel. Just like Piper's slinky sheaths wouldn't have fit in. "Regardless, I never came close to biting. I wanted to be in total control of a new business, with a new vision."

He seemed to be undermining my theory that he might've killed Abigail in order to take over a thriving company with an established clientele.

"She must've been threatened by your plans, right?" I asked. "I'm surprised you were able to work together at all, once she knew what *you* were up to."

I was fishing around, pretty obviously, but Dex didn't seem to care.

"Brides who would avail themselves of my services wouldn't go to Abigail," he informed me. "She knew that. She repeatedly expressed unhappiness about my plans—which were quite public, by the way. But she was far from threatened." He shrugged. "Why would she be, when she was planning a scam and, apparently, getting ready to flee town? In retrospect, I think that all the times she snapped at me and belittled my dreams, she was putting on an act. Covering her tracks while knowing all along that we'd never really compete, because she'd be off to . . . who knows where."

"So you've heard about the suitcases?"

Dexter's hand hovered over the selection of gowns, a pair of cuff links winking as he tried to decide what to show me next. He was very young, but had the suave air of an older movie star. If Moxie hadn't been in love with Mike Cavanaugh, I might've tried to pair *her* up with Dex.

"Yes," he said, his back still toward me. "The homicide detective, several insurance claims adjusters and some officers who investigate fraud have all mentioned the bag on the bed." I thought it was interesting that he only knew about one suitcase, when I'd seen two. "I understand she was packed and ready to go," he noted, "but never got the chance."

"Had you ever traveled with her?"

Dexter's hand dropped, and he turned back to me, temporarily giving up on our quest. He seemed understandably confused, and maybe intrigued, by the turn the conversation had taken.

"Yes, of course, we often traveled to destination weddings, expos and vendor fairs." He moved to a wheeled cart that held a bottle of complimentary champagne and wiggled out the cork. Pouring two glasses, he handed one to me. "Cheers."

We clinked, and I took a sip. The bottle had been open and was half empty, but the drink still fizzed pleasantly. When my nose stopped tickling, I asked, "What kind of suitcase did Abigail use?"

That question also probably seemed to come out of nowhere, but Dexter grinned. "Louis Vuitton. I can't tell you how many times I hauled her bags off airport carousels. She certainly never made a move to get them herself!"

"Did you ever see her carry a basic black bag? Plastic?"

He raised his eyebrows. "You're joking, right? Abigail Sinclair traveled in style. If her bags didn't match, she wouldn't have gone at all."

Having been part of one of Abigail's matchy-matchy events, I believed him. And I hadn't really believed the suitcase had been Abigail's to begin with. "Did she have a . . . partner?" I asked. "Someone she was involved with?"

Dexter still didn't seem to care why I was asking a series of questions about luggage and lovers. He seemed too taken aback by the idea of Abigail having the latter to consider why I might want to know, and he laughed out loud before telling me, "Oh, no. I don't know who in the world would be brave enough to pair up with Abigail romantically! God help the man who tried to meet her exacting standards on more than a professional level!"

I was pretty sure someone had tried to live up to Abigail's demands—and had maybe killed her, when she made too many.

"I see your point," I said, taking another sip of champagne. My *last* sip. I could already feel the bubbles going to my head. Before long, I'd be twirling on the dais in a gown, like Fidelia. I set my flute on the tray and, against my better, if slightly clouded judgment, asked a somewhat reckless question. "Dexter, what do you remember from the night of Abigail's death?"

He put down his glass, too. For a moment, we were close enough that I could smell his cologne, a distinctive sweet-and-sharp scent that I didn't like as much as I liked the masculine fragrance Jonathan always wore.

And I wasn't sure I liked the sudden shrewd look in Dexter's eyes, although I'd earned the suspicion I saw there.

"You have a reputation for solving murders," he said, in a lower, more even voice. "I'm fully aware that your questions haven't just been asked out of curiosity. I know you're trying to find the killer."

I couldn't deny that. "I'm just trying to get a clear picture of the events leading up to her death, mainly to help my future brother-in-law."

The sun was shifting, casting shadows on the white walls and seafoam carpet, so it seemed like we were in the center of a stormy ocean. I kind of wished Socrates was inside, instead of relaxing under one of the shade trees that grew near the schoolhouse.

I probably should've left, but I asked again, "What did you see, Dexter?"

"I'm under no obligation to tell you anything, Daphne," he reminded me, checking his wrist, like he had places to be. However, like Fidelia, he wasn't even wearing a watch, and he shook out his arm. "But I like Roger, and I can't imagine him killing anyone, so I'll tell you what little I know. Which is next to nothing. Because when the storm hit, I grabbed an umbrella and started helping guests to their cars."

"Who?"

"One guest," he corrected himself. "The groom's mother, who kept complaining that the water would leave marks on her silk blouse."

I could imagine Beverly fretting as she was hustled away to her vehicle.

"It was obvious that the event was over, and that we wouldn't even be able to clean up, so I left," he added, with the slightest lift of his shoulders. "It's pretty straight-forward."

His story was. Yet I felt like something was missing, either from the tale—or from our entire discussion of his relationship with his former employer. And the absent element was, I realized, *emotion*. Like any of the old-time movie stars Moxie so adored, Dex Shipley was almost too good at keeping his cool.

"Dexter," I said, cocking my head. "Can I ask one last question?"

"Yes," he agreed. One corner of his mouth lifted into a wry grin. "We've come this far."

"How did you manage to deal with Abigail for even a few years? She seems like a *very* difficult person to get along with."

I'd been trying to provoke a heartfelt response, and I got it.

Anger glittered in his eyes. Maybe toward Abigail. Or maybe toward me for asking nosy questions. Probably toward both of us. "If you're asking whether I ever wanted to kill Abigail Sinclair—and I believe you are—who wouldn't sometimes chafe under the control of a tyrant?

Which was, let's face it, what she was. But I used her, too. She taught me how to run a business without ever setting foot in a classroom. That's why *I* sought *her* out and endured her abuse. And I found my way out from under her thumb, as I'd always planned." He gestured around the shop. "A *nonviolent* way. Because I have goals that can't be achieved in a prison cell. But if you want to know if I ever daydreamed about doing away with the boss, as I've already told Detective Doebler, the short answer is *yes*."

There wasn't much more to say, so I didn't even respond. And within a few seconds, Dexter had regained his composure. Clearing his throat, he nodded to the rack of dresses. "Should we continue looking for something that meets your vision?"

"I'm starting to fear that the dress I imagine doesn't exist," I said, glad that the tense moment was over, even if I'd been the one who'd provoked it. There had been a few seconds, while he'd expressed his true feelings about Abigail, that I'd been tempted to run for the door. Relaxing a bit, I told him, "Or, if the gown I'm picturing is out there somewhere, there's only one, because I keep thinking it has to be vintage, or it will just look wrong on Moxie, and in the little chapel where Piper's now getting married."

Dexter took some time to think, then he snapped his fingers and said, "I might honestly have exactly what you're looking for."

I didn't want to get my hopes up, but it happened anyway. "Really?"

"Yes, come on." He started to walk away, beckoning me with one hand. His cuff links flashed again. "I'll show you."

I looked around the now-gloomy shop, which was still devoid of customers. Prom season had come and gone, and everyone with a summer wedding apparently already had the perfect dress. I really wished some fall or winter wedding parties would show up, but I supposed most brides

Chapter 24

"Oh, Daphne, this gown is perfect," Moxie exclaimed, smoothing a long, burnished-gold dress, which she'd hung on a peg in her garret apartment, located in a big yellow Victorian on Market Street, above my favorite bookshop, the Philosopher's Tome. Moxie always decorated for every holiday, and she'd put her unique twist on Independence Day, intermingling American artifacts with items like a string of old-looking red-and-yellow Chinese paper lanterns that were strung across the top of the open French doors that led to her balcony. I knew my best friend well enough to understand that she was honoring the Chinese origin of fireworks. "It's one of the loveliest dresses I've ever seen," Moxie added, "including the one that nearly got you killed, which was exquisite."

I had, indeed, nearly been murdered related to my purchase of a custom-made dress for last year's Bark the Halls Christmas ball. Socrates, who was observing me and Moxie from the balcony, considered the incident a cautionary tale against vanity. And I could tell he wasn't too thrilled that I'd ventured into a back room with a guy who

I *didn't* think had committed murder—although I wasn't entirely ruling Dex out.

"Well, if I was going to get killed over this dress, it probably would've happened already, back at Something Borrowed, Something New," I noted as I admired the gown, too. The dress had been hanging with a bunch of Tillie Martingale's old stock, which dated back to the boutique's grand opening in the 1960s. Among the castoffs had been a whole bridal party's worth of softly burnished umber, almost gold, silk sheaths with velvet detailing on the bodices. The gowns, probably from a canceled wedding, had mystery woven into their very fabric, which reminded me of a Tuscan sunset at the height of summer.

Moxie was smitten, too. "These *are* almost worth dying for," she said, earning a low *woof* of disapproval from Socrates. "I liked the Statue of Liberty costumes, but this dress is *really* special."

Giving up entirely on the conversation, Socrates turned to watch the sun setting over Sylvan Creek, while I wandered over to the big table where Moxie had created the elaborate gingerbread copy of the town that had helped solve a murder.

The detailed cookie sculpture was long gone—probably eaten by the white rat who currently sat on a sketch pad.

Gently moving Sebastian aside, which was a big step for me, I gasped. "Oh, Moxie! This is amazing!" I turned to my friend, who was beaming with pride over my reaction to her drawing of Piper's wedding cake. "Do you really think you can pull this off?"

"Yes, of course," she said, joining me. Her finger traced the outline of the three-tiered confection, which featured an elaborate, but subtle, design, as if she was drawing it again. "I told you that I've already finished the costumes for All Paws on Deck."

I still hadn't seen the outfits that Artie and Tiny Tim would wear.

Well, I had glimpsed a gold button when Moxie had whisked the costumes away as I'd entered her apartment. I had no idea where she'd hidden them in her crowded, charming home, and I knew they wouldn't reappear until I was boarding the *Tiny-tanic*.

"No need to worry," she added, with a smile. "I've got ages!"

"Um, no, you don't," I reminded her, checking the clock on her antique pink GE oven. Moxie's apartment was like a time capsule, stuffed from its sharply peaked eaves to its castle-like turret with all her favorite things from the past. A few objects, like a console television whose greenish screen had been blank for thirty years, were purely decorative, but I was pretty sure the clock kept perfect time. "And we are running late for the shower."

Moxie, who was fortunately already dressed in a suitable summer party dress, circa 1940, noted the time, too. "Oh, we do have to run!"

Socrates must've been listening, because he shambled in from the balcony.

Leaving the French doors open to let in a soft summer breeze, which carried the crackle of fireworks as the Fourth drew even closer, we all hurried down to my VW, where Moxie and Socrates engaged in a good-natured, if silent, debate about who would get to ride shotgun.

I hopped in the driver's seat and started to put the van in gear, only to notice that something was amiss in the back.

Hopping out, I opened the rear door, which was already ajar.

For a moment, I was delighted to see that someone had returned Piper's bicycle, if roughly, by jamming it awkwardly into my vehicle. The bike looked a bit worse for the wear, too.

Then I pulled off a note that was taped to the handlebars and read it quickly, thinking it would be an apology.

But it wasn't.

The message, scrawled with obvious haste on a crumpled piece of paper, was an unexpected farewell.

Chapter 25

The Owl & Crescent Art Barn was tucked away on the outskirts of Zephyr Hollow, a picturesque hamlet that drew the region's writers, artists and musicians with an almost mystical pull. The little structure, located behind a small, colorful Victorian house on the edge of a babbling brook, was an eclectic treat for the eyes, filled to the rafters with knickknacks collected by the owner, a pretty, dark-haired young woman named Willow Bellamy, who had a warm smile and an air of mystery herself.

That impression was probably enhanced by a book I'd spied on a high shelf when I was trying to get a better look at the inspiration for the barn's name, a white-faced owl named Rembrandt, who was perched in the rafters.

The dusty tome, titled *Bellamy Book of Spells, Lore & Miscellany*, seemed to hint that Willow's ancestors, at least, had dabbled in potions. And I wouldn't have been surprised if our hostess for the evening did a bit of conjuring herself, beyond whipping up some amazing summer hors d'oeuvres.

Moxie seemed to agree that the Owl & Crescent, which was also home to a sweet gray cat named Luna, who had a moon-shaped mark on her chest, was enchanting.

"I love this place," she whispered, waving a hand that held a Parmesan tuile topped with heirloom tomato salad. Her other hand was deftly wielding a paintbrush, dabbing oil onto a canvas, where a realistic rendering of the wedding-related objects Willow had arranged on a long farmhouse table was already taking shape.

I could make out the flowers, the top hat, the silken gloves—and the outline of two ceramic figurines: a basset hound and a white poodle.

Willow had thoughtfully purchased the miniature pups at a flea market after I'd mentioned that Socrates and Snowdrop, who was here with Daisy, would attend, if that was okay with her.

Fortunately, the Owl & Crescent was very pet-friendly. Along with the bird and cat, a rescue pig lived behind the barn in a pink children's playhouse, complete with a weather vane.

Glancing out a window, I saw Laci Chalmers, who'd agreed to photograph the shower for a less grand scrapbook I planned to assemble in lieu of the Magical Memories book that would never happen. Laci probably should've been shooting the guests, but she seemed entranced with the pig, Mortimer, who was posing in front of his house, his snout lifted high. I had a feeling he would be featured somehow in the *Weekly Gazette*.

Needless to say, the cute porker reminded me of Harley, who in turn made me think of Dorinda—and the note she'd taped to Piper's bicycle. I'd read it three times, and it was short and strange enough that I was pretty sure I'd memorized the whole thing, verbatim.

Sorry about your bike. It's a little messed up. A guy named Dutch wrecked it into a tree. If I were you, I wouldn't ask him to pay for repairs. Also, sorry

*I can't sing at the wedding or walk dogs. You
said I have a good voice, and I think so, too. I'm
leaving for Nashville today, and I'm not coming
back until I have a record deal. Or I punch another
cop. Whichever comes first.*

"She did have a country sound," I muttered, swiping
some paint onto my own canvas. Knowing my limitations,
I was focusing on one aspect of the scene: the basset
hound. Somewhat fittingly, the dog was shaping up to look
like a misshapen pony.

Glancing around the room, I saw that Piper's painting
was precise, in keeping with her analytical approach to life.

Fidelia, meanwhile, seemed to finally be channeling her
father, who'd been a famous, very wealthy portrait artist.
Her flowers looked like something Monet would've created.

Elyse Hunter-Black, whose easel was flanked by her
greyhounds, Paris and Milan, had rendered the scene in angular strokes, but it was clearly an artistic choice. I could
picture her painting on the walls of her modern Manhattan
loft, as featured in at least one design magazine.

And, while I couldn't see some of the canvases, I was
pretty sure the other guests, including Daisy Carpenter and
a handful of Piper's female friends, were all doing better
than me.

Adding a blob of brown to my poor dog's face, I shook
my head, both at my painting and at my uncertainty about
whether I should contact Detective Doebler to alert him to
Dorinda's departure. I could see him either being grateful
or accusing me of meddling in his investigation. I hadn't
told Roger, either. It seemed like Dorinda should share her
news herself, if she hadn't already. "What a mess."

"Oh, goodness, that is tragic!"

I turned to see Beverly Berendt looming over me, a glass of wine in her hand and an apologetic look on her face.

Not surprisingly, she was joined by fellow Realtor Maeve Templeton, who was also surveying my artwork with something close to a frown on her smooth face. "Yes, that is unfortunate," Mom agreed, swirling her pinot grigio, too. "Why are your flowers so brown, Daphne?"

"Because they're a *dog*," I explained, which didn't make matters any better.

I looked to Moxie for help, but she was taking a break, making her way to the buffet, which was set up on an antique sideboard. Socrates and Snowdrop had also abandoned me in favor of canoodling by the creek, which left me alone with Mom and Beverly, who leaned back and blinked at each other, their lips pursed to hold back laughter.

They were mocking me, in their mutual mime-like way, but to be honest, I was kind of happy that Mom had a friend, even if Beverly had likely chased her daughter first to a biker bar, then to a career in country music—which actually might turn out okay.

Not certain if Bev knew anything about Dorinda's move south, I didn't mention the bike or the note to her, either. Instead, I asked, "How's the lawsuit coming along?"

"I can't imagine how we'll lose," Mom said, fidgeting with one of her many oversized necklaces. This one had chunky red stones that glittered against her white blouse, which she'd paired with navy slacks. She was getting dangerously close to interpreting the rapidly approaching holiday too literally, perhaps taking over where Abigail had left off. She looked to Bev. "There's no denying that fraud occurred and money is owed."

"I feel like we're doing the other poor families a tremendous service by spearheading the effort," Roger's mother added. "It's practically charity work." She smiled at Mom.

"And several couples have expressed interest in investing any windfalls, beyond their recouped losses, in starter homes!"

I'd known they were both drumming up business with the suit.

"I suppose Abigail's mansion will sell at some point," I noted, using my brush to catch drips of white paint that were oozing from the dog's eyes, thanks to my attempt to add highlights. "Unless Abigail left it to someone?"

"The estate has not been settled," said Mom, who had some experience with circling, vulture-like, above murder victims' manses. "However, I will note that Dexter Shipley has already expressed interest in purchasing the place."

My hand jerked again. "Really?"

"Yes," Beverly said, wincing and taking a step back, because I'd accidentally flicked some paint off my brush. The spatter had landed dangerously close to her more subtly patriotic blue-and-white dress. Using her free hand, she swiped at an imaginary stain. "He's starting his own wedding planning business, and, needless to say, it would be convenient and cost-effective to use a space already set up for that exact type of enterprise, right down to the garden."

Mom shot me a pointed look. "Which is *perfect* for events, when you're not finding bodies there, Daphne."

I refused to react to my mother's attempt to get a rise out of me. Plus, I was preoccupied, recalling Dexter's comments about wanting to start fresh with his own vision.

So much for that claim.

I felt my shaky faith in Dex Shipley's innocence waver, even as I realized that it would be pretty gutsy for a killer to ask about purchasing the property where he'd committed homicide, and where he hoped to profit by rising from employee to owner in the wake of his victim's death.

I was so caught up in debating whether I believed Dex

was innocent or not that I jumped when I felt a firm hand clasp my arm, causing me to smear white all over the black smudge that was supposed to be my basset hound's nose.

Then Beverly surprised me even more by basically telling her best friend to buzz off.

"Maeve, dear," she said, still clutching my arm, with a surprisingly strong grip. "Would you excuse Daphne and me for a moment? I've been so looking forward to getting to know your lovely younger daughter!"

Mom seemed as stunned as I was by the turn of events. I supposed she'd assumed that I was the Templeton equivalent of Dorinda and not necessarily a person you seek out at parties, unless it was to criticize my artwork. But she graciously said, "What a lovely idea, since we all *will* be family soon."

Her tone was cheerful, but I felt like she was *warning* Beverly, who seemed a bit threatening herself when she leaned close the moment Mom was out of earshot and said, "Tell me, right now, if you think my daughter committed murder, as I suspect!"

"Why do you think Dorinda is guilty?" I asked once Beverly and I had stepped outside into the close, warm night. The moon was covered by clouds, but candles burned in lanterns that hung near the door and a moonflower-smothered arbor that arched above us was strung with twinkle lights, so I could read Bev's expression. She looked frightened—and frustrated. "Because, while I can't deny that she despised Abigail, I don't *really* think your daughter is a killer."

"Oh, goodness, I hope not," Beverly said, fanning herself. She stepped out from under the arbor, and I had no choice but to follow her. "But between the unsavory crowd she spends time with, and the tattoos—"

"The unicorn? And her *brother*?"

I was trying to remind Bev that the images were harmless, but she shot back, "And the *spiders*!"

I didn't think it was worth pointing out that many cultures considered arachnids symbols of good fortune. Beverly was shaking her head as we walked past a lush vegetable garden toward the creek, where two seats waited next to a ring of stones. "Not to mention her record, for police brutality!"

Bev wasn't using that phrase correctly, but I didn't mention that, either. "I know that some of the people at the Wild Hog aren't the most ethical," I conceded as the owl, Rembrandt, swooped out of a high, open window and off into the night. I admired his silent, majestic flight for a moment, then addressed Bev again. "But your daughter seems very nice. She returned the bicycle that was stolen from me when I visited the bar."

Bev overlooked the purloined bike. Her eyes grew wide for a different reason. "You've spoken to her? Recently? At that *place*?"

I was confused, and not just by the fact that I didn't see Socrates or Snowdrop anywhere. I wasn't really worried, though, and I told Bev, "I assumed you knew that. Why else would you ask my opinion about her as a suspect?"

"Because your mother said you were almost certainly investigating the murder, and Roger has informed me that he mentioned Dorinda's altercation with Abigail to you." We'd reached the chairs, but Beverly didn't sit down. "Since Maeve said you are a very astute sleuth, I assumed that you had looked into Dorinda's whereabouts, around the time of the murder. Although I didn't anticipate that you would visit that awful bar she lives above!"

We were supposed to be focused on Dorinda, but I was hung up on something Beverly had just said about me. "Mom called me *astute*?"

Beverly waved her hand. "Oh, she's forever bragging about you and Piper. Rambling endlessly about your business enterprises and your world travels and your handsome boyfriend. Honestly, as much as I treasure our new friendship and look forward to being family, your mother can be somewhat tiresome when it comes to you and your sister."

The wind blew, and chimes that were tucked around the property tinkled happily. "Wow. She never says that stuff to me."

"When you have a high-spirited child, prone to *adventuring*, you can't encourage them too much," Beverly confided. "A mother needs to keep her reckless offspring in check. And it's worked, hasn't it? Look at how successful you are!"

I didn't necessarily advocate the tough and hypercritical parenting approach my mother was *still* taking with me, and I thought she could ease up, but I had to admit that I felt like I'd turned out okay, and that she'd nudged—sometimes pushed—me in good directions since I'd returned to Sylvan Creek.

"If only I'd had the same success with Dorinda," Beverly added with a heavy sigh. "But, alas!"

"Maybe, just maybe, you could encourage her a *tiny* bit," I suggested, raising my hand and pinching my thumb and forefinger very close together. "She's a talented musician, you know. I tried to get her to sing at the wedding, but . . ."

I caught myself, before I mentioned Dorinda's abrupt move. But it was too late. Beverly was watching me with narrowed eyes. A few feet away, the creek burbled loudly, the sound dominating the quiet night until Bev demanded, "But what?"

"She's gone to Nashville," I said, not sure why I was keeping that news a secret. Dorinda hadn't asked me to do that. Not from her mother, her brother, nor Detective Doebler. "She wants to pursue a career in music. And I think she has a future."

That last part came out in a rush, because Bev's mouth was opening and closing. When I finally stopped talking she surprised me by saying, "Well, at least that's something. A step in some direction, away from the Wild Hog."

She shuddered, either at the dread name of the bar or because the evening was getting breezy.

I looked up at the sky again. The clouds looked darker, more threatening. "We should probably go back to the barn," I suggested, with a glance at Mortimer's playhouse. The pig had gone inside, and the weather vane was spinning. "It looks and feels like it's about to rain, and Dexter Shipley isn't here to escort us with an umbrella."

I was joking, but Beverly looked baffled. "Who in the world is *Dexter Shipley*? Some sort of sports player or 'hip-hop' person?"

I wasn't sure why she jumped to those two particular and strangely worded conclusions, but I told her, "He's the guy who helped you to your car when the storm broke out at Artful Engagements . . ."

I stopped describing him, because Beverly was pursing her lips and shaking her head again, more vigorously. "No. I ran to my car *hampered* by my brother, Alfred, who has grown portly, eating so much bread at the Gateway, and who was wearing, as usual, a ridiculous pair of sandals. He kept calling for me to wait up—he's never liked storms—and my blouse was ruined by the time I got into my Lexus."

I nearly asked Beverly if she was *sure* she remembered correctly, but she'd just described a pretty specific and plausible scenario.

And as I was trying to figure out why Dexter Shipley had lied to me—to cover up his role in a homicide was my first guess—I looked down the creek, in the direction the owl had flown.

I first spied a footbridge leading to a patch of woods.

Then I noticed two people who had crossed that arched wooden span and who were standing in the shadow of those trees.

Laci Chalmers. And Daisy Carpenter.

And it looked to me like they were *arguing*.

Chapter 26

"I'm telling you, it was weird," I said loudly, accepting another armful of bags from Piper, who didn't respond. She was hurrying through the rain from my van to her barn, where we were stashing the gifts she'd received that evening. Piper had wanted guests to come empty-handed, but, knowing they wouldn't do that, she'd suggested they bring contributions to local pet shelters.

The small gathering of animal lovers—discounting Mom and probably Bev—had been generous, and I'd spent the latter part of the evening loading up my VW, dropping Socrates off at Plum Cottage, then driving the short distance to the farmhouse, where Piper was helping me unload everything.

Normally, I would've just kept the stuff in the VW, dropping it off directly at Fur-ever Friends dog rescue and Whiskered Away Home, the shelter for cats. Unfortunately, I didn't expect to have time to swing by either of those places for at least a week, and I needed the space in my van to transport pet-sitting clients and hundreds of cookies for Wags 'n Flags—and possibly oars, boat decorations and the life jackets Mike Cavanaugh's cousin had *strongly* suggested the dogs and I wear during All Paws on Deck.

Burdened by the last two sacks of kibble, I waddled awkwardly around the tarp-covered antique truck, which had been pulled outside. Splashing through a puddle I'd already stepped in twice—I could have sworn it was moving—I again reached the door, which Piper had hauled open. Stepping into the dry, warm but dark barn, I picked up where I'd left off. "I couldn't see their faces, but Daisy and Laci were obviously arguing—"

Piper didn't say anything, but she managed to cut me off by flipping a switch.

"Oh, it's shaping up so nicely," I said, setting aside my story for a moment, and dropping the bags, too, with a pile of other stuff, including my horrible painting. I wasn't giving that away to the dog or cat rescue. I had just been hoping the blobby basset with the weepy eyes would somehow disappear in the barn, where tools and holiday decorations were usually tucked away everywhere, including under the floorboards, which would be a great spot for my artwork.

However, I suddenly doubted that I'd be able to ditch my shameful canvas in the clean, open space that stretched around me.

The floors had been swept of all dust, and the walls were bathed in the soft glow of two crystal chandeliers, which hung from the exposed beams. Strings of Edison lights crisscrossed the eaves, too, and the rain, pattering on the roof in a steady rhythm, made it easy to imagine people dancing in a space that had been cleared under the loft.

"Elyse has been busy," I noted, pushing some matted, wet curls away from my face and hoisting the bags again. I lugged them to the table that held the other presents, all of which would need to be tucked out of sight. But for now, the barn was a safe, dry storage place.

"Elyse's *workmen* have been busy," Piper clarified,

adding two cases of canned cat food to the table, too. I was impressed by the barn, but I got the sense that my sister was starting to feel guilty for having everyone going to such lengths for her and Roger. "I appreciate all this, and it's so much better than what Abigail was putting together. But it's really not necessary."

"I told you, Elyse was thrilled to pitch in. She lives to plan stuff like this!"

Piper still had a funny look on her face. "Daphne, I need to tell you something . . ."

"Can it wait?" I asked, brushing off my damp dress, which didn't help at all. Nor did stamping my feet, which were muddy from the puddle. "I'm kind of a mess."

"I think you look gorgeous."

The deep male voice came from the doorway, and I looked over, greeting our visitor with a question. "Jonathan . . . What are *you* doing here?"

"I really thought you looked fine before," Jonathan kindly lied, pouring two cups of tea from my kettle. He'd made himself at home at Plum Cottage while I'd gotten cleaned up, showering quickly and putting on a cozy sweatshirt, because the night air on the hilltop was cool after the rain. He carried the mugs to the living room, stepping over Ms. Peebles, who kept watching our visitor with something like awe in her wide eyes.

Tinkleston, who'd once attacked Jonathan, sat halfway up the spiral staircase, like he couldn't decide if he wanted to join the small party or if he should just go to bed, like Socrates had done.

Along with politely giving Jonathan and me some privacy, Socrates tended to stick to a routine bedtime, and it was getting late.

"So, how have you been since you ran from my house?" Jonathan teased, sitting down on my love seat and gesturing for me to join him. If his ego was bruised by my failure to respond in kind to his declaration of love, it didn't show, just like how he hadn't seemed embarrassed when I'd once turned him down for a date. On the contrary, I saw a glimmer of amusement in his eyes as I slipped onto the soft cushion next to him. The sofa left me no choice but to basically rest against him, which wasn't a bad thing. "And how was the shower?" he asked. "The one with the guests— not the one you just took."

I knew he hadn't traveled to Winding Hill to get an update on a painting party or my time in the bathroom, and I said, "Jonathan, about last night, and the stupid things that came out of my mouth . . ."

He'd taken a sip of tea, but he set down his mug and squeezed my wrist. "Daphne, it's okay. I didn't tell you that I love you to force your hand and make you say it back. I was just stating a fact. And I came here to make sure things are all right between us. Because you seemed a little spooked." He grinned. "A lot spooked."

"I was just caught off guard," I told him, thinking that was an understatement. I cringed every time I pictured myself babbling and darting to my van. "And things are fine. In fact—"

I started to tell him that I loved him, too, although it didn't seem like the right moment or mood. It was probably a good thing that he interrupted by pulling something out of the pocket of the soft, striped button-down shirt he was wearing open over a white tee that emphasized the tan he'd gotten in California. "Here." He shook out a folded piece of paper. "You wanted this, for some reason."

"What is it?" I asked, scanning the document, which looked like some kind of scientific report. I tried to make sense of the jumble of words and letters, which were like Greek, or at least a lot of Greek roots, to me.

Stereo microscope . . . FT-IR . . . microspectrophotometer . . .

"I'm reading, but nothing's registering," I admitted, before noticing one thing I could decipher: Coroner Vonda Shakes's name on the official letterhead. I shoved Jonathan's shoulder, because he was already laughing at me. "And don't say I'd be able to understand this if I'd attended the police academy."

"Well, that would probably be true," he said, taking the paper from my fingers and placing it on the trunk. He settled back again, and I sank even closer to him. "To summarize, it's the report on the fibers found on Abigail's body. Doebler shared a copy with me."

I was immediately intrigued. "So what did the strands come from?"

"The exact source hasn't been identified yet, but the fibers are a mix of blue and white silk."

I winced again as I recalled how I'd tried to strangle myself with a rag. That exercise seemed even more pointless in the wake of the report. "So they weren't fibers you'd find in, say, a dish towel from a restaurant supply company?"

"No, I imagine those would be cotton," Jonathan surmised, as Tinkleston ran down the steps, following Ms. Peebles into the kitchen. A moment later, I heard them both eating from their bowls, which were now side by side. "Why did you ask about a towel?" he inquired, seeming oblivious to the miracle of feline camaraderie I'd just witnessed. "And why did you want this report in the first place?"

I reached for my tea. "When Daisy Carpenter was considering fleeing town, I saw a stack of blue-and-white striped towels in a box at In a Pickle. And I later remembered that she'd been using one in the same pattern to wipe down the counter at Artful Engagements the night Abigail was killed."

Jonathan was giving me a look that said I probably should've shared that earlier.

"I didn't say anything because I didn't want to make things needlessly worse for Daisy if the report would rule out the towels—as seems to be the case," I reminded him. I felt some heat creep into my cheeks, but nevertheless confessed, "Plus, I tried to choke myself with a similar rag to see if it would be possible, and it seemed difficult to get a good enough grip."

"That sounds very scientific."

"Hey, I don't have an FT-IR, whatever that is," I pointed out, sipping my tea and placing the mug on the trunk, next to the report. "And you'll note that I reached the same conclusion as the doohickey—"

"The Fourier-transform infrared spectroscope."

"Yes, that. Which also ruled out the towel. If not Daisy."

I hadn't meant to mention my continued nagging, if weak, suspicion of Daisy, and, of course, Jonathan jumped right on it. He shifted on the love seat, facing me more fully and resting one arm across the back. "I thought you were fairly certain Daisy isn't the killer."

"For someone who's not on the case, you are very interested in my theories and observations."

He smiled, and I could hardly believe I'd managed to keep from blurting out that I was crazy for him when he'd whispered in my ear. But it definitely wasn't the right time then, and I stayed quiet as he told me, "We share an undeniable fascination with solving puzzles. So tell me more about Daisy."

I was glad Socrates was upstairs, because I didn't want to again worry him about Snowdrop's future, which would certainly be in jeopardy if Daisy Carpenter really was somehow involved in a crime. I lowered my voice. "I saw

Daisy tonight, with Laci Chalmers, in a shadowy spot near the woods. And, while I couldn't hear them, it looked like they were arguing." I pantomimed the hand gestures I'd seen both women use. "Laci was jabbing her finger at Daisy, and Daisy was raising her hands, like she was warding off blows."

"And you're linking this to the murder because . . . ?"

He'd connected the argument to Abigail's death, too. In the brief time I'd been talking, I'd seen the wheels spinning and associations forming in Jonathan's mind. He just wanted to know if I was drawing the same conclusions.

"They were likely the last two people at Artful Engagements the night of the murder—with the exception of Dexter Shipley, who outright lied to me about the events of that evening."

Jonathan leaned forward. I might as well have been under a spotlight down at the station. "How so?"

"He told me that he left the party after escorting Beverly Berendt to her car, because it was raining and he had an umbrella. But Bev says that's not the case." All at once, I doubted my doubts. "Then again, he might have mistaken Mom for Bev. They were both dressed almost exactly alike. And Mom *was* wearing a silk blouse."

Jonathan's arm, draped across the couch, moved slightly. Out of the corner of my eye, I saw that Tinkleston had slunk into the room at some point and levitated up from the floor, in his spooky way. He was perched on the back of the seat, allowing Jonathan to *scratch his ears.* Like Jonathan, I acted like this was no big deal. "Why is your mother's shirt important?" he asked as a faint mewling sound emanated from behind the overstuffed sofa.

Apparently, Ms. Peebles had tried to levitate, too, but had gotten herself wedged between the furniture and the wall.

Kneeling and reaching over the seat back, which disturbed

Tinks's moment with Jonathan, I reached down and pulled her free.

Both cats ran off again, yowling loudly to each other, but in a companionable way, while I settled back into my seat. "Dexter said the woman complained that the rain would ruin her outfit. It was a detail that made his story believable."

"That does sound like your mother," Jonathan noted. "So, forgetting Shipley for a moment, let's assume Laci and Daisy were the last two employees to leave the event."

"What if one of them saw the other do something fishy?" My repeated use of that phrase must've been related to my increasing concern over my looming boat ride, which I again shelved away in the back of my mind. "They might have fought about keeping it quiet."

Jonathan nodded agreement, but slowly. He was still thinking. Then he suggested a possibility that hadn't even crossed my mind. "Or what if they were both involved in the killing in some way? Conspirators who are now afraid one might sell the other out."

"That's a pretty classic scenario," I conceded. "But doesn't it sort of imply premeditation? It's hard to imagine two normal people getting blindly furious enough to kill someone at the exact same time. And the crime seems like one of passion, or at least done on impulse, right?"

"Yes, I don't think it was premeditated," Jonathan agreed. "And you're right. It's not likely that two individuals, however aggrieved with the same employer, would be pushed to commit such a violent act simultaneously."

The conversation lagged for a minute, but only because we were both considering other options. Jonathan was the first to speak, posing a question I had also failed to ask. "Do we know Laci's, or Daisy's, sexual orientation?"

Piper had reminded me that, if Abigail had been involved with someone, that person hadn't necessarily been male.

But I hadn't even considered Daisy or Laci as possible romantic partners for her.

Jonathan had suddenly raised so many possibilities that gears started spinning wildly in my head, too. And something Daisy had said the night of Abigail's murder suddenly took on a potentially different meaning.

Daisy had been angry with Abigail and had started to accuse her of something, saying, *"You keep holding me . . ."*

I hadn't known what to make of that when I'd witnessed the altercation, and it had only made sense when Daisy had told me how Abigail had basically blackmailed her. I'd assumed, then, that Daisy had been about to say "hostage."

But what if she'd meant "hold" in a different, physical sense?

Daisy and Abigail, or Abigail and Laci, certainly wouldn't have been the first people to engage in destructive, even abusive, love-hate relationships.

"You're thinking one of them might not have been leaving *at all* that night," I said, trying to put numerous disconnected pieces together. "Hence the suitcase on the bed. Or there was a love triangle. One in which Abigail was either the desired object, or a jilted party . . ." I rubbed my head. "You have really opened a possible can of worms. And given the way Laci and Daisy were huddled together in the darkness, I certainly can't rule out the idea of some sort of romantic entanglement."

"You've twice mentioned the woods. Where, exactly, were you all?"

"At the Owl & Crescent Art Barn—or, more accurately, behind the barn."

Jonathan suddenly seemed concerned. "That's where you held the shower?"

I nodded. "How do you even know the place?"

"There was a homicide on that property not too long ago. The detective on the case . . ." Jonathan took a second to recall the person's name, then said, "Turner . . . Lucien Turner . . . contacted me to ask if I had any suggestions for cracking the inner circle of a small town when you're coming in as an outsider. In his case, from New Orleans."

"What did you tell him?"

"Team up with a nosy pet sitter, if there's one around, and let her do half the work."

"Very funny," I said. "And I knew about the murder. The proprietor, Willow, mentioned it when I called to book the gathering. I told her that a homicide wouldn't scare off the Templeton party, then completely forgot about her concerns—even when I was down near the creek, talking with Beverly Berendt."

I could tell that Jonathan was thinking that I was expanding my range when it came to getting mixed up in murders and potentially falling into danger. "Why . . . ?"

"Bev wanted to pick my brain about Dorinda. To see if I believed *she* might be the killer."

Jonathan didn't seem surprised to hear that a mother doubted her own daughter. All he said was, "Doebler tells me Dorinda left town."

I was glad Jonathan's partner knew that. I'd still been debating sharing Dorinda's note with him. "I guess that doesn't look good for her."

"I really don't think Dorinda's a suspect," he said, surprising me. "A lot of people saw her at the Wild Hog around the time of Abigail's death."

"I think everyone agrees that most of those individuals aren't trustworthy."

"But some of them are, and I was able to vouch for a few of the witnesses Doebler tracked down. They all said Dorinda was in the bar until Roger showed up. Then they went up to her apartment."

"That's great," I said, not sure why he hadn't mentioned

this before. "That means Roger's probably off the hook, too, right?"

"I'm afraid not. There's still a gap between the time Roger was dropped off at his house and the time he showed up at the Wild Hog. A gap that includes a phone call to Abigail Sinclair."

I suddenly felt a little queasy. I'd considered the evidence against Roger before, but to hear Jonathan lay out the timeline so succinctly was unsettling.

"I'm sorry to burst your bubble," Jonathan said, rising, like he was leaving. "I know you're hopeful that Roger will be cleared soon. And, as his best man, I certainly feel the same way."

I stood up, too, and we moved to the door. "You don't think there's any chance he did it, do you?"

I was asking him to judge the facts and assure me that he had full faith in Roger before he stood next to him in the chapel.

"I can't argue that facts are stacked against him, and if I were on the case as an objective investigator, I would be watching him closely," Jonathan admitted. "But I'm not objective, and I can't seriously consider him a suspect. Which is why, for all our speculation and my conversations with Doebler, I'm not really on the case."

That reminder once again spotlighted the elephant that was always lurking in the room with us, unleashing it to rampage through my tiny home. However, this time, I tried to keep in mind that Jonathan wasn't looking for a reason to leave Sylvan Creek, or me—even if he did end up taking the job in California. In the meantime, I would try to take my own advice and live in the moment, honestly, with him.

I stepped closer to him and took his hands, for a change. "Jonathan, about what you said . . ."

"I don't want you to feel pressured," he reminded me. But I knew he realized I was letting my guard down, just like

I always wanted him to do. Still, he told me, more quietly, "You don't have to say anything."

"But I want to," I told him. "I wanted to last night. I was just so surprised."

Jonathan smiled down at me. "Really, Daphne? I've given you no hints? Not in the way I look at you, or work to win over a *cat* with a horrible attitude, just to make you happy?"

Tinkleston and Ms. Peebles had taken over our spots on the couch, and Tinks yowled in complaint.

Jonathan wasn't working *too* hard. He completely ignored the rebuke, telling me, "Not to mention the time I called in a bunch of favors to bring Socrates' 'girlfriend' back to town. And my arrangement of a sleigh ride for you, as well as the multiple times I've rescued you from perilous situations—"

"The rescues were all professional obligations," I reminded him. "I'm pretty sure you would've saved *anyone* from a locked walk-in refrigerator."

Jonathan unclasped our fingers and rested his hands on my hips. "Not with the same sense of desperate urgency, to make sure you were okay."

I slipped my arms up around his neck, enjoying the warmth and strength of his body against mine, and the way his voice was growing more tender and deeper. "You were really desperate?" I asked, my stomach prickling in a pleasant way.

"You're not going to make me admit that again, are you?"

He was grinning, but I'd grown serious. "How about what you said last night? Would you admit *that* again?"

His voice was even lower, quieter, and the warmth in his eyes melted me. "You *know* I love you, Daphne."

"I love you, too," I promised, as he bent to brush his lips against mine.

My heart was pounding, and, although I knew there was a good chance our deepening relationship might soon be tested by distance, a *tiny* part of me might've imagined the kind of future Piper was about to enjoy, with a wonderful partner by her side.

All at once, reality intruded on the moment Jonathan and I were sharing, and I rested one hand on his chest, stopping the kiss.

Piper can't marry Roger unless the real killer is found.

Someone used a blue-and-white weapon at an event where the water ran red.

White and blue, mixed with red water to make a pale shade of purple . . .

"What's wrong?" Jonathan sounded concerned.

I could tell that he thought I'd lost my nerve again and was going to run off. Or, more likely, shove him out the door, because we were at my house.

But I hadn't lost anything.

On the contrary, I was pretty sure I'd *found* something important.

"I love you," I repeated, a little breathlessly. I wanted him to know that I hadn't gotten cold feet before I shared some news that might really mess up a wonderful moment. Yet I had to tell him: "And I think the murder weapon is in Piper's barn."

Chapter 27

Jonathan wasn't even on the case, let alone the lead investigator, but he was in the thick of things at Piper's barn when Detective Doebler and some uniformed officers showed up to hunt for the silver gift bag that contained a damp, stretched-out purple garter.

Well, the garter was almost certainly dry by then, and I hoped that wouldn't mess up any attempts to confirm that it had been used to throttle Abigail Sinclair, as I suspected.

"How did I not think of that possibility?" I mused, shuffling and rubbing my arms, because the temperatures had dipped even lower, becoming unseasonably cool as the night wore on. "It was such a weird gift. Strange enough that even Moxie thought it was unusual. And she hardly raises an eyebrow at anything!"

Socrates, who'd reluctantly woken up and joined Jonathan's and my trek from Plum Cottage to the barn, yawned, like he wasn't surprised by anything humans did. He was also probably very tired, like me and Piper, who stood next to me near the antique truck, wearing a bathrobe and pair of rubber gardening shoes. We'd dragged her out of a sound sleep, too.

"This whole thing is exhausting," Piper said, folding her

arms around herself as yet another car rumbled up the drive, stopping near the cop cars. "I just wanted a nice, normal wedding."

"You'll have one," I promised, with more conviction than I felt. "I'm doing my best."

"I know, and I appreciate that," Piper said, talking to me, but watching Laci Chalmers hop out of a beat-up Honda. My sister flinched as Laci started snapping pictures on the run, trying to get some images before the cluster of law enforcement officers who were huddled just inside the barn broke up. The shiny bag dangled from Detective Doebler's gloved hand, looking paradoxically festive next to his sober brown suit. "I think that ship has sailed, though," Piper noted. "And with about as much success as I predict for the *Tiny-tanic*."

No one had high hopes for that boat, least of all me—and Socrates, who whined on my behalf.

Piper gestured to Laci, who continued to circle the meeting, half crouched down, the flash on her camera punctuating the darkness like fireworks. "Along with being part of what passes for a media circus in Sylvan Creek, Roger is still under suspicion, and we still have a cult leader for an officiant. In spite of your best efforts, things just don't seem to be working out."

"Let's just hope the garter is the murder weapon," I said. "Surely there couldn't be a connection between Roger and *that*."

Piper remained glum. "I'm hardly daring to hope at this point."

"Why don't you head back inside and go to bed," I suggested, not sure what else to tell her. I certainly didn't want to make things worse by admitting that I'd *completely forgotten about Alf Sievers*, whom I would contact the first thing in the morning. Plus, Laci Chalmers was stalking over to us, her camera still at the ready.

The meeting of professional investigators appeared to be wrapping up, so she probably wanted to get a quote or two from me and Piper.

"Hurry," I said, practically shoving my sister toward her house. "I'll handle Laci."

Piper hesitated, then she nodded. "Thanks. I am exhausted."

"Piper, wait!" Laci was waving a hand and calling to my sister's retreating back.

For once, my normally polite sibling strode on without replying.

Laci, who was less than five feet from me by then, raised her camera, as if she was going to snap a picture of Piper from behind. Then, at the last second, she changed her mind and snapped a shot of me, as I raised one hand, trying to ward her off.

I knew I would look guilty in the image if it ran in the *Gazette*, and I felt guilty, too, when Laci grinned at me wickedly, asking, "So, how did a death-dealing piece of lingerie end up in your swindled sister's barn?"

"First of all, my *mother* was swindled, not my sister, which is why Mom started the lawsuit," I reminded Laci, immediately realizing that wasn't much better. I'd probably just given Laci the opportunity to position my mom as a suspect. I could see the headline now: *Deadly Delicates Found in Barn.* Subhead: *Daughter of Woman Cheated by Murder Victim Recalls Mother's Personal Grudge.* I looked down at Socrates, who rolled his eyes, like he agreed I was making matters worse, before turning back to Laci and waving my hands, trying to erase my words. "Not that Mom killed anyone!"

"You said that, not me," Laci observed, her blue eyes glittering in the moonlight, while her torso disappeared into the darkness. She once again wore a black shirt and khaki cargo pants. Her short, dark hair was nearly invisible, too. "Maybe Maeve got her revenge before she tried to claim her share of the estate."

The sad thing was, that sounded like a plausible scenario. Then I remembered what Beverly Berendt had told me, about how my mother secretly bragged about me, and I felt disloyal.

"My mother has her faults, but she's no killer," I said, watching Detective Doebler climb into his unmarked sedan. The uniformed officers were getting into their squad car, too, leaving Jonathan alone in the barn. He stood bathed in the soft light of the chandeliers, his head bent over his phone as he repeatedly tapped the screen. Continuing to observe him, I asked Laci, "How did you even know to come here?"

"I was at the *Gazette*, working late, and Gabriel always has the scanner on. It's like working in 1953, with all the old papers and that crackling squawk box."

She was complaining, but I could tell she liked the atmosphere at the *Gazette*'s offices, which were stuck in time, from the old metal desks to a tray of linotype that I thought might still be in use. She grinned slyly. "So, sleuth-about-town—"

"Who calls me that?" I interrupted, still keeping one eye on Jonathan, who continued texting. He didn't even look up when the cars' engines turned over.

"Gabriel says you're the second-best amateur detective in town. After him, of course."

I was kind of flattered, although I considered myself number one.

"So, who's your money on, as the killer, if not your mother?" Laci asked, slinging her camera over her shoulder and crossing her arms. She cocked her head, her hair and shirt momentarily highly visible, illuminated by headlights beaming from the vehicles, which were turning around, heading down the hill. "Maybe your future brother-in-law? Or Daisy Carpenter?" When I didn't bite, she continued listing people who, I had to admit, were on my radar. "How about Dex Shipley? Or *me*?"

Needless to say, I'd been thinking about Laci's argument with Daisy and the possibility of some kind of love triangle among the women who had last been together at the mansion, right before Abigail's death.

Still, I told Laci, "I don't have a top suspect yet, because I'm not really investigating."

That claim earned a snuffle of reproach from Socrates. However, I felt like I was being honest. Speculating and sleuthing were two very different things. I hadn't done more than wrap a rag around my neck and offer a few people counsel.

Okay, maybe I was borderline sleuthing.

"At any rate, I wouldn't identify anyone," I said, wrapping my arms around myself. I'd made the mistake of pairing shorts with my sweatshirt, and I was getting cold. Then I nodded to Laci's camera. "You're a reporter. I wouldn't want my uninformed speculation showing up in the *Gazette*."

"Fair enough." A half smile played on Laci's lips. "But I bet you recall what I said the night of the rehearsal dinner. About how I'd probably have to pry my last paycheck out of Abigail's hands. And I bet you remember that I called her a witch, too."

I couldn't understand why Laci Chalmers was baiting me, trying to get me to admit that I *did* have some suspicions about her. Nor could I figure out why she would want to play up comments that would've caused anyone to doubt her innocence.

I glanced once more at Jonathan, who was slipping his phone into the back pocket of his jeans. I knew Laci wouldn't have a chance to answer the questions I was about to ask, but I posed them anyway.

"Okay, Laci," I said. "If you insist on discussing your possible involvement in Abigail's death, why don't you tell me what kind of suitcase you own? And I'd be interested to know what you and Daisy Carpenter were arguing about near the woods behind the Owl & Crescent, too."

I'd caught Laci off guard, and she stammered. "We . . . we were arguing about a story I'm writing. About how she poisoned a bunch of people with potato salad. I overheard her and Abigail whispering about it once. Daisy's completely covered it up."

"It wasn't her fault. And she's trying to make a fresh start."

"Aren't we all?" Laci said, with a grunt. I didn't know if she really had secrets herself or if she was making a general statement about human nature. "As for the suitcase, I think I know what you're getting at." She looked over her shoulder and saw Jonathan walking toward us. When she faced me again, she spoke quickly, her voice low, confidential— and urgent. "There's no time to explain. Meet me at Kremser's Landing, two nights from now. Ten o'clock. I'll share everything I know, if you'll spill, too."

I knew the spot she was referencing. It was a lonely stretch of gravel on Lake Wallapawakee, across from where the town's fireworks display would be launched. "Why there?"

"I'm shooting the fireworks for the paper. It's private, and I can kill two birds with one stone—talk to you, and get the images I need."

"But . . ."

Laci didn't give me a chance to ask more questions. She hurried off, brushing right past Jonathan, who turned to watch her jump into her car, rev the engine and drive quickly off.

"What was that about?" he asked, jerking his thumb over his shoulder as he approached me. "She left in a hurry."

"I'm not sure," I admitted. Jonathan didn't request further explanation, so I asked, "Does it seem like the garter might be the murder weapon?"

"Yes, it seems possible," he said. "The elastic was completely destroyed, and even to the naked eye, it was obvious that some of the fabric was stretched to, or beyond, its limits. It's also possible that the garter was initially blue, stained purple by the red water in the fountain. But that's all speculation. Doebler will need to order more tests."

We began the short walk back to Plum Cottage, where Jonathan's truck was still parked, and he rested one hand on the small of my back. Socrates trotted ahead of us, his white paws like ghostly, temporary footprints on the ground.

"When did the bag arrive?" Jonathan inquired.

"I'm not even sure," I said. "People were dropping stuff off at Piper's house, and some bags were left at the Sodgrass Club." I was struck by a sudden idea. "Gifts were left for other couples, too. It's possible that the garter wasn't even meant for Piper. It was such a mess when all the brides and grooms realized that the club was overbooked. And there was no card with the nondescript bag. Maybe we got it by mistake."

"I'll share that with Doebler."

"Why would someone put a murder weapon into a gift bag?" I mused.

"Maybe to cast suspicion on all the guests? Hide the weapon in plain sight? I'm not sure."

He was responding, but I could tell his mind was elsewhere, so I dropped the subject, letting him think. We walked together in silence, accompanied by crickets, until we reached the cottage, where he escorted me all the way to my front door.

Opening that, he let Socrates inside, but clasped my arm, holding me back.

I'd had a funny feeling growing inside me from the moment I'd seen him texting so late at night, and the sensation that something was amiss had escalated during our walk down the wooded path.

"What's up?" I asked, too casually.

"I'm really sorry, Daphne," Jonathan said, cutting right to the chase. "I just heard from NCIS. I'm leaving for San Diego again in the morning."

Chapter 28

I tossed and turned all night, replaying Jonathan's and my conversation on the porch. I was happy that there had been a break in the case on the naval base, which might bode well for wrapping up his obligations in California. Yet the fact that he was needed so urgently, and seemed indispensable—enough so that the navy was flying him across the country for just a few days—drove home the reality of our situation.

He should *take the job. It's a good move, and it makes sense. He'll regret any other choice.*

Those were my first thoughts upon waking up on the eve of the Fourth of July. Or maybe I hadn't really slept at all, and my resolution to *insist* that Jonathan accept the position was just a continuation of a full night's worth of jumbled musings.

Ms. Peebles and Tinkleston had been up into the wee hours, too. Thankfully, the cats seemed to be having a positive impact on each other after their rocky start. Tinks spent less time scowling in the herbs, and Ms. Peebles hadn't gotten stuck in the chimney for two days.

Only Socrates had slept soundly, as always. He stretched on his purple cushion while I swung my feet over the edge of the bed and rubbed my eyes against bright sunlight streaming in through the circular window behind us.

Together, we padded downstairs to the kitchen and I fed the cats, then filled a ceramic bowl for Socrates, too.

Putting on the kettle, I checked my phone, which I'd left on the kitchen table.

There was only one text waiting for me, from Moxie, and it made my heart sink, which was appropriate, given the contents of the message:

Setting down the phone, I went to the front door, thinking I'd open it to let some fresh air into the cottage before the day got too hot, as was predicted.

But when I opened the door, I was met by more than a cool breeze. I discovered that someone else had been restless overnight and had left me a package.

Not just a package, but a mystery to solve.

"Why do you think Jonathan gave you a big pile of newspaper clippings?" Moxie asked, over the sound of her own hammering.

Heeding her shorthand summons, which had been followed by directions, I'd met her at Mike Cavanaugh's cousin's lovely Sylvan Creek home, where a gray, weathered rowboat was dry-docked behind the garage, waiting on a trailer to be hauled to the lake. Moxie was bent over the rickety craft, affixing bunting to what I believed to be the hull. I thought adding *more* holes to the ancient vessel, even high on the side, was probably a mistake, and Socrates seemed to agree. He winced every time the hammer met wood.

Unfortunately, my best friend wouldn't be deterred.

She whacked the boat pretty hard, then looked up at me. "Wouldn't flowers have been a nicer apology for leaving?"

"The clippings are from Artful Engagements," I explained. "Detective Doebler doesn't think they're important, but Jonathan and I believe they might be related to Abigail's murder. He left them with me so I could read through them, looking for clues."

Moxie stopped hammering long enough to rest one hand on her chest, a dreamy look in her eyes. "Oh, he's finally teaming up with you—as an investigator! That's so romantic!"

I had also been oddly touched by Jonathan's inclusion of me in an investigation, which, strangely, spoke volumes about his increasing faith in me.

I wished I felt like I could trust the ancient boat that I was circling, pausing behind the trailer to note that someone had painted a black X over *Something's Fishy*. New red paint announced the vessel as the *Tiny-tanic*. Apparently the nickname had become ominously official.

"So, will Jonathan be back in time for the wedding?" Moxie asked, mumbling through two nails she held between her teeth.

"I'm not sure," I admitted. "And, to be honest, Piper seems like she wants to just give up on the whole thing. Or, at least that's how it seemed last night when police officers were raiding her barn, looking for a murder weapon in her gift bags. I think she's pretty discouraged."

"I don't blame her," Moxie said, giving the *Tiny-tanic* one more smack for what I thought was just good measure. Or maybe she hit it for good luck, the way one might break a champagne bottle over a ship. Straightening, she brushed some of her short, still-blue hair off her forehead with the back of her bare arm, although she didn't look sweaty at all in vintage, high-waisted shorts and a checked top that she'd knotted at the waist. "It was bad enough that Mike and I had to restart our relationship under a cloud of suspicion. I wouldn't want to start a life as husband and wife that way."

That was one of the most sensible things Moxie had ever uttered. However, Piper had also said being married to Roger before he left town was important to her.

"I think she'll be happy when it all comes together," I said, peeking into the boat, where more decorations, a set of oars and the promised life jackets, including two small ones for four-legged passengers, awaited. I saw a few spots that were quite obviously patched, too, and I didn't think the repairs looked very effective. Sunlight was streaming through a hole near what I believed to be the stern. I forgot about the wedding for a moment, because I feared my life might be in jeopardy, in spite of the safety vest that awaited me. "Moxie, the holes will all be above water when this thing is afloat, right?"

She didn't exactly answer. Clapping one hand on the side of the boat, she said, "I have been assured that this little craft is lake-worthy, if not seaworthy. I would not row out on the ocean."

Socrates made a groaning sound. I thought he was not only fearful for my well-being, but still expressing general dismay over the whole idea of the regatta.

"I'm going to need to do a costume fitting for Artie," Moxie added. "Will you be picking him up later?"

"He and Axis are staying with Elyse for the next few days," I told her. "Jonathan didn't want to add to my already overloaded to-do list."

Moxie dropped her hammer into a battered metal toolbox. "Oh, that was nice of him. I suppose I can run out to Elyse's house."

"Thanks, Moxie," I said, glancing into the boat again. Loops of lights, some streamers, pinwheels and sparklers were piled high next to the more practical gear. "And please don't feel like you have to go overboard . . . no pun intended . . . with decorating the boat." I was starting to worry about making a spectacle of myself before we even sank, so I tried to encourage Moxie to put her talents to use elsewhere. "I know you have a cake to bake, too. If the boat is a little understated, that's more than okay."

She waved off my concerns. "I told you. There's plenty of time for the cake. And there's no such thing as 'overboard' with All Paws on Deck—unless you lean too far starboard. From what I understand, the *Tiny-tanic* lists a little."

Socrates lay down and covered his muzzle with his big paws, like he couldn't endure the conversation for one more minute.

Luckily for him, we needed to get going. "Just please don't let the cake go for too long," I said, moving toward my van, where Moxie had painted the misshapen dog that was so often mistaken for an equally deformed pony. I sometimes feared haste had contributed to the mistakes, and I didn't want that to happen to Piper's cake, which was so beautiful on paper. I hauled open the passenger side door for Socrates, who gratefully lumbered inside. Then I slammed the door. "Please promise me the cake will be perfect."

Moxie joined me on the driver's side. "When the time is nigh, the cake will be as promised!"

She was being strangely cryptic. And her use of the archaic, biblically prophetic word "nigh" gave me a creepy feeling, given my next destination. The fact that the sky suddenly darkened, too, as if on cue, added to my sudden sense of foreboding.

Nevertheless, I climbed behind the wheel, prepared to drive to Graystone Arches Gateway to Eternity.

But first, I rolled down the window, because the VW

lacked air-conditioning, and Moxie was rapping to get my attention.

"What's up?" I inquired, since she looked very grave. Like maybe she honestly believed I might be held against my will—a concern that had crossed my mind several times that morning. I almost wished she'd talk me out of my errand, which I'd probably put off out of some subconscious concern. "Is something wrong?"

"Yes," Moxie confirmed, making me even more nervous. "There's something I need to tell you before you enter the gates to *forever*!"

Chapter 29

"I should've known Moxie wanted to add a loaf of pumpernickel to her order for sourdough," I told Socrates, who was staring out the window, watching the trees pass by as we climbed higher and higher up a road that snaked along the edge of Great Walnut Mountain, one of the highest peaks in the Poconos. Normally, a crest that size would've housed a ski resort, but from what I understood, an eccentric multimillionaire had purchased the entire mountain back in the 1880s to build a castle-like fortress, where he'd lived as a recluse. At some point, the property had been deeded in perpetuity to Graystone Arches Gateway to Eternity, and now the "monks" and their "acolytes" lived cloistered on the hilltop. I glanced over at my skeptic of a sidekick. "I don't know why I got so nervous when Moxie said *nigh* and *forever*!"

Socrates seemed to agree that I'd been a little too edgy, back in town. He continued to observe the passing foliage, while I finally spied a sign ahead in a gathering mist. It was like we were entering the cloud cover on that increasingly muggy, hot day, and I leaned forward, peering through the fog.

Not surprisingly, since nothing else was located on the

mountain, I discovered that we'd reached our destination, and I slowed to turn onto a bumpy lane, at which point I began to fret not about getting out of, but getting *into* the compound after our long drive. From what I understood, a gatekeeper was posted in a watchtower at the main entrance, and not everyone earned admittance. Supposedly, according to local legend, one had to be pure of heart in order to pass through the massive granite portal that loomed ahead, looking every bit as imposing as I'd expected, if not more.

Then again, local legends could obviously get totally blown out of proportion, because as I pulled up to a massive, but open, iron gate, I saw not a stern watchman waiting to turn us away, but a chalkboard sign, decorated with brightly colored, hand-drawn flowers and letters, that said, *Open House Today! Zither Demonstration 3 p.m. at Larison Hall!*

And below that was a notice that was going to make Moxie very happy: *Special on Sourdough—$3.49 per HEAVENLY Loaf!*

"Well, this is nothing—and everything—like I expected," I whispered to Socrates, whose head was swiveling back and forth as we walked the peaceful grounds of Graystone Arches. The compound, which was crisscrossed with paths linking pretty stone buildings, reminded me of a college campus, except, instead of chattering coeds, silent, robed figures moved slowly about, their expressions almost too placid. While their vestments were uniformly brown, the ropes that tied them came in a rainbow of hues, denoting rank—and financial contribution—if Piper was correct. "I thought it would feel like a prison," I added. "But I haven't felt trapped or threatened at all, with the exception of handing over my cell phone. That was kind of weird."

Socrates gave me a sidelong look, and I could tell he thought everything about Graystone Arches was a bit off.

"I know," I said quietly as a cloaked acolyte practically floated past us, carrying what I assumed was a zither. If the open house was a success, I hadn't seen evidence of that yet. I was the only person wearing anything but a belted muslin sack. In fact, the guest book I'd signed upon entering the compound only had about five signatures from the past two *weeks*. I'd read the whole list, reassured by the fact that everyone had signed out at some point. Still, as Socrates and I passed yet another resident who met my gaze furtively from under his or her hood, the sign inviting us through the gates increasingly seemed like a trap, and I fought to keep my breath steady. "I'm sure we are perfectly fine," I told Socrates. "We'll laugh about our nervousness on the way home."

In spite of acting nonchalantly on the ride, Socrates remained on guard, and I had to admit that worried me, even as we passed a cheerful bakery where I would need to stop on the way out to pick up a few loaves for Moxie and me. The person who'd given us directions to Brother Alf's "chambers" insisted that the bread froze well, so I planned to stock up, too.

Of course, that was assuming that Socrates and I survived our adventure. As we followed the instructions we'd been given, we were moving deeper into the compound, passing under a grove of ancient walnut trees, where the mist we'd encountered on the road swirled amid the trunks.

The biggest building I'd seen from across the grounds— one that I assumed, from its towers and turrets, was the original owner's home—loomed just beyond the grove, and we emerged in front of one of the property's signature archways.

We'd been instructed to pass through that portal and

follow a shadowed corridor that stretched beyond us. I surmised that the passageway, which led under the massive building, had once been traversed by horses and carts, and that a carriage house waited at the other end.

Socrates and I hesitated, sharing wary looks. Then I recalled that Roger had recently visited the compound and come home just fine. Moreover, Moxie knew where we were, and, if we didn't get back to Sylvan Creek, she wouldn't rest until her bread, if not her best friend, was delivered home.

"Those loaves are our safety net," I whispered to Socrates, as we both stepped into the semidarkness on an afternoon that was growing increasingly gloomy.

My basset hound sidekick didn't woof or wag a reply. His tail hung low and his head swiveled again as we made our way down the silent corridor, which reminded me of the skeleton-strewn catacombs that ran beneath the great cities of Europe. Water dripped from some unseen source, and a trickle of cold sweat ran down my back at the ominous sound.

"We should . . ."

I was about to suggest that Socrates and I turn back when, all at once, yet another robed and hooded figure stepped out of an alcove I hadn't even seen, stopping right in front of us and looking for all the world like the grim reaper.

I knew, because I'd played that role in a disastrous production of *A Christmas Carol*, thanks to Fidelia Tutweiler, who'd refused to play the part, in spite of acing her audition.

"Hello?" I ventured softly, when the individual who blocked our path didn't move or speak. "We're looking for—"

"I know who you seek, Daphne Templeton," the cloaked figure finally said in a low, deep voice. Without removing

Chapter 30

"Of course, you couldn't have known that Brother Augustus, who gave you directions, alerted me to your visit—and I'm sorry about wearing the hood," Brother Alf Sievers said, shaking his head with self-reproach. "No wonder you were unnerved!"

"I guess I didn't expect you all to have walkie-talkies, since I had to turn over my phone," I noted, watching him bustle about his "chambers," which weren't anything like the austere accommodations I'd expected.

Roger's uncle, who'd finally bared his balding pate, actually inhabited a quite comfortable apartment, which had been carved out of space on the top floor of the imposing main building. Mullioned, leaded windows overlooked the valley below, although the thickening mist obscured the view. Inside, where the air smelled of comforting yeast and flour—tinged, perhaps, with a faint odor I recognized as a pet sitter—Brother Alf's amenities included a clean, welcoming kitchenette with stainless steel appliances and a living room with a cozy sectional, where he'd gestured for me to sit.

Socrates, who wasn't yet succumbing to the ruddy-cheeked

cleric's hospitality, waited by the tall, arched wooden door that Brother Alf had closed behind us. I assumed that another matching door, which was also shut, led to his bedroom.

"It gets so chilly here on top of this blasted old mountain," Brother Alf noted, the mild oath offered affectionately and jovially. Rubbing his hands together to warm them, he plucked a whistling red kettle from the stove. "I forget that the cloak can be off-putting to outsiders!"

"It was a little spooky," I told him, wishing he'd accepted my offer to help with the snacks. But he'd insisted on brewing the tea and slicing up several loaves of bread without assistance. "Sorry if Socrates and I overreacted."

Over by the door, Socrates gave a low warning sound, almost like a growl. I guessed that he was trying to claim that he hadn't been concerned, but I knew otherwise.

"No worries, no worries," Brother Alf insisted, filling a bowl with water and taking that to Socrates, along with a dog biscuit on a plate. "I don't get many canine visitors— or visitors at all," he added, in a nevertheless cheerful tone. "But I keep treats on hand, just in case. We *are* close to Sylvan Creek, the pet lovers' paradise." Chuckling at his own turn of phrase, he set the bowl and plate down near the door. "Cheers, Master Socrates! Cheers, and welcome to my humble home!"

Socrates still remained wary, while I was charmed— probably too charmed—by Roger's relative, who had shuffled back to the kitchen to retrieve the tray he'd prepared for us. A part of me realized that charisma almost certainly played a role in luring people into cults, but with his twinkling eyes and apple-red cheeks, it was *very* hard not to like Alf Sievers. And my resolve to remain detached weakened when he set the tea and a selection of monk-baked breads, all slathered with butter churned on the premises, from Gateway Arches' own grass-fed cows, right in front of me on a low coffee table.

I kind of felt like I was already in heaven.

"Please, enjoy," Brother Alf urged me, waving his hands like a magician over the already enchanting tray of goodies. "You deserve a treat after navigating the mountain road to get here." He sat down on a section of the couch at a right angle to mine, blinking at me with happy befuddlement. "For what reason I haven't yet thought to ascertain."

I'd already helped myself to the pumpernickel—Moxie's last-minute request—and I'd closed my eyes for just a second to enjoy the divine, hearty taste.

"Oh, yes, about my visit," I said, my eyelids snapping open. I'd been close to asking where to sign on, if only for an instant. "I'm here because we bridesmaids are regrouping after the wedding disaster, and we're hell-bent . . ." I immediately regretted my phrasing. "We are *heck*-bent on getting Piper and Roger married before he leaves for Europe. We even have locations for the ceremony and the reception. Now all we need is an officiant." Licking butter off my fingers, I shrugged. "And about a dozen other things. But 'officiant' is right up there."

Brother Alf hadn't reacted to my mild curse, but as I'd been speaking, the light in his eyes had been dimming, and his apple-hued cheeks had faded from Red Delicious to Pink Lady.

"You . . . you still want me to perform the ceremony?" he inquired, resting his hands on his knees. He gave himself a nervous squeeze, knocking his legs together under his garment. "In spite of what happened with Abigail Sinclair?"

I didn't understand why Abigail's murder would have anything to do with whether he presided over Piper and Roger's union. And maybe he wasn't referring to the homicide.

He cleared his throat, trying again. "I mean, if you're planning an entirely new wedding—a fresh start—perhaps you, or should I say Roger and Piper, don't want any reminders of the whole sad mess at the Sodgrass Club, and the subsequent legal battle," he clarified. "To think of my sister, and your family, being swindled . . ." He sighed. "It broke my heart, and I would understand if my nephew and his lovely bride wanted to start their lives together with no vestige of that previous, let's face it, garish, event."

"You're not a 'vestige,'" I assured him, although part of me thought I should've just accepted his offer to stay away from the ceremony. Piper didn't seem to want him to preside. But his inclusion seemed to be important to her future husband and his kin, so I reminded Brother Alf, "You're family!"

"Oh, goodness." He continued to seem uncertain and fidgeted with his belt.

That was the first time I noticed the color.

Blue, braided with strands of white.

I kept staring at that long tie, trying to determine if there was any chance it was woven of silk. I didn't think so, but Graystone Arches certainly didn't seem to lack for funding.

And the longer I studied the belt, the more I wondered if I might've been wrong about a damp garter. Because the object wrapped around Brother Alf's expansive waist could easily be used to strangle someone.

In fact, I rubbed my throat, recalling that Beverly Berendt had mentioned that her sibling had impeded her progress to her vehicle. But Bev hadn't said anything about seeing him drive off . . .

"Is something wrong?" Brother Alf inquired.

I met his gaze, and it seemed to me that his eyes were a little less friendly.

"That's just . . . just a lovely belt," I noted, nodding to his hands, which continued to play absently with one of the tassled ends.

Could it be silk?

"I understand the colors are related to rank, right?" I asked, because he didn't thank me for the compliment.

Instead, he suddenly seemed to take a personal and suitably monastic vow of silence.

I looked over at Socrates, who had wisely remained near the door. His brown eyes were at once warning and resigned, like he knew things were going to get worse before they got better.

The silence stretched on until Brother Alf said, "I knew it. I knew all along that you came here in person because you're investigating Abigail Sinclair's murder. Roger and Beverly both said you're an amateur sleuth!"

"I have cracked a few cases," I admitted, finally setting down a piece of the sourdough. Moxie was right. It was amazing, and I'd kept eating, even when things had started to get uncomfortable. We'd probably reached a conversational tipping point, though, and I pushed aside my snack so I could concentrate. "But how did you make that leap? Why would my admiration of your belt mean I was looking into a murder?"

That question was either going to stump him or, quite possibly, expose him as a killer. Of course, there was a third option. The inquiry might also threaten him and cause him to strangle *me*. Unfortunately, I didn't think of that ahead of time, and I grew nervous when he stood up, telling me, through bloodless lips, "Wait right here. I have something to show you."

I should've bolted, and Socrates clearly agreed. He stood up and shuffled on his big dappled paws, pantomiming a run for the hills.

But Brother Alf was moving quickly for an older gentleman in Birkenstocks and socks, hurrying to the closed door. When he opened it, a fluffy calico cat slipped out, and I saw that I'd been correct. The door led to his bedroom, where I glimpsed something that I found very interesting, beyond the feline, who was running across the floor.

At least, I thought I'd spied an object that intrigued me.

Before I could be sure, Brother Alf, who had ducked inside the room, emerged holding not a weapon, as part of me had feared, but a *newspaper*. A copy of the *Weekly Gazette*, which he stuck under my nose, so I could see a front-page story with the headline *Cops Narrow in on Murder Weapon*.

The story, with Laci Chalmers's byline, described the events that had taken place at Winding Hill the previous night. At least, that's what I assumed. I couldn't read the whole piece, because it was pretty long, with a jump to another page, and Brother Alf's hand was shaking. I could barely make out Jonathan in the accompanying photo, which also showed Detective Doebler and the uniformed officers conferring in Piper's barn.

I looked up at Brother Alf, confused, excited by the prospect of catching a killer, and terrified that he'd silence me if I learned the truth. Yet I had to ask, "Are you trying to tell me that *you* planted the garter?"

"No!" He seemed exasperated with me and pointed at a different, smaller article. An investigative, *speculative* piece that was also by Laci, and which also featured a photo.

I quickly read the headline: *Is Lethal Lingerie Red Herring?*

Scanning the story, I caught the phrases "killed after over-the-top patriotic bash," "red, white and blue objects abounded," and "dish towel."

"She's very observant," I muttered, next checking the black-and-white photo, which was a blown-up and unflattering shot of Brother Alf's *waist*, with the caption *Blue-and-white belt, worn by member of Graystone Arches Gateway to Eternity elder to fatal soiree, among many potential weapons that could match fibers found in victim's wound.*

Laci, or more likely Gabriel, had been wise enough not to mention Brother Alf by name. But the image still seemed borderline libelous to me, and I thought Gabriel had taken a great risk by running it.

"I didn't even see the *Gazette* today," I told Brother Alf, whose hand had fallen to his side. He sank weakly back onto the sofa, absently stroking the cat, who had jumped onto her person's lap. Socrates relaxed a bit, too, although he remained close to the door. "And I don't know that you have any connection to Abigail Sinclair, let alone reason to kill her," I added. "It's one thing to wear a belt that might be a weapon—if it's silk, or a silk blend."

Brother Alf blanched, and I realized he believed that might be the case.

I tried to act like I hadn't noticed his reaction, telling him, "But people kill for motive, and, no offense, I didn't know anything about you before today, beyond the fact that your sister and Roger hoped you'd be part of the wedding."

Brother Alf wasn't sure if he believed me. And I wasn't sure I believed *him* when he said, quietly, "Of course I have no connection to Abigail Sinclair. None at all."

He'd protested a tiny bit too much. If Jonathan had been questioning him down at the station, he would've driven some kind of wedge under that flat denial and pried it open to reveal a secret, or maybe more than one, that Brother Alf was hiding in his twitching, pale blue eyes. I knew it. But I was alone in a castle-like building on a mountaintop where people were rumored to be imprisoned for doing far less than provoking a killer, and I stood up, forcing a smile.

"Why would you know Abigail, living out here?" I asked, moving toward the door, while Brother Alf kissed his cat's head and set the contented-looking creature onto the floor again. "You're pretty isolated."

I wished I hadn't emphasized that. Socrates must've been thinking the same thing. He made a sighing sound as I joined him at the door.

"Thanks for the bread, which is amazing," I told Alf, who'd trailed after me, the cat in his wake.

"It takes over *one hundred years*."

"What?"

I turned to Brother Alf, who had just mentioned that curious, and very long, time span, seemingly apropos of nothing, but in a very grave tone. And he looked deadly serious, too.

"Pardon me?" I asked, my mind struggling to find some connection between dense, delightfully sour bread and ten decades. But all I could think was, *Roger's uncle is going to trap me here for a century.*

The breath I hadn't realized I'd been holding came out as a burst of laughter when he explained, "That's how old the sourdough starter is. It's imported from France."

I glanced at Socrates, who rolled his eyes.

"About the ceremony," Brother Alf said as the cat rolled on the floor, rubbing her little cheeks against her person's Birkenstocks. "Where will it be held?"

I'd nearly forgotten that he hadn't yet agreed to be part of the wedding, and I said, "Oh, yes. About that. Piper and Roger are going to get married at an old chapel out on Crooked Creek Lane. It's being renovated as we speak."

I was about to explain more about the little church, on the assumption that Brother Alf wouldn't have any idea what I was talking about. However, his face turned a new apple-related shade: green as a Granny Smith.

"What's wrong?" I asked. "Do you know something about the church? Because there is some mystery surrounding it."

"No, no," he protested, his nervous eyes again telling a

different story. "I've no idea what you're talking about. Just please let me know when and where I should arrive."

"Yes, of course," I promised. "I'll leave a message with the switchboard operator when all the details are worked out."

He nodded. "That will be fine."

It wasn't fine. He was hiding something, either about the chapel or Abigail's murder, or both those things. Maybe more stuff, too.

I suddenly felt very hemmed in again, and Socrates was also eager to leave Graystone Arches. His nose was practically pressed against the tall, heavy door.

"It was nice finally meeting you," I said, reaching for the doorknob. "And I really enjoyed visiting your lovely home."

There was a tense moment during which Brother Alf watched me with a strange look in his eyes. I gave him time to reply, but he didn't say a thing. He just stood there in his belted robe, the calico kneading the air with her fluffy paws.

I finally turned away to twist the knob. But just before I opened the door, Brother Alf suddenly reached past me, braced his hand on the wood and said, "Wait. I'm afraid I *cannot* let you leave, Daphne."

Chapter 31

"That was the world's longest zither demonstration," I complained when Socrates and I were finally safe in my van, coasting downhill. Ten loaves of bread, procured with Brother Alf's discount, were perfuming the air, which grew warmer with each mile that passed, taking us closer to sea level. "That concert gave new meaning to the phrase 'captive audience'!"

Socrates sighed deeply. He'd tried to get me to leave during the first intermission, but I couldn't seem to find the right moment to get away.

And since we'd been stuck there, in a small auditorium that hadn't exactly been packed, I'd made a few clumsy attempts, between twangy sets, to get Brother Alf to admit that he had travel plans, because I'd seen a suitcase—a *black* suitcase—open on his bed when he'd ducked into his room and the cat had run out.

In retrospect, I probably shouldn't have been disappointed that my awkward questions about favorite airports and a personal anecdote about my food poisoning in Turkey hadn't elicited more than strange looks.

"I suppose he could've been *un*packing," I told Socrates, hitting the brakes to slow our retreat as we entered one of the tiniest towns in the Poconos: Hop Bottom, which was basically one block long. But an adorable block it was, with a Victorian inn, a coffee shop and a few other establishments selling gifts, like locally made bath products and pottery. "And, to be honest, I don't think Brother Alf and Abigail Sinclair seem like they would be lovers."

The very thought of that prospect made me want to both cringe and laugh, and Socrates woofed loudly.

Very loudly.

The sound was more than mere agreement. Then he barked again, even more insistently.

He almost never did that, and I knew he was trying to tell me something.

Slowing down more, I steered the VW to the curb, where we came to a stop right in the center of the town.

I first checked my gas gauge, because I did have a bad habit of letting the tank run dry.

But the needle was practically on full, so I next looked around the town, where the sun was setting behind the quaint rows of colorful shops that lined the street.

My gaze passed over the romantic Walnut Mountain Inn, with its private, shadowed porch, then a shop called Bubbles, which sold handmade soap. And across the street was a paper goods store I'd never seen before, because I rarely traveled to Hop Bottom.

I read the shop's name, and it rang a bell, but for a few seconds, I couldn't figure out why.

Then I grinned at Socrates, who normally frowned upon my sleuthing.

However, he also believed that justice should be served, probably even more so when his puppy love's person was suspected of murder, and he looked almost—*almost*—proud of himself when I said, "You found the Gilded Lily!"

* * *

The shop whose name was stamped inside the bag that held the stained, ruined garter couldn't have been more than ten feet wide. But every square inch was packed with party goods, ephemera and greeting cards, both new and vintage.

The store owner was also embracing the Fourth of July with floor-to-rafters enthusiasm. Red, white and blue lights crisscrossed the ceiling, and a deep gray candle in a strange but appropriate scent called "Gunpowder and Sky" burned on the counter next to a bell and a sign that urged customers to ring for service.

Not seeing anyone amid the cheerful chaos, I rang, then began to flip through a countertop display of antique Independence Day postcards featuring cherubic children waving flags and tooting horns, aggressive eagles clutching sheaves of wheat and militiamen playing fifes and drums.

"Moxie would love this place," I told Socrates, who was sniffing the air. The scent of gunpowder was probably overpowering his sensitive nose. I held up a postcard that featured a youngster in a sailor suit bursting out of a firecracker. The image struck me as a little creepy, but I could picture it on display in Moxie's apartment. "Should I get this for her?"

"Oh, lovely, lovely choice!" a gray-haired, rotund woman exclaimed, bursting out of a hidden back room, like *she'd* been launched from a firecracker. She rubbed her hands together, her long, voluminous white dress swirling around her as she approached us, smiling ear to ear. "All of those cards are just precious!" She looked down at Socrates. "As are you!"

I thought the compliment was nice, but Socrates clearly didn't consider himself "precious." He would've much preferred "dignified," and his head drooped, so his ears dragged on the floor.

"I'll take this one," I told the lady, setting my chosen gift on the counter. "And I also have a question that might seem kind of crazy."

"There are no crazy questions," she said, stepping behind the counter. "Just crazy people."

Yes, Moxie would fit right in at the Gilded Lily.

"I was wondering if you recalled someone buying a silver gift bag," I said. "It wouldn't have been anything too out of the ordinary."

"Unless one stuffed a murder weapon into it," the woman said, without losing her smile or the twinkle in her eye.

So, Doebler had already been there. I wasn't giving him enough credit.

"Are you another detective?" she inquired, accepting cash I'd dug out of my pocket. "Are you here to ask more questions about Abbie's death?"

I'd never heard anyone call Abigail by a nickname, and I certainly hadn't expected that in a tiny shop miles from Sylvan Creek. "Abbie?" I repeated, knitting my brows. "Were you friends?"

If so, the shopkeeper didn't seem terribly upset by her pal's demise.

"No, not friends," she said. "More like . . . colleagues. Abigail often bought paper goods here, for her theme weddings."

That made sense. It also complicated things. "So you know Dexter Shipley, too?"

She seemed delighted by my mention of Abigail's assistant. "Of course! Dex stops by often!"

"Interesting," I said quietly.

"I'm sorry, dear," the woman said, closing the drawer of an old-fashioned cash register and dumping some change into my waiting palm. "Did you say you're a police officer?"

"No, I've never been to the academy." I crammed my change into my pocket. "I'm just trying to solve the case on my own, in part to help my future brother-in-law so he can marry my sister and go to Europe. The silver bag that might hold the murder weapon was last seen in my sister's barn."

The cheerful shop owner didn't seem surprised by anything I'd just said. She was too busy surprising *me* by pulling a silver bag out from beneath the counter—a sack just like the one that held the garter—and plopping my postcard inside.

"I don't sell these bags, which I bought for the shop's silver anniversary," she said. "But they are nice, and some people no doubt repurpose them as gift bags—as I told the *real* detective who visited earlier today, asking a lot of questions about shoppers from Sylvan Creek."

No one ever seemed to tire of pointing out that I wasn't an authorized investigator, even when I admitted that right up front.

In spite of being embarrassed just a few minutes before, Socrates snuffled. A sound of barely suppressed laughter.

I pretended I didn't hear him. "Did you point out any potential suspects, if you don't mind me asking? Because I would *really* like to help my sister and her fiancé."

The pleasantly plump shopkeeper shoved the bag across the counter to me. "As a matter of fact, I did tell the detective about a very distinctive girl who stopped in a few weeks ago, looking for a unique wedding gift."

My heart started racing, and Socrates was tense at my side, too. "Did this girl buy a *garter*?"

The woman behind the counter shook her head and wrinkled her nose. "No, I don't sell those types of items. The young woman ended up buying something for herself. A string of antique paper lanterns. Red, with yellow Chinese characters."

My stomach turned to ice as I pictured a set of French

doors leading to a balcony, and I barely got my next question out. "And this person's hair . . . ?"

If the Gilded Lily's proprietor realized that I could hardly breathe, it didn't show in her expression. She continued to smile at me, her eyes still twinkling when she said, "Her hair was 'something blue'! She told me herself that she'd dyed it especially for her best friend's sister's wedding!"

Chapter 32

I tried all evening to get in touch with Moxie, but she wasn't answering her phone or texts.

I feared she was being interrogated by Detective Doebler, who would've easily figured out that Moxie was the blue-haired customer who'd purchased paper lanterns at the Gilded Lily.

I couldn't understand why Moxie hadn't identified the bag when I'd pulled the garter from the nest of tissue paper at Piper's farmhouse, and well after midnight, when Socrates was sound asleep, I kept pacing around Plum Cottage in my striped pajamas, struggling to make sense out of other fragments that all seemed connected to Abigail Sinclair's murder, but that didn't add up to a complete picture.

A silky garter of uncertain origin.

A black suitcase I'd glimpsed on Brother Alf's bed.

Dex Shipley's interest in the Artful Engagements mansion.

And Laci's aggressive, maybe reckless reporting . . .

Shaking my head, I tried to clear my thoughts, which kept circling back to Laci Chalmers, who'd promised to share information when I met her at the boat launch on the shores of Lake Wallapawakee.

In the meantime, I realized that I had another potential source of information that I hadn't yet mined.

Grabbing my cell phone from the kitchen table, I texted Moxie one more time. When she didn't respond, I climbed the spiral staircase to my loft, where I crawled onto my bed, cringing when I turned on the small lamp on my nightstand. I didn't want to wake Socrates, who was snoring on his cushion, stretched out to catch a breeze that was drifting in through the big, porthole-like window above us.

Being a deep sleeper, as well as thinker, he didn't so much as blink.

I'd tried not to disturb Tinks or Ms. Peebles, either, but to my surprise, neither one of the cats were in their usual spots. Tinkleston was missing from the foot of the bed, and Ms. Peebles wasn't curled up in the laundry basket.

"That can't be good," I whispered, glancing at the bridesmaids' gowns I'd hung over the door to my small closet.

Dorinda's dress wouldn't get used, but I needed to deliver Fidelia's the next day.

I took a moment to appreciate the way the burnished, umber silk fairly glowed in the soft light cast by the lamp. I knew the dresses would be equally pretty at Piper's sunset ceremony, and I selfishly hoped Jonathan would return in time to be my date. I was looking forward to seeing him in his tuxedo, too.

Sighing, I dragged my gaze away from the dresses and grabbed a stack of papers from the nightstand, setting them on the bed. Then I placed my phone in the space I'd cleared, only to snatch it right back when it pinged with a text.

I wasn't sure if I was happy or disappointed to receive a

message from Jonathan instead of Moxie. And I became more ambivalent when I read his text.

Can't talk tonight, but miss and love you.

I tried to focus on the reassuring part of the message, and I replied that I loved him, too. But I was worried that we'd only been apart for about a day and already there wasn't time for a call.

"That doesn't bode well," I muttered, replacing the phone near an old landline I hardly ever used anymore.

Then I bent over the papers that Jonathan had left on my porch before flying off and began to study them, starting with the photocopied clipping from the *Gazette*. The one that featured a grainy image of people standing on the shore of a lake.

Squinting, because the lamp cast the faintest puddle of light on my bed, I read the caption.

Hundreds gather for mass wedding on the shores of Lake Wallapawakee, an event sponsored by controversial local religious group Graystone Arches Gateway to Eternity.

"Why was Abigail interested in this?" I whispered, peering at it more closely.

I was pretty sure I spied Brother Alf Sievers in his robe, his arms outstretched, at the very edge of the water. He appeared to be standing on a platform.

Turning a few more pages, I discovered that Abigail had collected more articles on the group, most of them negative. However, bad press, including Gabriel's story, which was right below the mass wedding coverage, didn't seem to have hampered the group's growth. Flipping back through the clippings, which constituted something of a loosely organized reverse history, it was easy to see the organization gaining power and money.

Graystone Arches Members Swell to 300
Reclusive Group Claims Mountaintop Property

*Cool Millions: Tax Returns Reflect Graystone Arches'
Net Worth*

Beneath these was a more intriguing story.

Bequest Shocks Prominent Chestnut Hill Family

This small article, buried in a 1979 edition of the
Philadelphia Inquirer, featured the subhead *Siminski
Clan Vows 'Cult' Will Not Receive 'Blood Money.'*

"I know that name," I whispered. "But from where?"

I couldn't recall, so I tried to read the article, looking for
some clue. However, either the original, created before
digital archiving was standard, had been damaged, or the
photocopy had smeared. Either way, the print was illegible,
and I flipped to the next page—sucking in a sharp breath
when I spied the chapel on Crooked Creek Lane.

The photo, from a primitive edition of the *Weekly
Gazette*'s venerable society page, was also old, dating back
to 1978, but I could still tell that the building was well-
maintained. Then my eyes grew as wide as Ms. Peebles's
big saucers when I studied the image more closely, focusing on a group of smiling young women who posed in front
of the chapel.

Bridesmaids—who were wearing the *exact same dresses*
that were hanging in my room.

My gaze darted between the clipping and the gowns
hanging on my closet door about twenty times, until I noticed the bride, who stood off to the side, clutching a bou-
quet to the bodice of her simple empire-waist gown.

Her face was turned away, her solemn gaze trained
on something outside the photo's edge, but even in profile, she looked remarkably familiar, and I read that caption, too.

*Bride Desdemona Siminski's wedding party gathers for
photos on the eve of Sylvan Creek's most anticipated nuptials
of the year. Left to right, bridesmaids are . . .*

I had no idea what to make of the coincidence, nor

the second **appearance of the** name Siminski in the clips, and I didn't **have time to** piece together this new puzzle, because **all at once, I** heard noises I'd been bracing for ever since I'd brought Ms. Peebles into Plum Cottage:

A series **of sharp yowls, followed** by a tremendous crash.

Chapter 33

"Thank you so much for watching Ms. Peebles," I told Fidelia, as I stumbled through my part-time accountant's door, burdened by a cat carrier and a gown that was draped over my shoulder. Socrates was ahead of me, and when he stopped just inside the apartment, I nearly tripped over him.

I assumed he was taken aback by the strange combination of odors that met my nose, too. The first scent was a blend of roasted beans and chocolate, because Fidelia lived above my favorite coffee shop, Oh, Beans. But those pleasant odors were overlaid by whiffs of the sulfurous fireworks that kids were lighting off all over town in anticipation of Sylvan Creek's official show, which would start in about an hour.

Having never visited Fidelia before, I set down the carrier and had a look around, noting that she had actually hung the painting she'd created at the Owl & Crescent. Her rendition of the flowers, top hat, gloves and dogs—to which Fidelia had added a small heart, above the dogs' heads—occupied a place of honor just inside the door.

Beyond that, Fidelia's home was clean but austere, like she kept a tight rein on not just ledgers, but design. A small table and two chairs took center stage in a modest kitchenette, where two yellow mugs in a sink-side drying rack provided the only pops of color. The living room, painted pale blue, held nothing but a beige sofa, a small television and a low coffee table. And cheap plastic blinds, which covered all the windows, added to the impression that the space was temporary and utilitarian.

"Ms. Peebles was doing okay at the cottage until she jumped onto Tinks's herb garden," I explained as Fidelia unburdened me of the dress. "I think they could've become friends if she hadn't crossed that line."

"Oh, I'm happy to watch her," Fidelia promised, draping the gown over one of the kitchen chairs. She bent to unlatch the carrier. "Come on out, roomie!"

Ms. Peebles remained in the crate, mewing softly, like she did when she got herself stuck in bad situations.

"She's used to being trapped in places," I said, sympathizing with the poor cat, who had recently been zipped into a suitcase. "She probably thinks she can't leave of her own accord."

Fidelia straightened and waved at the carrier, dismissing my concerns. "We'll just give her time. She's probably unhappy because she's been through a lot of change, too." Fidelia frowned in her self-deprecating way. "And I know my apartment isn't as homey as Plum Cottage. She's probably disappointed."

"I doubt that," I said, even though I suspected that Fidelia's observation might have been close to the truth. The apartment, which suited Socrates' austere aesthetic, probably wasn't too welcoming from a cat's point of view. I knew from experience that they liked places to hide and climb, and Fidelia's home offered neither. I wished there was a way to tell Ms. Peebles that the situation was temporary, and she'd at least be safe, but I had no idea how to convey that, except to dig into the pocket of my light jacket, which I'd worn in anticipation of my meeting at the lake, and retrieving some Chicken Chompers homemade treats. I handed the bag to Fidelia. "These will help lure her out, when you're ready."

"Thanks so much." Fidelia accepted the bag. "I'm actually really excited to have her here. I set up a litter box in the bathroom, and Tessie Flinchbaugh is dropping off some bowls and food." She set the treats on the table, then lifted the dress off the chair, resting her free hand on her chest. She turned to me, practically beaming, to the degree Fidelia Tutweiler ever beamed. "Daphne, this dress is *amazing*!"

"I thought so, too," I told her. "Dex Shipley recalled that he had a bunch of them in storage not long after you left Something Borrowed, Something New."

Color crept up Fidelia's neck to her ears. "I know you think I like him." She didn't exactly deny that, but said, "I'm pretty sure he has a girlfriend, though. So it's stupid for me to even think about him, right? Plus, I'm not like you, who has handsome journalists and detectives falling all over you. Dex is probably just a pipe dream, right?"

She wanted me to confirm that she shouldn't pursue her crush. Yet she didn't want that at all. She had a hopeful look in her eyes.

"What makes you think he's seeing someone?" I asked, watching Ms. Peebles, who had poked her head out of the carrier before quickly retreating. "Has he said something?"

"No." She bit her lip. "It's more the way he kept looking at Laci Chalmers the night of Piper and Roger's dinner." Fidelia's shoulders slumped. "And, let's face it, Laci is beautiful and confident. I would never have the nerve to cut my hair that short!"

Outside, firecrackers popped and crackled, while a bunch of ideas exploded in my head, too.

What if Jonathan was wrong, and Laci and Daisy weren't conspirators?

What if Laci and *Dex* had teamed up to kill Abigail?

That made more sense.

They were more forceful personalities. The type of people who didn't let a wedding planner push them around forever without fighting back.

And I was going to meet one of them at a lonely boat launch . . .

"Daphne? Is something wrong?"

I shook my head, clearing my thoughts. "No, everything's fine." I looked outside and realized the sun was setting. "I do need to get going."

"Oh, really?" Fidelia sounded disappointed. "I was hoping you could stay for coffee. It's easy enough to run downstairs and get whatever we'd like." She looked at Socrates. "I could find something for you, too. I've gotten very close to the baristas there. We do each other favors all the time."

I got the sense that Fidelia was often lonely—because she frequently said so. She even sounded a little desperate about cozying up to her downstairs neighbors. I wished I could hang out for a while. However, I had promised to meet Laci, and I said, "Thanks so much. But we have an appointment."

Fidelia furrowed her brow. "So late?"

"I'm meeting Laci Chalmers at the fireworks," I admitted. I hadn't planned to share that information, but I could tell that Fidelia thought I was ditching her. And, in retrospect, it was probably wise to let someone know where I was going. There was really no reason to keep my destination a secret. It was just a bad habit I'd gotten into because so many people discouraged my sleuthing. Deciding to make my whereabouts very public, I told Fidelia, "She asked me to meet her at Kremser's Landing."

Socrates grumbled. He didn't want to go. And Fidelia still seemed confused. "Why?"

"She was in a rush when we set the time and place, but

she said she's shooting the fireworks from there, for the *Gazette.*"

"Well, be careful," Fidelia suggested, following me to the door. "I think it sounds a little odd. And someone was just murdered. I know I said I felt like we were all part of an Agatha Christie novel that might end with a big reveal at the chapel. But that was in broad daylight. And Laci was at Artful Engagements the night Abigail died!"

"Please don't worry," I said with a smile. "I've got Socrates by my side."

The dog in question made another groaning sound.

"There's a good chance other people will show up at the landing, too," I added, although I wasn't sure about that. Still, I reminded Fidelia and Socrates, "Everybody looks for good spots around the lake to watch the display."

Fidelia cringed. "I'd go with you, but I hate fireworks. They're so loud!" She looked at the carrier just as Ms. Peebles darted out and ran under the couch. "And I feel like I should stay with Ms. Peebles, who already seems a little nervous."

"I think that's a good idea," I said, looking past her to the living room. Big eyes fairly glowed beneath the couch. "You will probably hear some of the louder booms here."

"Well, have fun. And text me when you get home safely," Fidelia urged as Socrates and I headed out into the gathering darkness.

"I will," I promised, pulling the door shut behind us. "But I'm sure we'll be fine!"

Right before the latch clicked into place, I heard Ms. Peebles meow, a soft, mournful and strangely haunting farewell that almost made me feel like I might be wrong.

Chapter 34

"Cats in suitcases, cats in carriers, cats under couches and cats at cults . . . what am I still missing?" I asked Socrates, who hopped down from the VW, his paws landing silently on a grassy patch at the side of the road that wound around Lake Wallapawakee.

The night was clear and warm, the air tinged with sulfur even at the remote edge of Bear Tooth Forest. Atop a high hill, Elyse Hunter-Black's home, which most locals still called Flynt Mansion, loomed against a starry sky. And across the lake, people were gathering in a clearing at the edge of the water. I could see sparklers flickering and a fire burning in a pit that was also a popular gathering spot during Sylvan Creek's annual Tail Waggin' Winterfest.

Only a few of the most unflappable dogs, like Socrates, braved the fireworks, which were one of the community's few less-than-pet-friendly activities. Most pooches only attended the Wags 'n Flags picnic in Pettigrew Park and All Paws on Deck.

For once, Socrates, who usually enjoyed the artistry of a well-designed display of explosives, was among those canines who were less than enthusiastic about the loud light show.

I had to admit that I was also getting a bit uneasy, because it didn't seem like anyone else had come to the landing, except for Laci. Her old Honda was the only other vehicle parked at the top of the path that led to the launch.

"I'm going to let one more person know where we are," I told Socrates, just as the show started. A whizzing sound drowned out the loud hum of crickets and the sky was showered with glittering gold, followed by a thunderous boom. Pausing for a second to watch, I then pulled my phone from my pocket and texted Gabriel Graham, while big plumes of pink and green burst above us.

At Kremser's Landing with Laci, keeping her company while she works long hours for you!

I wrote that like I was joking, but in truth, I just wanted him to know that I was with his employee at an isolated location, in case he had suspicions about her. Gabriel also had a strong investigative streak, and I thought he'd alert me, or even come to the lake, if he had the slightest doubts about Laci.

That didn't seem to be the case. As Socrates and I began to pick our way down the dark path and the sky popped and crackled with festive lights, Gabriel immediately texted back.

She's a go-getter, no doubt. Stop by Elyse's later for a drink. Watching show from her patio with crazy Chihuahua.

I was reassured by his lack of concern—and the fact that he was close by, in case his faith in Laci was misplaced. I was also glad that Gabriel and Elyse continued to seem happy with each other after he and I had officially and amicably parted ways at the last Bark the Halls Ball.

"I feel much better now," I told Socrates, who couldn't read texts—at least, I didn't think he could—and who therefore continued to remain on alert. His tail was low and sweeping, and his nose was close to the ground, sniffing and scanning for danger.

Tucking my phone back into my pocket, I carefully picked my way down the dark path with Socrates by my side until we reached the inky water.

"Laci?" I called softly, batting at some mosquitoes. The landing, just a patch of gravel that led right into the lake, wasn't very big, but I didn't see her anywhere. "Hello?" I called, my nerves again jangling, just a bit. "Where are you?"

Laci didn't answer, and I couldn't help looking up again as the sky erupted in a cacophony of hisses and booms, while no fewer than four chrysanthemum-like fireworks arced and plumed downward.

I continued to follow the impressive pyrotechnics as they sizzled their way into the water, my eyes drawn downward until my gaze rested upon the gently undulating lake—where something nearly as dark as the water was bobbing.

Socrates had spied the object, too, and we both rushed into the lake, where Laci Chalmers floated facedown, her camera strap, minus her camera, pulled tight around her throat.

Chapter 35

"Oh . . . oh, goodness, Daphne, you poor thing!" Elyse Hunter-Black stammered when I reentered the kitchen at her gorgeous mansion, interrupting a quiet conversation she'd been having with my sister.

I hoped Elyse, who looked guilty, for some reason, felt sorry for me because I'd just found a body, and not because my hair was a mess and I didn't quite fill out the top of the incredibly soft velour track suit she'd loaned me while my wet clothes spun in her dryer.

After dragging Laci Chalmers's body to shore, I'd first called 911. Then I'd quickly texted Gabriel again to let him know what had happened. I'd done that as a courtesy to an employer. However, of course, he'd responded as a journalist himself and rushed to the scene, where he remained, after convincing Detective Doebler that I should be allowed to drive the short distance to Elyse's home to change clothes and wait for a debriefing.

I hadn't wanted to contact Piper, but Elyse had insisted, so my sister and Roger, who had been right across the lake watching the fireworks, too, were waiting for me at the kitchen table, where banquette seating overlooked the water far below.

The kitchen was also crowded with canines. Elyse's greyhounds, Paris and Milan, stuck close by her side while she moved about, putting muffins on a plate and refilling mugs. And Axis, Artie and Socrates hung out on an antique Persian rug that I always thought was a bold choice for a room where food might get spilled. The dogs seemed happy to be reunited, but all of them, including Artie, were subdued, reading off the collective mood of the humans, which ranged from shaken on my part to upset. That was mainly Piper.

"You are lucky you're alive," my sister told me. Her hands were on the table, next to a mug of coffee, and Roger squeezed her restless fingers, trying to restore her usual unshakable calm. "What were you thinking?"

"Easy, there, Piper," Roger soothed, while I made a shoo-ing motion, telling Axis, Artie and Socrates to go have fun. Socrates seemed reluctant to abandon me, but I kept brushing him along until he followed his friends. "Daphne's fine," Roger noted. "Let's not consider the what-ifs."

"Which could have been disastrous," Piper reminded him, her voice steadier. "Forget a wedding." She shot me a pointed look. "We could've been planning your *funeral*."

"I took some precautions before going to the landing," I assured her as the front door opened and slammed shut, the sound muffled by walls that separated the kitchen from the distant foyer. Setting one more steaming mug on the table, Elyse gestured to a chair, and I sat down, too. "I told Fidelia where I was headed, and I texted Gabriel."

"Yes, she did due diligence," Gabriel agreed, joining right in to the conversation without so much as greeting us. He smelled like pine and lake water and mud, although he'd had the good sense to ditch his shoes in the foyer. Pulling his own omnipresent Nikon from around his neck, he kissed Elyse on the cheek before setting the camera on the marble countertop.

Elyse Hunter-Black was almost always composed, but her fair cheeks flushed and her normally impassive eyes twinkled with warmth.

They were definitely having a good influence on each other.

Heading to a massive black Keurig that rivaled the Italian espresso machine at Flour Power, at least in size, Gabriel helped himself to coffee and leaned against a long bank of white cabinets. Taking a sip, he looked over the rim of his mug, watching me with his dark, intelligent eyes. "At least, I assume that your first text was meant to let me know where you were, and who you were with."

I nodded. "Yes. I was giving myself—and Socrates—a safety net when I realized that no one else had showed up at the landing, like I'd expected."

"You were also asking, without asking, if I thought you were safe with Laci, who'd disliked Abigail Sinclair, and who'd made no bones about that fact."

Gabriel was nothing if not shrewd.

"Yes, that's true, too. I was seeing if you'd warn me off."

My sister had mixed feelings about Gabriel, and he wasn't winning any points right then. "Why didn't you tell Daphne that she was in danger?"

"If I'd believed that, I would've told her to leave right away," Gabriel said. "But I worked with Laci every day, if only for a brief period, and I knew her to be tough. A little reckless, even."

That was a word I'd used to describe her, too. "How so?"

Gabriel grinned with grudging admiration. "She liked to upset the apple cart. I told her not to print the photo of the monk's belt implying it was a murder weapon. Laci went around my back and did it anyway." He shrugged. "The hazards of running a two-person operation, I guess. I had to trust her to take the paper to press when I couldn't be there."

Rule-following Roger appeared perplexed. "Why didn't you fire her?"

"I was a brash kid once, too," Gabriel said. "I wanted to give her another chance. Although I did warn her that she'd pay the legal fees and damages if we got sued. Which wouldn't have been easy on the salary I was paying her." He had momentarily forgotten why we were all gathered that evening, but quickly realized he shouldn't have made a joke. "The bottom line is, Laci was no angel. But I didn't believe for a minute that she was involved in Sinclair's homicide, or that you were in any danger, Daphne."

Elyse set the plate of muffins on the table, and Roger reached for one. Having eaten Elyse's baked goods, which were her Achilles' heel, I would not be making that same mistake.

"What convinced you Laci was innocent?" Roger asked Gabriel. "She was one of the last people to leave the party."

"For one thing, Laci was doggedly chasing down clues, with as much fervor as Daphne usually exhibits." Gabriel drained and set down his mug, which thunked on the marble. "I didn't think anyone would go to such great lengths to deflect suspicion. Especially since she wasn't above pointing out circumstances that indicated she might've done the deed."

"She did that with me, too," I said. "Or, at the very least, she asked if I thought she was guilty."

"In spite of everything, I'm still not convinced Laci wasn't involved somehow," Piper said, reaching for a napkin holder in the middle of the table. Grabbing a thick, white napkin, she handed it to Roger, who looked like he wanted to spit out the bite he'd taken. I had been there and actually done that. Piper turned to me again. "Why were you even meeting her?"

"Piper." Roger had managed to swallow, and his voice

Moxie and I both waved to Mike, who grinned and raised a spatula, and all at once, I figured out where she'd probably been the whole time I'd been trying to reach her about the silver bag. I could also guess why she hadn't been glued to her phone.

"You were with Mike when I was frantically texting you about the bag from the Gilded Lily, weren't you? And here I was a wreck, thinking you were being interrogated by Detective Doebler!"

"I don't know why you were so worried," she said. "I was able to show Detective Doebler that I still had *my* bag. And I texted you back to explain the next morning."

She had, but for once, I hadn't been able to interpret her emojis, which had included a striped container of popcorn, a collie dog and a wishing well. As we walked past a tent sponsored by Whiskered Away Home and manned by eccentric cat-hoarder-turned-decent-manager Bea Baumgartner, I finally figured out the symbols.

"You were binge-watching reruns of *Lassie*, weren't you?" I asked, waving at Bea, who didn't notice me. She was wrangling a basket of kittens, all wearing Uncle Sam-like vests. They looked adorable.

"Only the first twelve episodes," Moxie said. "We still have about five hundred seventy to go."

I couldn't believe there were that many. "That's a lifetime of kids stuck in wells."

Moxie grinned. "I hope so!"

I hadn't been positive before, but I knew then that my best friend fully intended to marry her high school sweetheart. I was confident they would live happily ever after.

I was feeling more optimistic for Piper and Roger, too, now that he'd been exonerated for one murder—Laci's—which was almost certainly tied to Abigail's death. There had only been a brief window of time between a sighting of Laci leaving the *Gazette*'s offices on the evening of the fireworks and my discovery of her body. Roger had been at the lake the entire time. Lots of people remembered seeing him and Piper sitting in matching lawn chairs, waiting for night to fall.

"Where are your sister and her betrothed?" Moxie asked, reading my mind, as usual. She tossed her picked-clean corncob into a bin. I assumed that our next stop would be Daisy Carpenter's tent, which was about fifteen yards ahead of us. I'd told Moxie she *had* to try one of the pickles displayed in glass jars that Daisy, who was smiling and chatting with customers, had artfully displayed on a rustic table. Stopping us both for a moment, Moxie wiped her fingers with a napkin and threw that away, too. "Piper and Roger are missing a crucial part of the Wags 'n Flags experience!"

"I think they're enjoying a quiet day together, celebrating the fact that Roger is a little closer to being off the hook for homicide."

"That is a good feeling," Moxie confirmed, speaking from experience.

"Hey . . . bridesmaids . . . wait up!"

Moxie and I both turned at the breathless sound of Fidelia Tutweiler's voice.

"Daphne, I heard about the latest body." Fidelia bent over and sucked wind. Then she straightened, still breathing heavily. "Is there . . . anything I can do?"

"Thanks, but I'm afraid not," I told her. "It's in Detective Doebler's hands now."

Fidelia got her breathing under control. "I was worried when you didn't text. Then I was relieved you were okay."

I'd completely forgotten that I'd promised to contact Fidelia, and I bit my lower lip. "I'm so sorry. I totally forgot. Things just got crazy . . ."

Fidelia rested a hand on my arm. "It's okay. I'm sure I wasn't a top priority at the time."

I still felt badly and worried that I'd bruised Fidelia's always fragile self-esteem.

Moxie was also concerned about my accountant, but for a different reason.

"What happened to you?" she inquired, gesturing to Fidelia's hand, which still rested on my wrist. Looking down, I saw scratches on Fidelia's fingers.

Although the wounds were far from severe, the lacerations were puffy and red, and I asked, "Are you okay?"

Fidelia removed her hand, seeming embarrassed. "Ms. Peebles got stuck on a light fixture. On the ceiling! I don't even know how she got there. And when I tried to get her down, she kind of panicked."

I felt terrible. "Do you need me to take her back?"

"No!" Fidelia cried. Her face fell. "I really enjoy her company, and I'm hoping she'll come to enjoy mine."

I had a feeling that Fidelia's apartment, more than her personality, was contributing to Ms. Peebles's uncharacteristic bad behavior. She was an accident-prone cat, but never mean.

"I still have a key to Abigail's house," I said. "I could stop by after All Paws on Deck and get some of her things. Toys, and her bed. Maybe it would help her settle in."

"Oh, that's way too much trouble," Fidelia protested.

"It's really not far out of the way," I assured her. "And it will only take me a few minutes."

"Well, if you're sure," Fidelia agreed, but uncertainly. She rubbed her scabbed fingers. "It might help."

"Pets do like to have their stuff," Moxie noted, holding out her vintage, woven basket purse and opening it so we could look inside. Sebastian was sound asleep on a soft scrap of fabric, his pink tail curled up over his nose. "Sebastian won't go anywhere without his wubbie."

I assumed his "wubbie" was the tiny blanket.

Moxie closed her purse, and I said, "Hey, Fidelia, do you want to get a pickle?"

"I . . . I don't know if that will be possible," she noted, looking past me with a funny expression on her face.

"What do you mean?" I asked, only to have the question answered when I turned around and saw that someone was about to cut into the line that had formed to buy briny treats.

Detective Fred Doebler, who was striding through the park, followed by two uniformed officers, all of them heading straight for Daisy Carpenter's tent.

Chapter 37

"I swear, I was working late at the restaurant," Daisy insisted, her gaze darting between me, Moxie, Fidelia, and Detective Doebler, who was sweating in his suit. The two uniformed officers, who barely moved, nevertheless stood out, and, noticing their presence, a crowd was gathering around the In a Pickle tent—and not to buy pickles. Daisy wrung her hands in one of her blue-and-white dish towels, wilting under what I considered to be unwarranted harsh treatment at the hands of Jonathan's partner. I didn't think Detective Doebler should be basically accusing Daisy of murder in public. "I didn't know anything about poor Laci," she promised, "until I read the *Gazette* this morning."

At that moment, Gabriel emerged from the milling throng, snapping pictures. I wanted to tell him to knock it off, but he was just doing his job, covering the latest development in murder investigations that now directly impacted his newspaper.

Snowdrop, Socrates and the other dogs had all run over, too, and all at once, the protective poodle snarled and latched onto Detective Doebler's pant leg, shaking it roughly.

Axis stayed quiet, while Artie and Tiny Tim yapped shrill

approval. I wished the pug wasn't wearing his *PUG NATION* T-shirt, but it seemed to be his only summer outfit.

"Hey!" Detective Doebler barked, too, when Snowdrop growled again. "Knock it off, mutt!"

"Snowdrop, no!" Daisy cried, her brown eyes wide with dismay. "Please, stop!"

Knowing that the once-spoiled pup was just slipping a bit, reverting to her former bad behavior, which had included some snapping, I swooped down, planning to scoop her up and gently remind her to mind her manners.

Socrates intervened first, calmly nudging Snowdrop until she let go, looking chastened. As the serene basset bumped his big, reassuring head against her delicate ear, she whimpered with fear and, I thought, remorse.

"It's okay, Snowdrop," Moxie promised, jutting her lower lip. She didn't like bullies, and I could tell she sympathized with the loyal, defensive dog.

Fidelia remained mute, as if overwhelmed by the whole chaotic scene.

"Snowdrop is sorry—and please don't treat her rudely," I told Detective Doebler. The perturbed poodle had misbehaved, but he shouldn't have called her a mutt. Not that there was anything wrong with mixed-breed dogs. I loved them. But he'd intended insult. I again bent to pick up Snowdrop, who was trembling, and Socrates stepped back, hanging his head in a gesture that looked like an apology for giving me the cold shoulder. He also should've known that, when push came to shove, I would protect our friends, but love had temporarily blinded him. I gave him a look that said he was fogiven, then returned my attention to the human drama.

"Miss Carpenter, I need you to come down to the station to answer some questions," Detective Doebler said, his face bathed in more staccato bursts of light from Gabriel's camera. Detective Doebler gestured for Daisy to walk with him. "Let's go."

Daisy looked too shocked to protest, her eyes silently pleading with me, as if I might have answers.

I only had questions myself, though.

Should I call an attorney?

Or was Daisy even under arrest? Because Detective Doebler hadn't said that.

And why was Jonathan's partner being so obnoxious, making a big scene?

I knew Jonathan would've approached Daisy quietly, in a more private setting, if at all possible. He wouldn't have strode through a happy event, humiliating someone who might very well be innocent. And he certainly wouldn't have mugged for the camera, like Fred Doebler was doing.

"Daisy, what can I do to help?" I asked, sounding like Fidelia, just minutes before. I stroked Snowdrop, who was wriggling to get down and follow her person. "Come with you? Or contact a lawyer?"

"Please just watch Snowdrop," Daisy requested over her shoulder. She wasn't wearing handcuffs, but it still looked like an arrest, the way the two officers walked closely behind her. "I know a lawyer, if I need one."

Detective Doebler moved to follow his fellow officers, and I fought back growing anger, because it wasn't a productive emotion and only clouded judgment.

Moxie wasn't quite so generous. "He's acting like a real big shot while Jonathan's away—for now," she grumbled.

Detective Doebler heard the comment. He turned slowly around, glancing at Moxie, then addressing me as Gabriel kept snapping away.

"You're lucky I'm not dragging *you* down to the station, Ms. Templeton," he said in a voice close to a growl. "And when Black leaves *permanently*, believe me, I'll look more closely at you the next time you find a body."

I didn't answer him, because I didn't respond to threats. And, even though I kept telling myself that it was best for Jonathan to move, I hated that Detective Doebler was rubbing that difficult reality in my face. He smirked, acting like he was doing me a favor when he told me, "In the meantime, you ought to be thanking me, because it looks like your brother-in-law, Berendt, will likely get off scot-free."

My heart thumped in my chest. "Why do you say that?"

His admission was grudging. "That storm the night of Sinclair's murder took down a tree on Route 23. It held up what little traffic was on the road that night. A flag man remembers waving Berendt by near the front of a line of cars. There's no denying that Berendt was stuck for at least a half hour, trying to get to his sister at her dive bar."

Detective Doebler left me to figure out that the delay would've eaten up time Roger would have needed to get to Artful Engagements, kill Abigail, and drive to the Wild Hog.

I wondered, for a moment, why Roger hadn't mentioned the fallen tree in his defense, then I realized he'd likely been keeping one last card close to his vest in case he needed to sacrifice himself to save his sister.

"He's got an alibi for Chalmers's death, too," Detective Doebler reminded me. "So your family is lucky again, if not your friends."

I should've been happy for Roger and Piper, who were finally free to marry and start their new lives without a cloud of concern and suspicion hovering over them. But as I watched Daisy slouch away through the crowded park, her head hanging down, guarding against the stares of curious onlookers, I felt the lowest I had since the whole wedding-and-murder debacle had begun.

I also felt an overwhelming urge to prove Sylvan Creek's increasingly power-drunk detective wrong about Daisy Carpenter, no matter what it took. Because Snowdrop, still wiggling in my arms, might've had her faults, but I trusted dogs even more than people, and the little white poodle was trying to tell me, with every fiber of her twisting body, that she believed in Daisy. And that, along with my doubt that Daisy could kill, was good enough for me.

Chapter 38

"Well, if you had to find another body, at least it didn't interfere with any sort of special occasion," Mom noted when we met for a late-afternoon coffee, following the community picnic.

Not surprisingly, my mother was completely over-looking the fact that I'd discovered Laci Chalmers's corpse during one of the town's biggest annual events.

Like Fidelia Tutweiler, Mom wasn't a fan of fireworks, which she called "much ado about literally nothing." Therefore, the celebration didn't even register with her.

Shaking out a sugar packet, she tore it open and dumped the contents into the already potent quadruple espresso she'd forced the barista at Oh, Beans to brew up for her, contrary to a store policy against dangerous levels of caffeine.

The always adorable shop was extra festive for the extended Fourth of July celebration. Along with serving holiday drinks, including one called John Hancock's Signature Blend—"a concoction writ large"—and Paul Revere's Midnight Ride—a mix of Oh, Beans' three darkest brews—the shiplap walls were festooned with classic reproduction artwork, including Leutze's *Washington Cross-*

ing the Delaware and a 1940s Rosie the Riveter poster. Candles burned in each of the twelve-paned windows, and I recognized the distinctive scent of Gunpowder and Sky, which I'd first smelled at the Gilded Lily.

The overall effect was charming, and I thought it was a lesson in how a theme could be taken just far enough.

"I do continue to worry about your deleterious effect on the local real estate market," Mom added, stirring the sugar into her custom drink. "There are limits on how many corpses a buyer will accept in one town before moving on to, say, Zephyr Hollow!"

That single reference to competition with a neighboring real estate market told me that there might be a *tiny* rift forming between two formerly chummy mini-moguls. I wasn't sure what would be worse for Piper—if Mom and Bev were thick as thieves, or at odds. It was probably a lose-lose situation.

I was also impressed by the vocabulary word—"deleterious"—that Mom had tucked into the middle of a completely unfounded correlation between my admittedly uncanny ability to unearth, or, in some cases, wade right into, homicide victims and the price of area properties. The conclusion seemed particularly off base since the Sylvan Creek market was, by all accounts, booming.

I swirled the straw in my tall glass, which held another holiday special drink, called Boston (Iced) Tea Party, which was a tart, cool mix of English tea and cranberry juice. "I don't think I'm hurting your business too much," I said. "And any damage I do is probably mitigated by Jonathan, who is apparently snapping up land right and left. Not that you'd ever mention that you deal with him on a regular basis."

"Realtor-client privilege," Mom reminded me. She might've disapproved of Jonathan's decision not to live on a golf course, like a "sensible bachelor," and she'd been unhappy when she'd believed he'd bailed on Piper and Roger's wedding, but she always appreciated a shrewd investor, and she nearly smiled. "I will say that he has a keen eye for potentially lucrative investments." The near smile turned into a near frown. "When he's making decisions with his head, for the good of his portfolio."

I gulped down a big sip of my drink. "What does *that* mean?"

My mother gazed out one of the windows, and for the first time in recent memory, her expression softened. Then she met my eyes again and, without answering my question, told me reluctantly, "I suppose you could do worse, Daphne."

There was a compliment, or perhaps insult, buried in there somewhere. Recalling how Beverly Berendt had claimed that my mother sometimes bragged about me, I decided to believe it was the former. Wanting to leave well enough alone, I changed the subject.

"Mom, about the land Jonathan bought on Crooked Creek Lane." I leaned forward. "Do you know anything about it?"

It took a lot to rattle my mother, but I saw a flicker of unease in her eyes, and she downed her espresso. Then she dug into her purse and slapped some money onto the table. "I don't even know what you're asking, Daphne. It's a lovely property, and it will be a wonderful spot for a wedding. Honestly, I can't fathom what compels you to go digging around, endlessly asking questions that don't need to be answered!"

With that, my flustered mother swept out of Oh, Beans, tossing a four-hundred-dollar bandanna-print scarf over her shoulder—"American cowgirl" as interpreted by Saint Laurent—and leaving me to wonder what the heck she was hiding from me related to the place where her favorite child would form a bond that was said to last for eternity.

Chapter 39

As evening settled over the Poconos the day after Laci Chalmers's murder—and the day before the rowboat regatta—I puttered around Plum Cottage, restless and ruminating about weddings, homicides and, last but certainly not least, going down with the *Tiny-tanic* in front of the whole town.

By all rights, I should've sat on my screened porch enjoying a glass of wine. After leaving Oh, Beans shortly after my mother's departure, I'd spent most of the day at Flour Power, finishing up the cookies for All Paws on Deck. I'd had some pet-sitting obligations, too, including three dog walks. And I'd stopped by the barn on the way home, checking the decorations for the reception.

Elyse and her crew had done a fantastic job, although I was a bit surprised by some of her choices, which weren't as romantic as I would've expected. In fact, she'd switched out the crystal chandeliers for wrought iron and added long, mismatched antique farmhouse tables instead of the smaller, round rentals covered with white cloths that I'd believed were part of her original plan.

I assumed that Piper, who wasn't fussy, would be just fine with the last-minute swaps. Not that I knew for certain.

I hadn't seen my sister since just after Laci's murder, at Elyse's mansion, and I assumed she was still decompressing with Roger before the coming round of more pleasant excitement the day after next.

I was looking forward to the wedding, yet I wouldn't have said I felt truly happy right then, and I could tell that Snowdrop and Socrates were unsettled, too. They kept wandering around the cottage, sniffing their food bowls, pawing at the door and trying, but failing, to nap.

Tinks was also disgruntled, pouting on the windowsill he'd refused to share, his smooshed-in face looking even grumpier than usual. I had a feeling he wished he hadn't chased his playmate away.

"If you stay on your good behavior, I'll bring Ms. Peebles back here after the wedding," I assured him. "Right now, I can't be here enough to supervise you."

My promise did little to placate the cranky Persian. Swiping his paw, he tried to push a coffee can full of sage off the sill. I caught it just in time, but missed stopping Tinks, who leaped over my free hand and ran up the spiral staircase.

That left me, Socrates and Snowdrop to pace around, with hours to go until our bedtime.

Joining them in the living room, where they were both lying near the hearth, their muzzles on their paws, I felt the urge to curl up, too.

Actually, I wanted to talk with Jonathan and tell him all about how Laci had been murdered, Roger had been cleared of Abigail's homicide, and Daisy was actually under arrest after failing to convince Detective Doebler that she'd been alone at In a Pickle at the time of Laci's death.

It was probably ironic that practically the whole town had been at Lake Wallapawakee, where the murder had taken place, so no one had seen any lights on at the restaurant.

I hated that I'd made Daisy's situation worse by telling Detective Doebler about her argument with Laci, although I still stood by my decision to be honest.

On the other hand, I *was* keeping information from Jonathan, who didn't yet know about my discovery of Laci's body. As much as I wanted to spill everything, I didn't want to worry him, so I'd kept my texts and voice mails upbeat, touching only on Roger's good news, and briefly, because Jonathan was obviously very busy, sending me repeated apologies for not being available.

I could feel myself drifting into a funk, when all at once, a warm breeze drifted in through the open windows, and I looked around my homey cottage, which was filled with creatures I loved. My sister was just a short drive away, getting ready for the happiest day of her life, my best friend was *hopefully* baking a cake, and my mother . . .

Well, rumor had it that she was proud of me, in her own way.

"We should not be moping around," I told Snowdrop and Socrates, who both raised their heads, the tags on their collars jingling in unison. As soon as I had their attention, I realized I didn't have a plan, but I quickly came up with one on the fly. Checking the angle of the sun one more time, to make sure we could reach our destination before dark, I asked one wary and one eager dog, "Who wants to go for a ride?"

Snowdrop, Socrates and I definitely would've made it to Crooked Creek Lane before sunset—if I hadn't gotten hopelessly lost in the mysterious valley, which still seemed like something out of a fairy tale.

As it was, the sun was just at the horizon, burnishing the summer foliage in a way that reminded me of my brides-maid's dress, as we bumped down the lane to the chapel.

"I'm not turning back now," I told Socrates, who was strapped into the VW's front seat with Snowdrop. The petite poodle was the only soul, animal or human, with whom he would willingly share his prized spot. He swung his head to look at me, and I saw that he believed we should just go home. Snowdrop, on the other hand, was panting eagerly in anticipation of an adventure. They were a classic example of opposites who'd attracted. "We won't stay long," I promised Socrates, who *was* the bark of reason in the vehicle. "I just feel that, since we came all this way, we should at least make sure the church . . . is not done!"

I changed my tune at the last moment, groaning with dismay, because when we emerged from the copse of trees to reach the dead end, I discovered not a picture-perfect little house of worship, but scaffolding, tarps and sawhorses—along with a shiny Lincoln Continental that seemed like an odd car for a contractor, and an expensive one for a recent ex-convict, to drive.

"I guess business is really taking off for the former inmates," I grumbled. I didn't begrudge their success. I was just frustrated that the job wasn't done, with less than forty-eight hours to go.

Parking my van next to the luxury sedan, I hopped out, then released the dogs.

We all proceeded to sniff around the property—literally, on the part of Socrates and Snowdrop. Glancing toward the pond, I saw that someone had added a small gazebo, which would've been nice if the rest of the work had been done first. But as I circled the church, I discovered that, while flower boxes adorned the windows and most of the painting was finished, there were still a few projects to complete. Coming back around to the front, I was happy to note that the steps had been repaired. But the door was locked, so I couldn't check the interior.

Stepping backward, I shaded my eyes, trying to see if someone was on top of the scaffolding. "Hello?"

No one answered, so I stepped farther back, looking all the way up to the steeple, which was among the unfinished projects. However, the plywood had been removed, revealing a black iron bell—and a figure in silhouette, backlit by the slanting rays of the setting sun.

"Hello?" I called again.

The person leaned out over the walled edge of the steeple. Dangerously far, in my opinion.

"Daphne?"

I immediately recognized the voice, as did Socrates, who'd trotted up next to me, along with Snowdrop. The low, almost growling sound that rumbled in Socrates' chest told me that he was not pleased to run across the man who continued to teeter above us in an unsound structure, where supposedly foul play had once occurred.

I, meanwhile, was mainly confused. And perhaps a little concerned. "Brother Alf?" I called. "What are *you* doing here?"

A long, long silence stretched between us. Then the man of the cloth confessed to us, "I've come to say goodbye— forever!"

Chapter 40

"I'm sorry I keep scaring you with my attire and flair for the dramatic," Brother Alf said, taking a seat next to me on the chapel's steps. "I assure you, I have no intention of killing myself." He twisted to look wistfully at the building behind us. "I'm simply saying goodbye to a spot that was once special to me, before I move on."

Having glimpsed a suitcase on his bed when he'd ducked into his room at Graystone Arches, I wasn't surprised to learn that Brother Alf was hitting the road. But I hadn't expected him to tell me that he was leaving the area for good.

Since he couldn't, or wouldn't, share exactly where he was headed, I instead asked, "What really happened here, back in the seventies?"

Brother Alf's response was a deep sigh that resonated with what sounded like a lifetime of regret, and I gave him a moment to reflect, thinking that Jonathan was right. The chapel was a good spot for contemplation.

The air was dark and soft and smelled of cut grass, mowed by the landscapers who'd cleared the area around the pond, so the water glistened in the moonlight. Frogs croaked and answered one another, and every now and then, I heard the faint hoot of an owl. The sound reminded me of Rembrandt, the bird from the Owl & Crescent Art Barn, although I doubted he ventured so far from his home. I was tempted to be lulled into complacency, but I still needed to understand why Brother Alf had made one last stop at the chapel, and why he'd reacted so strongly when I'd first mentioned it, back at Graystone Arches.

"You had something to do with a woman named Desdemona Siminski, didn't you?" I prompted softly, interrupting his reverie.

Brother Alf drew back gawking at me like I was a magician who'd just identified a card he'd pulled randomly from a deck. "How did you know that?"

"It was a guess," I admitted, glancing at Socrates and Snowdrop, who were sitting by the pond, their heads bent together. They looked like the basset hound and poodle figurines from the painting party, and I was glad Socrates had agreed to leave my side. He'd only done so after I'd contacted Moxie, telling her our whereabouts, and letting Brother Alf know, in no uncertain terms, that if we didn't get home by nine p.m., the cops would be looking for him.

Brother Alf had actually been happy to loop a third party into our meeting. He seemed a little wary of me, too, after reading about how I'd found Laci's body at the lake.

"Well, it wasn't a complete guess," I added. "I got hold of a bunch of clippings that Abigail had collected at Artful Engagements. They were all about Graystone Arches. Paging through them was like reading a history of your . . ." I almost said "cult's," but caught myself just in time. "A history of your organization's rise, in reverse. And one of the stories, near the very bottom of the pile, featured a photo of the chapel."

He knew what I was talking about. "Yes. Taken at Desdemona's wedding. Or, more precisely, the night before she was to be married."

His voice was quiet, almost hoarse. I could only see him in profile, but his expression looked haunted.

I spoke more softly, too. "Who was she?"

To my surprise, he shifted on the steps and suddenly smiled, laughter in his eyes. "Only the most beautiful, wildest thing you've ever met. That stuffy old-money family of hers could never crush her spirit!"

I tried to be tactful. "I take it you two were . . . ?"

His grin vanished, and he cleared his throat, like he was uncomfortable, too. "Yes. We were . . . an *item*. Drawn to each other like magnets from the moment we met. But the timing was bad. Very bad."

I was familiar with that situation, but at least Jonathan and I weren't involved with other people. Our situation wasn't quite so complicated, nor unethical. "How did you meet?"

Brother Alf hung his head. "She was planning her wedding. Her family, who hailed from Philadelphia—"

"Yes, I read that."

"They had a summer home on Lake Wallapawakee," he continued. "They decided that their favorite vacation retreat would be a lovely site for their daughter's celebration." He twisted to look at the chapel again, then faced forward. "I had just started here, a fresh-faced minister right out of divinity school, with all the best intentions in the world to save souls." He laughed, and it came out like a rueful, yet bemused grunt. "Then I met Des!"

An owl swooped over us, and in a flight of fancy, I really believed it was Rembrandt. Brother Alf followed the bird's progress, too, until I said, "The picture in the newspaper, where her bridesmaids are so happy, and she's alone . . ."

His hands drooped between his knees, to the extent they could do that, since he was wearing his robe. "I had already told Des I couldn't destroy her relationship with her family, because they suspected what was happening. And we were wrong to go behind her fiancé's back, too. I'd told her it was over."

"What happened?"

"She did not take it well. And being headstrong, not to mention armed with a trust fund that she'd gained control of at age twenty-one, she simply struck out on her own one night, leaving from the chapel, after saying goodbye to me, right here."

I wasn't sure I believed him. "But the rumor is someone died here. There's even a cold case file."

"The Siminski family tried to claim foul play, to save face. They insisted that Desdemona would never have left of her own free will. Even when Des donated generously to Gateway Arches, as a way of telling me that she still cared, in spite of all that had happened between us . . ."

I recalled the clipping about the Siminski family's battle to stop the donation of "blood money."

". . . Even then, the Siminskis swore an imposter had gotten hold of Des's identity and trust fund. To them, it was better to claim she'd been *murdered* than admit, publicly, that she'd walked away from her family, her future husband— and her infant daughter."

My eyes nearly popped out of my head, and Socrates and Snowdrop, whose keen ears must've been tuned in to the conversation, looked back at us, too.

"Desdemona Siminski had a *child*? But you said she wasn't . . ."

Brother Alf laughed again. "I'm the one who lives a cloistered life, but you seem very naive right now, Daphne Templeton. Surely you know that even in the late nineteen seventies, children were born out of wedlock. And, I told you, Des was quite wild!"

I pictured the old photo. I had thought the sad bride seemed familiar somehow. "I'm going to make another guess."

I didn't have to. Brother Alf rubbed his jaw. "Yes. That child was Abigail."

"But she didn't use her family name."

"From what I understand, she thought 'Sinclair' sounded classier for a wedding planner. She didn't change it until she started her business."

I thought back to the guest book at Graystone Arches, where Abigail had signed in with her *real* name. I hadn't recognized the surname itself. I'd thought the moniker looked familiar because I knew Abigail's distinctive handwriting from notes she'd left me when I sat for Ms. Peebles. The sharp, slanted way she wrote an "a," and the angular dots, like slashes, she'd placed over each "i" were unmistakable.

"She went to see you recently, didn't she?"

"Yes. While I'd sort of kept an eye on her, over the years, she suddenly seemed intent upon making an appearance in my life, letting me know that she had always blamed me for breaking up her family." His shoulders drooped. "And I suppose she was right."

"I don't know," I said. "It sounds to me like Desdemona wouldn't have been very happy, tied down to a child. Most mothers don't bolt that easily. And you ultimately tried to do the right thing."

He took a deep breath and exhaled. "Perhaps. But I must share some of the blame for the mess that left Abigail motherless." He nodded to his car. "And as you can see, even today, I have a difficult time resisting worldly temptations. I tried to cloister myself. Sought a new, more simple life, to atone for my sins, leaving this congregation behind and starting Graystone Arches. But, in spite of my best intentions, I ended up with a baking and zither empire!"

Brother Alf was exasperated by his own Midas touch,

and I wasn't sure what to say except, "The zithers do seem impressive. And my best friend is fanatical for the bread."

The dogs were still listening, and Socrates whined with embarrassment on my behalf. Then again, he might've still been complaining about the excessively long concert we'd endured.

"Getting back to Abigail," I said, hoping to gloss over my awkward comment. "Who raised her, if her mother was out of the picture?"

"Her father, Alan Ogilvie, who would've married Des, if she and I hadn't fallen so hard for each other. And I understand he was a devoted man. But I don't think it was ever enough. Abigail was determined to punish me for interfering with the dream she had of a perfect, happy family."

I considered Graystone Arches and its inhabitants almost unassailable. The place was literally a castle on a mountaintop. "If you'd wanted, you could've shut her out entirely. So how could she do that?"

"By telling a terrible truth." He shifted again to meet my gaze. "You know about the mass wedding, right? Just a few years ago?"

I nodded. That clip had been out of order, at the top of the pile.

"Such a stupid stunt, in retrospect!" Brother Alf groaned.

I didn't tell him that Piper and I both agreed.

"Abigail had enlisted someone to do some investigating, and they'd dug deep enough to realize that the acolyte who performed the ceremony—"

"I thought you did that," I interrupted. "I saw a picture."

He rubbed his balding head, getting agitated. "No. Brother Thomas looked like me." He grabbed part of his robe. "We all look alike, in these vestments."

That was true, and the photo I'd seen was grainy and shot from a distance.

"I was ill that day," Brother Alf explained. "So I told one of my followers to take my place and preside over the exchange of vows."

"But . . . ?"

Brother Alf buried his face in his hands. "Brother Thomas wasn't ordained. Had no authority!"

My eyes got big again. "So all of those marriages . . . ?"

"Shams," Brother Alf confirmed, in a whisper. "And Abigail was going to publicly expose me for the greedy, lustful fraud that I am. Even Beverly doesn't know the whole truth about me."

I had let down my guard as I'd listened to his fascinating story, but all at once, I felt a cold chill run down my spine, and I rose. Socrates and Snowdrop stood up, too, and joined us, both dogs on alert.

I didn't understand why Brother Alf had shared his secret with *me*, aside from the fact that he was leaving town anyhow. And I suddenly realized that he'd had a powerful motive to kill Abigail. Not to mention a colorful belt.

"The dogs and I need to go now," I said, clutching my phone. I tapped the screen. "I'm telling Moxie we're heading home."

Brother Alf stood up, too, and he stepped back, raising his hands. "No, you misunderstand. I wouldn't have hurt Abigail, physically."

I glanced at the woven rope around his middle, again doubting him.

"I'd harmed her enough, emotionally," he continued. He wiped his mouth with his sleeve, looking sick. "I didn't realize the extent until I spoke with her at the Gateway, and again at Roger and Piper's rehearsal dinner. She was living proof of the damage I'd done, so many years ago. So cold and angry!"

I still feared Brother Alf a tiny bit. But I felt sorry for him, too. He *was* deeply flawed. But he was also remorseful.

"We're more than just the product of our parents, if they leave," I assured him. "I'm living proof of *that*, and so is Piper."

He looked to his luxury sedan, a symbol of avarice. "I've done other harm, too. It's time for me to take Fifi—"

For a second, I regretted feeling sad for him, because it sounded like he had another paramour, to put it politely. "Who is 'Fifi'?"

"The calico you met," he informed me. "She's in a carrier in the car."

I noticed then that the windows were down. "Oh."

"It's time for me to take Fifi and move on," he continued. "I'm thinking of retiring to the desert. Someplace I can reflect and live more simply."

I was positive he'd start another cult, and so was Socrates. He nuzzled Snowdrop and they walked to the van, like he'd had enough of Brother Alf.

I followed the dogs. "What will happen to the acolytes? Aren't you kind of pulling the rug out from under them?"

"Spiritually, yes," he admitted. "But financially, they are in for a windfall. I've made provisions to distribute all assets from the pending sale of the mountain and compound among them. And the zither business alone could sustain those who choose to continue their spiritual journey together at some other location."

"You mean, they're all *rich*?"

Brother Alf nodded again. "Yes. And free to go about their lives—as they always were, you know. The rumors that I held anyone hostage were *never* true."

With that, he slipped quickly into his Lincoln and started the engine. But right before he drove off, he stuck his head out of the open window. "Daphne?"

"Yes?"

"We sell the sourdough starter, if your friend wants

some. It's ten dollars for an ounce—in really nice packaging, if you're looking for hostess gifts, too."

I wished he'd told me all that when I'd been at the compound. And as he drove away, I also wished I'd asked him to recommend another minister—an *ordained* one—to perform his nephew's wedding.

Last but not least, I regretted not inquiring about who Abigail had conspired with to dig into Brother Alf's past, because I had a feeling that person might've just been silenced, too, in the chilly waters of Lake Wallapawakee.

Chapter 41

"Brother Alf is a fishy character and a huckster, but I don't know if he's a killer," I told Socrates and Snowdrop as we crested Winding Hill in the van. "I just don't see enough motive for either murder. Between the zithers, the bread—and the mountain—he was literally sitting on a fortune, even if his reputation was ruined and he never lured . . . er, accepted . . . another acolyte into his flock. He could've just ignored Abigail and waited out the scandal about the bogus weddings."

Snowdrop barked loudly, like she still thought Brother Alf might be guilty of more than running his cult, while Socrates simply looked out the window at the dark night.

I took that to mean he either agreed with me or simply had no time for a snake oil salesman who peddled sourdough starter for more than five bucks an ounce. Decorative container or not, the price was pretty high.

"Well, at least we all got away alive," I noted, driving past the farmhouse, where most of the windows were dark. However, I did spy a light glowing in the kitchen, and I pulled into the gravel patch by the barn, next to Piper's Acura.

Socrates tilted his head, letting me know he didn't understand why we were stopping.

"I feel like I should tell Piper the chapel's not *quite* done," I explained, unhooking my seat belt. "And I want to ask if she has a *viable* wedding dress yet. Because we are nearly out of time." I opened my door. "You two can stay here. I'll just be a minute."

Neither one of the love-struck canines objected to some time alone, so I hopped out of the VW and hurried to Piper's back door. Raising my hand to knock, I realized that she might have turned in early, resting up for the coming big days. Deciding to make a quiet entrance, I used the key I still kept on my ring, for emergencies, and poked my head into the kitchen.

The room was warm and stuffy, all the windows sealed, which wasn't like Piper, who always liked to let in the summer breezes that cooled the hilltop.

The kitchen was also *too* clean, every dish put away, every scrap of paper gone, and the white bowl that always held some fruit empty.

I was struck by the crazy idea that my own sister had moved away without telling me.

Then I spied a note tacked to the refrigerator, and I suddenly feared that notion wasn't so crazy at all.

Chapter 42

"Did *everyone* except me guess that Piper and Roger were eloping?" I asked Mom the next evening, when she made a rare appearance at a Wags 'n Flags event, if only to tuck business cards into the bags of dog cookies I was handing out from a table on the lakeshore.

If Beverly Berendt hadn't insisted that Mom was proud of me, I would've thought my mother also looked forward to watching me, Artie and Tiny Tim go down with the *Tiny-tanic*. I still believed that might be the case, and part of me hoped that Moxie, who was running late, would fail to show up with the boat and the dogs in time for the parade. The sun had already set, and most of the other craft were lined up in the water, waiting to turn on their lights to oohs and aahs from the crowd before doing slow, small laps to more applause.

Socrates and Snowdrop had already picked a spot to observe the regatta, and I gave my basset hound buddy, who probably would've preferred to stay home, credit for indulging the poodle, whose person sat wanly in a lawn chair, trying to act normally while *out on bail*.

"Honestly, Daphne," Mom said, tucking yet another card into one of the cellophane pouches meant to advertise *my* business. "Did you really think your sister would have her reception in a *barn*?" Leaning over the table, she handed a cookie and her contact information to a man who was passing by with a Great Dane at his side. "How adorable," Mom cooed, pointing at the dog, which I knew for a fact was making her inwardly shudder. When the pair walked on, she changed her tone and told me, "It was a nice attempt dear, but I, for one, anticipated that Piper and Roger would fly off somewhere tasteful and romantic to be wed."

I secretly believed that, like me, Mom had not suspected a thing. And I knew for a fact that Piper hadn't objected to the spot I'd found for the reception—a location that had been endorsed and decorated by one of the nation's top tastemakers.

Elyse Hunter-Black, who was at the lake with Axis, Paris and Milan, *had* known all about Piper's plans, because my guilt-ridden sister had spilled the beans the night Laci had been murdered, right before I'd walked in on her and Elyse chatting quietly in Elyse's kitchen. That was why Elyse had looked so guilty, herself, when I'd entered the room.

Fortunately, she hadn't been upset about the wasted decorating effort. In fact, she'd happily switched gears, downplaying the romantic touches and setting up a more casual party for family and friends, who would still celebrate, albeit without the bride and groom physically present, the very next day.

"I really don't think the barn was the deciding factor," I said, glancing over my shoulder to see if Moxie was on her way in a borrowed truck with a boat in tow. I couldn't deny that I was relieved to discover that the *Tiny-tanic* was still nowhere in sight, and I turned back around. "The note didn't even mention the reception."

The truth was, when they chose to fly to the Virgin Islands and tie the knot, my sister and Roger had simply wanted to make a fresh start far from the drama of dual homicides and the suspicion that had hovered around Roger.

It was all clear in the very apologetic message Piper had stuck on her fridge.

Along with providing a rationale for the couple's out-of-character, impulsive and rebellious choice, my sister had explained why she'd tried on the skimpy gowns, thinking she should go with something "beachy" for the private seaside ceremony.

She had, of course, quickly realized she'd been wrong. In the photos she'd texted from an isolated cove, she'd worn a simple white sheath—and a *huge* smile on her face. Roger, slightly sunburned, looked otherwise blissful, too.

I'd kept the images on my phone, and the note in my pocket, because in it, Piper had asked me a question that she'd started to pose once before, only to stop herself.

I didn't understand why she'd finished her thought in a note of apology, and I believed that what she'd written about Jonathan's work on the chapel was wrong.

However, at least I finally understood why I'd seen travel brochures in her kitchen and why she'd been so rattled when I'd found her trying on the gowns I'd then returned to Something Borrowed, Something New.

"I knew something was fishy when I saw those dresses," I muttered—my timing perfect, because a truck pulling *Something Fishy*, aka the *Tiny-tanic*, was rolling down onto the beach.

My mother and I were silent for a moment, as were most of the people who'd turned to check out the late arrival.

Then the night air was filled with a sound I hadn't heard in years.

Peals of unrestrained laughter—coming from *my mother*.

Chapter 43

"I seriously doubt anyone but Mom and Moxie understood that you two are supposed to be characters from *McHale's Navy*—which was, against all reason, my mother's favorite show, back in the day," I told Artie and Tiny Tim, who stood proudly at the prow of our rowboat, which was bobbing on the dark lake, and which now had yet another moniker: *PT 73*.

I certainly hadn't recognized the name of the vessel from a 1960s sitcom starring Ernest Borgnine and Tim Conway. However, now that I had some context, I had to admit that Moxie had done a good job of casting Timmy, the wrinkled, snub-nosed pug, as Borgnine's character, Lieutenant Commander Quentin McHale, while skinny, shivering, overly enthusiastic Artie was perfect as Conway's Ensign Parker.

I knew the dogs' roles and ranks because Moxie had faithfully re-created the program's costumes, right down to McHale's hat and epaulets and Ensign Parker's narrow tie. Not that I still would've recognized the characters, if she hadn't made *dog tags* for both little sailors.

The mock PT boat was not quite as realistic, although Moxie had outdone herself in a different way by adding at least twenty red, white and blue pinwheels and even more strands of lights in the same colors, all strung between the sides of the boat and a tall flagpole she'd added to the very center of the craft, which did list a bit to one side.

All at once, on some cue I hadn't heard, the boats around us all lit up merrily, to the oohs and aahs I'd anticipated. The sounds carried from the shore, where lanterns and sparklers also glowed in the darkness under a starry sky.

I wanted to enjoy the view, but I was struggling to keep hold of my oars and switch on the *Tiny-tanic*'s battery-powered display. As the boat rocked, I managed to illuminate our entry in the waterborne parade, and it was impressive enough to earn a second round of gasps, and even some scattered applause.

Then, in keeping with tradition, the convoy of about twenty people-powered, highly decorated craft, most carrying dogs dressed like George Washington, Benjamin Franklin and Betsy Ross, began to move in a slow, erratic circle.

I had barely managed to get us out to the spot where the entries had gathered, and I got a little sweaty even before I'd really exerted myself.

"We can do this," I promised Timmy and Artie, who kept turning around, their matching, bulging eyes alight with excitement—or concern, because my efforts to stay on course in the choppy water were already failing.

Hauling on both oars, I tried to line up the *Tiny-tanic* with the craft ahead of us, which carried a golden retriever who was wearing an outfit remarkably like my Statue of Liberty bridesmaid dress.

"Lady, are you doin' okay?" someone from another boat called to us from across a dark stretch of water.

"We're fine," I promised, even as I realized the life jackets I'd wanted all of us to wear were stashed underneath my seat. I'd been so impressed with the dogs' costumes that I'd forgotten all about safety and hadn't even considered covering up Moxie's handiwork. Which was probably a mistake, since, just as I'd feared, water was seeping in around the pole that Moxie probably shouldn't have drilled into the already weathered boards.

"I'm heading for land," I told Artie and Timmy, keeping a wary eye on the small, but spreading, puddle at my feet. "We're perfectly safe, so don't panic!"

That was the wrong thing to say. Both dogs started barking wildly, their little voices high and shrill, which people on shore apparently believed to be part of the act. As I rowed harder, getting nowhere, and the water in *Tiny-tanic* rose, the audience on shore applauded again.

"We're actually sinking now!" I called, hauling on the oars with all my might. The pole Moxie had installed popped free and fell over sideways, the lights sputtering out and water burbling in through the suddenly empty hole.

Yapyapyapyapyapyap!

Artie and Timmy either knew something was wrong, or they were having the time of their lives. Either way, their barks were like machine-gun fire as we tilted dangerously leeward. Or maybe starboard.

"Mayday!" I cried, trying to recall a nautical plea for help. Artie and Tiny Tim spun around in the prow like the pinwheels attached to the sides of our doomed craft. "SOS! Ship down!"

I heard the creak and clack of oars against wood and more barking and voices as our fellow parade entrants tried to rush to help. But rowboats are not made for rushing, and it was too late for anyone to save us but me.

As the *Tiny-tanic* rolled completely sideways, I lunged for the dogs, scooping them up in my arms and leaping into the dark, chilly waters of Lake Wallapawakee.

* * *

"At least it was a warm evening," I told Socrates as we drove down the long lane to Artful Engagements. In all the excitement over the maritime disaster, I'd completely forgotten about my promise to pick up Ms. Peebles's bed and toys until Fidelia had texted me, asking if I could *please* bring some comforting items for the out-of-sorts little cat. Taking one hand off the wheel, I swiped my wrist across my forehead, getting some of my damp curls out of my eyes. "And it's a good thing I left my phone with Mom during the parade, too. Otherwise, it would be at the bottom of the lake with the *Tiny-tanic*!"

Socrates wasn't happy about our detour to the mansion, and he was worried about Snowdrop and her person, but he couldn't stop snuffling and huffing with what sounded like mirth—the canine equivalent of Mom's outburst when she'd spied a dark pug version of Ernest Borgnine.

I wasn't quite as amused by the memory of how I'd slogged through a muddy lake bed, after realizing the water was only chest high, with two bedraggled, costumed dogs, one of whom had lost the tiny hat Moxie had worked so hard to create. However, I *was* trying to look on the bright side of my second public humiliation at Lake Wallapawakee, which, like the first—when I'd been part of a polar bear plunge gone awry—had, of course, been captured on film by Gabriel Graham.

"Maybe I'll look heroic, like Jonathan did when he pulled me from the lake," I added. "I was carrying two dogs to safety."

Well, I *had* been carrying them, until they'd both wriggled out of my arms and begun swimming in gleeful circles before racing each other to shore, where they'd arrived about two minutes before me, because my feet kept getting stuck in the muck.

Socrates knew I was trying too hard to put a positive spin on things and that I wouldn't look anything like an action hero when the *Weekly Gazette* landed on doorsteps the next day. Even in the dark van, I thought his expression looked doubtful.

I pretended I didn't notice as I pulled up before an equally dark mansion, where a sign announced that the property was for sale—and that interested buyers should contact *Beverly Berendt Prime Real Estate.*

"No wonder Mom has cooled on Bev," I said, climbing out from behind the wheel. I went around to release Socrates, who reluctantly jumped down. "And I bet that's why she's not upset about Piper eloping, either. Mom probably wants to steer as clear of Beverly as possible until she can pull off her next real estate coup, which I guarantee will be in Zephyr Hollow."

Socrates had zero interest in petty feuds over property. And he had even less interest in entering Artful Engagements, although I'd reminded him, a dozen times, that the place was perfectly safe.

Not only was the big house empty, but, like Jonathan, I believed that Abigail's murder had been a crime of passion. The killer wouldn't be lurking around waiting for some random visitors to knock off, too.

"Come on," I told Socrates, leading the way to the back door, where my key fit the lock. "This will just take a minute."

He continued to hang back, but trotted after me. A few moments later, we were in the kitchen where I'd last seen Daisy Carpenter trying, and failing, to assert herself with Abigail.

As always when the building was quiet, I could hear the tick of the grandfather clock echoing through the whole first floor.

And as I stood there listening to that familiar sound, I flashed back to the day I'd discovered Abigail's body and the suitcases on the bed.

A missing timepiece—and perfect timing.
Messy brochures and overflowing baskets.
Ambition clashing with amour.
And a cat in a case, and at a cult . . .

"Why is this still not adding up?" I mused aloud, looking down at Socrates. "Just when I think one thing fits, it ruins another theory—one of which is laughable, because the person I'm thinking of *can't* be a killer."

Socrates wasn't laughing at anything. His tail dropped.

"Fine," I said. "Let's run upstairs and grab a few of Ms. Peebles's things."

He didn't look enthusiastic about that, either, but he trailed along behind me, both of us pausing while I found the proper switch to illuminate the corridor leading to the main staircase.

Flipping that, I again assumed the lead, only to stop at Abigail's office.

"Just a peek," I promised Socrates, who shook his head, making his long ears swing.

Ignoring him again, I stepped into the dark room and flipped another switch. Abigail's desk lamp turned on, and I noted that the brochures I'd seen were still near her computer.

"Mom would've tucked those away," I whispered to Socrates, who stayed near the door while I moved to the desk and picked up the pamphlets, one of which advertised a romantic couples-only destination in the Caribbean, not far from where I believed Piper was staying.

Studying the colorful photos, I finally realized that the brochures, which I'd assumed Abigail had collected for some other couple, were probably related to *her own* thwarted travel, and my pulse started to race.

"Some of this is starting to make sense," I told Socrates, dropping the fliers and turning to the messy baskets, which hadn't been tidied, either. "Seriously," I added,

"Mom would've been all over this. I hate to say it, but I think Abigail's estate chose the wrong Realtor."

If Socrates was listening, I didn't notice, because for the first time, the jumble of wedding paraphernalia also struck me as out of place. Not only would an organized person like Abigail have kept her emergency gear in order, like a firefighter, but she probably wouldn't have been rooting through the stuff right before she fled town.

Moving closer, I dug a hand into one of the baskets, which held cuff links, bow ties and cummerbunds.

Then I checked another, which held hair ties, bobby pins—and garters in an array of colors, from white to pink to pale yellow.

"There's no blue one," I told Socrates. "Don't you think that would be a very common color?"

Socrates woofed softly, and I thought he was probably trying to tell me that we should get moving, and that Detective Doebler would've already gone through the baskets, too.

"I'm not so sure about that," I said. "Fred Doebler's a *guy*, and he wouldn't think to even consider a stash of random wedding stuff. He probably didn't look in these baskets at all, and had forgotten about them by the time the garter showed up as the likely murder weapon." I recalled how Detective Doebler had let me go upstairs while the crime scene team was still in the garden. "The murder obviously took place outside, and that was his main focus."

Socrates looked doubtful, and I had to concede that maybe he was right and Detective Doebler was aware of what I considered to be a potentially important clue.

"Come on," I said, joining him at the door and shutting off the light. "Let's go upstairs and find Ms. Peebles's things."

Socrates dragged along behind me, resigned to the task at hand, but still clearly objecting to our adventure, which for once *wasn't* investigative.

Well, maybe it was a bit investigative. As we passed

through another corridor on the second floor I stopped once more at Abigail's bedroom, where the door was wide open. Poking my head into that chamber, I listened closely.

I didn't hear a thing, except the distant ticking of the grandfather clock downstairs.

"I swear, there was a watch on the nightstand," I told Socrates, peering hard at the small table. I could barely make out the outline of the book and tube of hand cream I'd seen before. "I'm sure that whoever came back to claim the suitcase took the watch, too."

Socrates, who'd often accompanied me to pet-sitting jobs at the mansion, responded by shuffling off toward the upstairs living room, where Abigail kept a basket of cat toys and a bed for Ms. Peebles.

Following him into the spacious, tasteful room, illuminated by moonlight streaming in through windows that overlooked the garden, I once again thought the messy baskets were an anomaly, and maybe a clue. A similar basket was neatly stacked with magazines, and the cat toys were arranged tidily, too.

Figuring I'd grab the whole stash, I walked across a thick carpet that covered an antique parquet floor. And when my steps were muffled, my ears picked up a faint sound I'd hoped to hear in the bedroom.

The tiniest ticking of a clock or watch.

Getting excited again, I knelt down by the basket, while Socrates stood in the middle of the floor, his paws sunken into the soft rug and his eyes trained on the door.

"Why are you so spooked?" I asked him, reaching into a bunch of catnip mice, plastic balls filled with bells and little birds with fluffy feathers.

And then my fingers found the watch.

Not just any watch.

The one I'd seen on the nightstand—and, I suspected, the one that had been missing from Dexter Shipley's wrist when he'd shown me dresses at Something Borrowed, Something New. He'd checked his empty wrist then, and at the Sodgrass Club, where he'd complained about doing that out of "force of habit."

Hardly anyone wore a watch on a regular basis anymore, when everyone's phone had a clock, and I turned over the masculine timepiece, examining the back in the soft moonlight. And, sure enough, my suspicions were confirmed, about both Dex as the owner and his relationship with Abigail. I squinted at a small inscription reading, *To D.S.— All my love, until the end of time. A.S.*

"Ms. Peebles *stole this*," I told Socrates, still staring at the somewhat cheesy note. "I bet she was purposely trying to leave a clue that would lead the police to Dexter!"

"That is the most ridiculous thing I've ever heard."

I always expected Socrates to talk one day, and when he did, he'd probably critique a theory like the one I'd just set forth. For a split second, I thought he'd actually responded, and I wheeled around, only to discover Dex Shipley, wedding planner on the rise, likely murderer—and Abigail Sinclair's partner in a romance that had somehow gone wrong—watching me from the doorway with a very funny gleam in his dark movie-star eyes.

Chapter 44

"I thought I'd left my watch up here the night poor Abigail met her demise," Dex said, leaning against the door frame, his arms crossed. A bemused smile played at the corners of his lips, making me keenly aware that he wasn't at all worried about the fact that I'd just identified him as Abigail's missing secret lover and likely killer. "When I came back to grab my bags the next night, I tried to find it, but I ran out of time. No pun intended."

Socrates still wasn't amused, and I wasn't laughing, either. I pulled my phone from my pocket—and Dexter pulled a knife from one of his, inside the blazer he was wearing on a hot summer night. Not so much as a bead of sweat dampened his brow.

Speaking over Socrates' low growl, Dex nodded to my phone. "I would toss that in my direction, if I were you."

It was the most cinematic confrontation I'd ever had with a killer, and I wished I wasn't afraid for Socrates' and my lives. As things stood, I couldn't exactly enjoy the encounter, and I surreptitiously tapped the screen with my thumb, hoping I'd hit the right app out of the few on my home screen, before bending over to slide the phone across the carpet. It spun to a stop near Socrates' big paws.

Dex let the phone lie where it had landed. He'd lost interest in the surrendered device and was studying me. "Why do you look like such a mess?"

I'd nearly forgotten about my damp clothes and tousled hair. I tugged at the soggy hem of my T-shirt. "My boat sank to the bottom of Lake Wallapawakee."

I thought that explanation begged for greater details, but Dex didn't seem interested in those, either. He shook his head with mock sadness. "So many tragedies at that lovely body of water lately!"

I knew then that he'd killed Laci Chalmers. And he wouldn't have done that if he hadn't murdered Abigail, too.

"Why don't you just let me and Socrates go, before you make things even worse for yourself?" I suggested, knowing full well that he wasn't going to listen to me. Still, I had to try. "I don't really know anything, and I just want to go home."

He knew I was lying, if only out of desperation, and he laughed out loud. "You want to run to the bumbling detective and share everything you *do* know. You have a reputation for digging up the truth."

"So what *is* the truth?" I challenged him. "Why did you kill Abigail and stuff poor Ms. Peebles in a suitcase?— which was really uncalled-for!"

Dex finally lost his cool, in-charge demeanor, if only for a moment. Confusion clouded his eyes, and not because I'd blurted that stupid thing about confining a cat, which was terrible, but not as "uncalled-for" as murder.

Dex knit his brow. "The *cat* . . . ?"

I was suddenly baffled, too. "Why didn't you take your suitcase with you the night you killed Abigail?"

I'd perplexed him again. "I . . . I . . ."

He didn't have to finish his faltering explanation, because all at once, the front door slammed downstairs, then heavy footsteps thudded up the steps.

Dex stepped into the room, concealing himself in the many shadows.

"Be careful!" I tried to warn the person who was hurrying down the corridor in our direction, and Socrates barked, too. "Don't come in here!" I again tried to caution the individual who had, hopefully, inexplicably come to our rescue.

I supposed I'd expected Jonathan Black to miraculously make yet another appearance in the nick of time, although a small part of me knew that was not a realistic belief, given that I hadn't told him where I was, and that he was three thousand miles away.

Yet I was still disappointed, if grateful, when *Fidelia Tutweiler* burst into the room.

"Fidelia!" I cried. "Watch out!"

She blinked at me in the darkness while I tried to figure out what was happening, because Dexter didn't threaten her, or say a word. He did step into the light so he stood shoulder to shoulder with my part-time accountant. Then the room got strangely, eerily still.

"Fidelia?" I asked, my voice a little choked. "Did you come here because it took me too long to get the cat toys, and you were worried?"

I already knew the answer, because I'd put some of the impossible-to-believe pieces together. And so I wasn't completely surprised when my fellow bridesmaid gave me a level stare and said, flatly, "No. I thought *Dexter* was taking too long. I was starting to worry that my plan had gone wrong, and *you* had killed *him*."

Chapter 45

"How long have you two been together?" I asked Fidelia and Dexter, who continued to hold on to his knife.

He alternated between tapping the blade against his palm and cleaning fingernails that I was sure were already impeccable, but I knew I'd have no chance if I tried to dart past him. Not with Fidelia at his side, blocking the door that led to the hallway.

So much for the bond between bridesmaids, not to mention employer and employee.

I glanced at Socrates, who also seemed to be weighing our options, in between shooting me reproachful looks. I hoped he was devising a better plan than I had formulated, because I had nothing. Our only hope, at that point, was my *mother*. I was pretty sure I'd complained about needing to stop by Artful Engagements on the way home. But there was no reason for Mom to follow up with me that evening. She would never know that Socrates and I didn't make it back to Plum Cottage.

I corrected myself:

If we didn't make it back. I wasn't counting us out yet.

"When did this all happen?" I asked, when no one answered my first question. "Did you even know each other before we started planning Piper and Roger's wedding?"

We were in a pretty grim situation, regardless of whether one was about to kill or be killed, but all at once, Fidelia Tutweiler beamed with happiness. "No, Dex and I had never met before your mother brought in Artful Engagements." She smiled lovingly at the handsome young man she'd sent to murder me. "It was love at first sight."

"So, all that stuff about Dexter being involved with Laci—"

"What?" Dexter sounded surprised.

Fidelia waved her hand at both of us, giggling like a schoolgirl. "That was just to throw you off the scent, Daphne. I knew you were investigating Abigail's murder, and I was afraid there was a chance you'd noticed Dex and me together at the rehearsal dinner."

I had seen them chatting, but had assumed they were two near-strangers making small talk.

Fidelia's cheeks flushed with anger, like she'd read my mind. "It was all too easy to convince you that I believed Dexter was too good for me—because you believed it, too!"

"That's not true," I told her. "I encouraged you to ask him out the day you were at Something Borrowed, Something New."

Dex smiled at Fidelia. "Yes. We were drinking champagne while Fidelia tried on dresses for *our* wedding."

Okay, maybe it was a little difficult for me to believe that my formerly mousy accountant and the Cary Grant look-alike were a couple, in spite of Fidelia's recent attempts to add some color to her wardrobe and her hair. Then again, the two had complete ruthlessness in common.

"You're really getting married?" I asked.

Socrates sighed deeply, like he thought that was a terrible idea. As did I.

Fidelia clearly disagreed. She moved closer to Dex and

slipped her hand around his bicep, resting her head against his shoulder and claiming him, although I, for one, had no interest in stealing him away. "Yes, we plan to wed as soon as all the unpleasantness over Abigail and Laci's deaths . . . and yours . . . is just a memory."

I stepped back at the blunt reminder of my looming fate and turned to Dexter. "Why did you kill Abigail? Why not just break up with her? I know she was domineering, but you could've just walked away."

There was a long pause, during which Dex and Fidelia shared meaningful looks I didn't understand. They seemed to be silently debating some point, Dex shaking his head and Fidelia starting to grin again.

I got the sense that Fidelia had won when she confided, with what I considered misplaced pride, "*I* killed Abigail."

My eyes must've been *huge*, and Socrates actually barked. Not one of his measured, almost human *woofs*, but a loud, doggy bark of surprise. After all, Fidelia had once tried to rob me at gunpoint—only she'd used a carrot, and her hand had shaken so much that she'd had trouble drinking the hot chocolate I'd offered her before she'd broken down and shared all of her perceived inadequacies with me. And there had been many.

I shook my head, trying to understand. "What the . . . ?"

"Dexter and Abigail were supposed to leave together in the wee hours of the night, before the wedding scam," Fidelia began to explain. "I had to do something."

I took an inadvertent step forward, my hands balling into fists. Not that I would've punched her. But I did feel doubly betrayed. "You *knew* about the swindle?"

Fidelia nodded vigorously, like she was proud of keeping that secret, too. "Yes! It was so funny to watch you all fretting about the horrible wedding Abigail was planning, all the while knowing it wasn't even going to happen."

I blinked at her, suddenly wondering why, and for how

long, she'd despised me, Moxie and Piper. There must have been signs I'd overlooked as I'd tried to befriend her and help her fulfill her dream of becoming an accountant.

"Anyhow," Fidelia continued, "Abigail had no idea that Dex and I had fallen in love. The plan was for him to get her and the money out of the country—"

"To the Caribbean, right?" I guessed, relaxing my fingers when Dex pointed the knife at me. A subtle warning gesture. I wiped my sweating hands on my shorts, which were finally drying in the warm, stuffy room. "I saw the brochures on Abigail's desk."

Fidelia's expression soured. "Yes. Unfortunately, the destination had to be romantic."

I suddenly remembered the big diamond ring I'd seen on Abigail's hand, sticking out from under the sodden flag. I looked at Dex. "You were going to marry *her*."

Dex opened his mouth, but Fidelia jumped in. "No!" Her protest was loud. "That wasn't going to happen. He was going to get hold of Abigail's financial information—account numbers, that type of thing—before it ever got that far. Then he would clean her out, taking everything, including the ring *I* would wear, and come back to me." She smiled at Dexter. "We'd start over, with Dex running the bridal shop and his new wedding-planning business, and me keeping the books."

"You really mucked up that plan, didn't you, Fi?" Dex grumbled under his breath, picking at his nails again. He looked his real age, for a change. Younger and less polished. "Cost us a ton of money. We never even got the ring back."

Apparently, not all was perfect in their homicidal little love affair. And, while Fidelia might've added some color to her clothes and hair, and murder to her brief résumé, deep down, she was still the same insecure young woman she'd always been.

"You didn't think he'd come back, did you?" I asked,

thinking that she would've been right. Whatever plans they'd hatched in the heat of the moment in Sylvan Creek would've dried up in the heat of the tropics, and Dexter Shipley would've just disappeared.

Under different circumstances, I would've sympathized with Fidelia. I certainly knew how difficult it was to let the love of one's life travel far away, with no guarantee of return—and I was fairly secure, unlike Fidelia, who clutched Dex more tightly, as if she needed to hold on to him for dear life even then. By the pale moonlight streaming through the windows, I saw her knuckles grow white around the dark fabric of his suit.

"Of course I knew Dexter would come back," she insisted. Her chin jutted, which only convinced me more that she was lying to me and fooling herself. "I just couldn't take the thought of Abigail even *believing* Dex was hers for one more day, let alone a few weeks or months. When he dropped me off at my apartment—"

I snapped my fingers, causing Socrates' ears to twitch. Then I pointed at Dex, who was pulling away from his girlfriend. "You didn't escort Roger's mother, or mine, to a car during the storm, did you? You had your arm around Fidelia."

Dex didn't try to answer, so Fidelia again responded for him, puffing out her chest. "Yes, of course, Dex took care of *me*. And when he drove me home, with plans to return to his own apartment to get a few final things for his trip, I made up my mind that Abigail's get-rich-quick scheme wasn't working for *me*. That love was more important than money."

Dex had a doubtful expression on his face, but Fidelia didn't notice. She was too enthralled with her own story.

"I went back to Artful Engagements and confronted Abigail in her office, telling her that she could carry out her swindle, but without Dex, because he was with me."

I swallowed thickly, knowing where the story was headed. I asked anyhow, if only to stall for time. "So, what happened?"

Fidelia lost a bit of her newfound bravado. "That old witch laughed at me and said that, even if I *was* younger, Dexter would never leave her for a 'schlump' like me."

"Fi, you're not . . ."

Dexter made a weak attempt to shore up his girlfriend's bruised ego, but to no avail. Fidelia spoke right over him, bitterness in her rising voice. "That's what she called me." The room was dim, but I saw spots of color on her cheeks, and her fists clenched, too. "A 'schlump.'"

If Abigail Sinclair had still been alive, I would've strongly cautioned her against calling people "trashy" and "schlumpy" in the future. Especially damaged young women. But it was too late. One of those words had already come back to bite Abigail, and hard.

"Then she had the nerve to walk away from me," Fidelia added. "She told me she was going to the garden to cool off and that I should let myself out when I was done being a 'ridiculous child' with 'pipe dreams' of romance." Fidelia spoke more angrily, and her hands shook when she gestured to Dexter, who drew back. "Abigail acted like I'd made up our whole relationship! Like it was just in my imagination!"

"Fi, you know that's not true."

Dexter sounded sincere. Almost hurt. But who knew what to believe from a scamming, cheating, murderous wedding planner?

I kept thinking he had to be with Fidelia for the same wrong reasons he'd been with Abigail. Yet, to my knowledge, Fidelia couldn't offer Dexter Shipley anything but love. She was a part-time accountant with student loans. And if he thought she was heir to her father Davis Tutweiler's fortune, he was mistaken. The artist whose paintings had sold for upward of a half-million dollars had left his daughter nothing.

Perhaps they really were in what passed for love between two heartless people.

"I take it you followed Abigail to the garden," I said, breaking an uncomfortable silence, during which I'd seen Dex and Fidelia silently communicating again. From the way Fidelia's gaze had slid to the knife, I was fairly certain they were asking each other if it was time to wrap up the discussion, so I tried to keep us talking. "Where did you get the garter?"

"From a basket in her office," Fidelia said, confirming my suspicion. "I started looking for something, anything I could use to kill her. I saw the baskets and rooted around until my hand hit the first thing I thought might be useful."

I cleared my throat. "And . . ."

"Do we really need to hear this?" Dexter sounded whiny, and Fidelia ignored him.

She'd done one, maybe two, bold things in her life, and she wanted to brag about her first intrepid act.

"I ran out to the garden, and I found Abigail by the fountain." Fidelia's eyes gleamed. "She couldn't believe I'd had the nerve to follow her, and she didn't even look scared when I got close—until I whipped the garter, which I'd twisted around my hands, around her throat and pushed her down into the water." Fidelia laughed, a short, mocking sound. "She had to wear those stupid stilettos all the time. I barely shoved her. And the rest was so easy!"

I didn't know if she meant physically or morally easy. I wasn't sure I wanted to know.

Socrates seemed to think it was the latter. Backing up next to me, away from the phone, which was useless, he growled, a low, deep rumble in his chest.

"Why did you give Piper the garter as a *gift*?" I asked. "Why not just burn it? Or bury it?"

Fidelia smiled again, smugly. "I thought maybe I'd frame Moxie Bloom, or, at the very least, muddy the trail of clues."

I must've looked confused, because Fidelia explained, "Moxie had mentioned shopping at the Gilded Lily one time when we were talking about possible wedding gifts for Piper. I had shopped there, too, buying some candles for my apartment and my *friends* at Oh, Beans."

I recalled the strange smell in Fidelia's home. The scent hadn't come from outside, where kids were lighting off fireworks. It had been Gunpowder and Sky.

"I stopped in the shop when Dex and I had a romantic night at the Walnut Mountain Inn," Fidelia added, reaching out to stroke Dexter's arm.

The gesture made me shudder. Dex didn't look too happy, either. I was starting to wonder if the bloom might be fading off the rose, at least for him.

"I stuck the garter into a silver bag, stamped from the store," Fidelia continued. "Then I dropped it off at the Sodgrass Club, with a bunch of other gifts that had been left in all the chaos."

Talk about bold acts. "Weren't you afraid you'd be noticed or remembered, either at the shop or the club?"

Fidelia's expression iced over. "I'm not memorable like you—or Moxie, whom I knew the Gilded Lily's shopkeeper would recall. Who has blue hair?"

I didn't say "lots of people," because it wouldn't have been helpful.

"No one ever notices me," Fidelia added, her eyes glittering again. "It's normally a curse. But it can be a blessing, too. Unlike you, I don't cause a stir every time I enter a room."

I was starting to understand the root of Fidelia's anger, toward me and Moxie, at least. She was jealous of the fact that people tended to notice us—if sometimes for all the wrong reasons, at least in my case. And she wasn't being fair. I would've gladly let Fidelia have my share of several recent spotlights. I'd begged her to play the role of the Ghost of Christmas Future in a performance that had drawn a lot of unwanted attention to me. And she could've rowed the boat at All Paws on Deck, too, if she'd wanted to make a literal splash.

If I hadn't been afraid to anger her more, I would've argued those points. Instead, I asked, "Why did you stuff poor Ms. Peebles into a suitcase?" I addressed not Dex, but Fidelia. "Because I know *you* returned to the scene of the crime. Not Dexter."

It was my turn to shock Fidelia. Her gaze darted between me and Dexter, who shrugged. I sensed that he was starting to see the whole chain of events more clearly as Fidelia laid them out and was realizing that, together, they'd made quite a mess. Fidelia, who didn't seem to grasp that, turned back to me. "How did you know that?"

"I actually first suspected you because of Ms. Peebles," I told her. "But I couldn't believe it was true."

"I don't understand . . ."

"She's a very friendly cat, but she wouldn't come out of her carrier at your house. And then she scratched you, which she's never done to me in all the times I've pulled her from sticky situations. I knew you must've done something to her to make her fear you. I just couldn't accept it." I hesitated, then admitted, "To be honest, I initially thought Brother Alf Sievers, who had his own issues with Abigail, was the killer. But he has a cat who follows him everywhere. I knew he'd never lock Ms. Peebles in a suitcase."

"Ms. Peebles is a horrible cat!" Fidelia insisted, stamping her foot. "Dex told me he'd left a watch on Abigail's nightstand"—she shot her lover a displeased, jealous look—"but when I returned to grab his things, the watch was gone. I knew that wide-eyed little feline brat had taken it, so I locked her away, to punish her."

Socrates barked again. He didn't like the cat, but he disapproved of cruelty in any form. I, meanwhile, got worried. "You haven't hurt Ms. Peebles, have you?"

Fidelia rolled her eyes. Like Detective Doebler, she was feeling her oats. "Your precious cat is fine. In fact, she served the great purpose of luring you here. I certainly can't destroy her before I tell the police how awful I feel about letting you volunteer to pick up some of her things— only to have you wind up dead."

"Fi, relax." Dexter chided his partner in crime for getting a little too obviously gleeful over their spree.

I spoke to him, realizing there was a slim chance I could convince him to be an ally. "Dex, why didn't you get the suitcase, like you originally told me? Why the lie?"

His gaze, under lowered lids, cut to Fidelia, and to my surprise, he answered me. "*I* wasn't going back to the mansion. Fidelia was the one who changed the whole plan, without my knowledge. It was her mess to clean up." His smile was forced. "Wasn't it, sweetie?"

I looked down at Socrates, and I knew he was thinking the same thing as me. Dex *wasn't* really loyal to Fidelia. And he might not have a taste for homicide. It was one thing to be part of a scam, and another to throttle someone.

Or maybe I was wrong, because I suddenly remembered Laci Chalmers, and one final piece of the puzzle fell into place. A piece that made my heart sink.

"You killed Laci, didn't you, Dex?" I asked, wanting to know the truth. I was also buying more time, now that I was starting to formulate a strategy. "Fidelia knew—from me—that there was a good chance Laci would be alone at the lake, if only during a brief window of time, and she contacted you the minute I left her apartment, telling you to hurry there and strangle her."

Some of the color drained from Dex's face, and I knew I'd been right. He didn't relish taking lives, like Fidelia apparently did. But that didn't mean he wouldn't do the deed, under duress.

"Fi thought Laci had pictures of us from the party and was just waiting to use them against us," he said, tapping the knife harder against his palm. "I had no choice but to kill her and take her camera. I was in too deep by then."

"Dex, sweetheart." Fidelia finally noticed that her man was getting agitated. She turned to him and rubbed his arm again. He once more recoiled. "We just need to take care of Daphne. Then *we'll* leave the country. It's all going to turn out okay."

Socrates and I were running out of time, and I dared to take a few steps closer to my phone. Socrates stayed by my side. Then I asked the most impertinent question of the night.

"Fidelia, how can you and Dex run away to a foreign country? He's a junior wedding planner whose little money, I presume, is tied up in a business he can't liquidate overnight. At least, not without raising suspicion. And you're a penniless—no offense—part-time accountant!"

"That's not true, Daphne." Fidelia glared at me with disbelief. She knew I was exposing her as a fraud, and it seemed that she'd somehow expected me to cover for her, right before she did me in. "You're lying!" She turned to Dexter. "You know I have money! My inheritance—"

"Is never coming," I interrupted, addressing Dex. "No matter what she told you about her father's millions being tied up in some legal battle that's nearly over, or a trust fund she's about to get control of . . . It's not true. *You've* been swindled."

Fidelia couldn't even deny it. "Dex," she moaned, clutching at him desperately, while he again backed away, twisting sideways to block her advances. "I can explain . . ."

It probably should've felt good to bring both of their lying, cheating worlds crumbling down, but it didn't at all.

I felt sick as Dex brandished the knife not at me, but at Fidelia, losing his movie-star cool entirely and screaming, "You! You've ruined a perfectly good plan that could've made me a rich man living on a tropical island. Instead, you've dragged me into *two* homicides—and you don't even have any money?"

It was Socrates' and my only chance. While Fidelia shrieked in reply, cursing Dexter, I bent to grab my phone, and Socrates and I both darted out of the room, shoving past the bickering couple, who immediately realized their mistake and again turned on us.

But they had lost their wits and stumbled against each other, giving me and a surprisingly quick basset hound the chance to tear down the hallway, bound down the steps and crash out the front door into the night.

My plan had been to jump into the VW, and I'd thought our chances of making it to safety were still pretty slim, given that I had to hoist a low-slung dog into his seat, even as I could hear yelling and footsteps right behind us.

Yet all at once, I quit running, and Socrates stopped short, too, because, just as Fidelia and Dex stumbled through the front door, finally united again in purpose, two squad cars that were rolling quickly down the lane, along with some unmarked vehicles, finally switched on their red dome lights and blared their sirens, lighting up the night like . . . well, the Fourth of July.

I'd never seen a more welcome parade.

Chapter 46

"You really cut it close this time," I told Jonathan Black, who was leaning against his truck. I was also resting against the pickup—and Jonathan. We were alone under a starry sky at Artful Engagements, after Detective Doebler and some uniformed officers had handcuffed and led away Fidelia and Dexter, who'd made a brief and embarrassing attempt to run off into the night on foot. Socrates had been so mortified on their behalf that he'd already climbed into the van, wiping his paws of the dysfunctional couple for good. Shifting, I looked up at Jonathan. "It was getting pretty dicey!"

"You should not be joking about that," he warned me, facing me, too, and crossing his arms. "If it hadn't been for your phone and your mother . . ."

I frowned, confused. I didn't understand how my phone had come into play, but I was more baffled by my mother's involvement in the evening's events. "What did Mom have to do with your arrival in the nick of time?"

Jonathan's eyes were dark with continued concern. "When I arrived back in town and couldn't find you or Piper, and neither of you answered your phones—"

"Piper's on her honeymoon," I interrupted. "She and Roger eloped."

Jonathan drew back, surprised. "Really?"

"Yes," I confirmed, smiling. "They're in St. Thomas. Piper sent some pictures of them both looking deliriously happy. Then she told me she'd be out of contact for at least a week."

Although that news meant Jonathan had fixed up a chapel for nothing, he grinned, too. "Good for them."

I didn't want to ruin the lighter mood, but he needed to finish explaining why he was even there. "So, getting back to my mother?"

His smile faded. "When I failed to contact you or Piper, I got a little worried, knowing that you were in the midst of a murder investigation." I opened my mouth, and he said, "Let's not pretend otherwise." I nodded agreement, and he continued telling his tale. "So I called Moxie, who said you'd been in a shipwreck." Jonathan looked me up and down. "Which was apparently true."

"Hey—"

Jonathan spoke over my second, louder protest, which still would've been weak. I was a mess.

"Since it's sometimes difficult to get clear information from Moxie Bloom"—he raised a hand—"charming as her colloquialisms are, I called someone who always gives me the story straight, even if we don't always agree on real estate."

"Mom."

"Yes. And she mentioned that you had planned to stop by Artful Engagements on your way home after, and I quote, 'offering a worthy tribute to the wonderful and underappreciated humor of *McHale's Navy*.' Whatever that means."

My heart felt warm, and I rested my hand on my finally dry shirt. "Mom said that?"

Jonathan arched an eyebrow. "Could I make it up?"

He really couldn't.

"I raced here because, as I made my way back from California, I kept piecing together the clues in Abigail Sinclair's murder," he continued. "I *thought* the killer had to be one of the three people who stayed the latest after the rehearsal dinner, and I was leaning toward Shipley. When I heard you had gone to a place where he might be gathering his things or erasing clues, I was afraid you might encounter him. And I assumed you'd reached the same conclusion as me, meaning that meeting wouldn't go well."

"I wish I could take that much credit," I said. "But, to be honest, I couldn't believe the clues that pointed to Fidelia, and I didn't so much solve the crime as get lured here as a potential victim." I paused to think for a moment, then asked, "So, what made you decide to call in reinforcements? That seems a little premature, based on what little information you had."

"I didn't do that," he said. "The uniformed officers were responding to a 911 call from your phone, which they traced to here. When they realized the request for help came from Artful Engagements, they contacted Doebler, too . . . What is wrong?"

Jonathan asked that question because my jaw had dropped to the ground. "That can't really be possible."

"What?"

"I tapped the panic button icon on my phone before I slid it across the carpet, toward Socrates. But I didn't get to tap again, actually placing the call. I was afraid Dexter would notice."

Jonathan and I both looked at the van, where Socrates was waiting patiently. Jonathan spoke first. "You don't really think . . . Could a paw even . . . ?"

"I have no idea," I admitted, nevertheless thinking someone had earned an extra treat that night. "Maybe *Socrates* should go to the police academy!"

I was trying to make light of what had been a bad situation, but Jonathan didn't laugh. He grew intensely serious and took my hands in his.

I searched his face. "What?"

"Daphne . . ."

I had finally reached a point where I could read the once-unknowable Jonathan Black like a book, and I swallowed thickly. "Just say it."

"I need you to be more careful, moving forward."

My heart felt like a chunk of lead, and I released his hands. "Why would you say that—beyond the usual reasons?"

He took a deep breath, then said, "Because, as it turns out, I won't always be here to save the day."

Chapter 47

"This is the best wedding reception I've ever attended where the bride and groom didn't even bother to show up," Moxie said, as if she attended similar events all the time. She clasped her hands, gazing around the barn, which was full of Piper's and my friends and family, and, of course, a lot of canines, including Artie, Axis, Tiny Tim, Socrates and Snowdrop, who were all mingling like the humans. "It's just smashing!"

The party did seem to be going well. The night was balmy, under a full moon that bathed the field of daisies in a wash of gentle light. More flowers overflowed from the bed of the antique truck, which was, as predicted, a popular spot for photos. And the barn's interior glowed softly with light from the chandeliers and hundreds of votives, which were tucked on the rafters, the windowsills and the long farmhouse tables, where guests were gathered, enjoying conversation and Daisy Carpenter's amazing food, which was drawing rave reviews, as was the decor.

I only had one complaint, related to Elyse's decision to hang the awful painting I'd created at the Owl & Crescent right above the buffet tables. But it was an honest mistake. Elyse had thought my canvas, which she'd found discarded in the barn, was some sort of quaint folk piece by "someone with raw, or perhaps, intriguingly, no talent," as she'd put it, before I'd claimed the work as my own. She'd still insisted upon displaying the blobby basset hound, promising me that guests would find the mysterious work "compelling." And, as usual, Elyse's sense of style was dead-on. I'd already received two offers to buy the painting from people who said they couldn't seem to look away from it.

"Daisy and Elyse did an amazing job," I agreed with Moxie, searching the crowd until I found the woman who was responsible for the ambience. Flanked by her grey-hounds, Elyse stood near the open barn door, talking with Tom and Tessie Flinchbaugh and Gabriel Graham, who had his arm around his gorgeous girlfriend.

They were a striking couple, and I was happy for them, if slightly miffed at Gabriel for running a photo of me slogging out of Lake Wallapawakee next to a story with the headline, *Local Pet Sitter Torpedoes Beloved Event.*

I turned back to Moxie, who had baked a cake—except it wasn't the multitiered confection I'd seen in her sketch-book. The simple but lovely chocolate dessert had only one layer and an appropriately basic border of flowers.

"How did you know not to make the real cake?" I asked my best friend, who'd washed the blue dye out of her hair. Her spiky locks were barn red, the perfect complement to a vintage gingham dress she'd altered to be formfitting, a playful balance between the rustic theme and an upscale cocktail party. "Did Piper tell *you* she was going to elope? Because I was getting really worried when you kept putting off baking."

Moxie's eyes sparkled. "Piper didn't say a thing. I just knew, from the moment I drew it, that the cake was meant for another couple." She *was* a bit psychic. "And there's not a huge hurry to bake it. There's still some time. Although, not *too* long."

"Is it for you and Mike?" I asked, thinking it would be strange for Moxie to bake her own wedding cake for her inevitable union with the man who was threading his way through the crowd, a big smile lighting up his face when he spotted the woman he'd loved since high school.

Moxie grinned, too, as Mike took her hand, wordlessly pulling her toward the makeshift dance floor. "No, silly," she told me, over her shoulder. "The cake is for you and Jonathan!"

I didn't have a chance to respond before she was out of earshot, and I wouldn't have ruined the party, anyway, by telling her that Jonathan and I would not be getting married.

I'd insisted, the previous night, that he take the job in California, refusing to even listen to his attempt to explain how maybe we could have the best of both worlds.

The last thing I wanted was to become desperately clingy, like Fidelia Tutweiler, and spend my days worrying about whether Jonathan was happy with a long-distance relationship that I knew in my heart wouldn't work for me.

In the end, I'd pushed him firmly away, telling him that I would prefer to end our relationship while we still loved each other, rather than watch it fizzle away slowly across three thousand miles until it sadly flickered out in an awkward Skype or phone call.

Standing alone in the crowd, I watched as Mike folded Moxie against himself, both of them swaying to a soft ballad sung by none other than *Dorinda Berendt*, who had returned to Sylvan Creek, mistakenly thinking the wedding was still on.

"She has a lovely voice, doesn't she?" my mother asked, joining me and handing me one of the signature Winding Hill Sunset cocktails Daisy had created for the evening.

To my surprise, Mom was sipping the tasty mix of orange juice, triple sec and peach schnapps. It was unlike her to drink anything but wine, let alone serve me—or compliment her once-best friend, now rival's rebellious child, who would soon return to Nashville, where she really was determined to make her mark.

"What's going on?" I asked Mom, who *looked* the same. She wore a cream-colored sheath dress that bared her still remarkably toned arms, with a silk scarf in a water-colored pastel floral pattern, an Impressionistic echo of the truck full of summer blooms that was parked outside. "Why are you handing me beverages and being nice about Dorinda? Because I know you're not happy with Beverly."

I searched the barn again and found Roger's mother in a small group of people I didn't recognize. I assumed they were part of the Berendt family. And from the way they were huddled together, I wouldn't have been surprised if they were discussing the sudden disappearance of Brother Alf Sievers and the imminent collapse of Graystone Arches Gateway to Eternity, where I needed to go ASAP and buy two sourdough starters before they were all gone. In retrospect, it probably was worth the price, and Moxie would appreciate the gift tin. I looked askance at Mom again.

"Knowing that Bev is handling the sale of Abigail Sinclair's mansion, I'd be surprised if you could think of something good to say about *Roger* right now."

"Daphne, Daphne, Daphne . . ." Mom shook her head at my ignorance, and I was relieved that she was acting normally again. "I have no issues with the Berendt family. Not the singer. Not the young man who stole your sister away." In spite of her claims to the contrary, she might've had a few issues with the elopement. "And certainly not with Beverly, who is free to go after any listing she wants."

I did not believe a word of that last statement. "Seriously, Mom? You expect me to believe that you have no problem with Beverly encroaching on your real estate territory?"

The corners of my mother's mouth lifted upward to an absurd degree, by her standards, and she got a sly look in her eyes. "Let's just say that Brother Alf Sievers is uncomfortable placing the sale of Great Walnut Mountain and the castle atop it into the hands of a sister who is currently very displeased with him."

I nearly dropped my cocktail. "*You're* going to sell an entire mountain?"

Mom sipped her drink, her dark eyes growing dreamy, an expression I'd never seen before. "I've had three calls from resort operators already," she said, smacking her lips. "And the property's not even on the market yet."

My mother was going to make a fortune off the commission, and, although I wasn't into material goods, I felt I had to congratulate her. I clinked our glasses. "Good for you."

"And good for you, not getting killed," Mom noted. "I suppose we should toast that, too. Although, I believe that I more than once tried to warn you that your accountant was not only unqualified, but sketchy."

I couldn't recall my mother ever using those exact words, but it would've made sense. She didn't trust anyone who wasn't born and bred in Sylvan Creek. And she was right about Fidelia's lack of qualifications. Yet, in spite of all that had happened, I didn't regret trying to help a fellow human being.

"Well, Fidelia and Dexter will likely be going away for a long time," I told Mom. "I think there's a pretty airtight case against them. And even if there wasn't, the way they turned on each other, I think they'll take each other down."

"Love is so messy," my mother said with an uncharacteristic sigh.

I gave her another funny look. "Is there something going on? Am I missing something here?"

Mom's hand, holding her drink, jerked, and some of her Winding Hill Sunset sloshed out of her glass. "I don't know what you're talking about, Daphne," she said, using her other hand to adjust the sharp edge of her already flawless bob. "What in the world would be 'going on'?"

She was hiding something. But I wouldn't get the truth right then, because someone else joined us, interrupting the conversation by asking us both a two-word question that wouldn't have made sense in most other contexts.

"Potato salad?"

Chapter 48

"I can't thank you enough for watching Snowdrop, and for solving Abigail and Laci's murders," Daisy Carpenter said, smiling first at me, then at the poodle, who, along with Socrates, had joined us outside the barn for a brief break from the party. The air was cooler and rich with the scent of flowers. "I was honestly starting to worry that I would be tried for homicide—a fear that grew worse when the truth about my argument with Laci came to light."

I cringed, nearly spilling what was left of the potato salad she'd offered me and Mom. "I'm sorry about that. I didn't mean for Detective Doebler to overhear. But once he had . . ."

"You had to tell the truth," Daisy agreed. "It just looked really bad for me. In a Pickle probably would've closed as quickly as it had opened if the story about the food poisoning got out, as it likely will someday. Hopefully after I've proven myself. In the meantime, your faith in me means a lot—whether it's in my character, or in my ability to succeed as a chef."

Actually, I had doubted Daisy at times when it came to murder, a fact I didn't intend to share. And, as I'd told

Jonathan, I didn't exactly solve the crimes, although I'd hoped to do that on Daisy's behalf.

"I can't take credit for solving anything," I admitted again, licking my fork to get the last bit of the salad, which was delicious. I was pretty sure I tasted dill in the mayonnaise, which would make sense, since Daisy's specialty was pickles. She was keeping the recipe a secret, though, even from me. I scraped the fork around the empty bowl one more time, telling Daisy, "And, to be honest, Snowdrop was the one who had full faith in you. I, in turn, trusted her instincts."

Daisy was okay with that. She beamed at the poodle, who was sitting next to Socrates, leaning against the basset's sturdy, trustworthy shoulder. I was increasingly convinced that he'd pressed his paw—or more likely nose—to my phone's screen, activating the panic button. The smear of doggy snot on the device seemed to be proof.

"I don't suppose you want an accident-prone, sometimes thieving cat, do you?" I ventured. "Ms. Peebles is up for adoption."

My offer was half-hearted. I had pretty much accepted that the wide-eyed feline would be part of an increasingly crowded tiny house. Tinkleston had tried to act like he didn't care when Ms. Peebles had walked back through the door, but when I'd left for the party, the surly black Persian and the clueless tan cat had been curled up together in the windowsill herb garden.

I was sort of relieved when Daisy said, "I'm sorry, Daphne. I'm working such long hours at In a Pickle. I barely have time for Snowdrop." She crossed her fingers. "And I think I'll be even busier after this event. The food seems to be a hit."

She'd given me no indication that she still planned to leave town, but I had to ask, on Socrates' behalf, "So, does all this mean you're staying in Sylvan Creek?"

Daisy smiled, and I was glad to see that her eyes were bright again, and her skin was rosy. "Yes. For now Snowdrop and I plan to stay put."

That was great news, and I was happy for both Daisy and the dogs, who seemed to understand. They were nudging each other, both their eyes alight, and I did my best not to think about another person who wouldn't be sticking around, only to fail miserably when my phone buzzed in my back pocket. Unlike Moxie, I hadn't dressed up for the shindig. Somehow, I just hadn't had the energy, and had gone with some nice jeans and a favorite shirt from a little consignment shop in France.

The phone buzzed again, and Daisy lightly touched my arm. "Take that. I need to get back to the buffet."

"Wait . . ." I didn't want her to leave, because if she did, I'd have no choice but to deal with the incoming text. However, Daisy was walking off, and against my better judgment, I checked the screen, which confirmed what I'd already known from the special tone I'd set. A series of notes I hadn't expected to hear again. At least, not for a long time.

I wasn't sure I even *wanted* to hear from Jonathan. Not until some time had passed. Yet, I couldn't help but be intrigued by his message, which said, *I'll be at Crooked Creek Lane for another hour, if you want to see me one more time.*

I read that message three times—then took a deep, deep breath and, with tremendous resolve, and more than a little regret, put the phone away.

Chapter 49

"I shouldn't be doing this," I told Socrates and Snowdrop, who bounced along next to me as we tore down Crooked Creek Lane, way too fast. The old VW was probably going to shake apart, but I had to keep my foot on the gas, because I feared we were already too late. More than an hour had passed while I'd debated, again and again, whether to go see Jonathan.

"He's not going to be here," I told the dogs, both of whom barked several times in raucous reply. Even Socrates seemed excited by the adventure. In fact, he'd kept following me around the party, nudging my leg and making a nuisance of himself until I'd broken down and piled him and Snowdrop into the VW for moral support. "Jonathan is long gone by now."

I said that so I wouldn't be disappointed when we emerged from the copse of trees to discover that the chapel was deserted.

Only that wasn't the case, and I suffered a whole mix of conflicting emotions when I saw Jonathan's truck parked near the church, where lights glowed dimly inside. All the scaffolding was gone, and in the moonlight, I could tell that the place was finished. The steeple gleamed bright white, and the flower boxes were filled with blossoms. The gazebo at the edge of the pond was also painted and strung with lights and lanterns that flickered with real candles. It seemed as though someone else, aside from Dorinda, hadn't realized that the wedding had been canceled.

Hopping from the van, I released the dogs with hands that shook for reasons I wasn't even sure I understood. I couldn't sort out my own feelings, which ranged from excitement to self-reproach to frustration and a frighteningly powerful *need* to see Jonathan Black, all of which served to make my heart stop in my chest when he stepped up behind me and clasped his hand on my shoulder.

I turned around, hating how happy I was to see him, and all I could stammer out was, "I . . . I thought you'd be gone."

He shook his head, not believing me. "I'm pretty sure you knew, by now, that I would've waited all night."

I didn't know what to say, and Jonathan took advantage of my rare silence, seizing an opportunity I hadn't given him the evening before, when I'd spoken over him, again and again, in an attempt to convince him that I was right about our futures, and how we'd be happiest apart, in the long run.

"Daphne Templeton," he said, taking my hand and leading me toward the pond, "now that you're not talking, for a change, will you please *listen* to me, for once?"

"I told you, I can't do a long-distance relationship," I told Jonathan, who sat next to me in the gazebo, our faces lit by the flickering candles. The dogs were taking a stroll around the pond, giving us some space. "I just . . ."

"You're talking again," he said, grinning, while I kind of wanted to cry. "You promised I could speak."

"I didn't really do that," I said, wiping one hand under

my eyes. Maybe I was crying, but laughing, too. "I just said I'd listen. There was no pinkie swear."

Jonathan crooked his finger. "Maybe there should be."

I wrapped my finger around his, and we shook pinkies. "Fine."

He released my hand and edged away from me, if only so I could see his eyes when he leaned forward. "If you'd listened last night, I would've told you that we *can* make this work. Because I've struck a deal with the Navy."

I forgot that I wasn't supposed to talk. "What kind of deal?"

"They want me in San Diego full-time."

I already knew that, and I had to bite my tongue so I wouldn't blurt that he hadn't exactly found a solution. And it was a good thing I kept quiet, because maybe he had.

"But they're willing to take me on as a consultant," he explained. "A freelance contractor. It wasn't their first choice, but they're willing to compromise, based upon my experience as a SEAL and an investigator, which they consider a valuable combination."

I tried to keep my heart still and dared to speak again, in spite of my promise, which I was keeping reasonably well. "And you'd be based . . . ?"

"Here. In Sylvan Creek."

My heart started pounding, and Jonathan must've seen my growing excitement. He squeezed my hand, urging me not to get ahead of myself. "There are a few downsides."

Of course there were. Clamping down on my tongue again, I let him explain them.

"If I'm a contractor, I won't just work at one base," he said. "I'll be expected to travel around the world. You'd have to accept that I would be gone at times. Maybe for extended periods. Although I've been assured that the San Diego stint was unusual. I'd more likely travel for weeks, as opposed to months."

"But you'd return here?"

He nodded. "Yes. Of course. To you."

The fact that he said he'd come back to me, not the town, or his home, was enough for me, but Jonathan continued explaining, laying out everything, so I'd have all the facts.

"The work wouldn't be steady. At least, not at first. But I think, between your businesses and my income from investing in properties, plus my trust fund—which I only use for investment—we should be fine."

I'd figured out that Jonathan came from a wealthy family, but I certainly hadn't known that he had a trust fund, and his admission reminded me of Fidelia's lie to Dexter.

I was glad Jonathan hadn't mentioned the money—though I didn't know why he would have done that before—because we'd both always know that he hadn't bought my love. Not that he could've done that anyway. He was well aware that money wasn't a priority for me.

"You're sure?" I asked. "About all of this?"

He grinned again. "San Diego's not for me. And it's time for me to part ways with Doebler, too. I can't work with a guy who insults dogs."

"I thought that was a one-time thing," I muttered, distracted as I replayed a part of Jonathan's and my conversation, latching onto something that suddenly struck me as odd. "You know, you just kind of combined our finances."

Jonathan leaned back and rubbed his jaw, a bemused gleam in his eyes. "You had to catch that, didn't you, detective?"

"What do you mean?" I studied his handsome face, which was matched by an even more beautiful and generous soul that he no longer hid from me. I wasn't sure how I'd managed to break up with him the night before. Then I shivered, because the night was getting chilly. "Maybe we should go inside to continue this discussion."

Jonathan was always chivalrous, and he surprised me by shaking his head. "No. You're not going back into the chapel until I'm waiting for you at the altar."

I heard what he was saying and understood the implication, and, even as my head reeled, part of my brain flashed back to Moxie's premonition about the cake, and the note Piper had left. The one that followed up on the statement my sister had started to make at the farmhouse when I'd caught her trying to elope.

. . . *you know why Jonathan brought the chapel back to life, right, Daphne? It's where he wants to marry YOU . . .*

"Jonathan?" My voice was breathless. "What are you saying?"

He leaned forward again, staring into my eyes and taking my hands in his. "I'm saying that I want to marry you, Daphne Templeton. That wherever life takes us next, whether it's San Diego or downtown Sylvan Creek for some crazy canine parade, I don't want to go without knowing you're by my side."

I let those words hang in the air for a long time, but not because I was unsure of my answer to his proposal. I just wanted to commit the moment to memory. The way Jonathan was looking at me. The words themselves. The warmth and sounds of the night, and the feel of his strong hands around my fingers.

I was also thinking about how Piper had wanted to marry Roger before he left for an extended period of time. I wanted to make sure I wasn't clinging to Jonathan. But as he held my hands, I understood that the bond wouldn't tie him to me in some desperate way. It was just . . . important. A means of being together when physical distance would keep us apart.

"I want that, too," I finally promised, smiling even as a few tears—the happy kind—slipped down my cheeks.

If I'd had any doubts about whether I'd picked the right guy, and I didn't, they would've been wiped away as Jonathan pulled me to my feet and gently swiped his thumb across my cheeks. Then, by the light of the candles and some summer fireflies, and to the music of the pond's croaking frogs, he drew me close and kissed me in a way that felt different, even better, if that was possible, than before.

Drawing back, Jonathan slipped a ring onto my finger—and the night erupted with overjoyed barks from two dogs who'd joined us at some point. A poodle with a starstruck look in her eyes, and a basset hound who, for the first time I could ever recall, lifted his muzzle and howled, his tail swinging wildly back and forth under the light of a full, and very auspicious, summer moon.

Recipes

Something's Fishy Cat Treats

There was definitely "something fishy" about the *Tiny-tanic*, in a bad way. These treats are a little "fishy" in a good way. By that I mean they contain fish, which your cat will love—and they sneak in some healthy veggies, too. Your favorite feline will definitely be "on board" with these snacks!

> 1 medium-sized carrot, sliced into coins
> 1 small sweet potato, cubed
> 1 can sardines in water

Steam or boil carrots and sweet potato until tender. Drain and place in a food processor.

Drain the sardines and add those, too.

Blitz into a nearly smooth puree.

Form into cat-bite-sized balls and store in your refrigerator for up to three days or freezer for up to three months, if they won't be eaten right away.

Fruity Pupsicles

My go-to summer pet treats tend to be easy to make, since they rely more on the fridge and freezer than the oven. These icy snacks will cool down your favorite pup while offering the healthy benefits of fruit. Socrates loves these treats on days when the mercury rises at Plum Cottage, which is air-conditioned the old-fashioned way—meaning the windows are open!

    2 apples, any sweet variety
    2 bananas
    1 cup strawberries
    2 cups natural coconut water
    1 tablespoon honey

Prepare the fruit by washing, peeling, coring or hulling, as appropriate.

Add everything to a blender or food processor. Process until a smooth puree forms. Add more coconut water if the mixture is too thick; it should be slushy, not like a paste.

Pour into ice cube trays or molds, depending upon how clever you want to get, and freeze. I like to use a paw-shaped silicone mold, but, honestly, Socrates is fine with a plain rectangle. He's not much for flashy presentation. If you want, you can also add "sticks" of your choice, like little pretzels, to make your pupsicles look more like the "real thing."

Store treats in your freezer for up to three months.

Meow Mash-Up Cat Food

Tinkleston and Ms. Peebles mainly eat high-quality cat food from Fetch! pet emporium. Those foods are formu-lated to make sure their dietary needs are met. But every so often, I like to treat them to a home-cooked dinner. If you plan to start feeding your cat a steady diet of homemade food, please check with your vet, who may recommend supplements. Oh, and why do I call it a "mash-up?" Because it brings together chicken and fish, and you literally mash it at the very end!

  1 whole chicken, without hormones or antibiotics
  4 carrots
  2 yellow squash
  2 cups brown rice
  1 hard-boiled egg
  2 ounces clams in juice

Rinse the chicken and get it boiling in a large pot while you chop the vegetables.

Add veggies to the pot and cook everything until the chicken and vegetables are cooked through and tender.

Meanwhile, cook the rice according to package directions. If you have a rice cooker, good for you! This step just got even easier!

Drain the chicken and veggies and let everything cool. When you can handle the chicken, remove the meat from the bone, being careful not to get any bone fragments in the food. (Poultry bones are dangerous for cats.) Discard carcass.

Use a pastry blender to combine the chicken, veggies, rice, hard-boiled egg and clams until the mixture is coarse enough to have a little texture, but fine enough for a cat's tiny palate.

Make sure the food is fully cooled before serving. You can also freeze the mash-up in sandwich or snack bags for up to three months so you have single-serving meals to thaw when you want to treat your furry friend.

Daisy Carpenter's
Secret Potato Salad with Dill

Daisy doesn't normally share this recipe, but since I did help to get her cleared of murder *and* save her restaurant, which was literally "in a pickle," I guess she took pity on me after I kept licking my plate clean at the barn party. She's assured me that I can share the recipe with friends, too. I guess the secret is out!

    3 pounds red potatoes, unpeeled
    3 eggs, hard-boiled and roughly chopped
    1 cup mayonnaise
    ¾ cup sour cream or plain Greek yogurt
    1 tablespoon apple cider vinegar
    1 tablespoon Dijon mustard
    2 tablespoons dried dill weed or 4 tablespoons fresh
dill weed, minced
    1 bunch scallions, chopped, white and green parts
    Salt and pepper to taste

Boil the potatoes until they are just tender. You don't want them to be mushy. When cool enough to handle, cut them into bite-sized chunks.

Mix together the hard-boiled eggs, mayo, sour cream, vinegar, mustard, dill and white part of the scallions. Add the potatoes and toss gently. Season with salt and pepper to taste.

Sprinkle the dish with green scallion tops for a pretty presentation that will wow guests at your next summer picnic or party.

Hint: If you love pickle flavor, skip the apple cider vinegar and add a few spoonfuls of pickle relish. Yum!

Don't miss the next adorable mystery
from the nationally bestselling Bethany Blake!

A Brushstroke With Death
An Owl & Crescent Mystery

Available in November 2019

Read on for a preview . . .

"Oh, goodness!" my friend Astrid Applebee cried, chasing her floppy straw sun hat down the stepping-stone path that led from my cottage to my studio, the Owl & Crescent Art Barn. The bat-like wings of Astrid's unusual poncho flapped as she scooped up the hat, jamming it onto her head and flattening her unruly, dark brown curls. Turning back to me and the third member of our small sorority, Pepper Armbruster, Astrid frowned. "Time to batten down the hatches!"

"It's definitely going to be a wild night," I agreed, hurrying after her and daring a wary peek at the darkening sky. Then I looked down at the path again, being careful not to trip, because I was carrying a basket that held freshly cut flowers, a ceramic rabbit, a flowerpot—and three sharp old garden tools, all props I'd use to create a still-life scene that guests to my upcoming wine-and-painting social could re-create in oils.

Joining Astrid at the studio door, I fumbled with the knob, while the wind, which was rising ahead of a storm, jangled the chimes that hung in my apple trees and rattled the shutters on my cottage. The rooster weather vane atop the pink wooden playhouse where my rescue pig, Mortimer, lived was spinning in wild circles. Finally managing to open the door, I gestured for Astrid to dash inside. "It feels like a tornado's coming!"

"Oh, there's a tornado headed our way," Pepper noted dryly, strolling right past me, too. She appeared completely calm, cool and collected in a pair of white jeans and a sleeveless black top, and the gusts weren't even riffling her perfect, blond bob—probably because she was quietly using her skills as an elemental, a witch tuned in to nature's forces and cycles. I stepped back farther to allow Pepper to pull a red wagon stocked with wine from her family's vineyard, Twin Vines, and food from her inn, the Crooked Chimneys, through the door, which I closed behind us all, shutting out the gale. "We should all brace for a flesh-and-blood cyclone," Pepper added, dragging the wagon toward a mustard-yellow, antique dry sink, where I usually served snacks during parties. "Or should I say, a category six *human hurricane*?"

"I thought hurricanes only went up to five," Astrid noted, shaking out her poncho, which featured elaborate zodiac-inspired designs. I suspected the garment came from the clearance rack at her quirky shop, Astrid's Astral Emporium, located in a narrow purple storefront on the bustling main street of our eclectic, artsy hometown, Zephyr Hollow, Pennsylvania.

Without waiting for instruction, because my friends often helped out with my gatherings, Astrid grabbed a porcelain matchbox holder from a shelf near the door and began to light the many candles I kept tucked throughout the barn. We were all fans of ambience, but, as the studio shook from floor to rafters, I thought the nonelectric light might come in handy.

"Can a storm really be worse than five?" Astrid noted again, striking a match and lighting a sage-scented candle I'd placed on a windowsill. Then she shook out her hand, extinguishing the flame. "And who is this terrible person who's about to blow us away?"

As if on cue, the wind howled angrily, and a petite, sweet gray cat with a white crescent-shaped mark on her chest—one of the inspirations for my studio's name—yowled in protest and jumped up onto the long farmhouse table where I planned to create the still life.

I smiled at the sleepy feline, who didn't like her naps to be interrupted, even by forces of nature. "It's time you woke up for a few minutes, Luna," I reminded her, setting the basket on the table. "You've probably been sleeping all day."

Luna flicked her tail and blinked her yellow eyes, seeming to ask why that might be a bad thing.

Over by the dry sink, where she was arranging a tempting display of treats next to equally inviting bottles of pinot grigio, Pepper grinned a bit wickedly and waggled her fingers, which were heavy with silver rings. "You know I could probably calm this tempest so poor Luna can get her beauty rest."

"Please, no messing with the weather," I begged my friend, smoothing my floral yellow spaghetti-strap blouse back into place. "Put those fingers away!"

Pepper laughed and waved off my concerns, again fluttering her hand. "Oh, I can't really banish a storm."

I wasn't so sure about that. Of me, Astrid and Pepper—the sole members of the world's least organized coven—Pepper was by far the most powerful witch. Female members of her family could trace their interest in magic and divination back to the Mayflower's arrival, and I suspected the Armbrusters' ancestral fortune was tied to the women's special abilities more than to the men's business acumen.

Meanwhile, most of what I, Willow Bellamy, knew about witchcraft came from a tattered family journal that contained a mishmash of recipes for everything from healing herbal teas to less-than-mystical Jell-O salads; handwritten "spells" with margin notes explaining when they had—and often hadn't—worked; and descriptions of rituals that seemed to enjoy roughly the same success rate as the spells, all collected by the last four or five generations of aspiring Bellamy witches.

My grandmother, Anna—quite the brewer of powerful, sometimes misfiring, teas herself—had quietly given me the *Bellamy Book of Spells, Lore & Miscellany* when, at age eighteen, I happened to rest a hand on a painting and found myself accidentally *sucked into the artist's soul*, making me, apparently, a witch of the arts-and-crafts variety, just like Pepper was an elemental.

I could still vividly recall how Grandma Anna, who'd also handed down the genes responsible for my thick, black hair and unusual green eyes, had pulled me aside and said, *"Your mother thinks this is all horse hockey. But, given that you obviously have gifts, I'd take a gander at the stuff in these pages, before you get yourself killed."*

I'd taken that advice and come to embrace a world that my mother, Mayor Celeste Bellamy Dinsmore Crockett Dinsmore Bellamy—who had a winding history of divorce and remarriage—did consider suspect.

In spite of lacking maternal support, I still had a stronger background than Astrid, who came from a family of determinedly mundane accountants, and who seemed to learn most of what she knew about her chosen path— astrological—from questionable Internet sites. However, what Astrid lacked in knowledge and experience, she made up for with clothing and jewelry.

Every so often, Pepper and I had to tactfully let her know that she looked a bit too much like a cartoon version of Merlin. In fact, we'd secretly taken away Astrid's purple velvet pointed hat, the ashes of which would forever rest at the bottom of my backyard firepit, surrounded by a cozy circle of Adirondack chairs that overlooked a bubbling stream called Peddler's Creek.

To quote a questionably wise axiom my Great Aunt Edith had added to the *Book of Bellamy*, *"It's not a crime if it's a favor."*

"Is anyone going to tell me who the hurricane is?" Astrid asked while I began to unpack the basket.

Glancing over, I saw that she was eating one of the watermelon-and-feta skewers Pepper had just arranged on a delicate white platter. Pepper had also supplied bruschetta, topped with basil and heirloom tomatoes from my garden, and Crooked Chimneys' locally famous pasta salad with grilled vegetables. I'd baked mini plum tarts topped with a drizzle of honey, the fruit and nectar gathered from my own trees and beehives. I was probably a borderline garden witch, if there was such a thing as borderline witchcraft.

While thunder rumbled in the distance, Astrid licked her fingers, which were covered in a tangy balsamic reduction. "Should I be worried about more than getting struck by lightning on the way home?"

"I would never let you get struck, Astrid," Pepper promised, pulling the cork from a bottle of wine. I had *no idea* if she was joking. I didn't see a twinkle in her gorgeous blue eyes as she poured each of us a small tumbler full of the award-winning pinot grigio that was adding to the Armbruster fortune. Joining me at the table, where I was arranging the flowers, Pepper slid the wine toward me, then gave Luna a quick scratch behind the ears. Luna tipped her head, practically grinning, while Pepper turned to Astrid, who'd grabbed a tart. "But I can't protect you from Evangeline Fletcher's lightning-sharp tongue tonight."

At the sound of my cantankerous next-door neighbor's name, Luna yowled and ran off. Astrid was also clearly stunned. Her brown eyes grew wide, and she thumped her chest, like she was choking on her bite of tart. "No!"

she cried, when she could finally speak. Her worried gaze darted between me and Pepper. "She's not really coming here, is she?"

All at once, I heard a loud rustle of feathers above us, and I looked up to the exposed beams to discover that the Owl & Crescent's other namesake—a majestic, suitably wise barn owl named Rembrandt—also seemed displeased to learn that our surly neighbor planned to join the gathering, which was sponsored by the Zephyr Hollow Small Business Alliance.

Narrowing his dark, intelligent eyes, Remi rattled his wings again, letting us all know that he'd be keeping an eye on the woman who'd once called a wildlife officer to trap the "pet" I was "illegally keeping" at my place of business.

Given that Rembrandt had lived in the barn before I'd renovated it, and came and went as he pleased, the accusation had, of course, been ridiculous. Just like Evangeline's claim that the *pig who lived in a pink playhouse*, complete with flower boxes, was "livestock," and therefore also suitable for seizure by animal control.

Evangeline had even called the authorities on Luna, insisting that my feline companion was feral because she sometimes napped on top of my potting shed.

And then there were the shadier rumors she'd spread about me . . .

"I can't believe Ms. Fletcher has the nerve to show up here," Astrid said, interrupting my thoughts and puffing her poncho indignantly. "I know she's responsible for that crazy tale about 'blood ceremonies' being held at the Owl & Crescent!"

Slipping into one of the antique ladder-back chairs that ringed the table, Pepper shook her head. "Such a shame that you had to spill red paint all over yourself, Willow. If only it had been blue!"

Astrid's cheeks were pink with outrage on my behalf. "And such a shame that Evangeline was, as always, spying when you went to the cottage to clean up, because that rumor cost you business for a good six months." She gestured to Rembrandt, then to Luna, who sat at the far edge of the table, licking her paws. "I swear, Evangeline Fletcher wants to get rid of all your poor animals and force you to move, too."

I was pretty sure that was the case. While most people in my quirky community—discounting my own mother—embraced the unusual, my neighbor had made it very clear that she wasn't a fan of my lifestyle or my colorful property. I knew from the Zephyr Hollow rumor mill that Evangeline wanted to buy my house herself and paint the pink, yellow and aqua Victorian cottage some dull shade, like brown.

From what I understood, she also hated Mortimer's playhouse and wanted to raze the barn, too. My small colony of bees were another source of aggravation, although they mainly just buzzed around my own gardens—which, if Evangeline ever did succeed in wresting my home away from me, would probably be replaced with the uniform, short grass that surrounded her own, much larger home, known locally as "Fletcher Mansion."

However, I would *never* sell my property, and there was no sense in fretting about things that wouldn't happen, especially before a party.

Taking a deep, calming breath—followed by an equally calming sip of wine—I continued to arrange my small scene, adding a rustic trowel, a hand rake, and an ancient, but wickedly sharp, pair of pruners that I'd used just that morning. Then I looked up at Rembrandt. "No one's going to throw a net over you again," I promised him, turning to Luna. "And no one's sending you to the pound, either, or—heaven forbid—turning poor Mortimer into pork."

Glancing out one of the barn's many windows, I saw that the black-and-white pig in question had ventured outside of his house, which was like a miniature version of my cottage. He was trotting around his enclosure, his snout raised as he watched the weather vane spin in the wind. I made a mental note to bring him inside the barn if the storm got too bad. Then I addressed my friends. "We *humans* also need to remember that, as a member of the Small Business Alliance, Evangeline has every right to join this gathering. She *does* own one of Zephyr Hollow's most successful restaurants."

Pepper rolled her eyes. "I swear, she gets half her business by leaving fake reviews—both good ones for the Silver Spoon and bad ones for every other place in town— all over the Internet. The Crooked Chimneys has received several *one-star* ratings in the last few months."

Astrid frowned. "Everybody knows your inn has the best, not to mention most romantic, restaurant around, and that there are lots of other good spots in Zephyr Hollow, too."

"*Locals* might know that," Pepper pointed out. "But tourists go by what they read online. And, I swear, lately somebody has been planting nasty reviews everywhere. Linh Tran, from the Typhoon, has noticed it, too. Her business is way down at the height of the tourist season. She only has twelve reservations for the night of the Gallery Walk."

I'd been adjusting the garden tools one last time, but I paused, surprised by that news.

"That is worrisome," I agreed as the barn creaked loudly, shaken again by the wind. The ten paintings I'd created for Zephyr Hollow's most popular summer event rattled against the wall, and for a moment, I thought one of them was about to crash to the floor.

The watercolor, depicting a tall, dark-haired man walking

a boxer-like dog down Main Street, had its own energy and always seemed restless to me. Thankfully, the piece, which I planned to price at three hundred dollars, stayed put and wouldn't need an expensive new frame before its sale. At least, I hoped the scene would find a buyer. I counted on selling all my works, which would be displayed at a shop called the Well-Dressed Wall, to boost my income, and I knew local restaurant owners factored the weekend's profits into their yearly budgets, too.

"Typhoon should be *over*booked by now," I added, growing more concerned for the owner, who was a friend. "Linh should be turning people away."

Pepper smiled, but wryly. "I hear the Silver Spoon, which is averaging *five stars* on every review site, is packing them in."

Astrid wandered over to the sideboard, where she helped herself to another tart. "Well, at least you don't have to worry, Pepper," she noted, taking a bite and talking through the crumbs. "I'm sure the Crooked Chimneys is booked solid, right?"

"Our dinner reservations are down a bit, but, yes, our rooms are filled," Pepper said, rising. Ever the hostess, even at my establishment, she moved about the studio, plugging in the fairy lights that were strung along the shiplap walls and draped from the rafters. The soft glow, like fireflies, made the always-festive space, which was cluttered with painted antique furniture, vintage Turkish rugs and little knickknacks I collected at the Penny For Your Stuff flea market, even more charming. As Pepper passed by the wall that held my Gallery Walk paintings, she paused, studying the watercolor with the dark-haired man and his dog. Then she turned to me. "Who is *that* guy?"

I shrugged. "Someone from my imagination."

Pepper grinned. "Do you have a spell in your 'book of

miscellany' to bring him to life? You do have some power with art."

"First of all, you can barely see his face," I pointed out, although I also thought there was something undeniably attractive about the man. Then I glanced at the painting and felt a prickle in the pit of my stomach. "And I'm honestly not sure if summoning him from that canvas would be a good idea."

My words sounded more ominous than I'd intended, against the backdrop of thunder that again rumbled in the distance. The light in the barn dimmed, too, as clouds rolled closer, and I wondered, briefly, if Pepper had anticipated the darkness, or if her decision to plug in the lights had been coincidental. Then, still feeling uneasy, I stepped back from the table and pulled a folded piece of paper from the back pocket of my jeans.

"I just hope my guests don't cancel tonight," I said, consulting a handwritten list of people who had RSVP'd positively. "This gathering isn't big to begin with. It would be a shame if the weather kept people away."

Pepper and Astrid didn't reply. Astrid was trying to rearrange the snacks, to fill the gaps she'd created on the platters, while Pepper began to set tubes of oil paint, canvases and brushes on the table.

"Thanks for all your help," I told my friends absently as I scanned the roster of about twenty local business owners. I knew everyone, at least to some degree, but a few names and notes I'd made popped out at me.

Evangeline Fletcher
Myrna Crickle—Owner of the Well-Dressed Wall
Linh Tran—Chef and owner, Typhoon
Penelope Dandridge—Penny for Your Stuff
Benedict Blodgett—Independent filmmaker (horror)
    and proprietor, Take Six Studio

was soothing but firm. He squeezed her hand again. "A young woman is dead."

That simple reminder drained my sibling of color and her anger, which was rooted in frustration with me. "Sorry," she said more quietly. But she didn't stop questioning me. "What drew you there, Daphne? What did you hope to find? Or learn?"

"I was hoping to uncover something that might help clear Roger's name," I said, wanting Piper to understand that, while I was driven by curiosity, I was also trying to be helpful. "The night Laci came to Winding Hill to get shots of the police taking away the bag with the garter, she told me two things."

The doorbell rang, and Elyse went to answer it, with Paris and Milan at her side. I could tell by the way she looked back over her shoulder that she was reluctant to miss key parts of the story, but she had no choice.

Roger leaned over his barely touched muffin, clearly curious. "What did Laci say?"

Gabriel was also listening intently, stroking his dark, devilish goatee and taking mental notes for a story that I was sure would appear the next day.

I pushed aside my mug, which I hadn't touched. I'd once had a bad beverage at Elyse's house, too. "I mentioned the suitcases I'd seen on Abigail's bed. One of which disappeared between the time I found the body and the time I returned to get the cat, Ms. Peebles."

I wasn't sure if this was new information for Gabriel and Roger, and I couldn't tell by their expressions, so I explained in detail.

"I'd noticed a Louis Vuitton and a plain black case. The black one was gone in the morning. Laci indicated that she might have some insights into the missing bag, and she thought we should compare notes."

Gabriel had lost a colleague, but he'd been a hard-boiled

crime reporter in Philadelphia, and his eyes gleamed with interest. "What else did she say? What's the second thing?"

I glanced at Piper, who was curious, but guarded. She wouldn't let herself get too enthusiastic about my sleuthing. Then I told everyone, "I also asked Laci what she and Daisy Carpenter had been arguing about near the woods at the Owl & Crescent Art Barn on the night of Piper's shower."

I expected someone to ask me about Laci's response. But no one had a chance, because at that inopportune moment, Detective Fred Doebler entered the room, telling me, "I'd like you to start that story from the beginning, please."

Chapter 36

"Poor Laci," Moxie sighed, batting away some wildly flapping helium balloons, clutched by a little boy who ran past us, dodging amid the many people and pets at the Wags 'n Flags celebration in Pettigrew Park.

The annual community picnic, always held the day after the fireworks as part of Sylvan Creek's extended July Fourth celebration, was one of my favorite summer events, and I tried to shake off memories of the previous night as we strolled past rows of tents set up by food vendors representing a whole melting pot of cuisines. I hadn't quite regained my appetite after finding Laci's body, but I had to admit that my mouth watered a little at the smoky scents of charcoal and barbecue sauce, mingled with Mexican, Thai, Mediterranean and Chinese spices.

"Does Detective Doebler suspect anyone—except you?" Moxie asked, nibbling on an ear of Mexican street corn, which was smothered in mayonnaise, cotija cheese and ancho chili powder. Somehow, she'd managed to finish half the cob without getting so much as a spot on her blue romper, which she'd sewn from a 1965 Butterick pattern.

"I think I've already been ruled out," I noted, glancing down at my sundress, which had gained a stain, although I hadn't even touched any food. "Jonathan was right. His partner has given up on investigating me and is starting to look at me more like a nuisance. Just like Jonathan used to do."

"Speaking of handsome detectives"—Moxie's segues to Jonathan Black were seldom subtle—"how are things shaping up in California?" she asked, giving me the side eye. "Has he wrapped up that case so he can come home?"

I shook my head. "No, Moxie. And I'm increasingly convinced he should take the job and stay out there. The alternative is to resent me for the rest of his life."

My best friend didn't answer, and, for the first time, I took that as tacit, if reluctant agreement.

I'd been trying to convince Moxie that Jonathan's best option was to seize the San Diego opportunity, yet it pained me to a surprising degree that she had seemingly caved in and conceded that I was right.

I was also bothered by Socrates' clear disappointment in me after I'd shared what little I'd known about the argument between Laci Chalmers and Daisy Carpenter with Detective Doebler.

My canine sidekick had accompanied me to Wags 'n Flags, but our ride to the park had been quiet, and he'd quickly darted off with Axis and Artie, who'd come with Gabriel, Elyse, and the greyhounds. Snowdrop had taken a break from hanging out at Daisy's tent, representing In a Pickle, to play, too.

I spied all the dogs, including Tiny Tim, running around near the creek, close to where Moxie's boyfriend, Mike Cavanaugh, was flipping burgers for the local VFW. As a veteran who'd served overseas and suffered an injury just before coming home, Mike was a member in good standing. Moxie believed that hanging around with other vets, including Jonathan, was helping him adjust back to civilian life after a rocky reentry.